Big Ice

By
Christopher Bonn Jonnes

PublishAmerica
Baltimore

© 2003 by Christopher Bonn Jonnes.

First printing

ISBN: 1-59286-587-9
PUBLISHED BY
PUBLISHAMERICA BOOK PUBLISHERS
www.publishamerica.com
Baltimore

Printed in the United States of America

For
Taylor, Abby, Jacob, and Susan

Acknowledgements

Without contributions of encouragement, information, and advice from others, this book would not exist. For that reason, I am profoundly thankful to the following people:

Beverly Bonn Jonnes
Arlene Robinson
Steven Jonnes
Burt Wilson
Susan Jonnes
Nelson Jonnes
Terry Robinson
Thanasis Syropoulos

Washington, D.C.: The National Ice Center — FOR IMMEDIATE RELEASE — An iceberg about as long as the State of Maryland calved from the Ross Ice Shelf in Antarctica last week. Iceberg B-15 is roughly 158 by 20 nautical miles in area, equivalent to about 11,000 square kilometers. The iceberg was initially discovered by National Science Foundation forecasters in McMurdo Sound and reported to the NIC for verification. The Ross Ice Shelf is the largest shelf in Antarctica.

CHAPTER 1

A rare Nor'easter dumped snow in earnest, flinging crisp little ice flakes at Seth Peterson's face like tiny Chinese throwing stars. Sleet froze on the sidewalk as the temperature dropped to near 30 degrees; but Seth loved it. Real weather had finally arrived in D.C., reminding him of his home in Minnesota, where winter was winter.

Few others shared his glee. Most saw the weather as a disastrous start to the workweek. If the wind and snow continued at this pace, the city would be incapacitated — with only seventeen shopping days until Christmas. Seth smiled, thinking how the rush-hour commute would go for the masses later that day, then remembered sadly that he'd be part of it. Easterners, to his mind, were woefully unprepared for such weather — not enough sand or salt, too few plows, and too many inexperienced winter drivers who were not aware of their inexperience.

Seth knew what to expect today. The night before, he had logged onto the National Weather Service radar via the Internet. To avoid morning delays, he left his home in Georgetown early — not because he couldn't handle the road conditions, but because he knew no one else could. He was right; traffic was snarled on the Beltway for miles. After a successful but frustrating commute, he parked his car in the lot at Iverson Mall in Suitland and walked the last mile to work for the exercise.

Easterners generally thought of Minnesota as that cold and barren land in the distant West where lutefisk and flaky politicians abound. Maybe ... but in Minnesota they know how to drive in snow — or at least, they *used* to. Before front-wheel drive and SUVs, Minnesotans drove old Camaros with manual transmissions: rusty, overpowered, ultralight rear-wheel-drive sleds with no ground clearance and windshields that never defrosted. Winter driving was an art, a study in momentum, probabilities, and fishtail grace. Never go too fast and never stop; those were the keys. It was an inborn talent, the result of natural selection. In Minnesota, when people spun out in the snow, they froze to death in the ditch. Now, even in Minnesota, winter driving was a dying art.

But in D.C., he thought with a wry grin, weathermen sensationalized one-inch snowfalls and 20-degree temperatures like the arrival of the next Ice Age.

Seth steered clear of the crowd emptying off the D-12 Green Line Metrobus at St. Barnabas and 28th Street, most of whom scurried for the Smithsonian's National Air and Space Museum at the Garber Facility nearby. He strolled northeast on Silver Hill Road, ignoring the scornful faces of those he passed, people bundled up as if they were taking on the Pole, and likely thinking he was a show-off in his flannel shirt and black St. Paul Saints minor league baseball cap like a shirtless drunk at a Redskins home game in December.

But they couldn't know that for a year he'd been trapped in a sedentary cycle: car seat to office chair to apartment couch. The opportunity to stretch his legs for a mile in the raw elements was refreshing. And he preferred dressing this way. If he got cold, he just walked faster.

He was judging whether the snow accumulation was a half-inch or inch when an older Chevy S-10 Blazer passed him from behind. He noticed because the light at Maywood Lane was yellow and the driver was still hitting the gas like an idiot, racing to the next light. Only now, there was snow on the ground with ice beneath. He caught a glimpse of the driver, a chubby woman of maybe fifty, wedged against the wheel with her seat slid forward, squinting into the snowfall.

Slow down, lady, he thought.

The light turned red. She was still a hundred feet from the intersection. Plenty of time.

Let off the gas now, and coast in.

Instead, the taillights came on and the vehicle lurched.

No. Ease off the brakes. Go easy.

She held the brakes firm, locking the wheels, causing the vehicle to slide sideways … right into the intersection.

There was no car waiting at Maywood when the light turned green, but Seth's view was blocked farther up the street.

Pump it, lady, pump it.

He could see she had no intention of letting off the pre-ABS brakes. They were locked, and she was riding it out no matter what. The Blazer swiveled 180 degrees, entering the intersection backwards. It had slowed quite a bit, down to about ten miles an hour, so it would stop just on the other side if it made it through.

But a Federal Express van had timed the light perfectly, and was moving at a fair clip. Planning a left turn onto Silver Hill, it appeared from south on Maywood and slammed into the front quarter panel on the driver's side. The van continued on, fairly straight, and stopped in the middle of the road just north of the intersection with minimal front-end damage. As far as Seth could

10

tell, the driver was fine.

Unfortunately, the impact sent the top-heavy Blazer spinning like a top. It did two 360s before the left rear wheel caught the curb, flipping it over awkwardly onto the sidewalk before sliding against a brick facade in a comet of sparks and snow and coming to rest on the driver's side between a building and a small aspen. Pedestrians scattered like penguins from a killer whale.

He was thinking the accident wasn't too bad when he noticed the smoke. He'd stopped to watch as the predictable scene unfolded before him, and was a hundred yards up the street from the scene, snow collecting on the bill of his cap. A small crowd inched toward the damaged vehicle. Was the orca dead? Half a minute passed.

Come on, lady. Get out.

There was still no movement from the truck when the smoke coming from under the hood thickened quickly and a small flame licked out from the wheel well. The crowd jumped back as one.

Seth had seen car fires before. They never seemed to happen with massive explosions as on TV or in movies. But what really happened was much worse for those trapped inside. He'd heard that burning to death was the worst way to die, each nerve slow-roasting — a gruesome death in which consciousness hangs on too long. He thought for a moment of religious zealots who choose self-immolation with gasoline and fire to broadcast their protest *du jour*. Those fools live long enough to regret their choice, he bet. They carry out Darwin's work. *Have at it*, he thought.

Yet the Blazer's driver had made no such choice. Just some poor woman who bought a four-wheel drive for security, or status, or because she believed the ads declaring it could drive up the side of sheer mountains. She obviously didn't know what every Minnesotan knows: that four-wheel drive only helps you *go* in snow, not *stop*.

And this lady wasn't getting out.

It was an electrical fire. Seth was certain of that, and the gas tank was still intact. But for how long? He didn't have time to wonder. The whole engine compartment was suddenly engulfed, with flames and smoke boiling from under the hood. In a matter of moments, he knew the entire vehicle would be fully involved. A few bystanders crept forward as if to help, but then withdrew, repelled by the flames.

No way was that woman dead in there, Seth thought. Injured or unconscious? Maybe. But she had to be alive. The crash wasn't that serious. Maybe her seatbelt jammed, or her foot was trapped. Maybe she'd had a heart attack or seizure. No matter what the reason, the fact that she was still in the car meant that she needed help. What were those people doing down there?

Suddenly realizing he was standing there doing nothing like everyone else, he broke into a slow run. Sprinting wasn't possible because of the poor footing, making the hundred yards seem to pass in minutes, not seconds. When he finally arrived, gasping for air, he slid around the front of the vehicle, where the fire was now escaping through the grill and gaps between the hood and quarter panels, and the paint was blistering like bad acne. The windshield was shattered on the driver's side at ground level, but still intact. Through the smoke and flames he could make out the figure of the woman, slack and motionless against her door. At first, kicking out the windshield seemed the best option to extricate her, but the smoke and heat there prohibited it. He ran around to the back and checked the rear latch.

Locked. *Damn.*

He looked around at the gathering crowd swarming out of the surrounding buildings and emptying out of cars in the growing traffic jam. No one was coming to help. A few people were waving at him to retreat. One heavily bundled figure yelled, "Get back!"

Like hell.

The rear wheel had just stopped spinning and he jumped up onto it, landing on his knees and then scooting up to check the side passenger door. It was locked as well. Without hesitation he got down on all fours and raised his right arm high in the air, swinging the bottom of his bare fist down on the door's window with as much force as he dared. It bounced off, leaving the window intact and his throbbing hand less so. Breaking car windows was another thing that didn't work as well as it did in the movies.

The fire was spreading. The cab filled with smoke. Inside, he saw the woman stir. She was alive, but not for long. He rapped on the window and screamed at her. She was incoherent, though. Alive and moving, but barely. This would not do.

He heard yelling now; not from the occupant inside, but from concerned onlookers astonished by his foolish perch on the would-be funeral pyre, sure that his fate, too, was sealed by the imminent explosion of the gas tank within. No one would step forward to help. It was up to him alone.

He focused again on the window. This time he raised his arm, but brought his elbow down on the window as a pro wrestler might do to the solar plexus of a prone opponent. Unlike a wrestler, he delivered his blow with every atom of energy his large frame could muster. The window shattered and his elbow punched through. He withdrew his arm and exposed a grapefruit-sized hole in the now concave glass, out of which a plume of acrid smoke and heat

12

escaped. His elbow felt broken, and his shoulder felt dislocated.

Jumping to his feet on the snow-slickened side panel, he proceeded to kick out the rest of the window. Reaching in, he located the door-lock button and pushed it. To his surprise it clicked, and the latch released. Standing again, he lifted open the side door, which was undamaged except for the window he'd knocked out. Unfortunately, because of the vehicle's side-lying position, the door wouldn't stay vertical without being held. So, gulping a deep breath of fresh air and holding it, he lowered himself into the cab, holding the door open above him and then setting it gently down, making sure it didn't latch. There would be no time to figure out how to reopen it, or squeeze back out the window either.

But door or no door, he had no idea how he'd carry the big woman out with him. Inside, the heat was intense and the smoke worse. Flames had breached the firewall and were lapping at them from beneath the dash. He stooped inside, standing on something soft, which he concluded was the woman's hip. The air by his head couldn't sustain him, nor could he hold his breath any longer. He kneeled over the woman and sucked in a lung full, relieved to find the air down low breathable, if barely. He shouted in the woman's ear and shook her. She mumbled unintelligibly, still out of commission.

Have to do it the hard way, then.

She was still in her seatbelt. Luckily, the latch was on her right side, not beneath her; he undid it without difficulty and threw it off. A moment of indecision struck as he remembered the perennial caution against moving the injured lest you further the damage and render them paralyzed. Considering that sure and torturous death soon awaited her, the thought was fleeting. He wedged his left foot between her back and seat, straddling her in the cramped compartment. Taking what he thought was his last half-clear breath, he squatted low, slid his arms under her armpits and heaved her up so that she half-stood with him in a crouch. The effort took tremendous strain. The position was all wrong for proper leverage, and though short, the woman was well packed, probably weighing in at 160 pounds or more fully clothed.

The crucial moment had arrived. Unable to breathe, holding the deadweight before him, feeling the heat beginning to tickle his skin with urgency, and with no means to open the door above or drag the woman out if he did, the thought suddenly occurred to Seth that it might have been a good idea to heed the warnings of those safely outside.

Just as he was about to drop his load and make a desperate attempt to save his own life before his breath gave out, the door above him opened and a rush of heat and smoke escaped, allowing him one more smoky gasp of oxygen.

Through smoke-dimmed eyes he saw a young woman up there, on the side of the burning truck, holding open the door. Never was there such a welcome sight.

But the problem of how to extricate the driver still loomed. Taking advantage of the open door, he stood to his full height now, lifting his arms and forcing hers up so he could grab farther down around her waist, hoping to do a clean-and-jerk move that would get her far enough out the door so that he could push her up by the butt. She was too limp, though. If he released her chest, gravity would take her down as fast as his arms came down.

He was about to panic again, when suddenly the load lightened. He looked up and saw that a hand had grabbed one of the woman's raised arms and was pulling her up. Another stranger had come to the rescue, this time a man. The savior got his other hand engaged, and the woman's body began to rise. Seth used the opportunity to shift his hands lower to get better leverage. A moment later the woman was dragged out, and a swarm of other helping hands swept her and the man carrying her off and away from danger.

The young woman holding the door barked a warning for Seth to get out fast. With the older woman safe, he didn't need to be told twice; moving quickly, he leaped onto his belly and pulled his legs clear. The woman let the door fall shut and the two rolled off the inferno into the melting snow, scampering away on hands and knees.

Seth lay in the wet street face down, coughing and spitting, allowing the snow to squelch the fire on his skin. Hands patted him all over and words of congratulation floated down with the snow from the impressed audience. Sirens blared suddenly, and noise and shouting rose to a din around him. An EMT knelt and looked him over. Seth answered some questions, complained of pain in his right arm but proclaimed good health, and was left alone.

Recovering his breath and composure, he stood and brushed himself off. Now wet with snow and perspiration, the adrenalin rush gone, the cold was settling in. That, combined with the creeping reality of what he'd just done, set him to shivering. He thought of getting closer to the heat of the burning wreckage, but a pumper truck had arrived and was making short work of the flames. So instead he turned and walked toward the crew of EMTs working on the victim, already strapped to the board and ready for the ambulance.

Pushing through the crowd of gawkers, he looked her over. Her eyes were open, though glassy. An oxygen mask covered much of her face, but she seemed to be breathing on her own. The crew was cutting away her full-length dress coat to get at her arms for an IV hook-up and blood pressure check. The coat was charred in places with spots of burned skin visible

14

beneath, but nothing that looked serious. He leaned in and asked an EMT how she was, having to speak loudly to be heard over the surrounding commotion and annoying sirens. The distracted EMT afforded him no more than a glance back over his shoulder with a nod of his head and a thumb up.

It was all Seth needed. As he rose to leave, he saw the man and woman who'd helped save her standing near the circle of observers. Just as he was about to turn away, hoping to avoid them, the girl made eye contact and nudged the guy next to her, pointing Seth out. They made their way over to him. The woman was a shorthaired redhead, an athletic type in sneakers and earmuffs, wearing a red Nike running suit with black stripes. He guessed she'd been out jogging.

As she approached Seth, he offered her his hand. She ignored it and gave him a hug instead. "You saved her life," she said. "That was the bravest thing I've ever seen. Are you okay?"

His shoulder felt like the time twenty years earlier when he'd launched his BMX bicycle Evel Kneivel-style up a neighbor's lawn embankment, successfully clearing the lilac bush ... but not the elm tree. He still waved off the man's question, saying only, "I couldn't have done it without you two." Then he reached his hand out toward the man, who thankfully wanted no more of him than that. The guy was maybe forty-five, pudgy, balding. Dressed like a lawyer, the poor guy had destroyed an expensive-looking suit in his efforts, but the huge Schwarzenegger-for-a-day grin of satisfaction on his face showed he didn't care. The event would probably play well for him at home and the office for years to come. Even so, he may as well have been Arnold when he squeezed Seth's damaged hand.

"Thank you," Seth said, wincing and then managing a weak grin.

"You are one dumb son of a bitch," the guy said as his own smile continued to grow.

After exchanging a few more kind words they parted, and Seth decided to head for work. The ambulance was leaving and the police were dispersing the crowd, trying to make room for a flatbed wrecker that arrived to remove the wet and blackened Chevy carcass. He'd nearly left the scene when he saw a woman pointing at him and talking to a short, stocky policewoman writing in a notepad. The cop then pointed at him, too, and motioned with her finger for him to come over. He looked around to make sure she was gesturing at him, and then pointed at himself with a questioning expression. She nodded, already walking toward him. He waited where he was, wishing he'd cleared out a moment earlier.

"Excuse me, sir," she said. "You were involved in the rescue?"

"Well ... yes, but there are two over there who could probably tell you more." He waved his head back toward the scene.

She looked up at him, open disbelief in her expression. "That's not what everyone else says."

Seth shrugged.

"Did you get some medical attention?"

"I'm fine."

"You don't look like it," she said, making a squeamish face.

Biting back a sarcastic "thank you," he said only, "May I go?"

"I just need some information for the report, sir," she said, applying pen to paper again. "What's your name?"

"Peterson."

She looked up again and squinted. "Would you mind elaborating, sir?"

"Seth Cooper Donner Peterson."

"Two middle names?"

"Yes, ma'am."

"Do you know the driver?"

"No."

"Did you see what happened?"

"Yes."

She peeked up at him from the pad again. "And would you like to share what you saw with me, sir?"

Seth sighed. "She got sideways and slid through the intersection, trying to stop for the red light. The van clipped her in the front, spun her around and she flipped over onto the curb. A fire started, and some of us pulled her out."

She started spending more time looking at him than at the paper. "What's your address?"

"Georgetown, but I'm thinking of moving."

"Can we be a little more specific?"

"Is this necessary?"

"Do you have some reason to be evasive, sir?"

"I'm cold, wet, and late for work."

"Where's your jacket?"

"Home."

"Where's your car."

"Iverson Mall."

She was getting exasperated. "How did you get here?"

"Walked."

"With no jacket?"

"I didn't plan on being out here this long."

"Let's have your address."

Reluctantly he supplied his address and phone number.
"Where do you work?"
"Spring Hill and Swann Roads."
She thought about it. "The Suitland Federal Center?"
"Yes."
"Naval Intelligence?"
He shook his head. "N-I-C."
"Which stands for?"
"National Ice Center."
"Ice Center?"
"We track icebergs."
"Ah, that would explain your personality. Did you have car trouble?"
"No."
"Don't they have parking at the Federal Center?"
"Yes."
"So why were you walking in a blizzard?"
"Exercise."
"Would you like a ride there now, sir?"
"No, but I'd like to start walking there," he said, suddenly aware that he'd lost his favorite hat in the melee, but unwilling to go back for it.

"Very well," she said, sounding anything but satisfied. "Thank you for your cooperation. If there's anything else we need, someone will call."

Seth moved off quickly. *Never should have gotten involved*, he told himself.

The NIC facility was still a good distance away, and he was shivering harder now, so he began jogging to get his heart pumping.

CHAPTER 2

Despite his appearance, Seth's ID card allowed him to pass unhindered through the Gate 5 guard station, and he arrived at Federal Office Building 4, with its array of satellite dishes, only a half hour late. He slipped by the guard desk and into the stairwell unnoticed, hoping to reach the restroom on Floor 2, where he could spruce up unseen. When he entered the hallway, however, he confronted the NIC's receptionist and liaison officer, Sandy Page, who reeled at his appearance. He didn't blame her: His clothes were soaked with sweat and melted snow; his chestnut hair, usually well kept, was wet and matted; his face and hands were streaked with dirt and blood.

"What the hell? You look like a sewer rat." She waved her hand back and forth in front of her wrinkled nose. "And you smell like napalm." Everything she said seemed to relate to armed conflict. But that, too, Seth understood: Her husband had been killed during the 1968 Tet Offensive in Vietnam. As though reading his mind, she added, "Is there a war going on out there?"

"Just snowing hard."

Bill Steiner, the Center's newest hire, approached them. "Jesus, Seth, were you in a plane crash?"

Seth started up the hall, trying to lose them, but they and their questions followed.

"What happened to your forehead?" Bill said, pointing.

Seth touched the spot and came away with a blood-dabbed fingertip. He must have scraped himself in the car or getting off. "I slipped."

"Did you fall into a furnace?" Sandy said. "You smell like my mother-in-law's cooking."

"I stopped to see a car fire on the way in."

She stepped forward and felt his sleeve, indicating the singe marks. "You must have been pretty close."

"I got downwind, I guess." He slipped into his cubicle and grabbed a gym bag stuffed with a tank top, shorts, tennis shoes, and a change of street clothes. He'd stashed it in a corner six months earlier when Dr. Dave Thornton, one of the Center's physical scientists, would occasionally invite him to play tennis or basketball on the campus courts. The clothes had sat unused, until now. He brushed past Sandy and Bill, who still stood in awe of his appearance and enigmatic answers, and made his way down the hall to the men's room. "Look, I've got to get into some dry clothes. Do you mind?"

He knew he was being rude, but his skin was already crawling from the unwanted attention. If he didn't clean up and get past this event before the news permeated the building, it would ruin his week. He smiled as best he could at his confounded coworkers and backed into the restroom, leaving them alone with their bemused wonder.

After washing up in the sink and changing into dry clothes, he returned to his cube and passed a few uneventful hours at his desk. As he hoped, his return to normal appearance quelled the interest his entrance had generated earlier. The questions tapered off as he continued to downplay the actual events to the point of denial. Eventually he was left to work alone, as was his habit.

Seth didn't accomplish much that day. The accident kept replaying in his head. He found himself staring at the wall for long periods, daydreaming what-if scenarios, and thinking about how close that woman — and he — had come to dying. It was strange how calm and automatic his response had been. He couldn't get over it. Why was it he could face such terror without flinching, yet could barely function in day-to-day life?

Would that question ever be answered?

He shook off another trance and glanced at the wall clock, suddenly remembering the two o'clock staff meeting he was to have attended three minutes earlier. In a flash, a terror worse than anything he'd felt earlier that day gripped him. He was late again. Under the circumstances, it was a meeting he wasn't sure he would survive.

Circumstances, hell. He knew that had nothing to do with it. He'd burned through every reasonable excuse to miss previous meetings, and it occurred to him that by downplaying the morning's event, he'd blown the chance for another. But now he was desperate. There was no time to conjure a new excuse. He rose and slipped out the rear entrance, hoping to evacuate via Gate 2 onto Suitland Road. He'd have to come up with something later.

Halfway down the hall he bumped into Bernard Harris, Ice Center's Commanding Officer and his 5'6" supervisor, almost knocking him to the floor.

"I can have you fired for that," Harris said, straightening his Navy uniform.

"Sorry, Bern."

Bernard hated his name, and the nickname Bernie was worse. Bern was an acceptable tag, though he preferred "Sir" or "Commander."

"Yep," the shorter man said, "Lawsuit too. That's at least six figures. I can see the headlines now: 'Large, disgruntled white male accosts diminutive

African-American boss in retaliatory rage.'"

"I didn't see you."

"Negligence. You admit it. Treble damages."

Part of him wanted to stand pat, continuing the sporting give-and-take his manager was so good at, but Seth needed out. He pressed on toward the door. "I'm late," he lied.

"Damn right, you are, Peterson. Get your ass back here."

"I've got to get something in the car." That didn't sound like much of a delay, but the car was a mile away.

Harris got serious. "*After* the meeting, Seth. You're not missing another one." He wasn't joking now.

Seth stood for a second, torn by indecision. The door at the end of the hall beckoned freedom, but he knew it was too late. He was caught. To go now would create a scene worse than the meeting itself. There would be questions, suspicions, explanations required. After all, he'd done the meetings before. He could survive another.

"Oh, yeah. Forgot the meeting," he said. "I can go out later. I'll be right along." He turned and headed up the hall in the opposite direction, bypassing the door to the meeting.

"No you don't. Follow me. I'm personally escorting you to this meeting."

"But my papers."

"We'll send Sandy for them. Come on, we're late."

Bern opened the door that Seth had skipped and held it for him, arm extended in invitation. "Coming?"

Seth felt the flush. He wasn't ready. He would *never* be ready. He forced a smile. "After you, Commander."

They retraced Seth's escape route and continued to the conference room. Along the way, Bern stopped and peered over the portable privacy barrier to Sandy Page's office cube, standing on the tips of his dress shoes and hanging on with his hands to help his nose over the top. "Sandy, can you get Mr. Peterson's file for the meeting and bring it in? We're late."

A soft voice floated up out of the cubicle. "Whatever you say, Kilroy, sir."

Seth stepped to the barrier and peered in at Sandy, his chin easily clearing the top edge. "It's on the left side of my desk. It says 'Big Ice' on the tab." He Cheshire-smiled and bounced his eyebrows, pretending his best to hide the horror he felt.

"Survival of all mankind hinges on its contents, I'm sure," she said, rising to go.

"If you only knew," Seth said.

As they neared the conference room, a cute young woman from Wing 1, wearing black tights and a pink wool pullover, walked past, smiling at them. Bern gave Seth a wild look and whispered something crude.

Seth looked away. He appreciated the humor, but his mind was preoccupied by resigned dread at the moment.

The conference room smelled of stale coffee and erasable marker. Twelve colleagues were already seated. Sandy delivered the file and it was passed hand-to-hand down to Seth, who sat at the far end next to Carl Maddox, Satellite Specialist, a big friendly guy who attracted attention like a black hole sucks up light.

Bern stood at the other end of the large oak table. After asking Sandy to hold all calls he got everyone's attention, interrupting a heated discussion on the likelihood of a Redskins Super Bowl win. "We've got another one, folks. Data from the Landsat 7 satellite shows B-22 calving off the Ross Ice Shelf at 170 degrees, 22 minutes west longitude." He glanced at his notes. "And that's at … 77 degrees, 49 minutes south latitude. Dave, what are the dimensions on this one?"

Dr. Dave Thornton was the National Ice Center's most senior physical scientist, an M.I.T. graduate with a personality like cold oatmeal, but an intellect like no other. He'd hung a miniature orange "Men at Work" traffic sign in his cubicle, on which someone had added the stick-on letters "s" and "a," so that "Men" was now "Mensa."

"Nine by two," he said in plastic monotone.

"That's miles, people," Bern added. "This ain't no growler. Dave, I want projections on speed and direction to Sheila by 8:00 a.m."

Sheila Kirby was the NIC Media Spokesperson. A Grambling graduate, she was competent, glib, and good-looking as well. "I'll set something up for midmorning," she said.

Bern turned to the youngest and newest member of the team, pointing a stubby finger. "Bill, you get out the standard notices. This looks as though it may be headed for rush-hour traffic."

Bill Steiner was a communications specialist responsible for reporting the findings and appropriate warnings to the Navy, Coast Guard, and National Oceanic & Atmospheric Association. The idea was to keep ships in the Southern Sea lanes from ramming into the enormous floating ice cubes that regularly break free from the various Antarctic ice shelves. Unfortunately, his IQ seemed to be only half that of Dave Thornton's. To no one's surprise, he only nodded vaguely.

Bern addressed other mundane policy issues in his standard, no-nonsense, efficient manner. His ability to address the group with such confidence

21

always impressed Seth. His boss was a well-respected, fair and effective team leader.

Near the end of the hour-long meeting, the thing Seth had hoped to avoid happened. After another discussion on perennial traffic congestion and its effect on employee tardiness, Bern turned to him, a nonparticipant to this point, and said, "Mr. Peterson, how's your special project coming? What have you got for us?"

Someone at the opposite end of the table chuckled sarcastically, and a few other stifled laughs followed. Then silence hit, and all eyes were on Seth. A palpable tension flooded the room as a familiar feeling swamped him. He struggled for rational thought.

"Actually, it isn't ready for a report yet," he said. "Friday looks better right now."

Someone muttered something he didn't hear, but a few others did and laughed.

Bern stared at him in silence for a long moment. Seth fought with full strength to keep his heart in his chest and his eyes off the floor.

Bern finally spoke, mercifully rescuing him. "That's fine, Seth. We'll expect the report on Friday. You'll be the headliner." Then he clapped his hands and said, "Okay, people, let's get out there and save the world."

Notebooks slammed shut and people stood, ready for the door. Before anyone moved, though, Sandy Page knocked lightly and poked her head into the room. "Are you guys almost done?" she said.

"We just finished," Bern said. "What's up?"

"The phone's been ringing off the hook. For Seth."

This statement got everyone's attention, especially Seth's. He rarely took calls; just the thought of them sent his blood pressure soaring. "Who was it?" he said.

"Every reporter in town."

Oh no.

"Why are they asking for you?" Sheila asked. She normally handled media interaction.

Sandy stepped all the way in, put her hands on her hips, and saved Seth the trouble of thinking up an answer. "Well, it seems that while he was out walking in the snow this morning, our Mr. Peterson witnessed a serious traffic accident and jumped into a burning vehicle to save a woman's life. The press is calling him a hero. They're swimming the moat to talk to him. They all want the exclusive. If I can't start putting some of these calls through, I wouldn't be surprised if they storm the building."

As one, all eyes again fell on Seth, who nearly collapsed into his chair.

Bill pointed at him. "So that's what it was. 'Downwind' my ass."

"It's not what they're making it out to be," Seth shot back, defensive. "Two other people helped the lady out. I just assisted. It was no big deal." Then he made himself the first one out of the door, leaving the others standing dumbfounded.

Before the door swung shut behind him, he heard Carl Maddox ask the group, "Why wouldn't he just tell us this morning?"

Because no one must know, Carl.

Finally free of the meeting, Seth sated a coffee craving with a cupful from the machine in the lunchroom, savoring it like a smoker's first cigarette of the day. He paced an empty hallway, breathing deeply, then retreated to the solitude of his cubicle, where he thought the day might begin to ease.

Wrong. Bern Harris was waiting for him.

"Sit down and talk to me, Seth."

Seth laid his folder atop a file cabinet, pushed his keyboard across his cluttered desk to accommodate his coffee, and sat with false leisure in the oldest office chair in the facility, the one with squeaky casters he'd inherited as a new hire but kept rather than unload on the newcomer, Bill Steiner. "You're not going to try to set me up on another date again, are you, Bern? Or try to sell my story to *The National Enquirer?*"

Bern pursed his lips and adjusted his tie. "We need to get what you've got in that file made public, Seth. You've had a year to develop your theory. It's important, worth reporting. You get this project summarized or I'm pulling the plug. Or is there something else going on?"

"You're upset because I wasn't ready today?"

Bern slammed his palm down on the desk. "Cut the crap, Seth. You know we're both too smart to fall for it."

Seth looked into Bern's piercing brown eyes, noting how comical the smaller man looked in the chair across the desk. His feet barely reached the floor, reminding him of Lily Tomlin as five-year-old Edith Ann in the rocking chair on *Laugh-In*. But Seth was well aware that his boss had power, mysterious power that transcended the social stereotypes of white over black, big over small, old over young, educated over uneducated. In Bern Harris, Seth saw a face capable of masking the vulnerable man beneath, of capping the well of terror that under similar circumstances would gush in Seth and render him incapacitated. Seth's respect for him went beyond his ability to express it … just as Bern's ability to read Seth exceeded Seth's ability to hide from it.

"Bern, I've made huge progress," he ventured. "I'm just careful. I don't want a big splash if I can't convince others."

Bern's long stare conveyed more than skepticism. "Look, Seth, here it is. I like you. I hired you. The concept in your preliminary report was fascinating." He motioned toward the manila folder Seth had just placed on the file cabinet. "You know your stuff. But you've played this cat-and-mouse game for months. People here think you're a complete fraud. You know they're laughing and whispering behind your back. I can't keep carrying you. I believe in the team, and I won't allow a rotten apple. I need your final report." Seth started to answer, but stopped at the wave of the man's hand. "It doesn't have to be perfectly polished. We're scientists, not showmen. If you blow me off again, or I find out you've been picking your nose in here, running the clock for a year and stringing me out with a dead-end idea, I'll fire you. You understand me? I don't want to do that. Don't make me."

Seth was oddly calm in a way he'd have given anything to have been fifteen minutes earlier in the conference room. "I understand. Sorry to make you look bad. I'll do the report Friday." Then, with eyes drifting to the walls decorated with a calendar, satellite images of polar ice, and various data charts, he added, "I like it here, Bern. Trust me, I've done the work and we're onto something big. I'm just careful, I guess."

"Are you sure it isn't something else?"

Seth brought his eyes back to Bern's and shook his head.

Bern was measuring him, nodding. "Friday then," he said, "or else." He stood to go, but paused. Seth expected more, perhaps something friendly to offset the harsh threat just leveled. Instead Bern said, "You should know, I signed you up to deliver your presentation at the Earth Environment Conference a week from Friday at the Washington Hilton and Towers. This is the conference's first annual meeting, and there will be a lot of press attention. This Friday is your warm-up. We need this information made public, Seth."

Then he disappeared up the hall, expensive shoes vocalizing his unique, short-stroke cadence on the tile floor.

Seth stacked his fists on the desk in front of him and crowned the tower with his forehead. There *was* something else. It had been there his whole life. He bounced his head a few times. How wonderful it would be to share the mysterious burden with Bern, with anyone.

But that must never happen.

Every fiber of his being screamed, *Hide it*!

CHAPTER 3

Seth shared a shadow with the alleyway across from The Igloo Bar & Grill in Woodley Park, trying in vain to blow smoke rings with his breath. Diesel fumes hung in the windless air. The temperature had returned to the forties after yesterday's storm, and the snow had turned into filthy mush. Crisp winter air amplified the ceaseless traffic noise, unlike the August nights when the oppressive heat and humidity suppressed everything, including sound itself. He hated Washington, D.C. — hated all cities — but he'd landed a dream job here and managed to get lost in a sea of cold strangers. No matter where he hid, he could never escape what chased him. He was so tired of running. Yet Friday, there loomed another challenge. And beyond that an even bigger one, imposed by Bern, for the following week.

Even tonight was a trial.

Yesterday afternoon, following Bern Harris's warning, Seth took the first of many calls from reporters. They continued even today, running the gamut of media forms: newspapers, magazines, radio, and television. Some only had questions. Most tried for face-to-face interviews. A few dangled vague but provocative financial incentives as bait for exclusives. One tabloid representative virtually guaranteed "six figures" for book and movie rights to his "incredible story of personal heroism in this time of pagan self-worship."

After early waffling — and once familiar with this new type of call — Seth developed a standard response. He bluntly told callers that he adamantly opposed self-aggrandizement and would accept no accolades, financial, symbolic, or otherwise, for an action that any bystander would have done eagerly and without hesitation. Please don't call again.

Every word was true, but also masked a harder fact: even if he found the money or fame inviting, he couldn't do an interview.

Except for one clever, perceptive reporter who quickly countered with the notion that Seth might help elevate society by sharing his I'm-no-hero message, most callers were either stunned to silence and apologies, or steamrolled right over his objections, absolutely indifferent to his wishes. The latter he hung up on. Eventually he had enough, and made a personal visit to Sandy's cubicle, asking her to dump all calls into his voicemail without screening them — no exceptions. He knew she felt this was

25

discourteous and improper, but despite a nasty look, she said nothing.

That evening was spent in dark solitude at his apartment. He threw his collection of Mozart CDs into the changer and sank into the couch with a full pot of extra strong Earl Grey. For the next three hours he wrestled with the demons in his head.

Keeping his job meant doing the presentation on Friday at work, and at the conference on the nineteenth. They were things beyond his ability, impossible to complete, yet he must attempt them. Again he committed himself to the fire.

Starting tomorrow, things will be different, he told himself.

How he could expect the result to be better than in the past, he didn't know. But he would try.

Tonight was a first step in that direction, a small challenge before the big test. If he could tackle increasingly difficult trials incrementally over the course of the week, he'd be better prepared for the big one at the end. He could ease into it, rather than take one giant leap.

So here he stood on a Tuesday night in December in a part of the dark city where he might be mugged at any moment, dreading the thought of crossing the street and seeking shelter in the safe haven of The Igloo. He feared the cold, the threat of physical harm, and the idiotic loneliness of his whole miserable and enigmatic condition less than what he'd come for. He felt the dizziness rising, telling himself it was the cold, the pollution, the coffee, an allergy — anything except what it really was.

Baby steps, he thought. *Put one foot in front of the other, or you'll never get through the next two Fridays.*

He crossed the street, dodging cars, hopped up the four white-carpeted steps beneath a white awning, took a deep breath, and headed into the bar. He knew that Bern, Sandy, and the others were already inside; he'd watched them go in ten minutes earlier. So he walked in with bold motions and looked for the group.

The bar was loud, crowded with young jocks from Georgetown and urban professionals in suits. *ESPN* blared on TV sets hung in all four corners. A harried waitress in a risqué uniform of black-and-white penguin-décor T-shirt and *faux*-caribou-skin miniskirt swayed through the packed tables with a loaded tray of Blubber Burgers and fries. The room was a fog of cigarette smoke, backlit by Santa's North Pole theme lights.

He walked into a wall of heat. The furnace had long since won the battle against the 40-degree weather outside; but despite the combined forces of furnace, overworked kitchen, and sweltering body heat, the crowd yelled at him in unison to shut the door. Laughter followed that, as if all newcomers

26

were greeted similarly. The place was full of parkas, hats, and mittens, like happy hour on a polar expedition.

As he removed his wool shirt and pulled the cuffs of his long-sleeve T-shirt to his elbows, a lovely lady in a pink tank top glanced up at him, and then looked again and smiled. The crew cut next to her scowled. Seth looked away and moved further into the bar.

He spotted the NIC gang against the back wall, which had been painted to look like blocks of ice and decorated with various Inuit artifacts, such as harpoons, knives, ivory implements, and polar artwork depicting Eskimos, dogsleds, orcas, seals, penguins, and narwhals. Bern and Sandy were there with Sheila, Bill, Dave, and Carl Maddox, all at a table for six. With no place to sit and no free chair in sight, Seth panicked. He should have come in sooner. He strode to the table and slapped Carl on the back.

"Seth, you made it," Carl said in his foghorn voice, crushing his hand like a salesman. Carl had joined the Center only months before Seth, but was the type everyone liked immediately, as if he'd been there forever.

Bern stood and reached his hand across the table. "Mr. Peterson, glad you could join us. The waitress won't be back here until closing. Get yourself a beverage at the bar and pull up a chair."

Seth did the right thing and asked whether anyone else needed anything, then headed to the bar with a drink order for seven. The monstrous wooden bar, with its hanging, sealskin-lined kayak canopy, stuffed-penguin and polar-bear-head mountings and surrounded by leather-bound stools of dubious Aleutian origin, was standing room only. Getting a drink was difficult for all but the loud and expert. Seth was neither. The sweaty bartender finally acknowledged him and grudgingly filled his order, explaining that tray orders were for the waitress. He wasn't making any friends with the patrons, either, as he muscled through to retrieve the drinks. The front door beckoned strongly. He considered abandoning the drinks and regrouping in the bathroom, but fought off the urge.

Eventually he returned with the tray to a grateful gathering. A nearby chair became available. In a few minutes he was seated, into his second beer, and feeling better about himself.

The Igloo was conveniently located on Connecticut Avenue near the Woodley Park-Zoo Station on the Metrorail Red Line. The group worked late, and made the rail commute together from the station on the Federal Center campus. All but Seth. He made an excuse and drove separately. He'd never been crammed in with the crowds on the Metro, and never intended to be.

The gathering was a weekly ritual, a team-building activity encouraged by Bern, with a location likely frowned upon by official policy. His repeated invites for Seth to join them had finally paid off, and success showed in his face. Most of the drinks were on him, which looked to be the norm. Bern was a big believer in getting along, especially with him, but Seth knew, too, that he was capable of doing whatever was necessary for discipline and policy. He was fair and likable, but tough — a good mix for a manager. That earned him respect.

Seth used a lull to break into the conversation. "Is this place your choice, Bern?" he said, looking around the crowded bar.

"Yes. The polar theme was an obvious choice for the Ice Center crew. Do you have a problem with it?"

"No, but has anyone noticed the incongruity here?"

"What?" Bill Steiner, a new guy who tried too hard, interjected. "Heat and ice in the same room?" He laughed at himself.

"No, Bill, I meant the penguins and polar bears thing."

Bill looked at him blankly and said, "What about them?" as Sandy tried and failed to suppress a laugh.

Seth's response was innocent. "They don't belong together."

Bill laughed again. "Yeah, the polar bears would eat the penguins, I guess."

"No," Seth said slowly, beginning to realize Bill's ignorance. "The only place a polar bear would see a penguin is in the zoo."

"What are you talking about?" Bill said, giving Seth a beery scowl.

"Polar bears live in the Arctic, like the Eskimo. Penguins live in the Southern Hemisphere. Never the twain shall meet. Penguins and Eskimos only play together in cartoons."

Sandy couldn't resist. "You didn't know that, Bill? How'd you get a job with the Ice Center, studying Antarctic ice, thinking polar bears live there?"

"I didn't think that," he said sarcastically. "I only thought there were penguins in the North. Sorry that I'm no expert on both poles."

"Well," she persisted, "There are no penguins in the North, and never have been. They're all in Antarctica."

"Actually," Seth added politely, "the South has seventeen or eighteen species of penguins. But they're spread out. One group lives as far north as the Galapagos Islands. Of course, *most* of them live in Antarctica."

Bill and Sandy sneered at each other.

Bern spared the group more bickering by changing the subject. When he did, Seth wished he'd kept his mouth shut. "So, Seth," he said, "have you surrendered to the press yet?"

"Never."

"Why are you avoiding them?"

"I know why," Bill said. "He's holding out for the highest bidder."

"Yeah," said Carl. "You're one smooth operator, Peterson. How much will it take to buy your story? What will you cave for?"

"It's not for sale at any price," Seth answered, forcing a calm he didn't quite feel.

"What do you have against talking to the press?" Sheila asked.

"He's camera shy," Bill said, and they all laughed, including Seth.

"No, it's just none of their business. So I helped somebody. So what? What's the big deal?"

Sandy, taking his comment more seriously than the others, said, "Saving someone's life under fire is always a big deal."

"Yeah, okay," he conceded. "I think it's important too, or I wouldn't have done it. I just don't think I'm obligated to parade all over town, boasting and selling out for something anyone would have done."

"*No one* would have done, you mean," Sandy corrected him.

"False modesty, I say," said Bill.

Sheila joined Sandy in Seth's defense. "Shut up, Bill. You've got spaghetti for brains. As if you'd ever do something like that. It's his own damn business if he wants privacy."

Bill placed his thumb on the end of his nose and wiggled his fingers at her, demonstrating the reason he hadn't made many friends in his short time with the Center.

"Come on, people," Bern said. "We're here for team building. Save the personal attacks for the office."

After a moment of respectful silence, Carl said, "Did you guys hear the news?" They all shook their heads. "They're really making a story out of Seth avoiding the limelight. They're calling him 'The Shy Samaritan.' But they add the qualifier 'so-called,' like they're pretending they didn't make it up. They're just reporting it, of course."

Bern said, "I can see it now, Ted Koppel saying, 'The Shy Samaritan — day 418. Still he remains silent.'"

They all laughed and gulped their drinks in unison.

Stone-faced Dave Thornton had remained quiet thus far, as was his way, concentrating his efforts on the free popcorn. Yet he was respected for his intellect, if not his personality. His nickname was "Hut," for the old E. F. Hutton television commercial: when he talked, people listened.

So when Sandy asked him, "What's your take on this, Hut? Is Seth's modesty right or wrong?" Dave said nothing for a moment, as was also his way, displaying the emotional intensity of a brick. Only past experience told them that he was, indeed, thinking through the matter, and would in time respond. When the response came, he didn't bother to look up or slacken his popcorn-stuffing pace, answering instead with his mouth full. Little bits flew back out onto the table as he spoke.

"There's no right or wrong in it," he said. "It's his choice. Nevertheless, his choice of silence may be misguided." He stopped and chewed, annoying the others who were curious to hear his reasoning. Finally he looked up, as if just realizing they expected more. "Well, that is to say, if he just doesn't give a damn about what others think, fine, that's one thing. An admirable trait." He glanced at Seth, who remained silent, before continuing. "But if he thinks he's somehow sending a morality message by trying to downplay his heroics — the old lesson that good deeds are their own reward — I think that'll fail. First, the public will reserve final judgment on the purported good deed until they've actually seen him and heard the facts verified in his own words. We're all accustomed to the media blowing things up a bit, no?"

His rhetorical question brought murmurs of agreement.

"Second, if his motive is to seek anonymity, his silence may backfire on him. Ironic, but true enough. As Carl pointed out, they've already named Seth The Shy Whatever. In only thirty-six hours he's become a local media sensation. But that's due more to his silence than to what he actually did ... which isn't entirely unprecedented, despite its virtue."

A few raised eyebrows was his only response this time. Undeterred, he carried on: "Third, if Seth is disgusted by the notion of 'selling out' as he calls it — which I presume is what he thinks he'd be doing by accepting money in exchange for an interview — he has to realize that many people are already making money over his action ... more specifically, his *non*-action. The media is selling advertising at premium rates to companies desperate to put their commercials in front of a public mesmerized by coverage of the Shy Savior. They'll milk this thing and overplay it until it's a sickening, shriveled cliché. When the local media is through, they'll sell it to other outlets for megabucks. Seth might be better off taking that money up-front himself and distributing it to the charity of his choice.

"But regardless of the choice he makes, it's sad that the focus has shifted from his selfless act yesterday morning to measuring his sincerity after the fact." He stopped chewing for a moment and shook his head in disgust. "And some will always doubt his motives — especially if he chooses not to talk to the press. On the other hand, if he chooses to speak publicly, others will doubt him, too. Disgusting."

That said, he went back to his silent munching.

The group eyed one another, nodding at Dave's wisdom. Seth was astonished by what Dave had said, but he had to admit it made sense. "Hut, you're saying I have to go public to stay private?"

"An interesting paradox, no?"

"Maybe I could just change my name."

Bern, having enough of the current subject, used that as his cue: "Speaking of names, tell us again how you got that middle name, Donner. I love that story."

Seth was thankful for the topic switch. "It was my dad's idea. He developed a morbid fascination with the plight of the Donner party, after whom Donner's Pass is named. He said that he was too busy to eat during my mom's three days of labor before my birth. One thing reminded him of the other, and he named me accordingly." He grinned. "My mom liked the name until she discovered the connection — too late."

"See, this is what always amazes me," Bern said with three-beer sincerity. "You get a couple of hungry white people and it's a tragedy. Monuments are raised. Passes are named. But black folk were starved by the boatload, and nothing."

Everyone at the table threw popcorn at him.

"The Donners weren't 'hungry,'" Seth said. "They were *eating* each other."

"That's a white thing, Peterson."

"What's the origin of 'Bernard'?" Bill asked, unaware that the subject of his full name was taboo.

"That's *Bern*," Harris said to a table full of snickers. "But I'm proud to say that it's a German name meaning 'bold as a bear.'"

Seth considered that silently. It was an appropriate label for Bern. The short man was bold beyond his stature. He knew the origin of his own given name — "The Appointed One" or "The Chosen" — but was far from living up to it. The thought depressed him.

"What about your last name, Bern?" he said, determined to fight off the rising melancholy. "What does Harris mean?"

"It's a British patronymic just like yours," he said with obvious smugness. "Peterson is 'the son of Peter.' Harris is 'the son of Harry.'"

The beer had taken full effect. Someone said, "The word in the office is that it stands for 'None of Hairy,' loosely translated as 'He of the Bald Scrotum.'"

Following that, too quickly to identify the speaker, came: "Ask any woman on Wing 2 about that."

"It's a black thing, right?"

"Okay, you degenerates." Sandy emptied her glass of Chardonnay and

31

stood to leave. "I've got grandchildren waiting for me at home. There better be no 'headaches' tomorrow for reveille." With that, she waved and left.

Seth watched her exit. His mind momentarily left the party with her, thinking of the family he might have had. Carl brought him back. As though he had heard his inner thoughts, Carl asked, "Is it true that you have two middle names, Seth? What did you do, keep your maiden name?"

Seth knew that coming here tonight after so much time would subject him to personal scrutiny from coworkers who barely knew him after more than a year, but he never imagined this much grilling. He'd been the focus since he arrived. And he hated the topic of marriage more than The Shy Samaritan. "Cooper is my mother's maiden name," he said, with as much politeness as he could muster. "My parents couldn't agree on whether to use that or Donner, so they put both names on my birth certificate. A bit long, but classy."

"Gay, if you ask me," Bill blurted. An awkward silence descended like a lead weight on the table. Eyes flitted back and forth. Bill, suddenly a little more sober, flushed and stammered an apology. "I didn't mean anything by that, Seth."

Dave's chewing was the only movement at the table until Sheila banged Bill on the arm. "Way to go, asshole."

Seth now clearly saw what he'd long suspected, and laughed aloud. "You all think I'm gay, don't you?"

"Nobody cares," Bill said, trying to minimize his gaffe.

"Maybe not, but you shouldn't make assumptions."

Bern was expert. He raised his hand in the air and swung it in a circle, wordlessly ordering another round of drinks from the passing waitress. Only then did he say, "What else should we think when a guy with quarterback looks wears no ring, has no pictures on his desk, and rejects the blatant advances of the sweaty-hot goddesses on Wing 2?"

"What goddesses?"

"Beth, for one."

"She has teeth like a baleen whale."

"Big flippers, though. Nobody said you had to kiss her."

Seth thought the whole matter quite funny, but knew that it would ultimately lead the conversation down a dark path. "You've got a big blowhole," he said with a chuckle, throwing down forty dollars and rising to go. "Don't worry about my preferences."

"You don't have to pay the whole tab here, Mr. Peterson," Bern said, scooping up the bills and holding them up to him.

"That's okay," Seth said, smiling. "I was named in the Versace will."

He left behind a ripple of nervous laughter and made for the door, riding a euphoric wave. He'd accomplished the evening's goal, tough as it was, even managing to have fun. The lady in pink had continually peeked at him all night, making him feel vital and attractive. The crew cut glared at him as he swept past, and that gave him the courage to glance her way once more. He hit the street feeling gloriously normal.

But the moment evaporated. It always did.

The effort required was anything but normal. Had crew cut been gone, what would he have done about the obvious opportunity with the pink lady? And the little step taken tonight, though successful, took him only to the base of the wall towering over him, the wall separating him from the rest of civilization, from normalcy. It was like a million other small steps taken before, steps ultimately repulsed by the great wall. Today the gauntlet was again laid down. In three days he would die a spectacular death, like those he'd suffered before. No number of small steps could get him over the wall in time.

His life's goal — ice in his veins — was beyond reach.

By the time he reached his car, Seth was nauseated by smoke, drink, and the omnipresent fear.

CHAPTER 4

By Wednesday morning Seth's gloom lifted a bit. Work seemed normal, except that several people stopped by his cube to relive their favorite moments from the night before, threatening to cut further into the limited time allotted to his salvation. He needed to work diligently on the presentation due Friday. Preparation was his only hope.

Sheila commented on the suspicious coincidence of Bill and Carl's "illnesses," which had forced them both to call in sick. "How late did they stay out?" she wondered aloud. Seth, passing by her cube, smiled but decided it was safer to not voice his own suspicion. Bern was out of the building for the day at a Coast Guard briefing. Dave took the afternoon off, starting a prescheduled vacation. Other than a few early-morning interruptions, the office was quiet and the day ideal for productivity. He set about preparing his notes for Friday's presentation.

Sandy stopped by with the daily mail. Since Seth rarely corresponded with anyone, he rarely received anything other than the occasional seminar junk mail. Today he received a pink, squarish letter, like a birthday card. Sandy dragged it past her nose before handing it over.

"Oo-la-la," she said, wiggling her hips, "It's perfumed. Someone has a fan." She smiled and moved off, continuing her delivery rounds.

Seth looked at the envelope. It was return-addressed to an Emily Corbin. He didn't know an Emily Corbin. He opened it anyway and pulled out a Hallmark card. It was a multipurpose card with no text, the kind on which the sender supplies the message. The front cover was a beautiful iceberg scene: clear blue skies, dark calm waters, white monolithic ice. Inside was written, in near perfect penmanship:

> *Not in some great deed of heroism; not in some great speech or act that may be pointed to with pride — but rather in the little kindnesses from day to day. —3795-1.*

Below that, written more haphazardly, was a large *"Thank You!"* and the scrolling signature of Emily Corbin.

Probably the woman from the Blazer, he surmised. Must have located him through the media. But how did she get a card there so fast? Could mail service deliver by morning of the second day? Perhaps, he thought ... but only if she was discharged from the hospital on Monday and rushed to a card shop. She hadn't looked that healthy. Of course, hospitals have card shops too.

He read what she'd written again, trying to relate it to their meeting. He preferred to think of his actions in the Blazer as a "little kindness" rather than as a "great deed of heroism." He wished others would too. The cover photo was apropos as well, considering his profession. Clever choice.

He shrugged and stuffed the card back in the envelope, just then noticing it had no postage. It had been hand-delivered. *That's how she got it here so fast.* A chill struck as he realized how close he'd come to having a visitor. Glad that she'd chosen to avoid a personal meeting when she came to call — and creating a scene — Seth dropped the card in his portfolio and forgot about it.

He'd been first into the office that morning, brewing a pot of coffee. He preferred it too strong for the others' tastes. The solution to the problem was supplied by Sandy: a white index card marked "MUD" in black magic marker and kept in the spoon drawer. When his mix was in the pot, the sign was taped to the front of the machine, warning all comers to dilute their mugs with water as necessary. He was deep into his third cup by late morning, and his supercharged mind was making great progress in the layout of his notes and the key points to be made at the meeting. It would be an impressive show — if he could pull it off. But that was always the question.

He worked right through the lunch hour, blindly masticating a homemade tuna sandwich at his desk with pen in hand, as usual. His focus today was so completely on the project that he was virtually unaware of his chewing, and later wondered whether he'd eaten at all.

He'd just opened a warm cola from his reused lunch bag when Sandy called him on the intercom. "Seth, there's a caller on Line Two with questions. Can you help him?"

He made a habit of avoiding the telephone. "Let Hut take it," he said. "He's got all the answers for me."

"He's already gone for the day. Besides, it's not about the Shy Samaritan stuff. This is NIC business."

Seth glanced at the wall clock for the first time in hours, surprised at how fast the day was going. "How about —"

Sandy cut him off. "Sheila is out to lunch, and so is everyone else. You're point man."

In addition to loathing phone conversations, today he was particularly anxious to avoid interruption, and his mind instantly and instinctively went into excuse mode. Before he opened his mouth, however, the thought of the "daily step" formed, and he pictured this challenge as fitting the bill.

"I'll take it then." With effort, he said the words as if taking the call were no problem whatsoever.

Sandy, her relief obvious, said, "Line Two."

He poked the button below the flashing light on the handset parked at the farthest reaches of his desk. The button was seldom used, and had collected dust until the reporters forced him to smudge it clean the day before.

"N-I-C, Seth Peterson speaking. May I help you?"

The caller said something, but Seth couldn't make it out. The man's voice seemed muffled, and there was quite a bit of background noise, so he pressed the receiver tight against his ear, pushed the volume button up full, and switched off the little radio on the cabinet behind him. "I'm sorry," he said. "Could you repeat that? We seem to have a bad connection."

"Yes, sir," said the caller, who could now be heard, though with difficulty. "I'm a staff writer for Eastern Environmental Corporation, a nonprofit environmental watchdog organization, and we're doing a piece on the National Ice Center. I was hoping I could ask you a few questions."

Seth was unaccustomed to taking such calls. His mind spun wildly, and he tensed as he searched for what he should or shouldn't say. "What kind of questions?"

"Just basic background stuff on your operations there. We're focusing on the effects of global warming on various aspects of the environment."

This hit home for Seth. "I'll answer what I can."

"The National Ice Center tracks every iceberg in the world. Is that right?"

"Not exactly. We use satellites and onsite craft to monitor the location of all the significant icebergs, make predictions on future movement, and generally analyze ice conditions — but just in the Southern Hemisphere."

"What about the Northern Hemisphere?"

"That's the responsibility of the International Ice Patrol out of Groton, Connecticut. Different organization. They've been around a lot longer. They were organized after the Titanic sank, I believe. The NIC has only been around since the seventies. Their funding source is different, too. They're sponsored by seventeen different countries: we serve only the Navy, Coast Guard, and NOAA."

"NOAA?"

"The National Oceanic and Atmospheric Administration. It's in the Commerce Department. That's the agency I work for."

"Not the NIC?"

"Well, yes, but NIC is a tri-agency effort. Most people here are Navy.

We're also referred to as the Naval Ice Center. But there's also a member of the Coast Guard here, plus a handful of civilians like me representing the NOAA."

"You said 'significant icebergs.' What makes an iceberg important enough for you to study?"

"We don't have the resources — or the need, really — to track every ice cube in the Southern Seas. There may be as many as three hundred thousand at any one time. The idea is to monitor and forecast movement of the largest pieces of ice. They're the ones most likely to threaten navigation. We track everything but growlers."

"What's a growler?"

"Sorry. That's NIC jargon for a small ice chip the size of a car. The next size up is the 'bergy.' That's more like house-sized."

"And how big do the real icebergs get?"

"Bigger than a small country."

"Really? That must displace a lot of water."

"If you only knew."

"But why the separate agencies? If you have satellites, can't one agency track both hemispheres?"

"Well, there are important differences. Southern bergs tend to look different. Arctic bergs are tall, peaked, easier for ships to see. Antarctic ice — that's what we monitor — tends to calve in flat sheets that float low in the water."

"Calve?"

"More NIC terminology. Calving is the breaking off of a slab of ice from a larger piece."

"And I assume their source is the Antarctic glaciers?"

"Yes, massive glaciers called ice shelves."

"This is great stuff," the man said, pausing as if he were taking notes. "What happens to one the size of a small country?"

"It moves, melts, calves, and generally makes a nuisance of itself in the shipping lanes."

"How fast do they move and melt?"

"That depends on a lot of factors: wind direction and velocity, water temperature, solar radiation, ambient air temperature, ocean currents, and other factors." As Seth spoke, he ticked each one off on his fingers. "Under the right conditions, they can move up to five miles a day. Melting occurs faster as they move north toward the equator. But bigger bergs like a B-15 or A-38 can last ten years."

The caller whistled. "The 'A' and 'B' are assigned names?"

"Correct. Just names for monitoring purposes. Antarctica is divided into four quadrants, A through D. If a berg breaks off a shelf in map quadrant B, it might be named B-15. The number is based on the order of its discovery. When a smaller chunk calves off that, it becomes B-15B, for example."

"Can you describe the formation of these ice shelves?"

"The ice doesn't come from the ocean, as some think — at least not directly. The climate on the continent makes it too cold to rain, but it does snow a bit each year. It piles up year after year, eventually compressing into ice. After eons of accumulation, this forms sheets of ice, literally miles thick. Our knowledge of sub-ice geology — what goes on under the ice — is limited, but science is making progress."

"What could go on under a solid sheet of ice that thick?" the reporter asked, incredulous.

"Plenty. For instance, we know that, in some spots, glaciers can form ice streams that can move a half-mile per year. Those ice streams eventually reach the sea and actually extend over it. Those are the ice shelves. Ice shelves extend hundreds of miles off land, grounded at the coast but floating on the sea. They keep flowing into the sea until warm conditions finally cause them to calve and float away."

"Is that what causes icebergs?"

"Well, there are other ways. Like sea ice. That's frozen seawater. It can get up to thirty feet or more thick, although most of it is only a few feet deep."

"So this sea ice isn't dangerous to ships."

"Well, no, it's at least as dangerous. It can melt in the spring and break into chunks. The chunks get pushed around by wind and waves, grinding together like a colossal slushy. Many an early explorer learned the hard way what this kind of ice does to ships caught in it."

The caller pressed on. "How do you study the ice? You mentioned satellites."

"Our roof holds quite an array of satellite dishes. The NOAA's National Environmental Satellite, Data, and Information Service operates here, but we also get feed from Landsat 7, Magsat, Meteosat, NASA's QuikSCAT, Canada's Radarsat-1, and the Danish geomagnetic satellite Orsted, as well as others. I could throw out more acronyms than you'd care to hear. We supplement that with aerial reconnaissance and on-location reports from ship captains. We take all the data we receive, record it, chart it, and analyze it. And from that, we note the trends of the iceberg movement."

"Let's see," the reporter said. He paused again, and Seth could hear something that sounded like scribbling. "You mentioned a couple of different

38

kinds of ice. Are there more?"

"There's a wide range of ice forms: new, pancake, brash, big, vast, giant, fast, as well as the bergies, growlers, and more. I could go on."

"Well …" another pause, then the voice continued: "This is all going to be very useful. But our real interest is in the reports we're getting that global warming from the Greenhouse Effect is threatening the polar ice caps."

Seth was in his glory now. "Well, not officially." The only response was silence, so he tried to clarify: "The evidence tying the Greenhouse Effect to polar ice melting is inconclusive. Especially Man's contribution to it."

"So, you dispute the theory that Earth's temperature is rising?"

"No," Seth said. "That's not what I mean at all. Mainstream science pretty much agrees on that."

"So it isn't true that an increased number of icebergs are breaking off ice shelves recently?"

"I wouldn't say that, either," Seth answered, reaching up to rub his suddenly weary eyes. "The numbers don't lie. That's true, especially in the past decade."

"So what's causing that to happen, if not climate change?"

"Look, it's really nothing new. Earth has undergone a great many global climate changes over the eons. Obviously, these can't be blamed on Man's influence, since they predate his existence."

"Is this something the Center investigates? Global warming, I mean?"

"Definitely. Well … no … I mean … I should say, our primary mission is sea ice analysis. Part of that work is analyzing changes in the polar climate, but NIC doesn't study or have a position on global warming. I know it's a political hot potato now, but global warming already gets a good deal of attention from other parts of the scientific community."

The caller paused for a moment, mumbling uh-huh's in assent. Seth could hear him shuffling paper again, obviously taking more notes while considering his next question.

"So these climate changes would take many centuries to affect the Earth? I mean, to have a catastrophic effect on civilization."

The question took Seth completely by surprise. "Uh … not necessarily."

Another pause, then the caller said, "Look, I know you said this isn't really your field, but … are there studies on this?"

"Well," Seth replied carefully, "for the past year, I've been working on a project designed to predict future ice breaks — at least, those caused by warming. Actually, it's been more like two years of effort, counting the time I put in on it at home."

"Predicting where icebergs will break? From what you've told me, that would be great. Have you been able to predict any yet?"

"Let's just say there's cause for concern."

"Really? Is that public information yet?"

Seth suddenly regretted broaching the subject of his study. Bern's open-minded acceptance of his research proposal stretched the Agency's limited scope. He hadn't even shared his final report with his boss yet. He doubted they'd want it revealed to anyone, even if they knew what he had found out. But enthusiasm loosened his tongue: "No, my study isn't public yet. We serve only the three agencies I mentioned. What they share, or ask us to share, is up to them."

"I see. And what was your name again?"

"Seth Peterson."

"Ice, nature, and God to you, sir. Thank you for your assistance."

Before Seth could say another word, the phone went dead.

Rather abrupt, he thought. He had no idea what kind of tree-hugger oath the man had signed off with. *Must be from California.*

He didn't think of the call again for several days, but the opportunity to discuss his research aloud with another person seemed to help him organize his thoughts for the group presentation ahead, and he was able to fly through the rest of the work.

CHAPTER 5

The week passed too quickly, and when Friday came, Seth still felt anything but ready. He'd focused all his time and faculties on perfecting his presentation, practicing his written speech, spending hours each evening presenting it to the bathroom mirror and an imaginary audience on the living-room couch. The material was accurate, well organized, and compelling, and he knew it by heart. Knowing that reading a prewritten speech from a sheet of paper held in one's hand was hardly an acceptable form of public speaking, he outlined the key points on cue cards, planning to jog his memory with them as he spoke.

None of that mattered, though. He still wasn't ready, and never would be. He'd barely slept in four days as a result. To complicate matters, Emily Corbin was starting to worry him. He'd discovered another card from her, sans postage, in his apartment mailbox on Thursday. This one had a cute scene of Emperor penguin chicks in a crèche on pack ice, with the icy peaks of the Admiralty Mountains in Victoria Land, Antarctica in the background. The inside yielded another quote:

> *Worry will only unfit and prevent the body from meting out the best in self and for others, and in this respect, will must manifest and not be pulled about by circumstance, as it were. — 39-4.*

> *Eternal Gratitude,*
> *Emily Corbin*

He'd worried less about climbing into the burning car than about giving today's speech. Worry was the definitive word of the day.

It was unnerving that she had tracked him down at home. Just that morning he found another card slipped under his front door. This card carried yet another panoramic view of Antarctica he recognized as the Siple Dome Research Camp, home of the largest ice corer in the world. Inside the card was another quote:

> *Fear is — as it ever has been — that influence that opposes will, and yet fear is only of the moment, while will is of eternity. — 1210-1.*

Love,
Emily Corbin

So now we've gone from "Thanks" to "Love," he thought. A chubby woman twenty years his elder who quotes a weird kind of scripture was stalking him. *That's great.*

Something else about her bothered him. The whole thing was creepy: how she found him so quickly, sneaked around to hand-deliver her messages, chose photos all relating to his research. But mostly it was the quotes. They seemed somehow more appropriate for that day's challenge than for his actions on the day he'd pulled her from the burning truck. But that was impossible. Today's quote was on overcoming fear with will. This, coming on the day of his presentation, was unnerving. Even reading it made him shiver. Mere words could not save him now, though. In fact, these particular words added to his guilt. He lacked the will to overcome the fear.

But, since he could find no easy answers, he finally tossed the card onto the counter with the other ones and put them out of mind.

The morning at work was a foggy, disjointed world. People spoke to him in vaguely familiar voices about distantly recognized topics, but he was barely aware. Unable to sleep, he'd been the first one there, again filling the machine with "MUD." He drank another cup to lift his spirits and raise his mind from the sleepy haze. Coffee was a habit, a welcome refuge, a liquid security blanket.

But it didn't help. He couldn't keep his mind from the sure tragedy ahead. His breathing was erratic. His heart raced. With an hour to go, panic hit him full-force. Thoughts filled his head. Voices spoke to him, screaming warnings of the inevitable outcome, of the sheer folly of his effort, reminding him of past failures and foretelling certain disaster.

Today was different, though. He'd promised Bern, and he always kept his word. No matter what the odds or what the voices said, no matter what the outcome, Seth would not turn back. He was tired of running. Running had ruined him. The threat was always there, but this time the consequences were immeasurable. This wasn't about him or his wants and needs, not even his life. It was about the lives of millions, maybe billions. He couldn't turn away.

He repeated these thoughts as he floated in ethereal haze down the gray-carpeted hallway with the white-block walls toward the conference room. He swung open the door and saw that others had already arrived and were conversing pleasantly. What he wouldn't give to be like them: carefree, normal. As the crypt door swung shut behind him, the wave hit. The incessant buzz of stress swelled to dull terror. *Trapped.* He sat at the end of the table furthest from the others, avoiding conversation. He couldn't have carried on an intelligible one now if he tried.

He opened his leather portfolio and occupied himself by rifling needlessly through the papers inside. Removing his cue cards and arranging them neatly before him, he looked them over without seeing, trying to get his exploding mind under control.

Sheila entered and sat in her usual spot. Bill soon followed. Each person who entered turned the fear-ratchet up another level. Each body further filled the claustrophobic room. Soon, only Bern was missing. When he came, it would be too late. Then it would happen. He heard nothing but the voices. *Go now*, they said. *It's not too late. Leave the building. Leave the city. Never come back.*

Bern Harris walked in and threw down a stack of papers on the table. "Hello, people. Are we all ready?" He glanced at his watch. "Look at that. Thanks for being on time."

That's what everyone else heard. Seth saw Bern's lips move, but the words didn't register. He'd kept his word, and the trap was sprung. There was no way out now. He'd accomplished the first step: staying. Now all he had to do was await the outcome.

"I've got a long list of short items to cover, but I thought first today we'd cover the bigger subject." He looked across the long table at Seth. "Mr. Peterson, you promised a report today. If you're ready, we'll hear that now." He sat down, and all eyes turned away, landing directly on Seth, each pair weighing tons, pressing the breath clean out of his chest.

"I'm ready to go." It felt like someone else inside his body saying the words. He stood and fumbled with the cards already properly set before him. "Okay," he said, glancing up at the eyes smothering him, "As you all know I've been developing a method to predict the location and timing of ice calving, as opposed to using the current Ice Prediction Modeling method to forecast berg movement *after* the fact."

He felt the flood rising in him. The invisible tide rose beneath his skin, past his belly and chest, and into his neck, choking him. His eyes lost peripheral vision. It rose further, past his nose, compressing all life and conscious thought into the remaining cranial cavity. The pressure forced his temperature to skyrocket. Heat flashed like a gasoline fire across his head. His face flushed and he was sure everyone saw it, saw that even now, just one sentence into his perfect presentation, failure was imminent, and he was going down.

"And I'd like to report that I've had tremendous success. I think you'll find my data quite intriguing."

43

Suddenly his brain cramped. This was as much of his speech as he remembered by rote. He glanced at his cards, adjusted them with tremulous fingers, trying to collect his thoughts. The delay was obvious. They knew. It was happening. He glanced up. The eyes were waiting. *Look at the cards*, he told himself. *Read the first line. That's why you made them. It will remind you of what to say, help you get going.*

But it was no use. He couldn't concentrate, not enough to read. The words made no sense. The speech was lost, hopeless. There he stood, three sentences into a half-hour oration, and he was through. The flood surged now, pressing instantly with explosive force to the top of his skull. It doused the fire and he could feel heat, color, and life drain from his face. The room spun, and he knew he was going down.

He must have only blacked out for a second. Next thing he knew, he was sitting in his chair. Bern was rising, and Sheila was already out of her chair and moving toward him around the table.

"Are you okay, Seth?" she said, placing a gentle hand on his shoulder and stooping to look at his eyes. "You don't look so good."

The worst was over, but now he was shaking, hard. There was no going on. "I don't feel good. Sorry, guys. I need to lie down, I think."

He stood again and gathered his things, sweeping them into the portfolio in one shaky motion and making for the door. Beyond the door were light and air and freedom. An army couldn't have stopped him.

"Will you be all right, Seth?" Bern said. "Do you want us to do something?"

Seth paused at the door, not bothering to look at anyone. "No, I'm fine," he said with a wave of his hand. "Just a touch of the flu ... or too much coffee."

He left them in silence and escaped the eyes.

CHAPTER 6

An hour after the conference room debacle, the call Seth expected rang like a fire bell in his closed-in cubicle, startling him despite its anticipated arrival. The pencil he'd flipped aimlessly for an hour dropped to the idle desktop. Without hesitation, he took the call.

"Seth, this is Bern. Can you come to my office? I need to see you. Bring your project file."

Seth said he'd be right along, and set the receiver gently back on the set in slow motion.

Feelings are strange, he thought. He was about to walk the proverbial plank to the privacy of Bern's office, past the infamous conference room where his recent undoing had played out publicly, past the knowing stares of coworkers to experience the ultimate confidential employee meeting. Inexplicably, he was dead calm.

How could that be?

He knew: because nothing compared to what he'd faced and failed at earlier that day, not even the prospect of losing another job and having to move and start over with another group of strangers.

Why had he chosen to stay in the office and "recover" while the gang continued their meeting? He wasn't sure. Why not go home and make a sick-day or two out of it? With luck, time off would allow the storm to blow over. It might help him keep his job. The impulse to run was strong.

But no. That only delayed the inevitable. There'd be another presentation required another day. And Bern had been very specific. He wasn't a manager who made hollow threats. He meant what he said. Seth would be forced out anyway. So why wait around for additional public humiliation? Why not spare Bern the unpleasant task? Why not leave a written resignation on the desk, pack his measly personal articles and go? Never look back. He'd done it before.

Answers were in short supply. What he knew was that the terror had passed. Running was something he did only when the monster was at his throat. He could handle anything, anywhere and any time when he was normal. Staying to face the consequences was the right thing. It was payback, self-flagellation, punishment for failure; ointment for the oozing wound of guilt.

God, how he wished someone understood. He wished *he* understood. There was another compelling reason to stay: the information in his folder was important. It must be shared, pursued, developed further. Lives depended on it. The data needed explaining to someone at the Center, someone knowledgeable enough to comprehend the significance. Then, he could leave. Bern's asking for the project materials was a good sign. Maybe he only wanted them handed over, but Seth's goal in the little one-on-one ahead was to convince Bern to hear him out — not to save his job, but to make the presentation he'd failed at earlier.

Laying his leather Oleg Cassini portfolio open on the desk, he methodically loaded his file, speech, crib notes, and raw data inside, throwing the flap over and snapping it shut. The portfolio was supposedly a gift from the NIC staff on the day he joined. He later learned it had been a unilateral action by Bern; no one else there knew anything about it. That was how Bern operated: always sharing the credit. Seth didn't want to appear ungrateful, but the gift seemed wasteful. All he could think of was the cost of the opulent tote and how many perfectly good manila folders the same money could buy. It suited Bern's tastes, not Seth's. But Bern couldn't have known that then. Probably still didn't.

Seth sat a moment, looking about the cube, his home for over a year. He didn't delay purposely; in fact, he intended to reach Bern's office quickly. No reason to let the stress build for poor Bern. Only doing his job. He'd undoubtedly told the truth earlier: he didn't enjoy firing people. Who would, anyway? Some people, Seth supposed, but not Bern. He wasn't the type. Bern was good-hearted. Seth hated letting him down like this. It was Bern who'd hired him, assigning him the special task Seth pitched him on. This would be a professional failure for Bern, failure to hire right, failure to manage right. He deserved better.

Seth mentally inventoried the personal items he would come back to retrieve in a few minutes, judging how many awkward trips to his car it would take past staring eyes in the office. Radio, portfolio, Carhartt jacket. What else? Used lunch bag? No, that could stay. It had served him well and could be retired now, just like him. No art on the walls. No galoshes on the floor. No pet plants. No favorite pen. He opened all six drawers. A Butterfinger bar. Bring that. And his weathered copy of Roland Huntford's *The Last Place On Earth*, his cherished tale of Robert Scott's ill-fated race against Roald Amundsen to the South Pole. He'd been trying to read it for the fourth time over lunch breaks. Little else; one trip would do. He traveled light. Habit, he supposed, or necessity.

Here we go, then.

Toting the portfolio, he left the cube and made his way down the hall with long, muscular strides. He whistled a loud tune, affording those he passed an aural warning of approach. It helped. Sandy was coincidentally on the phone. Bill was looking out the window with his back turned. Carl focused on a satellite image. Awkward eye contact was avoided. *Did they do it for his benefit or theirs?* he wondered.

At Bern's office, he knocked and walked in without hesitation. Bern looked up stern-faced and pointed silently at the door, his coded way of saying, "Shut it for a private meeting."

Bern's office was as well-dressed as Bern was in his naval officer's uniform. A fine swivel chair matching those in the conference room accommodated the small manager like a veritable throne. Two stationary leather armchairs were positioned for visitors, symmetrically facing the desk front, matching pillows wedged in their corners. A distressed-pine credenza to the left held a flourishing philodendron, an exquisitely framed action photo of Bern committing his one and only tandem skydive on his thirtieth birthday, a vase with three fresh red roses, and a smooth wood carving of an African elephant. On each wall hung matted reprints of abstract art, expensive-looking stuff Seth couldn't appreciate. A bank of file cabinets to the right held healthy potted plants. All drawers and doors were closed. The desk was tidy: phone, pen set, computer, and a calendar placemat with one ominous-looking manila folder centered on it.

Bern motioned him toward a chair with another silent gesture. No friendly nicknames now.

"Seth, remember our talk earlier this week?" Bern's voice wavered, though he made an effort to appear controlled.

Seth tried to help him along. "It's okay, Bern. I know what this is. I don't hold it against you."

"Damn it, Peterson. Why do this? Why let it get to this? I don't understand. I misread you. I thought you were the real deal."

Bern's disappointment was palpable, painful. Seth wanted to explain, but how could he?

"Give me an ear long enough to go over this stuff before I go," he said.

"Hold off on that a minute. Something isn't right here, and I want to understand it. I haven't talked to anyone yet. Nothing is set in stone. You and I both know what I said I'd do, and — *damn it* — what I should do. Now talk to me. Give me a reason I shouldn't fire you."

Seth leaned back in the chair, pleasantly surprised by his calm under the circumstances. This appeared more difficult for Bern than it was for him.

"I can't explain it, Bern. Just do what you've got to do. I understand."

Bern yelled at him, "*I* don't understand! I thought you had it. You're smart, educated, likable. Why piss it away? Did you even *do* the research, or was it all a waste of time?"

"I did it," he said — calmly, not defensively. "It's all here. I want a chance to show you."

He pulled the file from his portfolio and set it on the desk. Bern opened it and took a cursory look, enough to see that a large volume of work had been done. Then he closed it and fixed Seth with a familiar, piercing stare. "You don't present it to me, Seth. I'm the commanding officer, an administrator. You present it to the Science Department, people who can interpret it and corroborate its significance and help decide what direction to take from there, the people who give me second and third opinions on its veracity and the advisability of making it public and seeking funding for additional research." He had allowed his eyes to drift, but now his gaze snapped back to Seth, ensnaring him. "No," he said, "it's something else. Tell me why you make up one stupid, phony excuse after another to miss meetings."

Seth sat stoically, saying nothing. He knew the truth. But he wouldn't share it.

"Seth, do you know what I was going for in my Ph.D. program at Florida State in Tallahassee before I gave up and went Navy?"

Seth shook his head.

"Counseling Psychology. It helps a lot with this job. I know what makes people tick. Now, you fooled me, I'll admit that. But I don't think you're the loser you appear to be. So, out of professional courtesy, please tell me where I went wrong."

Seth's will weakened. What a relief it would be to share the burden. But when one knew, then everyone knew. He turned away, saying, "It doesn't matter."

"It matters to me. I've got over a year invested in this."

"It's all right there," Seth said, pointing at the file.

"Not that. *You*."

"You wouldn't understand," Seth said in nearly a whisper.

He shouldn't have said that. It implied that Bern was right; that there was, in fact, a problem. A problem he could — and should share. Now more questions would follow. Bern was chipping away the wall of resistance. He felt himself slip. What would it matter if he told someone? How could that hurt more than what he'd already endured, or was about to?

"Seth, as a friend, I'm asking you to tell me what the deal is. There's a reason for this self-destructive behavior. Just tell me. I want to help."

48

Still Seth held out. The need to hide the secret was strong. He'd practiced the deception to perfection over a lifetime. But this time something was different. No one had ever challenged him directly before. No one had openly sensed the thing he hid so well, so deep. No one had ever appeared to care.

But no one must know.

"Last chance, Mr. Peterson. Something's going on here. You've as much as admitted that. Maybe your job can be saved. Maybe I can help — but only if you tell me what the problem is. Hell, if I can't help you, telling me won't change anything we're about to do here. You have nothing to lose."

Seth looked at his hands, clasped tightly in his lap, fighting the urge to begin wringing them. He felt Bern's stare, felt like a kid in the principal's office being asked to rat on a friend, to break a blood oath. But the wall was tumbling fast.

Bern waited a few more seconds, and then could wait no more. "Okay then. I'm sorry, Seth, but —"

"Wait."

"Yes?"

It was coming. He could feel it rising. A Mount St. Helens of flowing words, spewing emotions. He stood and turned toward the door, but didn't go through it.

It was some time before he spoke. But that was all right. Bern was willing to wait now.

"I did the work, Bern. It's all there ... just as we agreed. Good stuff. The results are more startling than I imagined. You're right. It's important, and must be told. I don't want to lose my job. I like it here. But ..."

He stopped. Bern said nothing, waiting him out. Seth would have to say it now, but this was a thing that must be said face to face. He pivoted and stared Bern in the eye, choking on emotion.

"I'm a coward."

Bern's eyebrows went up. He frowned and spit an exasperated laugh. "Yeah, you're a coward. Mr. Superhero. He who flies into burning cars to save helpless souls is a coward. What's this crap?"

"You don't understand."

"We agree on that."

"I can't do the presentations because I'm too scared."

Bern's eyes narrowed. "Stage fright? Is that what you're saying? You've been pulling all this because of stage fright?"

"It's bad."

"Buy a book, listen to a tape, take a class. There's tons of stuff out there to help you with public speaking. It's the most common fear in the world.

Everybody has it. Get over it."

"I've done the tapes and books and seminars. It's about more than just giving a speech. That's just the worst. I'm scared of everything, everyone. I've been running from people my whole life."

"So you're shy. Take some assertiveness training. We can spring for that."

"Been there, done that. Didn't help. I know the tricks, just can't use them. Nothing helps."

"What does your doctor say?"

"Haven't been to a doctor in thirty years."

"Too scared?"

"Exactly."

Bern started nodding his head. "And you don't have many friends."

"Have to talk to friends."

"And you almost never go out in public."

"That's where the people are."

"And you avoid phone calls like the plague."

"They have a cure for the plague."

"And this is why you're militantly modest about saving that woman?"

"I prefer modesty to horrible death, yes."

"And this explains your apparent disinclination toward the hot women you could so easily have?"

"They're considered people too."

Bern nodded slowly with a keen eye.

"It's starting to make sense to you now, right?" Seth said. "You saw the weird quirks, but never understood the cause. I can't cope with it. I'm a coward."

"What happens when you try?"

"I fall down."

"Like today?"

"Like today."

"But you were a meteorologist. You did weather forecasts in front of millions of viewers back there in ... Missouri."

"Minnesota."

"Same thing. How could you have done that?"

"I didn't."

Seth hated to see the look of shock fall over Bern's face. "Oh, no. Did you lie on your application?" His voice, normally strong, had fallen to a whisper. "I'll lose my job. Incompetence. Bad hiring practices. Failure to perform due diligence. You son of a bitch."

"I didn't lie. I just didn't tell the truth."

50

"What's the difference?"

"I was a meteorologist, but I quit before I ever gave a forecast."

"Why's that?"

"I had an ... episode."

"You were scared of something?"

Seth returned to his chair. "My life's ambition was to be a weatherman. I earned my degree in the meteorology program at the University of Wisconsin at Madison, and then got my seal from the American Meteorology Society."

"An obsession?"

Seth shook his head and was surprised to feel himself grinning. It didn't last long. "It's hard to understand in other parts of the country, but weather is everything in Minnesota. It's bigger than sports. A third of every newscast is devoted to it. Skiers watch it, farmers worried about rain for their crops. *Everybody.* You go into a restaurant, a bar, a gas station, and people are talking weather. And no wonder. The temperature there can range from sixty below to a hundred and ten above. You can have ten feet of snow in winter. Easy. People freeze to death there, or they fall through the ice and drown."

"I had no idea the weather could get that serious up there."

"It can. In Minnesota, weathermen are kings, celebrities. And I was good. I knew my stuff."

"But you quit?"

"I couldn't handle it. I thought that because I practiced hard and loved the career, I'd be able to get through it."

"Something happened?"

"On the morning of my debut, a Saturday morning — when they start out the rookies — I came out of makeup, gathered up my notes, sat down on the set, hooked up my mike, watched for the producer's hand and the little light that indicates you're live, and ... I froze."

"You choked. That probably happens a lot the first time."

"That's not all. I couldn't move, couldn't function at all. I saw the producer rolling his arm for me to get with it and read the damned TelePrompTer, but that only made it worse. I could feel a hundred thousand people staring at me through the camera."

"Didn't they break for a commercial?"

"They tried. Didn't make it. Before he could cut over I wobbled a few times and passed out cold. Fell right out of the chair under the desk on live TV. Everyone I knew on Earth watched it happen."

"Ouch."

"Exactly."

"You never went back?"

"Give me a burning car any day."

"But quitting and moving out here? That's a bit of overkill, don't you think?"

There was more, but that incident Seth would never share. The humiliation was too profound, the pain too deep.

"You don't understand what it's like," he said. "I'm allergic to people. I feel intense fear whenever I meet someone, or the phone rings, or the doorbell dings. And if things like those are bad, you can imagine what happens in a crowd, or when I'm expected to face a camera or address a group. I've told myself a million times it's all in my head. Grow up, Seth. Be a man. Deal with it. Ya-da, ya-da. But these are physical symptoms. It feels like I'm about to die. My heart tries to jump out of my chest. I get this rush — adrenalin, I guess — and the lights just go out. It's beyond bad."

"How the hell do you get your groceries?"

"I shop in the middle of the night when no one is there. Believe me, I've walked out of stores before, leaving a cart full of food behind in the aisle because I couldn't face the checkout line."

"You're able to come to work and get along with everyone. They think you're a fake, a bit eccentric, or ... that Bill thing ... but I doubt anyone has a clue you're like this."

"It's not something I'm proud of," he said, shaking his head. "I've managed to cover it up all my life. You're the first person I've ever told."

"Not even your family?"

"What would I say? 'Mom, Dad, I'm a loser.'"

"Don't they have any compassion?"

"It's not that. Why put them through it? It's my problem, not theirs. I'm not this way because of anything they did. I wasn't abused as a kid. They didn't store me in a closet and give me cold-water enemas, or anything."

"Maybe you're suppressing that part." Bern smiled.

That broke the tension, and Seth managed a weak grin in return. "I've been able to get by, hiding, lying, running. I'm okay with people one-on-one, especially people I know."

"What are you doing in Washington, D.C.? It sounds like you ought to be living in a cave in ... Montana, or something."

"Minnesota. The city is tough for me, but it's easier to get lost in a crowd of a million than in a small rural town of a thousand. Besides, I'd never have a job like this anywhere else."

Bern pushed Seth's personnel file to the side of the desk, disrupting the symmetry of the surface, and stood, pacing behind the desk. Occasionally he stopped to look out the window behind him, watching the shuttle bus delivering another group of visitors from across campus to the main entrance below.

"Hasn't there ever been a woman in your life, Seth, someone you could talk to, someone to support you, someone you loved? I mean, you're not going to sit there and tell me you're a thirty-six-year-old virgin, are you?"

"No, Bern."

"Well?"

"There was a woman, a special woman, but that was long ago and far away."

Bern turned and looked hard at Seth, his instincts apparently telling him that he'd waded into taboo territory. A squint in one eye revealed his curiosity, but perhaps the volume of personal secrets he knew Seth had already revealed was enough for one day. He dropped the subject.

Seth sighed deeply. Oddly, he felt relieved rather than embarrassed by his admission, as though a burden had lifted. Poor Bern, though. Seth had dumped his problems and now sat staring vacantly at him as if expecting a solution. So he jumped back in and tried to end the awkward silence. "Well, that's it, then. Let me explain this stuff," he said, pointing at his work file, "and then I'll go."

"Now just hold on there, Seth. I told you I studied psychology, remember? I'm no psychiatrist, but what you've described here with your panic attacks is a fairly common condition. I recall them referring to it as social phobia. Maybe it's called something else now, I don't know. But social phobia comes in varying degrees. Sometimes it's so serious, people are literally scared to leave home. You obviously don't have it that badly, because you're able to function in day-to-day life."

"You're saying I'm nuts?"

"I'm saying you have a mental ..."

"Illness."

"— condition. It's more common than you think."

"I think I'd rather be a coward than be deranged."

"Just because you have a phobia doesn't mean you're a coward."

"What's the difference? It means you're scared of something."

"Cowards run from things — real or imagined — that they might otherwise be capable of handling if they had the nerve to face them, but they don't. They choose the easy way out and run."

"I've run."

"Perhaps. But the difference is that you have physical symptoms beyond your control. You aren't capable of handling the terrifying situation, whatever it may be. Your reaction is out of your hands. You can hardly be blamed for avoiding situations where experience has repeatedly shown what the outcome will be. And who's to say who's a coward and who's not? You've probably faced and defeated more fear in your lifetime than a hundred people who are —"

"Normal?"

"— not so afflicted. Fear and courage are relative. You may have run before, but you came to that meeting today. You must have known it was going to be a problem for you, right?"

"I thought today was the last day of my life."

"Exactly. Yet, you came anyway. What brought you there?"

"You."

"No, courage. From what you're telling me, it took all the guts you had to attend that meeting and to even try to open your mouth."

Seth liked the sound of that, but he wasn't ready to buy it. "Well, my definition of courage is mustering what it takes to overcome something. I've never overcome it."

"No, courage is in trying."

"It's very noble to hold an intellectual debate about definitions and fine lines, but the bottom line is the same: I can't do the job. Quit patronizing me, and let's just get this over with."

Bern looked at him and laughed.

"What's so funny?" Seth said, not bothering to hide his hurt. "Do you *enjoy* eviscerating people?"

"You big dummy, they have a cure for what you've got."

"Frontal lobotomy?"

"*No,*" Bern said, still chuckling. "Medication."

Skepticism replaced Seth's hurt. "What? Valium? Methadone? I won't walk around like a zombie for the rest of my life."

"No, No. Not narcotics. They have specific drugs, with minimal side effects. They counteract the cause in your brain. If you'd ever bothered to talk to a doctor, he could have told you this stuff years ago."

Seth was intrigued, but still skeptical. "What's this stuff called?"

"There's more than one drug. It's a class of drugs called SSRIs. Don't remember what it stands for. Prozac is one."

"Prozac? That's for freaks."

"Oh, really?" Eyebrows raised. "What do you know about it?"

"It's prescribed for people totally off their rocker. I read that some people even commit suicide or murder after taking it."

"The media blew a couple of cases out of proportion. Sure, many patients

54

on Prozac are suicidal. A few are probably homicidal, too, statistically speaking. But they were that way *before*. It helps most of them. As for it being just for loonies, twenty-eight million Americans take antidepressants. That's like one in ten. You can't tell me that many nuts are out there. Besides, Prozac is just one example. I don't think it's the one usually prescribed for social phobia anyway. There are plenty of others."

"Well, thanks for the tip. I'll keep that in mind for my next job."

"Good, because your next job is to schedule an appointment with a psychiatrist who can give you a real diagnosis and prescribe medication before you try your presentation again."

"You're not going to fire me?"

"Of course not. You don't need disciplinary action. You need *medical* action."

The notion of a miracle cure, some magic potion or pill that could render him normal was tantalizing, but even the thought of seeing a doctor set his heart racing. He rose and again paced the room behind the two matching chairs, crafting reasons Bern's new plan wouldn't work.

"What'll everyone else in the office say? They expect you to fire me."

"It's none of their business. Besides, that's my problem, not yours."

"I have to work with them too."

"Give them a chance. They're a decent bunch. They'll put up with you for another few months."

"Knowing I need a shrink?" He shook his head in disbelief. "They'll probably stone me. And Bill will throw the first rock."

"Are you going to tell them you're seeing a shrink?"

"I wouldn't have to. One word from you and the scandal would spread like wildfire."

Bern stretched himself to his full height, and Seth knew he had touched a nerve. "I thought you knew me better than that. Successful managers don't spread gossip about subordinates. Your personal medical information is absolutely confidential. Even if I wanted to — *which I don't* — I can't discuss your psychiatric visits."

"I didn't say I was going yet."

"Are you trying to talk me into firing you?"

"No."

Without warning, the power that this man had so often displayed came to the fore, and if Seth hadn't already had known what fear felt like, he would have at that moment.

"Let's make something perfectly clear," Bern said through gritted teeth. "You don't have a future here, or anywhere else I can think of, including serving the public at McDonalds, unless you do this. I can't force you to go, Seth, but I can make your continued employment contingent on it."

Seth took a deep breath and paced faster.

"Why even give it a second thought? Don't you want to take control?"

"The cure sounds worse than the disease."

"Can't you swallow pills?"

"It isn't that."

"What then?"

"They always try to shrink your head in group therapy. I've never understood why sitting around talking to a bunch of other psychopaths is supposed to help someone get his head together. Anyway, it's the facing a group I can't do. If I could handle group therapy, I wouldn't need group therapy."

"I'm sure that's voluntary. They might recommend it, but they wouldn't force you to participate."

Seth remained unconvinced. "Just seeing a doctor is bad enough."

"Have someone go with you. You do have at least one friend in town here, don't you?"

Seth shrugged and shook his head. Friends were a burden.

Bern returned to his chair, sighing. "Okay look, I'll help you. I'll call our insurance carrier, pick a psychiatrist from our HMO network, set up an appointment for you, and take you in. How's that?"

Seth paused and stared unseeing at the wall. He knew he had no reasonable alternative. To say no meant losing a job he liked. Then again, to say yes might mean ... something worse. "You go ahead and set up something if you want. I'll try to go. But alone. The more people, the worse it gets."

"Okay, Seth, consider it done. I'll let you know when and where on Monday. Let's be clear, though. You have to do this, or else."

He turned and looked Bern in the eye. Understanding passed between them. "I know it's your problem," Seth said, "but I'm curious. You won't get an appointment for me on Monday. It'll probably be a week or three before I get in. What will you say to people here? And what should I say?"

Bern leaned back in his chair and rocked. "I don't know yet. If you had any plans to fall down and break a leg, now would be a good time — anything that keeps you out of the office for a while."

Seth harrumphed, but didn't protest. "That leaves the matter of the research then. Will you keep that file?" he asked, pointing to his folder, still sitting on Bern's desk. "Or should I take it?"

"It won't do me much good." Bern pushed it across the desk. "You keep it for now. Is the research done?"

"It'll never be done. But there's enough to tell an interesting story, one that screams for more study by a wider scientific community."

Bern rubbed an earlobe between thumb and fingers. "You're scheduled for the Earth Environment Conference next week. I thought it might do our funding some good if we had something meaty to introduce, something showing that taxpayers aren't being ripped off by their investment in the Center. That, and saving the world from a global warming catastrophe." He looked at Seth. "But I suppose you won't be ready by then."

Seth made a horrible face. "No way. You saw what happened today in front of a dozen people I know. Don't think that next week I'll miraculously be able to face a hundred strangers because we talked about my problem here today, even if I did take a pill by then."

Bern Harris's mind was spinning. "Yeah, but I really want this report to grab some attention at the conference. Maybe I'll have you brief Bill, and have him make the presentation. That'll give me an excuse to keep you around a few more days."

Seth winced. "As long as I already have one foot in the grave, let me be frank — this may be over Bill's head. Let me work with Dr. Thornton on this."

Bern's expression changed from compassionate coworker to stern manager in an instant. "I'll make the assignments. This is what Steiner was hired for. He majored in Mass Communications. And Sheila is swamped."

"He's a talking head at best. This data isn't the present-it-and-go-drink-beer kind. There'll be questions — tough ones. Without a TelePrompTer, Bill is toast. But you're the boss."

Bern thought a moment. "That makes sense. But Dave is a satellite jockey. You've seen him with people. He might get through a presentation, but I'm not sure his audience would. You'll have to make it work with Bill. Give him a full briefing on Monday."

Seth should have felt relief. He had not only avoided the axe, but also gotten a lead on a solution to his worst problem. Yet at one level he was disappointed that Bern hadn't fired him. It would be so much easier just to skip town and leave it all behind again. His old scandal was surely a distant memory by now in the Midwest. Maybe he could even slip back into Stillwater, his artsy hometown on the Minnesota side of the St. Croix River, and maintain a low profile. Maybe even build a new life.

Minnesota was calling him home.

CHAPTER 7

The day had grown unseasonably warm. Seth broke a sweat while his sun-heated car idled in traffic on the commute home to Georgetown. Despite the frustration of city traffic, he preferred driving to work over riding the Metrorail, even though there was a conveniently located station on campus at the Suitland Federal Center. His fear of crowded mass transit dwarfed all other concerns and inconveniences.

He planned to spend the weekend summarizing his report in outline form, hoping that would simplify its explanation for Bill Steiner. Bill could also use the notes in his presentation. By the time he climbed the six chipped and worn concrete steps to the entrance of the red brick quadraplex that housed his second-floor apartment, he was mentally organizing the year's research. He checked his mailbox there, and carried the handful of letters and pizza coupons up to his door, planning to look at them when he got inside his apartment.

With envelopes tucked in an armpit, he readied his key with his right hand and placed his left on the door handle. As his right hand approached the keyhole, he instinctively twisted his left wrist. The knob didn't turn, but the door opened at the slight pressure from the weight of his hand.

What the hell?

He was sure he'd locked the door when he left for work that morning. *Everybody* locked their doors in the city.

Wary, he pushed the door open and immediately sensed trouble.

The one-bedroom apartment was once attractive, but had seen many landlords and tenants over the decades. Most of the latter were college students. Too many parties, décor changes, and short-term-profit-minded owners had rendered the place borderline slum. That made it affordable, and Seth rarely entertained anyway.

But this evening he had a guest.

On first glance, the living room was as neat as a thirty-six-year-old bachelor could make it — just the way Seth left it that morning — but drawers were open in the kitchen to the left, and the hallway to the bedroom on the right was piled high with stuff, as if someone had stood in the bedroom and tossed everything out.

That someone must have heard Seth enter the apartment, because within

58

a split-second of his taking in the disarray, a large man about Seth's size exploded from the bedroom and charged for the exit. He crossed the twenty-foot distance between bedroom and front door in four bounds.

Seth still stood there with one hand on the knob and the other holding up the key, ready to open the lock, his left armpit still snugly clutching the daily mail. If his high school football coach had succeeded in talking him into playing linebacker for the team, facing a crowd of 5,000 screaming fans each Friday night, Seth might have had the skills to counter what happened next. But the coach had failed. An extra split-second of reaction time would have helped too. He didn't get it.

Rather than slowing, the intruder accelerated as he approached the door, launching his broad shoulders like Lawrence Taylor into the man with quarterback looks and hitting him square in the midsection. The 200-pound impact drove Seth straight out the door, bending back the handle as it was wrenched from his grasp. The key fob took flight from Seth's right hand and landed a dozen feet away, sliding along the floor and over the edge of the stairwell. Letters flew like feathers in a pillow fight.

But this was no pillow fight.

Seth left his feet and fell on his back with nothing to break the fall. The full weight of his assailant landed on his exposed thirty-something belly, momentarily stunning him. The two slid across the hallway until Seth's head stopped them against the far wall. The other man rolled off onto his back and scrambled to rise and go. Seth was barely able to breathe, but still conscious enough to respond to the adrenalin flooding his veins. He tricked the man who was now sitting up and turning away as he rose to escape in one fluid motion.

"Hey, look at this," Seth gasped.

The man fell for it and turned to look just as Seth rocked forward and swung his right elbow up into the man's face. The move was a Muay Thai martial arts move he'd learned from a Bruce Lee video on Jeet Kune Do and Thai Boxing. When Seth was in his early twenties, Lee had inspired him to practice such moves on a heavy bag in his Main Street apartment in Stillwater; at least until the restaurant downstairs complained of noise. That ended his fitness training; joining a public gym was out of the question.

But that move was enough. The man grunted and fell away, then rolled to his stomach and continued to advance toward the staircase, trying to reach his feet.

Deep in pain and barely functioning, Seth managed to sweep his right arm out and grab the hind foot of the burglar, tripping him and laying him face forward on the unswept hardwood floor of the hallway. Encouraged, Seth sat up, still holding his foe's ankle, and tried to lean forward over the bottom half of the other man. If he could get over the guy, he could begin applying more Thai Boxing elbows and forearms.

That was not to be.

As he used the ankle to pull himself up, the last thing he saw before he was knocked unconscious was the bottom side of the man's other boot coming at his face like a strong and well-placed horse kick.

CHAPTER 8

When Seth woke, he was still on his back in the grubby hallway. A big-boned black woman he recognized later as his neighbor Charlene was leaning over him, pressing a towel to his face. Suddenly recalling the struggle a minute earlier, he flailed out in panic. The surprisingly strong woman held him down firmly.

"Whoa there, Mister. I might be ugly, but I ain't Mike Tyson and you ain't the Great White Hope. You proved that well enough. Just lie there and relax. Help is on the way."

Seth stopped thrashing around, but went ahead and sat up despite the neighbor's protests. He leaned his back against the wall his head had tried to move a few minutes earlier. He took control of the towel, pulling it away from his face long enough to see that it was blood-soaked.

"That nose is broke for sure," Charlene said, kneeling next to him.

Seth grunted in assent, taking mental inventory of his various injuries. The bloody nose was most obvious. His free hand located a good-sized lump atop his head where it struck the wall. The skin had held; his fingers came back dry. His heavy wool shirt prevented abrasions on his elbows during the fall, but they hurt anyway. Bruises would appear later. The worst pain centered in his chest and abdomen where the mysterious intruder had tackled him. It hurt to breathe or move; both of which were hard to avoid for long. He looked at Charlene and saw her wincing in unison with him.

A man who'd quietly climbed the stairs, presumably curious about the commotion above, peeked up the hallway at them, then quickly retreated. Charlene yelled after him: "I've got it under control here, Dexter. No reason for you to get involved. Thanks for your help." Then, to Seth she added, "The worthless scumbag."

Seth recognized him as another neighbor, but wasn't as bothered as Charlene seemed to be. It was a cold city with plenty of crime; many were reluctant to get involved.

"I'm your neighbor," the woman offered.

"I've seen you," Seth said. He realized he wasn't being generous with words, considering she was only trying to help, but he wished none of this had happened. He'd managed to live there a year without having to meet anyone. And now this. Then he remembered the name on her mailbox downstairs. "You're Jackson," he said.

"That's right. Charlene Jackson. I'm flattered you took notice of my name. And you're Peterson in Number 4. Glad to finally meet you."

He raised two fingers in a weak wave and decided it was time to get inside the apartment and out of the limelight. He started to rise.

"Oh, no you don't, Peterson," she said, gently applying a hand to each of his shoulders, but holding him in place like a concrete wall. "I called the police when I heard the thumping out here. They'll be arriving within the hour, I guess. Let's wait for them."

Seth didn't like that. "I don't need any cops."

No sooner had he spoken than he heard a siren wailing up the street, stopping out in front of the building.

Charlene Jackson shrugged at him. "Too late now, honey. Hope I didn't cause you more trouble than you've already got."

Seth grunted and shook his head.

A minute later two cops marched up the staircase, not in any particular hurry. The first to appear was a well-built white man in his late twenties. He had a hand on his gun holster, at the ready, and moved quickly yet stealthily along the opposite wall toward them.

"The bad guy got away," Charlene said. "If you'd actually come when I called, you might have caught him."

The all-business officer sneaked a careful peek into Seth's open doorway, as though wishing to prove to his own satisfaction that the threat had passed. He slipped inside the apartment and disappeared without saying anything to them.

The second cop, a mid-fortyish black man with a potbelly and standard-issue cop mustache had reached the second floor and responded to Charlene: "We were doing undercover work on a gang of serial jaywalkers, or we'd have been here sooner."

He stopped at Seth's feet and looked over the scene. "You two have a domestic here?"

His neighbor laughed. "I don't go much for white guys," she said, "although I'm willing to make an exception with Mr. Peterson here. If this were my man, there'd be no time for disputes. He's cute — at least he used to be."

Seth's face turned red beneath the towel and smeared blood.

"I live next door here," she said, pointing down the hall. "I called in a burglary. I assume you already know that."

Cop One reappeared from the apartment. "Clear," he said. Dropping to one knee, he looked closely at Seth's injuries. "He'll live," he said after finishing his cursory examination, "but you'd better call in a 10-52, George. The nose could be broke, and he could have a rib."

"What's a 10-52?" Seth asked.

Now George did all the talking. "We'll call an ambulance for you." He reached for his collar-mounted radio and mumbled "10-52" and something else unintelligible.

"I don't need an ambulance."

"Just for your safety, sir."

"I won't go with them."

The cops looked at him strangely, and then at each other. "Let's see what the EMTs say first," George said. "Do you live here?" He tossed his head toward Seth's open door as he took out a pencil and notepad.

"Yes."

"Alone?"

"Yes."

"What's your name?"

"Seth."

George looked up from his notepad. "Is that like Liberace, or do you have a last name too?"

"Peterson."

"How long have you lived here?"

"A year."

"You say you were coming home from work. Where's that?"

"The NIC."

"Come again?"

"National Ice Center."

"You guys deliver?"

"We track icebergs."

"A lot of call for that here in D.C., is there?"

Seth ignored him.

"Why don't you tell me what happened then?"

Charlene started in. "Well, I heard some awful big thumps —"

George cut her off. "Let's hear from the victim first, ma'am."

Seth thought for a second. "I came home from work and found the door unlocked — or opened somehow. I walked in and surprised this guy robbing the place. He got anxious to leave and plowed me over on his way out. That's about it."

"You don't know him?"

"No."

"What's he look like?"

"Bruised."

"You got in a few shots of your own?"

"One good elbow."

"Uh huh," George said, taking notes. "Would that have been to the thorax or the head?"

"Head."

"Black guy?" Cop One asked.

"White guy," Seth said.

Charlene sneered.

The ambulance arrived and the EMTs, a young male-female tandem team, approached them, ridiculously overloaded. They studied him as the interview continued.

"How old?" George said.

"Maybe thirty, thirty-five."

"How big was he?"

"About my size. I didn't get a good look at him."

"Anything memorable about him? Long hair? Beard? Tattoos? Scars? Piercings? Weird clothes?"

"No, just normal."

"That *is* normal around here."

"Then he was from out of town."

"Call in the description, Dwayne," George said to his partner.

"Did you see him?" he asked Charlene.

"No. He was gone by the time I got out here."

"So you heard a ruckus and called it in."

"Right. I knew he wasn't dropping groceries out here. Somebody hit my wall there." She pointed where Seth's head hit. "I thought they were coming right through."

The male EMT stood. "I'll get the stretcher."

"Wait," Seth said. "I won't go to the hospital. I already told these guys that."

The EMTs looked at the cops and then at Seth. The woman spoke up. "Look, sir. Your nose is broken and —"

"What are they going to do about that?" Seth asked.

"Tape it up with a splint."

"I can tape it up."

"Well, you've got a rib or two that may be fractured, but we can't be sure without x-rays."

"No bones are sticking out. They're cracked at best. All the doctor is going to do is tape those up too, and send me home with a huge bill."

"It's just to be safe," she said. "Besides, they'll give you painkillers. Ribs hurt."

"I've got tequila. Forget it. I'm not going. You can't make me, can you?"

The cops looked to the EMTs for a ruling on whether the severity of his injuries justified overriding his right to choose. The woman shook her head reluctantly.

George shrugged in response, and the EMTs packed up and left.

"Was the guy carrying anything?" he said after the EMTs had lumbered away.

"Not that I saw. Couldn't have been anything big if he was."

"Do you have any valuables he could have been after? Cash? Drugs? Weapons?"

"There isn't anything in there worth more than fifty bucks. Except maybe my computer, and he surely wasn't carrying that."

"If you're all healthy then, Mr. Peterson, why don't we look inside and see whether anything is missing."

Seth struggled to his feet with help from Charlene and Dwayne, noticing that the nosebleed had slowed to a trickle. His head throbbed and his torso ached when he stood, but he did it without complaint to avoid giving the cops second thoughts about the hospital.

They all stepped into Seth's apartment, including Charlene, who must have felt her involvement thus far allowed or required it. Dwayne wordlessly stopped her just inside the door. She called out, saying, "Seth, if you need me, I'm right across the hall, okay?" Then she turned in a huff and headed home.

While George did a quick visual inspection of the living room, Dwayne inspected the door for clues to the intruder's manner of entrance. The door handle was locked and the deadbolt still extended, but holes in the doorjamb and bits of splintered wood on the floor indicated that the locked door had been simply forced open. "Nothing fancy," he said.

George agreed. "These doors are awfully weak. Probably just laid a shoulder or boot to it."

They looked in the kitchen next. The drawers had all been pulled and left open. Otherwise, there was nothing unusual to see. The living room seemed untouched.

His bedroom was another matter. It was completely ransacked. To get in they had to climb over the pile of stuff the burglar had thrown into the hall. Giving the heap a wary eye, George said, "Looks like a process of elimination here. Are you sure you didn't have valuables in here? You see anything missing?"

"No, nothing," Seth said. "Probably just a random burglary. Broke in and figured I stashed my cash in the bedroom. That's all I can figure."

The cops headed for the exit. "You're probably right," George said, "but your description of the perp doesn't exactly fit the standard neighborhood profile, and from the looks here, he was after something more specific. We'll write up our report. If you think of anything else, give us a call."

They stepped into the hall and aimed for the stairs. Seth stepped out to watch them go.

Dwayne suddenly stopped and spoke, "It's him."

George looked at him.

"It's him," he said again, nodding his head toward Seth. "The Shy Samaritan. Seth Peterson. I recognize the name now."

They both looked at Seth, and he could feel the flush building.

As he stepped backward into his apartment, he heard George say, "Well, I'll be damned," just before the door swung shut.

CHAPTER 9

After showering off the sweat and dried blood, Seth treated his wounds. He wound an Ace bandage around his chest to protect his ribs, and used masking tape — the only thing he could find — to cover and stabilize his nose.

Scrounging in the freezer — also untouched by the intruder — he found a Swanson Hungryman frozen dinner of boneless white fried chicken, vegetables, and a brownie. Throwing it into the microwave and grabbing a fork, he used his left hand to shut all the drawers in the kitchen. The sun was setting by then, and darkness filled the apartment fast. He flipped on the light switch for the overhead fixture, but nothing happened.

Damn it. The day was setting records for bad luck.

He tried the other switch sharing the same wall plate, the one that operated the living room fixture. Same thing: no light.

What the hell?

He looked at the digital clock on the microwave, and saw that it was glowing; it wasn't a power outage. Irritated, he stomped to the only other light in the main room, a cheap lamp on an end table by the couch. As he reached to turn it on, he saw broken glass by its base, something he and George and Dwayne had missed earlier. He peered over the top of the shade at the socket, and discovered that the bulb was broken.

He went to the hallway. The switch there had failed too. Same thing with the overhead bedroom fixture and the reading lamp on his nightstand. There he found more glass. That lamp's bulb was broken as well. Not one light in the apartment worked.

It was getting dark quickly. He returned to the kitchen and opened the refrigerator door for temporary lighting as he searched drawers for the flashlight he'd bought a year before, just after arriving from Minnesota. He hoped it still worked; not much camping in Washington, D.C.

He found it at the back of one of the same drawers he had slammed shut minutes before. To his surprise and satisfaction, it worked. He shined it up at the kitchen fixture, but couldn't see through the opaque white glass covering the three sockets. Grabbing one of the folding chairs from the table, he set it below the kitchen fixture and climbed aboard, reaching up to feel the bulbs above the covering. All three were broken.

He duplicated the routine in the living room, and made the same discovery, as well as in the hallway and bedroom. Every light bulb in the apartment was broken.

Someone had committed felony breaking and entering to vandalize his light bulbs? *Whatever.*

Knowing the batteries wouldn't last long and that he couldn't leave the fridge open all night, he searched the apartment for spare bulbs. He hadn't seen any in the kitchen drawers. That left only the hallway closet as a likely spot to look. Behind a stack of ragged towels he found a single dusty bulb in a box of miscellaneous junk left by the previous tenant.

After remembering the hard way to turn off the light switch before removing the base of a bulb from a light socket, Seth installed the new bulb in the bedroom lamp and was amazed — considering how everything else was going — that it worked.

With the pressing demands of the upcoming Earth Environment Conference and his obligation to transfer the report to Steiner on Monday morning, he decided against a trip to the store for more bulbs and spending the evening undoing the burglar's mess. Both would have to wait for another day. Tonight he'd spend at the computer organizing the report. Monday he'd begin explaining it to Bill.

He fetched his dinner and dragged the office chair back from the heap in the hall into place at his computer desk. Sitting was a slow, painful process. Minutes after booting the PC, he had eaten his dinner and was absorbed in his work, manipulating the report summary for Bill's presentation. Following his habit — and another lesson learned the hard way — of backing up his work frequently, Seth reached for the floppy drive to push in the disk that always rode there half-inserted, at the ready.

It wasn't there.

He hadn't noticed it earlier, but immediately thought it strange. He quickly searched around the PC, desk, and floor. No good; the backup disk was missing. Sighing, he tackled the heap in the hallway, eventually moving virtually everything in it and creating a new pile in a vain search for the disk. As he suspected from the start, it wasn't there, either.

After minutes of indecision he did what he didn't want to do. He called the police and reported a burglary.

Fifteen minutes later, Seth carried his dimming flashlight to answer a loud knock on the front door. He opened it to find officers George and Dwayne standing on opposite sides of the doorway, hands at their holsters in case someone decided to come out shooting.

George was again spokesman. "Mr. Peterson?"

"Yes."

"Did our guest return?" He peered into the darkness.

"No," Seth said, backing up to allow the pair to follow him inside. "I found something missing. You said to call if I did."

"So you called in another burglary?"

"I didn't know the proper procedure. Something wrong?"

"Nothing serious, but now we've got two reports of burglary when only one occurred. You need to be careful with that. You'll skew our crime statistics and get someone elected."

Dwayne laughed.

"Are you having a séance here, or can we get some light?" George asked, reaching for the light switch and finding that it didn't work no matter how many times he flipped it.

"The guy broke all my light bulbs."

George and Dwayne exchanged glances and simultaneously produced their Streamlight police-issue flashlights. Dwayne's had a blue strobe light attached to the handle end, which startled them all.

George snapped at his junior partner. "Shut off that damned strobe," he said. "What is it with white guys and gizmos?"

Dwayne hit the off switch but otherwise ignored his partner, flashing his light around the main room and moving off to investigate the broken bulbs they'd missed on the first visit. George flashed his light at Seth, looking at the masking tape on his face.

"Nice HMO you got. Is that the best they could do for you?"

"I didn't go in."

George harrumphed. "You're a real tough guy. Burning cars and broken ribs are all in a day's work, huh?"

Seth ignored him and led the way into his bedroom.

"The light is on in here," George observed as Dwayne joined them.

"I stuck my only spare in here," Seth said. "Why do you think he knocked out the lights?"

Dwayne spoke up, talking to George only, as if Seth wasn't there. "Must've climbed up and reached over the fixtures to break the bulbs. He had to be pretty careful to not smash the fixtures, though. Very curious."

"Maybe he was worried about making too much noise," George said. "The bulbs would break fairly quiet-like, but bashing the fixtures is another matter."

"After rhinoing the door?"

George puzzled over it.

Seth, less worried about the noise factor, said, "But why take the time to knock out the lights, anyway?"

George shrugged. "Probably didn't want anybody seeing him."

"It was broad daylight. I thought maybe he'd planned to hide out until dark and then do the robbery, but why break in and wait hours for the sun to fall, giving me a chance to get home and find him? I mean, he wouldn't do it just to be sure that if he got a brain cramp he wouldn't accidentally turn them on himself."

"Maybe he thought he might be there a while looking for something, and was worried that you might turn on the light and see him as he dashed out. A positive ID wouldn't help his cause in court, you know."

Seth thought about it but shook his head, still unconvinced. "How could he do his looking in the dark?"

George rubbed his chin. "Have to admit, that's a question I'll be asking this character when we get hold of him. One of many. This whole burglary doesn't fit any pattern I'm familiar with around here. Now, you say something was stolen?"

"Yes."

"I thought you said he wasn't carrying anything."

"A computer disk. It's small. I wouldn't have noticed he had it."

"Like a ... floppy disk?"

"Yes."

"Like one of those?" George said, pointing at a stack of disks on the computer desk.

"Exactly."

"And what are those worth these days? A dollar?"

"No, this one is important."

"A special gift?"

Dwayne laughed again.

"No. It has all my research on it."

"How can you be sure it's that particular disk?"

"It's labeled."

"What does the label say?" George reached for his notepad again.

"Big Ice."

"Just 'Big Ice'?"

"Yes."

"I remember now. You work for the National Icemakers Association."

"National Ice Center."

"That's right. Maybe you just misplaced the disk or it's in this pile of stuff in the hall."

"I looked. It's not. I always left it right in the drive."

"You're that sure?"

"I'm a single guy. I have habits."

The officers exchanged glances again. George looked for the right words. "Mr. Peterson, are you sure you don't have an ex ... roommate ... who is a bit upset or ... jealous, maybe trying to mess with you?"

"For God's sake, why does everyone think I'm gay? I'm not gay."

George held up his hands in defense. "We're not here to point fingers. We serve all kinds. Something here doesn't add up, and I was just thinking out loud. It seems possible to me that you, as a single guy — if you *were* gay — could have had a falling-out, and as a way of retribution, Tinkerbell sneaks back into the apartment and steals your most prized research disk."

"That's clever thinking, but wrong."

"Well, here's another idea then. You have a secret admirer, someone who heard about you being The Shy Samaritan. He thinks you're cute, but he's a little weird. So he sneaks in and steals a memento."

"What about the lights?"

"Like I said, he's weird."

Realizing he could be right, Seth rubbed his face with both hands in disgust. "I hate this city."

George kept hypothesizing. "Of course, that would mean that taking that particular disk was purely coincidental. Because if it wasn't, then someone who knows you and your research has a beef with you. How are you getting along at this National Ice Cube Council?"

"National Ice Center."

George nodded and slapped his head as if he were forgetful.

Seth went on. "Seventy-some people work there, and I know or recognize them all. The guy that hit me was a stranger."

"An ex-employee?"

Seth shook his head. "I've seen pictures."

"It could have been a third party hired to do the dirty deed. Does anybody down there at the ... wherever ... want to take credit for your work, maybe?"

"Most don't even know what I do."

"What about outsiders? Would anybody else have an interest in this?"

"I can't imagine why. Not enough to steal that disk, anyway."

"What exactly is the research on that disk?"

"It's a summary report with supporting spreadsheet graphs and charts and the raw data on ice conditions in Antarctica."

George pursed his lips and raised his eyebrows. Dwayne wandered off and put his flashlight to work again.

Seth saw that his description wasn't enough. "I'm working on a method to predict major breaks in the Antarctic Ice Sheet, with the goal of understanding the full impact of global warming on the polar caps."

George's pen stopped. "Yep, The Shy Samaritan. That's my hunch. You've got yourself a fan."

"What? A love-struck penguin?" Seth waited, but a better explanation wasn't forthcoming.

"How much is the loss of that disk going to set you back, Mr. Peterson? Is it possible for you to put a dollar amount on it?"

"Well, nothing really. That was only a backup disk. I still have the original on my hard drive here, so I haven't lost anything. I thought I would call though, since something was stolen and it involved government research."

George nodded slowly. "Maybe you should report that down at ... work next week." Then he closed his notepad and said, "Okay. I think we have what we need. We'll update our report. 'Big Ice' was that filename, right?"

Seth nodded and accompanied the two to the door. "What about fingerprints?"

Dwayne snickered. "Yeah, George, maybe we could get some of the perp's DNA off Mr. Peterson's elbow."

George struggled to keep a straight face. "Mr. Peterson, that level of investigation is normally reserved for homicides."

Seth gave them a grin, feeling ignorant.

"If you think of anything else important, give us a call."

Seth watched the two descend the staircase, talking in undertones and smiling.

CHAPTER 10

Seth left for work early Monday morning, hoping to arrive before the others and slip into the safety of his office unseen. He planned to pretend he was busy on the phone every time someone walked by, and avoid the scrutiny of coworkers most of the day.

But traffic on the Beltway had other ideas.

He finally entered the facility in Federal Office Building 4 ten minutes late, and was again the center of attention. He'd left the masking tape off, but the swollen and probably broken nose left him with two black eyes, which led to shocked looks and questions from everyone he met. Friday night's excitement would not be easily minimized.

Like a replay of his disheveled arrival at work a week earlier after the burning car incident, Sandy Page was the first to meet him, followed shortly by Bill Steiner. "My God!" she said, grimacing at the sight of his damaged face. "What sort of battle have you been in now?"

"Geez, Seth," Bill added, "did you have to save more lives on the way to work today?"

The commotion caught the attention of Carl, Dave, Sheila, and Bern. A small crowd was soon confronting him with concerned looks and probing questions.

Seth squirmed in the spotlight, but realized an explanation was necessary to satisfy their curiosity, and he ought to get it over with sooner rather than later. Doing it with all of them at once made the most sense.

"I surprised an intruder when I got home Friday night," he said matter-of-factly. He correctly assumed that this terse explanation would be inadequate.

"What was he doing?" Carl asked.

"Burglarizing the place," Seth said, choosing to leave out details on the stolen disk for a later conversation with Bern only.

"I told you there were bad people in that PSA," Bill said.

"In that what?"

"Police Service Area."

Seth knew what that alluded to. He'd defended blacks against Steiner's veiled racist comments before. Silently he wondered why Bill, feeling as he did, chose to live in D.C., a city that became a haven for newly freed slaves after Lincoln's Emancipation Proclamation, and where they now represented

73

a population majority. How could Bill be so stupid to think his own boss, a black man, was oblivious to the hidden meaning of such statements? Seth thought.

"Yeah, the cops should crack down on that white trash," Seth said.

That shut him up.

"What did he hit you with?" Sheila asked.

"A boot."

"Did he get away?" Bern asked.

"Not before I shared an elbow."

"That's our hero, The Shy Samaritan," Bill said. He laughed and slapped Seth a good one on the back.

The pain almost dropped Seth to the floor. He grunted and couldn't prevent a twisted grimace of pain.

"Good move, Bill, you idiot. Can't you see he's hurt?" Sheila shoved him aside and held Seth gently by the elbow to steady him.

Bill shrugged and went defensive. "How was I supposed to know? What's the matter with you, anyway?" he said to Seth.

"I got nicked in the ribs too."

"The boy seems to have a flair for the understatement," Dave Thornton said.

"I'll be fine," Seth said, recovering quickly and holding up his hands to fend off Sheila and Sandy, who were both intent on aiding him.

"What did your doctor say?" Sandy asked.

"I didn't go in."

"Are you crazy? Your nose must be broken. You could have internal injuries."

"I played hockey back in Minnesota. This is nothing."

He saw Bern trying to mask a smile. "Yeah, Sandy, don't you know that doctors are only for when you're coughing up blood or the bones actually poke through the skin?"

"You men are nuts."

Seth answered a few more questions and then moved toward his office, using his best body-English tricks to signal an end to the meeting.

As the parties dispersed, Sandy called after him: "For a civilian, you surely lead an interesting life."

Seth, who wished life was a lot less interesting, did his best to smile.

The upside of the latest episode was that his bizarre behavior at the staff meeting Friday and the strange looks and questions he expected as a result were forgotten. After filling his coffee cup and waiting for everyone to settle back into a work routine, he visited Bern's office at the end of the hall.

"Come in," Bern said, dropping his pen and leaning back in his chair. "I've got two things for you."

Seth set his mug on Bern's desk and adjusted one of the perfectly placed chair cushions so that he could ease himself into the chair without yelling.

"Are you ready to meet with Bill today?" Bern asked.

"Yes. But I should tell you something first. There was something weird about that break-in Friday night. The only thing stolen was a floppy with all my research on it."

His boss's eyes flashed. "Damn it, Seth, don't you pull the dog-ate-my-homework stunt on me. This report is going to be given one way or another."

Seth shook his head. "No. It's not like that. This was only a backup disk. I'm just telling you because it could be important."

Bern scrunched his forehead, causing a furrow to appear between his brown eyes. "You're serious? Someone broke into your apartment only to steal a computer disk containing data on polar ice?"

Seth nodded with a grim smile.

"What the hell would he want that for?"

"I have no idea, but I thought you should know."

Bern nodded thoughtfully. "Did you work up the nerve to call the police?"

"Yes."

Bern threw up his hands. "Well? What did you tell them?"

"At first I didn't think anything was stolen. I had to call them back. But I told them about the disk being gone and roughly what it contained."

"And?"

"And nothing. The cops didn't have much interest in ice research. They think I'm either a homosexual having a falling-out with a jealous lover, or some crazed fan is stalking The Shy Samaritan."

"That makes more sense to me too — the latter, that is," he said, smiling. "I take it they didn't catch the guy."

"No, sir. And they didn't exactly instill confidence that they ever would."

"Hmm. I'll think about this."

Seth sipped coffee. "You said you have 'things'?"

"Yes, here," Bern said, standing and handing a four-page fax across the desktop. "I got the name of the closest psychiatrist from our HMO network directory. I called and requested an expedited appointment for you. Normally it'd be three weeks before you could get in, but they agreed to see you Wednesday. The appointment is only tentative until you call to confirm it, which you must do today or they'll fill the time slot with someone else. You're an adult. I can't commit for you. This form is a prescreening questionnaire they want filled out and faxed back before your first visit. The name, number and address are at the top." He paused a moment to let Seth look over the form before adding, "Remember our agreement. This is mandatory."

Seth didn't say anything for a minute or two, choosing instead to study the questionnaire. Though his eyes scanned the sheet, his brain absorbed none of its content; the thought of facing a doctor dominated all thinking. Still, he grunted absentmindedly and nodded assent. "What's his name?" he asked, looking for something constructive to say.

"It's right there on the sheet. Dr. Dong."

"Dong? What is he, a sex therapist?"

Bern grinned. "I assume he's of Chinese descent."

Seth grunted again, then rose and headed for the door.

"Peterson," Bern called after him. "Last week I was only kidding when I said now would be a good time to break a leg."

No matter what it cost him, Seth had to smile. "I thought you were serious," he said. "I negotiated with the burglar for that, but the bastard insisted on kicking me in the head instead."

An hour later, after two more cups of java and more questions from curious coworkers, Seth called Steiner over the intercom. "Bill, did Bern tell you you're supposed to give my presentation on Friday?"

"Yeah, I just got the word. That's short notice, but I'll do my best."

"We'd better go over the material ASAP. Are you ready?"

"I'll be right down."

Five minutes later, Steiner sat in Seth's cube with a legal pad on his lap, ready to take notes.

Seth plopped his file folder on the desk in front of him and flipped it open. He hesitated, expecting some comment from Bill on his ridiculous failure to make the presentation himself, but it didn't come. After a moment's thought, he decided to find out how much he knew.

"Did Harris say why he wants you for the presentation instead of me?"

"Sure," Bill said easily. "He said we can't send mutilated employees to the podium. Not professional. And your celebrity status would detract from — as he put it — 'the significant message we have to deliver.' He didn't say so, but I also think he wants me to bone up on Antarctica after that penguin and polar bear thing the other night. Probably sees this as a good way to force the issue."

Seth smiled inwardly. Bern was a genius. The guy probably spent a sleepless weekend trying to figure a way to handle the politics, yet came to work ready to face the problem with no solution in hand. Then the perfect rationalization dropped right in his lap.

76

Seth decided to help him further. "Ha," he said, "when he told me about it, he left that last part out. He told me flat out that you're more qualified for public speaking." He tried to look hurt by their boss's decision.

Bill ate it up. He sat straighter in his chair, not bothering to hide his smug smile.

"Oh, well," Seth said, "I can see his point, I guess. It's what you went to school for. This report is important. We need our best person presenting it, and sending a mangled rookie up there to do it probably isn't the brightest idea."

Bill tried but failed to assume a modest demeanor. "Well, let's do the data transfer," he said. "I don't want to let him down."

Seth nodded, and then set out his charts and data on the desk for Bill to see as he began to explain the research. "Bill, let me tell you what I know about Antarctica — or at least, the short version. Despite millennia of speculation on its existence, the continent wasn't actually discovered until the nineteenth century, and was first explored only a hundred years ago. The name itself is of Greek origin. They believed there must be an 'Anti-Arctos,' a southern version of the great bear constellation, 'Arctos.'"

"Pretty dry," Bill said.

Seth nodded in agreement, then continued. "But then you can pick up the pace by telling them how Antarctica is a continent of extremes. There's a lot of fascinating trivia to pick from. It's a place no country owns or rules. You don't need a passport or even permission to visit, just the right job or a lot of money. Since all the time zones converge at one spot there, the whole concept of time there had to be rethought. They finally agreed to use New Zealand time.

"It's the coldest continent, colder than the North Pole — which isn't a continent anyway — because, although it gets seven percent more solar radiation, it's at a higher, colder altitude. The Russian station there at Lake Vostok is considered the coldest spot on the planet."

"How cold?"

"A world record minus 132 degrees Fahrenheit."

"Ooo. That must make a nasty windchill."

"Yeah. The average temperature there in December — that's their polar summer — is negative 27 degrees, and minus 92 degrees in August."

"Whew!" Bill paused, then added, "You said there was a lake?"

"Yes. There are actually many lakes there, preserved under the ice. But Lake Vostok is one of the greatest discoveries ever. It's a 124-mile-long, freshwater lake under a two-mile thick canopy of ice."

"Liquid?"

"Incredibly, yes — with life! Its waters are heated — to maybe 70 degrees — by geothermal activity, plus solar radiation through the ice. And this is really bizarre: right smack-dab in the middle of a place where temperatures haven't risen above freezing for millions of years is a ... I guess you could call it a sealed time capsule of prehistoric microbes. Those microbes may offer clues to development of life on Earth. It may be the only place on the planet unaffected by Man. It's like another world."

Bill whistled.

"Antarctica also has the world's largest ice shelf — Ross Shelf, the size of France. Lambert Glacier is there too ... another world record. The ice is nearly 16,000 feet thick at Wilkesland. Antarctic ice is so thick, it literally depresses Earth's crust 2,000 feet. It's hard to envision, but the mountains would actually rise if the weight of ice were removed by melting — or shifting. There's enough ice there to give every person on Earth an ice cube as big as the Great Pyramid."

"Whew. Manhattan would get crowded," Bill said. "Do the Guinness Book people know about the place?"

"If they did, I doubt they'd be willing to go there to verify it. If the cold doesn't turn them away, the polar night will, 182 days of 24-hour darkness. Fewer than a hundred thousand humans have ever touched the continent, and it has zero permanent residents. There's not much other life there either — only thirty-six species of birds, two species of flowering plants, and no land animal larger than a small insect. Just birds and sea creatures. Hell, you can't even have dogs there anymore because they aren't native, and they're too dirty. They were banned by the Madrid Protocol On Environmental Protection."

"But won't the conference attendees already know these facts?" Bill asked.

"A few of the scientists will be familiar with some of this, but not all. Remember ... the conference is on the environment in general, not just the Antarctic." Recalling the reporter he spoke with, he added, "Besides, half the attendees will be press and politicians. They know nothing."

"This is some amazing stuff."

"Yeah. People think of the Antarctic as a boring slab of ice, but it's really beautiful, fascinating ... and important."

"Important?"

"Yeah, considering the changes that are occurring there now, and that have been for millions of years. Antarctica was once lush and green, teeming with life."

"Earth used to be that much warmer?"

Bill's surprise was genuine, but Seth expected it. "Warmer *and* colder. But when it was warmer, it was probably crawling with dinosaurs. The South Pole was like the North Pole then: frozen ocean with a snow topping. Geologically speaking, the continent hasn't been there long, and will eventually be gone. Just passing through. But in the millions of years it's been there, many things have happened. For example, the Pleistocene Epoch two million years ago had up to ten ice ages, each lasting thirty to forty thousand years, and the periods in between were warmer than today. The last ice age was only twenty thousand years ago. During those interglacial periods, there's evidence that the ice sheet completely collapsed. We're in a warming period now."

"Global warming?"

"Yes, but ... global warming hasn't been going on for a hundred years, but for twenty thousand years. And it's been doing it over and over again."

"So it isn't all hairspray and automobile exhaust?"

"Not likely. The evidence of Man's impact is inconclusive. But regardless, it appears that global warming is very real, very natural, very cyclical, and unfortunately, very deadly. The crusade for emission controls may be in vain. I think it would do us more good to study the ice for weak spots."

"Is it really that serious?"

"Antarctica is a volatile place, Bill. The climate is dynamic, transitory. *Very* transitory. And there's so much ice there that if it all melted, sea levels would rise two hundred feet worldwide. Ordinarily, it would take thousands of years for the ice sheets to melt."

"So if it's thousands of years, why are we worried?"

"Unfortunately, the record shows that rapid and catastrophic changes sometimes occur. We don't fully understand these, but at some point the large calving of ice shelves becomes the complete collapse of whole sheets. There's plenty of evidence that it has happened before."

"A shelf isn't the same as a sheet?"

"No. Ice *sheets* blanket the continent. Ice *shelves* extend offshore. They float, grounded only at the coast. That's where they connect with the sheets."

"So, melting icebergs aren't the problem?"

"No. A melting iceberg doesn't threaten ocean levels — the ice has already displaced the water — ice shelves, and especially ice sheets do. But today we've got chunks the size of states calving off shelves. If the shelves themselves go, you've got ice cubes the size of countries displacing water. But those aren't the killers. They're already displacing a good portion of their potential."

"So what *is* the problem?"

"The real threat is the West Antarctic Ice Sheet itself."

"Why just the West?"

"The West Antarctic Ice Sheet is smaller than the Eastern Sheet, but not by all that much. It's younger and less stable, too. Most of it is located on the bedrock below sea level. If the sheets collapse, this one goes first." Seth dreaded saying what he had to say, but if Bill were going to take his place at the conference, he had to know: "Unfortunately, the collapse of the ice sheets is not a question of if, but when."

"And you think you know when." Bill's face was as dubious as his words.

"Not so much when as *where*. Today, with the exception of an occasional crack detected by a satellite such as NASA's Landsat 7, all we're doing is reporting the location and movement of icebergs *after the fact*, and then trying to forecast where they'll go next. As you know, I spent the past year trying to find a pattern to the calving of ice shelves. Most scientists consider that a random phenomenon, but the truth is, we don't really know for sure why it happens. The goal of my study was to develop a way to predict the location of major ice faults. By doing that, I hoped to be able to predict future breaks, too."

Uncharacteristically, Seth looked directly into Bill's eyes. "What if — what if we knew in advance that a sizable chip — say, the size of a small country — was about to break off? We could be there to conduct studies beforehand. If we could do that, we could improve our tracking accuracy, and be able to better focus our research on the forces behind it all."

Bill Steiner was rapt.

"Now, that alone might justify my work, but there's more. I ... I believe I've identified two dozen of the most likely major fault locations." He paused a moment, then quietly added, "One of these may be the one that allows the entire West Antarctic Ice Sheet to break off and slip into the sea."

Bill Steiner set his unused pen down. "You really think that's possible?"

"Not only is it possible, it has probably already happened ten times or more in the past."

"In the past." Bill scowled.

"It's a natural cycle, Bill. Polar ice sheets come and go."

"So ... so you're saying that history could repeat itself anytime? We have proof of this?"

"Yeah," Seth said, and his words sounded heavy in his ears. He pointed to the file lying between them. "And it's all in there. Every proof anyone could ever need."

"Okay, so it could happen. But how long does it take for a broken ice

80

sheet to slide into the ocean? A thousand years? I mean, who cares?"

"Look, Bill, I don't see a sliding ice sheet as a one-day event that causes a big splash and creams the globe with the mother of all tsunamis. But it might happen over a short period — as small as fifty to a hundred years. Maybe even one year. Bam!"

"What could trigger something like that? I mean, it would have to be something huge, huh?"

"That's the question we need answered. Nobody knows for sure, but possibly several things. Rapid climate change is one candidate. That could be caused by events like earthquakes, volcanoes, magnetic flux, changing ocean currents. Or it could be a whole slew of things — multiple events at once. There's also proof that extraterrestrial events have caused catastrophic climate changes."

"Meteor impact?"

"Exactly. Or comets, solar phenomena, or things we don't yet know about. Virtually all those could have a more direct influence on destabilizing the sheet."

"How?"

"Vibration. A meteor or exploding volcano wouldn't need to melt the ice sheet. It could just shake the damn thing loose. There's one other thing, too. It may not be common knowledge, but Antarctica has active volcanoes."

"Volcanoes? You've got to be kidding!"

"Nope. But that's not even as worrisome as this." Seth flipped through the pages in his file and retrieved a sheet of paper. "Let me read you a quote," he said.

"'In a polar region there is a continual deposition of ice, which is not symmetrically distributed about the pole. The Earth's rotation acts on these unsymmetrically deposited masses [of ice], and produces centrifugal momentum that is transmitted to the rigid crust of the Earth. The constantly increasing centrifugal momentum produced in this way will, when it has reached a certain point, produce a movement of the Earth's crust over the rest of the Earth's body, and this will displace the polar regions toward the equator.'"

Bill cocked his head and with a smirk said, "Did you write that?"

"I wish. No, that was Albert Einstein."

"Really?"

"Surprising, right? You get to read this to the audience and get the same reaction."

Bill smiled at the thought of that power-moment.

"There's another theory," Seth said. "Whether or not polar ice throws it off kilter, Earth's rotation is unstable. It actually fluctuates. That's called Chandler's Wobble, and it was discovered by a guy from Boston named Seth Carlo Chandler in 1891. Actually, he only proved the earlier prediction of a Swiss guy named Leonhardt Euler way back in 1765. But Chandler was clever. He invented a device called the almucantar, which measured the position of stars relative to a circle centered at the zenith rather than at the meridian."

Bill's eyes glazed over.

"Well, don't worry about that," Seth said. "Just know that the Earth essentially spins like a top, wobbling about its axis. When the wobble hits its maximum distance off center, there are extraordinary centrifugal forces at work. And that's not all. There's another abnormality that affects the Earth's tilt toward the sun, and this one has an even greater effect on the climate. It's called the Milankovitch Cycle, after the guy who calculated it, a Serbian mathematician named Milutin Milankovitch. He discovered that the Earth shifts 2.5 degrees on its axis every 20,500 years, and then back again for a full cycle every 41,000 years."

"Hmm."

"That's enough to move the Arctic Circle twenty-five feet per year."

"Oh!"

"The crux of it is that many powerful forces are at work on the ice sheets."

"Man-made greenhouse gases being one," Bill said.

"Yes, but more than 95 percent of greenhouse gases *aren't* man-made. Did you know that the volcanic eruptions of Mt. St. Helens, Mt. Pinatubo, Krakatoa, and Laki in Iceland have released more greenhouse gases than have all the cars in the world since they were invented? We're not supposed to get excited about that, because they also release great volumes of aerosol particulate, which block sunlight with a cooling counteraction. The trouble is, the particles fall out of the sky within maybe a week or two — while the greenhouse gases are there for centuries. But the world has fifteen hundred potentially active volcanoes, with eight to ten erupting at any one time. What are we supposed to do about those?"

"But we *can* control our production of greenhouse gases."

"And we should. But this climate change has been building a lot longer than what Man has been doing. I'm not convinced that our efforts will make any difference one way or another. I'm less worried about our influence on greenhouse gases than I am about the inevitability that the Western Sheet will slip into the ocean."

"I guess so." Bill looked at him with awe. "You came up with all this on your own?"

"Me?" Seth gave him a rare smile. "I'm not the first to propose it. Hell, there are a dozen federal agencies and universities studying this right now. It's been written up in scientific journals, and there was even a *Nova* documentary about it on *PBS* a few years ago — although that focused on rapid melting and calving rather than on a wholesale slide. I'm just the first to identify the possible location of major fault lines."

"Where would something that big go? It's not as if ships won't see it and ram straight into it."

"That's not the danger, Bill. We're talking about a block of ice the size of Mexico slipping into the sea. The water displacement would result in ocean levels rising sixteen to twenty feet worldwide."

Bill shrugged as if to say "so what?"

"Bill," Seth said, trying to be patient, "a twenty-foot rise in sea level would wipe out New York City, Boston, Baltimore, L.A., New Orleans, San Francisco, and virtually all of South Florida, including Miami. Not to mention Hong Kong, Tokyo, London, and on and on. Every coastal city on the planet would be under water. More than half of the world's population lives in coastal regions. We're talking global catastrophe here. Imagine sixty percent of the world's population suddenly moving inland. Well over half."

"That's a serious traffic jam."

Seth laughed, but then worried that might be the extent of Bill's understanding.

"Bill, try to imagine where those people are going to settle. How do you relocate four billion people? How do you feed them with every port in the world destroyed? With transportation and agriculture crippled? Whole economies, and then entire governments would collapse. Famine, chaos, and war would follow. We're talking about the Apocalypse here."

Bill went serious then. Seth could see his weak brain working as if his skull were transparent. But with his next words, Seth had no doubt that Bill had already warmed up to the idea of being the person to report this to the world. He leaned forward over the desk and looked at Seth's materials. "Show me what you've got," he said.

CHAPTER 11

Despite Seth's mental attempts to prevent it, Wednesday came on schedule. He'd mustered the courage to call the psychiatrist's office and confirm the appointment Bern made for him. He also completed the survey, faxing in that as well. The only task left was to survive the visit itself.

The morning at work was a total waste. Other than answering a few clarifying questions for Bill he accomplished nothing. His shirt was wet with perspiration. His hands felt like a corpse. The drive across town went too quickly. Suddenly he was in the clinic parking lot. Time had moved too fast, and he wasn't ready.

But then, he never would be.

After several false starts and a few near retreats, Seth finally headed for the clinic door, his mind swimming with irrational terror.

A pleasant, attractive blonde worked the reception desk. She looked up, did a double take at his black eyes, and greeted him.

"May I help you?"

"I have a one o'clock appointment."

"With which doctor?"

He'd hoped to avoid saying the name aloud. "Dr. Dong," he said quietly, expecting her to burst out laughing.

Instead, she calmly looked at her schedule book and then back at him. "Mr. Peterson?"

"Yes."

"Why don't you have a seat? Dr. Dong will be with you in a moment."

She gestured toward the waiting room to her right. Three other people already sat in the small room; each spaced as far as possible from the others and avoiding eye contact. Seth fit right in.

After five yearlong minutes, an Asian man in slacks and sweater appeared and called his name. Seth rose, shook his hand, and followed him to an office down the hall, teetering on the edge of consciousness the whole way.

The doctor, who spoke with no hint of a foreign accent, invited him to sit. Then he, too, sat and observed Seth in silence for an uncomfortably long time before speaking. He had the questionnaire on a clipboard, which he propped on his lap after crossing his legs old-man style.

"So, Seth, why are you here?"

"Under threat of termination by my boss." His heart was pounding out of his chest.

Dong nodded … something he was apparently going to do a lot of. "So you're having trouble with public speaking?"

"Yes." He looked at the door and thought about how it would feel to get up and walk out. He might have done it, except that would attract even more attention.

"Have you sought professional help before?"

"I used to go to the dentist." The tension was easing, as it often did after weathering the first onslaught.

Dong smiled. "Did you form any impressions about our meeting from this questionnaire?"

"It's hard to get enthusiastic about meeting people who want to know what color my stool is."

Chuckling, the doctor pointed at his clipboard. "Your answers indicate skepticism over whether we can help you here. What did your boss tell you to expect?"

"He seems to think I have some mental disease that you can cure by having me pop a few pills."

"You don't think so?"

"I can't see how a pill will make me want to get up and give a speech, no."

"Let's get some background. Are you taking any medication?"

"No."

"Do you have any medical conditions we should be aware of? Any allergies?"

"None that I know of."

"When was the last time you had a physical?"

Seth had to think. "In 1979, probably."

Dong squinted. "When was your last doctor visit?"

"In 1979."

"You haven't seen a doctor in decades?"

"No need."

"I take it you don't believe in preventive medicine."

"I don't like hypochondriacs."

Dong scribbled notes. "Tell me about your upbringing. How was your childhood?"

"Normal."

"Can you expand on that? Did your parents stay together? Was there any abuse, alcoholism, or other dysfunction?"

85

"No. My parents were normal. They're still together, I think."

"You're not sure? When did you last see them?"

"A little over a year ago."

"Did you have a falling-out?"

"No. I moved away."

"Have you called them or written?"

"No."

"Not even at holidays?"

Seth was getting exasperated. "It's complicated, but no, I haven't spoken to them since I left. But they're not the problem. If I'm crazy, it's not their fault. They never did anything wrong."

"Fine. We'll come back to that." He looked at the form again. "Let's focus on your anxiety over speaking in public. Is this a new problem, or something you've always dealt with?"

"Always."

"I can't help notice that you keep your answers short. Why do you think that is?"

"My main goal in every conversation is to end it."

"Why is that?"

"Because when you talk, people look at you."

"So you feel uncomfortable being the center of attention. This isn't just about public speaking, is it?"

"No."

"Would it be fair then to say that you tend to take steps to avoid being the center of attention?"

Seth's head bobbed around noncommittally, but mostly up and down.

"Well, Seth, I'm going to ask you to describe some specifics on how you avoid being the center of attention, and at the rate we're going with your one-syllable answers, I'll be retired before I can help you. I want you to take a deep breath and try to make a paragraph out of it."

Seth got the hint. For some reason he couldn't identify, Dong's words put him at ease. He took a deep breath as instructed and surprised himself by what came out next: "This has been going on my whole life. I'm terrified of the stupidest things. I can't do stuff a little girl can do. I hate crowds. I don't know how I got through school. I hate funerals, parties, *any* social gatherings. I do my grocery shopping in the middle of the night when there's no one else there. I haven't been to a barber in decades. I cut my own hair. I can't cope with people. I get scared. I'm a coward."

"Do you have many friends?"

"None, really."

86

"Does that bother you?"

"Not much. Life is easier that way."

"Have you ever considered suicide?"

"Is that your professional recommendation?"

Dong laughed. "No, just a question."

"Well, I've thought about it, but no, that's not me. I'm actually happy — when I'm not scared to death."

"What happens when you get scared?"

"I get these ... episodes. A fear comes over me. It can happen in an instant. I can't control it, no matter what I do. When it's really bad, I go down."

"Go down?"

"Pass out."

Dong scribbled hard now. "So you've literally fainted?"

"A few times. That's what I fear most."

"Tell me about an incident where that happened."

Seth related his disastrous debut doing the weather in Minnesota. Dong was obviously intrigued, but to Seth's surprise, didn't act as if it were abnormal. "You must also occasionally do things that give you pleasure or that you feel have socially redeeming quality, actions you're proud of, or that took some courage to accomplish. Tell me about one of these situations from your past."

Seth frowned and thought for a moment. This was a painful subject. All his life, it seemed, he had craved the recognition and praise he felt he deserved. But to accept it meant drawing unwanted attention. As usual, he minimized. "Well, there was the time I climbed the neighbor's tree to get their daughter's cat down."

"How long ago was that?" Dong said as he wrote.

"I was seven."

Dong stopped writing. "How about something a bit more recent."

Seth sighed heavily and thought harder. "I suppose you've heard about that woman who was pulled from the burning car recently?" he said reluctantly. "The one the media makes such a big deal about?"

Dong looked at him blankly for a second. Then his eyebrows went up. "You're The Shy Samaritan?"

Seth nodded slowly. "Psycho Samaritan is more accurate."

"Congratulations," Dong said. "That certainly qualifies. I've never treated a celebrity." Seth began to blush and regret that he'd mentioned it.

"You must feel very good about what you did. You saved a woman's life."

Seth shrugged. "Sure. But see, that's the problem. Burning cars are fine, but warm spotlights are a real killer."

Dong smiled an understanding smile. "I see you're still a bit sore from that ordeal."

Seth was unable to control the occasional wince his ribs produced, and obviously couldn't hide the damaged nose and eyes. "It's not from that. I tussled with a burglar a couple of days ago."

Dong shook his head in amazement, and Seth sighed inwardly: another person in awe of his crazy life.

They chatted for another half hour about specifics in his past before Dr. Dong began to sum things up.

"Okay, Seth, you claim to be a coward. Let's analyze the word. According to the dictionary, it's a person without courage. Courage is the capacity to meet danger without yielding to fear. Fear is the instinctive emotion aroused by impending danger, pain, or evil. Now this may be a bit of Clintonian parsing, but despite your assertion that burning cars are fine, we can both agree that you had some fear during that rescue, right?"

Seth nodded.

"The impending danger and pain were real, so your instinctive emotional reaction was rational. Yet you did not yield to it, which required courage. Thus, quite literally, you are not a coward. The dictionary has another word: phobia, a morbid and often irrational dread of some specific thing. Morbid describes something as not natural or healthy, unwholesome. Your mind is deceiving you, making you more terrified of imaginary or irrational things than of real threats."

"So you don't think I'm a coward," Seth said eventually, "but I *am* insane."

"Not quite. I think you work for an intelligent fellow. You should be grateful he did what it took to get you to come in. You have a rather severe case of what we call Social Avoidance Disorder, also known as Social Phobia, or SP. The worst version of this is agoraphobia, which you obviously don't have. That's when social anxiety is so intense one is unable to function at all. People with this condition find it difficult to hold down jobs, and are literally scared to leave home.

"Symptoms of SP can manifest themselves in a variety of ways. Common ones are irrational fears that trigger anxiety attacks. These 'episodes,' as you call them, are false alarms, responses to warning signals sent out by one of the noodles in your brain called the amygdala, which releases stress hormones and glucose into the bloodstream. These produce intense physical reactions such as sweating, shaking, elevated heart rate and blood pressure, loss of bowel control, nausea, dizziness, and so forth. Right or wrong, a memory of the frightening event is imprinted on your brain, which primes it to repeat the reaction when facing similar stimuli in the future. Your condition is serious enough to cause loss of consciousness, but you're lucky."

"Yeah, I'd rather pass out than fill my pants."

Dong smiled. "No. I mean numerous medications are available today that can control this quite effectively."

"You can cure me?"

"'Cure' isn't the right term. These drugs, called selective serotonin reuptake inhibitors, or SSRIs, are taken indefinitely to control the symptoms, and they work roughly two-thirds of the time."

"Prozac?"

"That's an example. It isn't the one I typically prescribe first for SP, however. I prefer Paxil. If that doesn't suit a patient, I switch to Zoloft, Celexa, Wellbutrin, or Luvox. There are other options as well: Buspirone, or the monoamine oxidase inhibitors such as Nardil, Parnate, or Marplan. Side effects vary from drug to drug and patient to patient, but they're usually minor."

"Like what, loss of bladder control? Projectile vomiting?"

"Nothing so drastic. Usually only temporary gastrointestinal discomfort, drowsiness, weight gain, libido changes, other such stuff."

Dong went on for another minute, losing Seth in his recitation of the known list of tricyclics, MAOIs, novel antidepressants, and SSRIs. Seth brought him back.

"I don't like the idea of taking happy pills to solve problems."

"SSRIs aren't mood altering. Besides, is rigid conformity to your principle worth the pain you cause loved ones?"

Seth fingered an earlobe. "Just a pill and I'm okay? No head shrinking? No group therapy?"

"We could supplement your treatment with hypnosis, and there are Social Phobia support groups you can join."

"Those must be some lively meetings."

Dong smiled as he opened a drawer and retrieved a small pharmaceutical package. "This is a starter kit of Paxil. I'll start you on a modest dosage of five milligrams per day for one week. Then you'll jump to ten milligrams for another week. I'll meet with you again in two weeks. Then we'll assess what to do next. The typical full dosage is forty milligrams. Realize that this doesn't produce overnight results. It may be weeks before the desired result is attained. Also, it's important to challenge yourself along the way, taking on things you wouldn't otherwise believe you could do. Once you see that

89

they're possible, the brain begins to reprogram itself accordingly, and future anxiety attacks become less likely. In that, a 'cure' is possible."

Seth read the back of the package while the doctor wrote a prescription. "What about coffee consumption, Seth? Do you drink it?"

"Oh yes."

"Much?"

"Way much."

"Regular or decaffeinated?"

"La Brea Tar Pits."

"I recommend switching to decaf. Caffeine exacerbates anxiety."

Seth wrinkled his nose. Doctors always wanted you to give up the good stuff.

"What about illegal drug use, Seth? Do you have any history of that?"

"I smoked pot once at a party, but it freaked me out, made me even more paranoid. I had to sneak out and go home. Never did it again."

"How about cocaine or LSD or heroin?"

"No way. Drugs were never my thing."

"How about alcohol? Do you drink?"

"Well, yeah. I mean, I'd probably still be a virgin if it weren't for beer courage. I've done my share of boozing, but I wouldn't say I'm a drunk. I prefer my orange juice straight."

"You're lucky that way. Many people with Social Phobia are drawn to chemical dependency as a crutch, which of course compounds their problem. When it comes time for them to seek help for the phobia, we're treating two problems: anxiety and dependency — and the latter can be much more difficult to overcome."

"Hmm."

"Speaking of virginity, you have been intimate?"

"I don't have fallow crotch, if that's what you mean."

"I'm sorry?"

"Oh, my dad grew up on a farm in western Minnesota. He used to refer to impotence as 'fallow crotch.'"

Another smile. "I see. You're not married, Seth?"

"No."

"Never?"

"No."

"Girlfriend?"

"No."

"Do you find it difficult to date?"

"Yes."

"You do realize that you're a fairly handsome man. I can't imagine you'd have much trouble getting dates if you tried. I would guess it's the 'trying' that's hard. The Paxil should help you there."

"Not interested."

"Did you have a bad experience?"

"You could say that."

"Do you want to talk about it?"

"Not particularly."

"Well then, let's return to the question of your parents. I find it enigmatic that you haven't communicated with them in over a year, though you maintain they were fine parents and you blame them for nothing. There's an inconsistency there, and I suspect this topic might be important, something we should be talking about. You're here for help, not to be judged. Don't hold back. And, Seth, your answers are becoming short again. Let's try for another paragraph here."

Seth fumbled with the package in his hands, avoiding Dong's eyes. This was a subject he did not want to discuss. He'd never mentioned it to anyone before.

No one must ever know.

Dong waited patiently. Seth knew his delay was telling, that the longer it went on, the more obvious it was that Dong had correctly identified a festering sore. He struggled a full minute in silence, and his heart began to pound again. But he seemed to gain strength from the drugs in his hand — even before taking them — as if they were helping him through osmosis, as if just knowing there was hope and that he was heading in the right direction had already begun the healing process.

Suddenly he decided to tell his story, but a wave of emotion hit and he had to wait more seconds or he was sure his voice would crack and tears would well in his eyes.

"Here's the deal," he said at last. "My TV weatherman fiasco wasn't the only public debacle I've had. In fact, it wasn't even my worst." He paused again, but Dong was a patient doctor. "In Minnesota I fell in love with a wonderful woman. She was a news reporter for WCCO, a rival station to KSTP, where I was hired. We met at an industry get-together. I loved her right from the start, but of course had trouble doing anything about it. Luckily, she was a very self-confident, assertive woman. She basically did all the work getting us together. It was hard overcoming my fears, but she was persistent and I really liked her. I think that gave me extra courage. Anyway, we became an item and eventually got engaged."

He looked up finally, and Dong's eyebrow was raised. At least he wasn't boring him. "Was this before your debut?" he said.

"Yes, I worked quite a while behind the scenes before getting my break at the weather."

"So you were engaged at the time you fainted on air."

"Uh huh."

"And I assume your fiancée was watching?"

"Oh yeah."

"I see. And this ended your relationship?"

Seth saw where Dong was headed. "No, it wasn't like that."

"What happened then?"

"My passing out on TV didn't seem to bother her. It didn't affect our plans. But the engagement happened before I realized how important it was to her to have a big, traditional wedding. I knew from day one the wedding was going to be a problem, but I was trapped. I loved her, and wasn't about to lose her. I tried subtle tricks to downsize the ceremony, which was about six months after the debut, but they all failed.

"The nub of it is," he said after a stumbling pause, "the fear just built up and built up until the day of the wedding, when the time came to step out of the back room at the church and walk up in front of those two hundred people and face them all for that intense ritual ..."

He had to hesitate again.

"... The terror just took over. I had no control. I slipped out another door and left the church. At first I told myself it was just for a breath of fresh air, but I kept walking. I meant to go back, but then I knew too much time had passed, and they all had to know something wasn't right. Now I'd created a scene, and it would've been even harder for me to face that situation than face the wedding. It was too late. So I panicked and ran. I didn't even take my truck. I ran home, packed my bags, went to the bank, closed my account, took a cab to the airport, and took the next flight to anywhere. It happened to be here."

Seth put his head in his hands. "I left her there. I left them all there, my parents, too. How could I have done that? That's cowardice."

After a moment he looked up to see an enthralled Dr. Dong.

"And now here I am blubbering to a complete stranger."

"It feels good, doesn't it?"

It did, in a strange way. Yet in the telling of it, Seth realized again the totality of what he'd done a year earlier, how he'd destroyed his life, dashed his dreams, and worst of all, hurt his family and the woman he loved. "It all just snowballed on me. I kept making one bad move after another, each one meant to avoid the consequences of the previous one."

Dong scribbled long and furiously before responding.

"Seth, didn't it occur to you that six months after your humiliating experience doing the weather, your fiancée still wanted to marry you, and your parents and two hundred other loved ones still thought enough of you to share in your wedding celebration?"

"What do you mean?" Seth already felt bad enough.

"You see it's typical of Social Phobia sufferers to have a distorted view of social embarrassment. We all suffer embarrassing moments. *Your* mind simply blows them out of proportion."

Actually, it had not occurred to Seth exactly that way. "But the TV thing didn't affect them directly. Going down at my own wedding would have been ten times worse."

"For you only, Seth. Now, nobody would dispute that it would be embarrassing, but it does happen. People wake up, get back on their feet, and the ceremony goes on. Some even have a good laugh about it later. You compounded your problem."

Seth was pensive. The truth hurt.

"We know your fear is irrational," Dong said. "It affects judgment. But ultimately you're responsible for those actions. The road to recovery requires enlightenment. You must become more aware of how you react to uncomfortable situations. Listen to your body. Your fight-or-flight mechanism is out of whack. It has you reacting as a wild animal to situations that don't require such a response. Stop and think about the worst possible outcome of your fears. As you've learned, facing them is rarely as bad as running from them. The medication will help you with this, but alone it's no cure. Without challenging yourself and reprogramming your mind, you'll continue to avoid normal life situations and fail to attain your full potential in career, love, and life goals."

"Hmm." Dong was good. He made a lot of sense. But whose cruel joke was it that forced him to face a fear to defeat it?

Why can't they just go away?

"You haven't communicated with anyone from Minnesota since?"

"Not a word."

"How do you feel about that?"

"Guilty as hell."

"Is your plan to hide from your family and ..."

"Campbell. Campbell Morrison."

"...forever?"

"I'm sure they wouldn't want it any other way."

"We might assume that's true for Campbell, though not necessarily. But do you really think your parents want that, or are you still thinking of yourself by running?"

Seth didn't want to think about it.

"We're out of time, Seth, but I'd like to see you again in two weeks. Begin taking the medication, and I'd like you to think about Campbell and your parents over the two weeks. Think about whether continuing to hide is helpful to either of you. Think about what it might take to bring yourself to contact them and face whatever venting they feel justified in doing."

Seth left the clinic drained. He wasn't expected back at work, so he used the early hour as an opportunity to beat the rush-hour traffic home.

The only good news lately was that Emily had apparently called off the chase. It had been five days since her last card. But, like a mysterious omen, waiting for him at home was another pink envelope. He opened it downstairs in the entryway to find more Antarctic photography. She'd obviously bought the complete set. This one was a tender scene of a pair of king penguins nuzzling in the snow. Not wanting to but unable to resist, he read today's message:

The influence or force that motivates the life of each soul is love!
But it may be love of self, of fame, of fortune, of glory, of beauty, or of
self-indulgence, self-aggrandizement, or the satisfaction to the ego! —
1579-1.

Your Friend,
Emily Corbin

His mind jumped back to his discussion of Campbell and his parents: love. It was as if Emily was talking directly to him.

Who was this woman?

CHAPTER 12

Damn psychiatrists.

It had been two days since Seth's visit to Dr. Dong, and the medicine had done nothing. But, he forced himself to admit, the talking had. The guilt he'd almost learned to live with now consumed him again. A hundred times each day, he was haunted by the image of the lovely Campbell Morrison, dressed in white and holding a bouquet of flowers, standing at the altar without him, facing the crowd and taking the brunt of humiliation alone as she and all the guests realized there would be no groom.

And Dong wants me to think about this? He might as well have recommended suicide.

The doctor had to be wrong. Making contact with people from his past couldn't possibly help anyone. How could they forgive him? They would want to kill him. Forget that. He had other problems now.

Seth breathed deeply, gathered his courage, and walked through the large glass doors of the Hilton Towers Hotel north of Dupont Circle to watch Bill Steiner make the presentation. He dreaded going. There was a crowd, and the speakers — nerve-racking just to watch — and the guilt of knowing it should be him up there. It was overwhelming to imagine himself up there at the podium facing the audience.

Bern had asked Seth whether he planned to attend tonight's conference, and whether he wanted to meet and ride together. Seth was convinced the invitation was a veiled ploy to ensure his attendance.

He considered skipping the conference; so strongly, in fact, that he rejected Bern's offer, saying he'd come along on his own, holding the possibility that fear would keep him away. It was always necessary to ride solo in case a quick exit was required.

But he forced himself to do the honorable thing and show up, crossing Rock Creek on the Dumbarton Bridge. Curiosity over how Bill would perform was one reason. Seeing the audience's reaction was another. That was key. More study was required on the weakening Antarctic Ice Sheets. A large group of environmental journalists, scientists, politicians, and other related money-holders was in attendance. These were the movers and shakers who could make stuff happen. He hoped Bill could capture their attention with the compelling research.

Passing through the marble and tile lobby, he followed the accumulating crowd toward the hotel's concourse level. His internal tension rose as he queued with the clot of people waiting to slip through the meeting-room door. As he entered, he glimpsed a poster advertising the "1st Annual Earth Environment Conference" and "EEC — World in the Balance" on an easel to the side of the doorway in the hall. His name was still one of the six listed speakers, but a red highlighter had been used to draw through his name, and Bill Steiner's was written beside it. It was an unprofessional modification; the transparent ink failed to mask his name printed in black beneath. Given the short notice, the quality was understandable; nevertheless, he wished they'd done the alteration in black ink so his name didn't appear at all. Many of the guests were out-of-towners unfamiliar with The Shy Samaritan, but his name had been in the news enough lately. The last thing he wanted was more attention, especially in a large public gathering.

He dismissed the concern as he entered the room. No one paid any attention to the poster. After all, it was the topic of the speeches and prestige of the National Ice Center and other organizations that attracted attendees, not unknown speakers.

Seth chose an aisle seat near the doors at the back end to allow a hasty exit and sat hunched forward, pretending to peruse the program he was handed at the door, hoping no one would recognize him and initiate conversation.

Against his wishes, the large room slowly filled to capacity, and soon all the chairs around him were occupied. A threesome of Asian men wearing fine business suits took the seats next to him. He was relieved to hear them respond in Chinese patter and lots of nods when he raised the courage to smile and greet them as they squeezed past. No conversations there, he thought, relief washing over him.

A woman approached the dais, and Seth's blood pressure rose incongruously as the crowd noise diminished. She welcomed everyone and matter-of-factly introduced the first speaker, a boring, hem-hawing, bespectacled representative of the Oceanographic Society who spent a half hour updating the audience on global warming's latest statistics: a mind-numbing mountain of data prompting climatologists to declare with confidence that the past year was a record-breaker for the planet, the warmest in 1,200 years. Most of his material focused on Man's influence on climate, stuff Seth was already all too familiar with.

Continual burning of fossil fuels was polluting the atmosphere with carbon dioxide, causing the average temperature over the past hundred years to rise a full degree off the norm, and it was now projected to rise as much

96

as nine or ten more within the next century. If this happened, catastrophic ecological changes would occur. Species would expire at an ever-increasing rate. Deserts would spread. Forests would die. Crop yields would fall, with devastating repercussions for world food supplies and the global economy.

It was good stuff, the perfect precursor to Seth's material. Get the crowd worked up and then deliver the big blow — one that most here had never considered — that a hunk of ice a mile-and-a-half thick and as big as Mexico could slide off the Antarctic continent and end the world as we know it. And this could happen in a period as short as one year, and might begin any day.

But never fear; Seth Peterson had developed a method to predict the location of likely faults in this ice. This knowledge, if properly applied and supported by well-funded research, could lead to possible remedies. Would mankind reverse global warming in time? Could he patch the weak ice and prevent catastrophe? Would he take precautions in anticipation of total destruction of every coastal city in the world? Who knew the answers to these many and complex questions? But the logical start was notification to the scientific community of impending doom — and the glimmer of hope that Seth's research held.

In spite of the gnawing stomach it caused, Seth wished he were up there instead, delivering the message with the passion and conviction it deserved. But this was Bill Steiner's mission. His presentation was next, and the stage was set as well as Seth could hope.

The speaker finished and left the podium to a smattering of applause. There was a one-minute interim before Bill appeared, and the crowd noise rose slowly as pockets of discussion broke out. Seth tried to return his focus on the program, but his heart pounded in anticipation. The anxiety was quickly becoming intolerable. He shifted his feet and leaned forward and back, trying to find a body position in which his heart could beat comfortably. He was so terrorized to watch someone else speak publicly that what he had suspected all along sank home in irrefutable truth: He couldn't have done the presentation on his own, medicine or not. This event would have been another debacle almost as bad as the wedding, and far more public. As this thought compounded his fear and forced perspiration out of every pore, Bill Steiner walked confidently to the podium, and the crowd din subsided.

Bill stood Al Gore-erect at the dais and smiled politely while waiting patiently for the room to come to order. He adjusted the microphone and managed only to say "Good evening" before the trouble began.

First, the power failed. The room went black and emergency lights in the upper corners came on, providing a dim, séance-like aura. A hum came up from the crowd, and then a hush settled as everyone paused to ponder why the lights had gone out in good weather, and when they'd come back on. Someone laughed. Someone else let out an eerie "oooh-wee-oooh" that generated more chuckles.

Five seconds after the lights went out, there was a bright flash along the wall to Seth's left, accompanied by a strangely muffled yet vaguely familiar sound. A commotion began at the front of the room by the podium. Seth's first impression was that an electrical problem with an outlet or light fixture had caused the flash, and that maybe a fire would break out.

At the front of the room, a woman began screaming, setting the room to panicked motion. Chairs banged around as people frantically strove for the aisles, then the one known exit at the rear of the room near Seth.

He could have been first out the door, but something about the nonstop wailing at the front compelled him to force his way against the grain of the human stampede toward the exit. He used his large size and strength to part the crowd, drawn by the urgency of the woman's distress.

Finally he broke through the pack and rushed to the podium, the source of the screams. By the time he got there, his pupils had adjusted to the diminished light. As the crowd fought and clawed their way from the room, Seth alone knelt to help the incoherent woman on the floor by the podium.

The focus of her attention and grief was a human body. By her side, splayed on the floor behind the podium, was Bill Steiner. His brains were splattered over a wide area.

CHAPTER 13

The next morning, there was a loud knock at Seth's door.

He'd barely slept at all, finally drifting off in the wee hours, sprawled on the couch. He glanced at the kitchen clock through glazed eyes and thought he was a half hour late for work before remembering it was Saturday.

Too groggy to peek through the peephole or pull a T-shirt over his bare, once-muscular chest, he shuffled over and removed a wooden chair he'd used to wedge the broken door shut.

Two grim white men in gray suits greeted him. The older one, a frumpy, fiftyish man with a comb-it-to-hide-the-bald-spot haircut, produced a badge and introduced himself as Detective Newman, Metropolitan Police Department Violent Crimes Unit. Newman's suit fit poorly over his puffy body — so badly, he must have preferred it that way. He introduced his partner as Detective Marvin Roach, a smaller but athletic man who probably shaved on weekends.

Seth stepped back and they entered silently, without invitation. Just as uninvited, they followed him into the small kitchen, where Seth winced again as he poured himself a glass of orange juice and downed his third dose of Paxil. The pain in his ribs hadn't diminished; he leaned against the counter, awaiting their questions.

"We've been assigned to the Earth Environment Conference shooting, Mr. Peterson," Newman said it as if he expected Seth to resent it.

There was no antipathy in him. Though nervous, Seth was glad they'd come. "Any leads yet?" he asked.

Newman ignored the question. "Were you there last night?"

"Yes."

"Is that where this happened?" He pointed at Seth's two black eyes, now a fading but still-noticeable shade of purple.

"No, that was last week."

Newman adjusted his belt and cleared his throat. "You were originally scheduled to speak at the conference last night. The deceased took your place. Is that correct?"

After determining that Bill Steiner was beyond hope, Seth fled the scene quickly the night before, unable to cope. The situation had quickly dissolved into chaos. Panicky people, flashing lights, sirens, EMTs pumping a dead man's chest, cops running helter-skelter, shouting, brandishing guns and trying to preserve the crime scene. Yet other than the murder of Bill Steiner, no one knew what had happened. The police could do no more than detain witnesses and gather information. Seth decided unilaterally that he'd answer questions later. He slipped away through the crowd and headed home, shaking uncontrollably and grappling with the realization that it could have been him on the conference room floor.

"Right," he said. "It was my material Bill was going to present."

Newman nodded at Roach, who magically knew this meant to start taking notes.

"Why the change of plans?"

"My boss thought he'd do a better job."

"When was the schedule changed?"

"I don't remember. Monday? You'd have to ask my boss, Bernard Harris. He made the call."

"We already talked to Mr. Harris."

"What did he say?"

"This works better when we ask the questions."

Seth took a deep breath. His ribs didn't appreciate it.

"Where did you disappear to last night, Peterson?"

"Home."

"You shouldn't have left the crime scene. Didn't it occur to you that we might want to ask a few questions?"

"I didn't know I was a suspect."

Newman smiled cutely at an expressionless Marvin Roach. "Even if you're only a witness, we like to ask questions. We're funny that way. But since you mention it, yes, it does seem you'd have motive, and you did flee the scene."

"What motive?"

"Maybe you think that should've been you giving the speech. Maybe you didn't think Mr. Steiner was doing well with your material."

Seth shook his head and picked up his prescription of Paxil. "No. See this? These are scaredy-cat pills. I've got some kind of phobia they just told me about. I didn't *want* to give the presentation. Couldn't have. Too scared. That's why Bill did it. He was helping me. Beside, why the hell would I just come home and wait around to be arrested?"

The notion that he'd just spoken a "paragraph" without having it pried out of him, while revealing his mental infirmity to two complete strangers after holding it secret for thirty years, suddenly occurred to him.

Newman was unmoved.

100

Seth pressed on. "I was the one who tried to help the woman screaming at the front of the room when everybody else bolted for the door."

Newman cocked his head. "You don't know who she is?"

"Should I?"

"Rachel Steiner. Bill's wife."

Oh, no. Seth had never met her during her husband's short stint at the Center. He tried to conceal his shock as he realized she'd been in the front row to cheer on her young husband as he eagerly took advantage of the career opportunity offered by Seth's weakness. Seth tried to ignore the issue. "Well ... if I killed him, don't you think I'd be the first to leave?"

Newman ignored the question. "Do you own any weapons, Mr. Peterson?"

Seth was getting upset: a mixture of anger over the accusation, grief over Bill's death, and guilt that maybe it should have been him instead. He swore and threw the prescription on the counter. "No. I've never owned a gun in my life."

"Do you mind if we look through your apartment?"

He smirked. "Be my guest. It's a bit messy. I still haven't cleaned up from the burglary."

Newman and partner eyed each other in silence.

"What burglary?"

"What do you mean 'what burglary?' Don't you guys know what the hell goes on in your own police department?"

Newman and Roach stared at him stoically.

"I interrupted a burglar here a few days ago. We had a two-molecules-can't-occupy-the-same-space confrontation in my doorway."

"Looks like he carried more atomic weight than you."

"He took an electron to the face."

"Ah. Did they catch a suspect?"

"Not that they told me."

"You called MPD?"

"Yes."

"Do you remember the officers' names who responded to the call?"

Seth scrunched his forehead in thought, but stopped because it hurt his nose. "George and ... Dwayne. Don't know their last names."

Newman nodded at Roach, who jotted the names on his pad. "Did he get anything?"

"I didn't think so at first, but yeah, he stole a computer disk with my research on it."

"What research?"

Seth sighed and dropped his head. He didn't want to go through it all again. "The research that Bill Steiner was ... presenting last night." The last few words came slowly as a strange thought occurred to him and a chill went up his spine.

Newman must have had the same thought. His eyebrows went up and he told Roach to call in a request to the Second District for the police report on the burglary.

Newman peered down the hallway and pointed at the pile of debris the burglar had thrown from the bedroom. "He did all that and came away with only a computer disk with environmental research on ..."

"The methodology for location and prediction of Antarctic Ice Sheet faults."

"Uh huh. And a few days later the guy presenting the same research is gunned down? Does this sound a bit odd to you, Mr. Peterson?"

The quiver in his spine worked its way to his knees. "Quite a coincidence."

"Only defense attorneys believe in coincidences. I'd call it a clue to who's behind the murder."

"I thought you said I did it."

"Just checking stories. Witnesses had you on the wrong side of the room. You're not our number one suspect — at least as trigger man."

Seth poured himself more orange juice. Suddenly he didn't feel well. "What happened there last night?"

"You tell me."

Seth described where he sat and what he'd seen and heard.

Newman nodded while Roach scribbled. "Same story as everyone else. Damnedest thing. Someone slipped in a side door to the conference room when the lights went out and drilled a perfectly placed hole through your friend's head with a rifle."

"It was awfully quiet for a rifle."

"We can't be sure until we find the weapon, but I'll stake my career that it was an AR-15 fitted with a silencer."

"What's an AR-15?"

"An American-made assault rifle, better known as the M-16, the weapon made famous by GIs in Viet Nam. It's possible to convert them to full automatic, but he only needed the one round in the guy's head to make him D-R-N. A longer burst would be a waste, since the body would be collapsing before subsequent rounds could hit accurately. Full automatic is strictly for deforestation."

"D-R-N? What's that?"

"Dead Right Now. That's what we call Steiner's kind of injury. We picked up a full metal jacket Winchester five-fifty-six casing." He looked at Seth as if that was supposed to explain it all. Seth's blank stare said it didn't. "You're not a gun guy," Newman said.

Seth shook his head.

"Ah. Winchester is the ammo manufacturer. Full metal jacket means the soft lead bullet is fully encased in a copper metal jacket, primarily to allow piercing of tough objects such as steel helmets, car doors, and flak jackets. With a headshot, it virtually guarantees a clean-through wound. He could have gone with a hollow-tip, which flattens on impact, or a round-tip, which does a 90-degree swivel at entry and travels sideways through the body. Both those are intended to rip a wider path through flesh. Five-fifty-six means a 5.56-millimeter round — a .22 caliber."

"Aren't those pretty small?" Seth said.

"Sissy ammo in a handgun, but this was a fifty-five-grain rifle cartridge with a muzzle velocity of 3,200 feet per second. It enters the skull in the front through a hole the size of a spring pea, and exits the rear with a hole the size of a fall tomato — sucking out a good portion of the brainpan along the way."

Seth recalled more of that scene than he cared to. "I thought silencers and automatic assault rifles were illegal."

"So is murder. Actually, as long as you have the right permits, those things aren't illegal. My guess is that they didn't bother to pay their fees, though. Perpetrators such as these don't join the NRA or observe gun laws."

"How did he manage to aim accurately with the lights off?"

"Assuming his target wasn't random — and I doubt it was — only one way: night vision scope or goggles. We found a lens cover by that side door. Have to prove it yet, but it looks to belong on an AN/PVS-4 Model 700 Series night vision scope."

Roach broke in, "With catadioptic lens, adjustable internally lit reticle, and twenty-five millimeter third-generation image intensifier tube."

"Thank you, Marvin," Newman said in patronizing tone. Then to Seth he said, "It's a state-of-the-art accessory for the AR-15 — expensive, but legally available through any number of sporting outlets."

Seth shook his head in disbelief. "Sounds as though he was taken out by the FBI."

"No way. They only shoot redneck survivalists and Christian fundamentalists."

Roach laughed.

"Who the hell is it then?"

"Don't know. I wish we had a witness who could at least tell us skin color. Something tells me this one is white. Not your typical crack hit."

"I thought you weren't supposed to do racial profiling."

"We have roughly 15,000 violent crimes per year in this city. Over ninety percent are committed by one ethnic group, Peterson, including murder. Most cops — black and white — are only interested in bagging bad guys, not in getting color quotas to please the press. We deal with reality, and that's that most crimes and arrests aren't racially motivated, they're drug related. The racial aspect is largely a myth perpetuated by the media. Eighty-nine percent of black murderers kill other blacks. Seventy-one percent of whites kill whites — probably a lower percentage only because whites are the minority here. But which murders make the news? The rare one where a white kills a black or vice-versa. And the media accuses *us* of bias. Do you know what the next coming scandal is? Gender Profiling. Males are twenty times more likely to commit violent crime than women are. Cops know this and act accordingly. Just wait until the media gets wind of that 'injustice.' We'll have to start busting more women just to be fair."

"Very enlightening," Seth said. "That rules out Arab terrorists, so what kind of white male would do this?"

"I'd guess environmental extremists or disenfranchised Florida voters."

"Plural?"

"At least three players by our count. There's no light switch by the door the shooter entered. Someone else did that. In fact, they didn't turn out the lights. If you noticed in the commotion afterward, the power was off in the whole wing."

Seth nodded, remembering now.

"Weird thing is," Newman continued, "the accomplice that got into the utility room didn't bother to throw the main breaker ... he shot the hell out of the circuit box as though he were mad at it. We found twenty-six casings on the floor. There's your full automatic."

That was it. Seth went pale, and barely made it to the living room, where he eased himself onto the small sofa.

Newman followed. "The whole thing was well timed. I figure there was at least a third perp driving. Of course, no one saw a thing. We didn't have much to go on until we came here. You shouldn't have left last night," he repeated.

"You know what I think?" Seth said hesitantly.

"I would love to know what you think."

"I think they meant to kill me, not Bill."

"You just figuring that out now?"

104

"I assumed it was a robbery or something and Bill got caught in a crossfire, or some homeless lunatic was shooting randomly at the podium or, as you said, a Greenpeace freak was there exterminating scientists to save the world. I just thought I was lucky to be in the audience."

"You were."

"Yeah, but they must have been planning to shoot *me*. The program change to Steiner was done late. I don't think it was advertised anywhere except on a poster by the front door, which they could have easily missed. What's eerie is that thing with the lights. The burglar here went to the trouble of breaking all my light bulbs as if he had something against them."

Newman had no comment on the lights, and didn't seem surprised by Seth's revelation that he was the target. "That's the most likely scenario I've heard so far. Now we just need to find out who and why."

A uniformed officer arrived and delivered the one-page report on the prior burglary. Newman scanned it quickly and then swore. "Get forensics up here pronto. I want this whole place dusted for prints."

As the cop left, Seth caught a glimpse of the neighbor lady Charlene standing in the hallway, observing the activity. He shook his throbbing head. Murder attempts, and now more attention. Things were spiraling out of control.

Newman took a seat opposite Seth while Roach continued to stand and look on. "Let's go over this again. You say that in broad daylight, while you're at work, some stranger breaks in here to steal a disk with ice research that you're going to present at a science conference in a few days. You plan to go ahead with the presentation, only you're too shy to do it yourself. So a coworker does it for you, and gets killed."

Seth nodded pensively.

"Sounds as though someone very mean and nasty didn't want that information to go public."

"Someone very well armed," Seth added.

The mention of "shy" rang a bell for Roach. He spoke again, pointing at Seth. "Seth Peterson," he said.

Newman looked at him as if he were crazy.

"Seth Peterson," he repeated. "The Shy Samaritan. That's the guy's name. I recognize it now. He's The Shy Samaritan."

"Is that true?" Newman asked.

"Yes," Seth admitted reluctantly.

"Well, goodness gracious. This gets weirder all the time."

Seth wanted them to leave. A familiar claustrophobic feeling came over him. Suddenly he wanted out to fresh air and wide-open spaces. But he was trapped.

"I think we need to retrace your life a bit further back," Newman said.

Seth spent the next hour reviewing the burning car incident and the minutia of the previous two weeks. Before he finished, the forensics specialist arrived, dusting every surface in sight. Three other uniformed officers showed up, too, conducting a search for clues and taking orders from Roach.

Newman scratched his stubble. "Has anyone contacted you? Leveled a threat?"

"No. Nothing."

"No calls at all?"

"I generally don't get many calls, and I don't answer them anyway."

"Too shy?"

Seth shrugged.

Roach wandered across the room toward the telephone on a pine end table. A seventies-vintage answering machine was attached to it. "I didn't think they even made these anymore," he said.

"They don't," said Seth.

The detective pulled out a pencil and poked a button with the eraser end. The tape rewound with a whir and, after a few clicks, replayed a dozen messages Seth didn't know existed. Most were older calls from reporters hoping to interview him shortly after the burning car incident. But two calls stood out.

One was from Emily Corbin, a sweet, older-sounding woman with a rasping cough she'd probably picked up from smoke inhalation. She thanked him profusely, called him an angel, and otherwise thoroughly embarrassed him in front of the officers.

The other call was quite different.

"Peterson," a rough voice said, "Skip the Earth Environment Conference or you'll die. Drop the research altogether or you'll die. Ice, nature, and God to you, sir."

"Good detective work, Marvin," Newman said.

Seth immediately recognized the voice, especially after the bizarre sign-off at the end. It was the same caller who a week earlier phoned him at the Center for information on global warming.

The mysterious threat was followed by recent calls with friendly concern from Bern Harris, Sheila Kirby, and Carl Maddox, each curious to know how he was.

Roach poked the stop button, ejected the tape, and placed it in a plastic baggie, using the sharp end of the pencil to avoid touching it.

Newman gestured with his thumb at one of the uniformed officers. "Mr. Roach, will you have one of these gentlemen dredge up the last two weeks' phone records here ASAP please?" Then he turned to Seth. "You're telling me you didn't know about these messages?"

Seth was rocking back and forth with his elbows on his knees and his hands combing his hair. "The ringer volume is turned down."

Using his trusty non-fingerprint-smudging pencil again, Roach squatted so that the tabletop was at eye level and tipped the SlimLine-style phone up from the bottom to peer beneath at the volume control. He nodded to Newman, then went to the door to deliver Newman's order.

"Maybe your new pills will help with your phone answering problem," Newman said. "I'm not sure you want to miss too many of those calls. Bad for your health."

Seth wanted to give the guy the finger, but knew he was only trying to help — and he was right.

"I don't suppose you know the caller, Mr. Peterson?"

"Yes and no."

Newman wiggled his finger for Roach, who had just sent an officer after the phone records, to return from the front door. "Need your notepad again, Marvin. I have a feeling this case is about to go strange. Proceed, Mr. Peterson."

"I'm pretty sure this is the same guy who called me at work about a week ago."

"Damn it." Newman punched his knee. "Marvin, call ahead and have that officer include every line they've got at the National Ice Center for the same time period. Go on," he said to Seth.

Roach tossed the notepad and pencil in Newman's lap, then moved off to call the station on his cell phone.

"Maybe you didn't understand my earlier question about calls," Newman said.

"I had no way of knowing it was related until I heard his voice and that ice and God thing, whatever that is."

"Who is he?"

"I can't remember. I'm not sure he told me, but he did say whom he worked for," Seth rubbed his temple, trying to stimulate memory recall. "Eastern something."

Newman tried to smile patiently.

"Eastern … Ecology Council, or something similar — no, I remember, Eastern Environmental Corporation. He said it was some kind of watchdog group. He was writing an article on the Center for his newsletter."

107

Newman wrote it down. "What did he want to know?"

"Normal stuff. What the Center did, the latest on global warming, *et cetera*. As we talked, though, the discussion led to my research and I started blabbing about that. He was very interested."

"Do you get many such calls at the Ice Center?"

"I usually don't get *any* calls, but this was right after the burning car thing and the press was calling nonstop. I assumed it was another reporter."

"Did he ask for you specifically?"

"No. I remember him asking my name right before he hung up. I think he may have just been fishing and got lucky, caught the big one."

"Then what?"

"Then nothing. We're talking along and all of a sudden he drops that Ice God thing on me and hangs up. I thought he was a kook. Never even thought of it again until just now."

"Didn't call back?"

"Never heard from him before or since."

"Think it was the burglar?"

"I didn't get a good look at his face on the phone, and he didn't say anything at the apartment. Hard to get a good match."

"What about this issue of the lights?"

Seth explained the condition in which he'd found his light bulbs.

"Interesting," Newman said. "The obvious reason is that they broke them instead of shooting out the breaker box for the cover of darkness. But why not just flip the switches?"

"And they didn't get darkness here, even with the lights off," Seth added, gesturing with an open hand at the two windows along the wall. "So why do it?"

Newman tapped the pencil on the pad. "We'll have to think about that one. Feels like a clue to me."

The fingerprint expert approached them and asked Seth to ink his fingers and make imprints on a piece of paper he was carrying, explaining that this way they could rule out his prints all over the apartment, using them as comparison to identify alien prints. That done, he told Newman he was finished there, and would call in the morning after checking the FBI's Integrated Automated Fingerprint Identification System.

"Let's talk about motive," Newman said, focusing again on Seth. "The burglary report says that you're a single white male, never married. A good-looking guy such as you must have broken a few hearts along the way. You got any enemies like that?"

"Nope." The painful memory of Campbell intruded yet again. Surely she had motive enough to commit murder, but this had nothing to do with her. She didn't even know where he was. And he wasn't about to share their sordid tale with the detectives.

"Are you dating anyone now?"

"Nope."

Newman scratched his neck and looked skeptical.

Seth helped him out. "Too shy, remember? Anyway, this doesn't strike me as a lovers' quarrel. I'd say it has something to do with my research."

"Agreed. How's your relationship with coworkers? Any jealousies or animosities there?"

Seth shook his head. "I'm not the most popular guy there, but no way. They're all decent, hard-working people."

"Tell me about this research."

Seth grimaced. "You won't want to hear it. It's pretty dry technical stuff. When I explained it to your friends George and Dwayne, their heads began to overheat. I thought George was going into spontaneous human combustion."

Newman smirked. "Try me. I got a 'C' once in college."

Seth sighed. "Don't say you weren't warned. Here it is in a nutshell. The media has been preoccupied with possible world calamities lately, ozone depletion, meteor impact and such, but I think the most critical is global warming. As you may know, this is caused by increased carbon dioxide in the atmosphere. According to many scientists, man's burning of fossil fuels — automobile exhaust, industrial emissions, *et cetera* — has caused a twenty-five percent increase in greenhouse gases in fewer than two hundred years. Carbon dioxide is the main one. Carbon dioxide allows solar radiation to penetrate through the atmosphere, which warms the Earth, but absorbs infrared radiation on the way out. This effectively traps heat on the planet surface."

"Better known as the 'greenhouse effect,'" Newman said smugly.

"Right. And CO_2 isn't the only culprit. Methane is worse. It absorbs ten to twenty times more heat radiation."

"Methane, huh? Maybe we should outlaw beans."

Seth grinned. "I don't think that's necessary. The evidence tying this to human activity is still weak and politically controversial."

"Yeah, I read the paper."

"But some studies show a connection between the increase in underwater volcano activity to global warming. We've got hard data that as seismic and volcanic activities have increased, so has global warming. But no matter what the cause, the rise in global temperatures poses plenty of future problems for the Earth, and anybody on it. A little-known possibility — one that Bill was going to bring out at the conference — is that a major section of the Antarctic ice cap — a three million cubic kilometer ice cube, you might say — might slip off into the ocean."

"So don't we have stuff like that happening all the time? Like earthquakes?"

"Not like this. If this happens, it will raise the ocean levels high enough to flood every coastal city in the world."

Newman's eyes were big. "Washington, D.C.?"

"Fish food."

"I wonder if my homeowner's policy covers this."

In spite of the seriousness of the situation, Seth laughed. "My research is a study of this ice. And I ... I mean, Bill ... was going to make a big announcement about it." To the detective's questioning stare, he said, "I believe I've developed a method for predicting the location of faults. In fact, I think I know where it's going to break next. If I'm right, this would allow us to bring other scientific disciplines to bear on the question, with the ultimate goal of formulating a remedy, or at least providing advance notice."

"Something like earthquake predictions."

"You should have gotten a C-plus. And speaking of earthquakes, they could easily be what eventually triggers the movement of weakened ice."

"And this is all supposed to happen when?"

"This afternoon maybe."

Newman dropped the pencil.

"Or maybe never. This isn't a sure thing. There's quite a bit of agreement among scientists, though, that it could happen sometime in the next one or two hundred years."

"So the faster scientists know about this, the better."

"Right. The idea last night was to stir interest and get better heads working the problem. If we don't turn this around soon, your grandchildren — or even you — will be able to surf on San Bernardino Beach."

"I don't get it."

"San Bernardino, California? It's presently fifty miles inland."

"Aha."

"It may be too late already. California's entire coastline and a majority of its population are at risk. Based on what I found out, they should take a break from their crusade against Big Oil and Big Tobacco and focus their resources on Big Ice."

"Why the hell would someone want to stop you from sharing this with the world?"

"I have no idea. I would think environmentalists would urge me to hurry up."

"How about competing agencies or governments? Maybe someone else wants the glory."

"I don't know much about cloak and dagger, but it occurs to me that releasing the information after the way it was taken would be a problem for them. Wouldn't they immediately become murder suspects?"

Newman nodded. "There must be a reason. Who stands to benefit either financially or politically if it happens?"

"From global catastrophe? Nobody that I can think of. Even the right stock market investments wouldn't pay off if money suddenly had no value."

"Hmm. A real mystery. No disrespect intended toward your friend Steiner or you, but I like this. Most of our work involves ginning up evidence to convict those who we already know did the dirty deed. It's a refreshing change."

"Sorry if I don't share your glee."

"Understandable."

After a measurable silence, Seth asked, "Where do we go from here?"

Newman pored over the notes. "We follow up the clues. We'll try to locate this Eastern Environmental Corporation. We've got the voice on tape, phone records, the lens cover, ballistics to run, maybe some fingerprints if we're lucky. Was the burglar wearing gloves?"

Seth thought back to the fight in the hallway outside his apartment. "It happened so fast. He didn't hit me with his hands, but yeah, I have the impression he wore gloves. Just don't know for sure, though."

"Damn guys with night scopes always seem to go that extra mile and buy the gloves, too."

Marvin Roach drifted over after sending off the three other officers. "You about ready?" he asked Newman. "They didn't find anything."

Newman stood and handed an MPD business card from his well-worn wallet to Seth. "Call us if you think of anything. I'll double the patrols on your street. I noticed that at least one of the papers got the story wrong and said you were the victim, not Steiner. There's some chance the perps still think you're dead. For all we know they may be in Iran by now, so you may be out of danger. But I'd be careful. Lock your door, look over your shoulder, chew each bite twenty times. That kind of stuff. Checking into a hotel might not be a bad idea. Up to you. I'll call or stop by tomorrow if we've got anything to report."

The wraithlike notion that he might still be in grave danger suddenly coalesced into a hard kernel of fear. He saw the detectives to the door, feeling vulnerable and alone. He replaced the chair wedge under the front door handle after they left and paced for an hour, his emotions shifting through confusion, fear, grief, and anger. His entire head hurt, half from the nose injury, half from a stress headache and too much thinking. His chest ached continually. His coworker had been murdered. He was probably next. And now the damn Paxil had him constipated. He stood at the window and watched the sun setting across the Potomac in a polluted kaleidoscope of pinks and oranges that he was in no mood to appreciate.

Things couldn't get much worse.

Newman's hotel idea was logical, but the same fears that kept him from regular doctor visits ruled that out as well, at least tonight. Instead, he took his knife set off the kitchen counter and distributed the contents strategically throughout the apartment, hiding a blade under his pillow, between couch cushions, and in other places where a weapon might become handy during a break-in. He found a large folding electrician's knife in a drawer and carried that in his pocket. What that might do against the AR-15 he'd seen in action the night before was unclear, but he felt more secure nevertheless.

He spent a second fitful night on the couch, with only the television for comfort.

CHAPTER 14

Seth woke late Sunday morning with a start. He'd finally drifted off to sleep hours after midnight, now waking to a dreary, gray-clouded day. He instinctively checked the chair at the front door, which had held fast overnight.

He was still alive.

But Dong's "minor side effects" were oversold, at least in Seth's gastrointestinal tract. He headed to the kitchen for a glass of OJ, which he assumed must be good for regularity since it seemed to be good for just about everything else. Whenever something was wrong, he drank orange juice as if it were medicine.

Returning the carton to the fridge, he noticed his Paxil prescription on the counter where he'd thrown it. After taking his daily dose, he recalled Newman's comments on taking phone calls. He walked over and switched the ringer on.

Following a shower and change of clothes, he peered out the front door peephole and, seeing the coast clear, removed the chair and walked catlike down to his mailbox on the first floor. On the return trip, he ascended the stairs slowly, looking over Saturday's mail, which he'd forgotten to get yesterday.

He groaned with frustration. In the stack, positioned among free credit card offers and the inevitable pizza coupons, was another pink envelope from Emily. He'd hoped that foolishness had passed. The picture this time was a windswept image of the United States' McMurdo Station, a "city" on the icy plains of Antarctica where hundreds of National Science Foundation members lived and worked. The station was located on Ross Island near Hut Point, where Robert Falcon Scott's supply hut still stood intact, housing a ghostly stock of goods since 1904, six years before his ill-fated polar expedition. Today's message read:

There is too much unrest; there will continue to be the character of vibrations that to the body will be disturbing, and eventually those destructive forces there — though these will be in the next generation.
— 1152-11.

Thinking of you,
Emily Corbin

Seth continued to climb as he reread her ominous message, but two steps from the top he froze. As if Emily's card wasn't enough, he'd opened the Sunday newspaper and stood staring in disbelief at the headline in the local metro section: *"Shy Samaritan Strikes Again."*
Things just got worse.

A door opened loudly above him, down the hall, and Charlene appeared, startling Seth so badly he dropped the mail and nearly fell down the stairs as he fumbled in his pocket for the electrician's knife. Seeing who it was in time, he left it there.

"You're a little jumpy, aren't you?" Charlene said. "What was all the commotion here yesterday? Did you get burgled again?"

Seth couldn't tell whether she'd made the connection with him as Shy Samaritan and the murder on Friday night. From her demeanor, he guessed not. "No," he said. Four days ago he'd have left it at that and retreated to his hole, but after being startled, his heart had settled nicely and he felt she deserved something more. After all, she was only being neighborly. "A friend of mine had some trouble night before last. I was helping the police with information." He moved toward his door, his conditioned response to conversation.

"You aren't dealing drugs out of there, are you?" she said. "We've had to run that type out of here before, and we ain't about to put up with it again."

"Do I look like a crack dealer?"

"No. But you look like you went three rounds with Tommy 'Hitman' Hearns."

She headed downstairs as Seth opened his door. He stopped, though, and called after her. "Charlene?" he said.

She peered up through the spindles in the railing. "Yes, dear?"

"Thank you for the other day." He found it awkward and difficult to say.

"My pleasure, honey." She nonchalantly descended and exited the building.

Inside the apartment, Seth dropped the *Washington Post* on the stained and scarred linoleum countertop and read the metro section lead article incredulously. Once again, complete strangers had decided to make him a news item and use his private life for their personal financial gain. Others might be proud of what they read. Seth felt invaded.

The article was fueled primarily by the effusiveness of Rachel Steiner, Bill's widow, who took time from her grief to extol the virtues of Seth's exploits at the conference, declaring that he'd disregarded the unknown danger and fought against the grain of a stampeding mob to come to the aid of her dying husband, and then selflessly disappeared into the night, interested only in doing the right thing and receiving no accolades for it. The article went on to point out that Seth had been the intended speaker, and was fortunate not to have been the victim himself.

Seth shoved it aside in disgust. The reality was that he hadn't done anything at all. Bill was already dead when he got to him, and patting the deceased's wife on the shoulder hardly seemed worthy of front-page news. The press was blowing it up to sell copies. They could have at least tried to get his side. Of course, as Dr. Dave Thornton had accurately pointed out, they *had* tried; it was Seth's refusal to respond that created the fiasco in the first place. Now the media circus would raise their tents outside the Center, and the pressure for him to come forward for public examination would increase to fever pitch.

Worst of all, there could now be no mistaking the public pronouncement that Seth Peterson still lived. If his would-be killers were still near and literate, he was in danger.

The chilling fear of this realization was punctuated by the loud ring of the phone, something Seth hadn't heard for some time. The noise caused him to jump in fright. He approached it and hesitated, finally picking it up on the fifth and final ring before the answering machine took over.

"Seth? Bern here. Where the hell have you been?"

"Busy."

"I've been calling for two days. What happened to you Friday night?"

"I came home."

"Can you believe it?" Bern's voice wavered. Seth could tell he was taking Bill's death hard.

"Worst thing I ever saw," Seth said, trying to disconnect from the horror. "I don't know how somebody could do that."

There was an awkward silence as both grappled with emotion and a complete inability to verbalize anything timely or appropriate.

"I feel like I assigned him to die," Bern admitted, obviously dealing with more than just Bill's death.

"I suppose you'd feel better if they'd shot me," Seth said. It didn't sound the way he meant it, but figured it might help Bern deal with the guilt nevertheless.

"Did the police contact you?" Bern asked.

"Yeah. They were here almost all of yesterday."

"And?"

115

"It's beginning to look as though the disk stolen from my apartment and Bill's murder are related. They went from thinking I did it to thinking I was the intended target."

"Oh boy."

"That's what I said."

"That seemed to be the way their questions were going," Bern said.

"They talked to you, too?"

"And everyone else from the office. Who did you piss off?"

"It would appear that somebody has reason to shut down my research. But who and why are a big mystery."

"They got any leads?"

"Yes, but no suspects."

"Are you sure it's not some crazy fan of The Shy Samaritan? Seems he hit the news again."

"I heard."

"Rachel had good things to say about you."

"I don't know why. I didn't do anything. I'm just like everybody else."

"Actually, I think it's because you're like *nobody* else. You ran toward the trouble when everyone else ran away in panic. And once we were safely outside, we hung around, getting in the way long after the cops were through with us, too scared to go home. You didn't even wait to be questioned. Rachel wanted your phone number, but I didn't give it out. You should call her, though. I think she wants to thank you personally."

"Mmm."

"The cops weren't the only ones who called. The reporters are at it again too. You're playing well with the public, and they can't seem to get enough. Did you see the line in the *Washington City Paper*? They compared you to Batman."

Seth just moaned.

"What happens next?" Bern said.

"The cops hinted that the bad guys may have unfinished business. They said I might want to check into a hotel."

"And you're still sitting there?"

"Haven't had a chance to make any plans."

"Well, don't plan on coming in to work tomorrow."

Seth was stunned. "You're firing me now?"

Bern laughed. "Did you go see that shrink like I said?"

"Yes."

"Then you're not fired. I just want you to stay away for a day or two, until they get somebody behind bars for this thing. I can't put the other staff in jeopardy. Some of the others have hinted around. Attendance might be low tomorrow morning if you come in."

The potential threat to those around him hadn't occurred to Seth. He was offended at first, but then thought of Bill and Rachel. "I see your point."

"Call me tomorrow afternoon. We'll see where we're at."

The phone rang again within seconds after Seth hung up from Bern's call. With more reluctance than usual, he reached for the phone. The caller introduced herself as a *National Enquirer* reporter. Without a word, Seth hung up and switched the ringer off again.

CHAPTER 15

With the door again wedged and knives planted throughout the apartment, Seth wasted the rest of the day waging internal debate over whether to check into a hotel or brave another night barricaded in the apartment. By the time he decided prudence demanded overcoming his agoraphobic behavior and abandoning the false security of the apartment, it was too late in the evening to do so — or so he convinced himself. The threat of death still couldn't compete with fear of a night on his own in the big city: taxi drivers, hotel concierges, and who knew what else. Maybe tomorrow. He wasn't expected at work in the morning, so sleep wasn't required. Vigilance was. The new plan was to stay awake all night and vacate on Monday.

The Paxil had other plans.

A side effect of the medication was drowsiness. That and the lack of sleep the two previous nights knocked him cold by nine o'clock. He woke in the morning on the couch again, with the TV on and a butcher knife by his side. He sat upright and shot a glance over the back of the couch at the front door. The leaning chair was still in place.

Now what?

He swung his legs down and rubbed his face. Matt Lauer and Katie Couric were prattling on about some popular young sitcom actor he'd never heard of. He grabbed the remote off the floor and changed the channel to the local news. The weatherman was a bad actor who wore mascara. Seth loved to hate him. In typical oversell he warned of a Gulf Stream low-pressure system spinning counterclockwise up the coast toward them, pulling warm air and moisture. This was in imminent danger of colliding with a clockwise-spinning Arctic high-pressure front descending from Canada. At a minimum, temperatures would drop into the low forties with overcast skies and gusty winds, with rain or sleet possible. Like clockwork came file video of a huge American flag waving wildly in a stiff breeze at Arlington National Cemetery, and wind-whipped whitecaps off the Atlantic coast. Seth scoffed at the dire prediction. The Perfect Storm this was not.

The national weather included a flash of radar over the Midwest. A following Canadian air mass deposited a swirl of clouds over southern Minnesota and was expected to drop three to four inches of snow, with overnight lows in the high teens. The meteorologist took a few steps toward

118

the camera and hammed a big shiver. Seth wanted to wring the geek's salon-tanned neck.

The traffic report detailed a couple of crashes on the Beltway. Nothing new. He aimed the remote to shut off the set.

What he saw next stopped his finger and his heart. The screen filled with a special graphic of artsy text saying "The Shy Samaritan — Where Next?" Then the camera returned to the news anchor speaking seriously from his wood and Plexiglas throne, with an image of Seth Peterson superimposed in the space above and to his left like he was Yasser Arafat or Alan Greenspan.

Where the hell did they get that? he thought. Then it occurred to him; it was the photo from his Ice Center ID card. Coworkers were feeding the media, probably thinking they were doing good … with no idea how wrong they were.

Next the anchorman explained that sources within MPD had confirmed that the murder of Bill Steiner at the Earth Environment Conference three days earlier may have been a case of mistaken identity, and that Seth Peterson, a staff meteorologist and research scientist for the National Ice Center — the city's Shy Samaritan — may have been the intended target.

Mr. Freeze was out to get Batman.

The TV went off and Seth stood, feeling his pockets for Detective Newman's business card. Before dialing the number, he replayed the answering machine tape again to check messages. After hearing eight more calls from reporters and one from Newman the day before, saying he assumed Seth was in a hotel, that he had nothing to report, and that Seth should call at his convenience, he shut the machine off and dialed the printed number.

Detective Newman answered the direct line to his desk on the second ring.

"Nice leak," Seth said.

"Mr. Peterson?"

"How'd you guess?"

"I thought you might call."

"Does this fall under the heading of 'To Protect'? Or 'Serve'?"

"These things happen."

"I'd like to happen a few things on whoever's trying to get me killed down there."

"It's probably someone who doesn't realize the problem he's causing. He's just gabbing, or maybe owes a favor."

"What are you going to do about it?"

"What do you want? Nobody is going to admit it, and the reporter will never reveal his source. It's over, done."

"So am I."

"Let's not overreact."

"Sure. Some guy with a vendetta against light bulbs is trying to sacrifice me to the God of Ice with an AK-47, and *I'm* overreacting?"

"AR-15. The AK-47 is a Russian —"

Seth interrupted him with a flurry of four-letter words.

"Okay, okay," Newman said.

Seth took a deep breath. He hadn't used such profanity in a long time. Never, in fact. Either the Paxil gave him courage, or the situation provided enough anger.

"Did you catch anybody yet?" Seth said.

"No, but I was going to call you this morning. We have a few interesting tidbits. You were right about that caller at work. Both calls came from the same phone, a payphone at the Dulles main terminal. They were charged to separate phone cards, both stolen."

"Which tells us what?"

"We're on the right track."

Seth moaned.

"No luck on the fingerprints, though," Newman said. "The FBI computer didn't find a match. Of course, we didn't really find anything other than yours and ours. Looks as though the bad guy wore gloves or wiped up after himself — and you don't do much entertaining. Our expert said he'd never seen a place so full of only one person's prints."

"I'm new in town."

"Uh huh. Well, we also got the autopsy report and ballistics on the round they removed from the wall after going through Steiner's head. No surprises. They confirm one shooter firing a single .22 caliber rifle round. He painted his sight dead center in the forehead. Death was instantaneous. I doubt it was the first time this individual fired a gun. AR-15 is still the suspect weapon. It's a good choice for this type of hit: accurate, powerful, easily accessorized, relatively compact. At thirty yards like that, handgun accuracy gets pretty iffy. The target practice in the utility room was also done with an AR-15, but not the same one, which confirms at least two players. We still have no witnesses on who they were or how they got weapons in unnoticed. One interesting thing we learned is that your Eastern Environmental Corporation doesn't exist, at least as far as we can determine. Are you sure about the name?"

"I'm sure. You couldn't find them?"

"If they exist, it's with an unlisted phone number. We made a few calls to some environmental organizations that ought to know. None had ever heard of the outfit. I'd say it was an alias, just an appropriate-sounding front the caller used to get through and get the info he wanted."

"Now what?"

"We need good leads, but we aren't getting any. We're taking a lot of calls. Unfortunately, most of them are nut cases calling to claim responsibility for killing The Shy Samaritan, or fans wanting us to put you in touch with them. A woman called this morning to see whether you could appear at her son's birthday party. Last night they picked up some nut on Pennsylvania Avenue carrying a huge samurai sword. He said it belonged to The Shy Samurai and he wanted to collect the reward for finding it. Turns out he was a little confused about the difference between samurai and Samaritan. This always happens with celebrity cases. It gets hard to separate fact from fiction."

"I'm hardly a celebrity."

"Don't you watch the news?"

"Bastards."

"Hey, look on the bright side. If you live through this, you can write a book and make a million, go on tour with Monica Lewinsky."

"If?"

"Where are you now?"

"At home."

"Did you stay there all weekend?"

"I was armed."

"I thought you didn't own a gun."

"Ginsu knife."

"You may be shy, Peterson, but you've got walnuts. Didn't you see what was left of your friend's head? I don't care if you're Daniel Boone. Two guys with full automatic AR-15s could cut you in half before you got that blade out of your little leather sheath."

"I thought I was receiving extra police protection."

"Mr. Peterson, sending a squad up your street an extra time or two doesn't necessarily constitute adequate protection. If I were you, I'd be making myself extra scarce right now."

Seth hung up after promising to vacate the apartment — at least temporarily — and check in by telephone daily from another location.

After showering, Seth dressed in jeans and an old gray University of Minnesota sweatshirt with the bucktoothed mascot Goldy Gopher on the back. He was on the couch, tying his tennis shoes, when a knock on the door startled him. He fumbled quickly for a knife between cushions, then sat

121

frozen in indecision, his heart practically exploding in his chest.

The door knock came again, louder this time.

It occurred to Seth that if they busted through the door, he was a sitting duck there on the couch directly in front of them. Then again, there was no safe place in the apartment. Suddenly he wished he'd heeded Newman's advice earlier.

Fighting panic, untied shoelaces trailing behind, he moved stealthily toward the door, staying to one side in case a burst of gunfire suddenly crashed through. He leaned his head over and peeked out the peephole. An attractive and well-dressed blonde woman filled his view. Next to her was a sloppily dressed, longhaired man carrying something that looked like a small suitcase. It took a second, but Seth recognized the woman. She was a reporter for one of the local TV stations. It dawned on him that the man accompanying her was a cameraman toting his professional digital video camcorder, a Panasonic AG-DVC200, a unit Seth had seen at the station in Minneapolis.

He breathed deeply, trying to quell the flood of adrenalin pumping through him. They were only there to interview The Shy Samaritan. Then he leaned back against the wall next to the door and waited them out.

A third and final knock made him jump again, but he wasn't about to answer it. He heard the two talking and then walking down the stairs. He quickly finished tying his shoes, slammed back a glass of orange juice, grabbed his keys, and left the apartment before anyone else showed up to talk … or worse.

He had closed the door and taken two steps when Charlene appeared in the hallway from her apartment. "I *thought* you were in there," she said.

Seth cringed, but stopped and looked at her.

She walked slowly toward him as if wanting a closer look. "You're not taking visitors today?"

"Probably just salespeople," he lied. "You keeping track?"

"I heard the rapping. Considering all the strange goings-on lately, I suppose I have a right to be curious. Neighbors have to be looking out for one another in this city."

This was weird. What did she want? Seth wanted badly to leave. A week ago he'd have simply walked away from her, leaving her with the impression that he was an arrogant SOB, maybe prejudiced too. But Charlene had never done anything but help him. And after all, she *was* his neighbor. He tried to face her and remain polite. "I owe you for that, don't I?"

She smiled a mouthful of very white, large, and crooked teeth.

He returned the smile and waited out an awkward pause. "I'm late. Guess

122

I'll get going."

He took the first step down toward the exit, but Charlene wasn't done with him. "I can't believe it's you," she said.

Oh no.

"Pardon me?" Seth said, looking up at her.

"I saw you on TV," she said. "Here I've been living next door to a hero for a whole year and never knew it. Damn near choked to death on my eggs this morning when I saw your picture there on the tube. You're The Shy Samaritan, you silly man."

Seth forced another smile. "You won't tell anyone, will you?"

Charlene belly laughed. "You're too much. If that was me, I'd have been on *Oprah* by now, tooting my horn and trolling for rewards."

"Not as much money in heroics as you'd think."

"Well, don't you worry. I'm fixing that."

Seth raised an eyebrow. "What do you mean?"

"Those weren't salespeople knocking at your door. They were from Channel 5. I called them this morning. They already interviewed me."

The other eyebrow went up too. "Charlene, they call me shy because I'm trying to stay anonymous."

"Too late for that, honey. You're bigger news around here than an Al Gore recount. Time for you to get something for your efforts."

Seth looked hopelessly into her eyes. The poor, misguided but well-meaning woman actually thought she was helping. The last thing he wanted to do was hurt her feelings. But without knowing it, she'd put them both in more danger.

"Charlene, I appreciate what you tried to do for me, but you've got to listen to me. The television may not have made it clear, but the police think that robbery attempt here the other day was related to the murder at the conference the other night. In fact, they think it might have been *me* they were trying to kill. We don't know why, but there's a good chance they'll come back here with their machine guns to finish the job. I don't plan to be here for that. You need to be careful yourself, and more ... discreet."

Seth watched as her expression dissolved. Suddenly it looked as though her eggs might threaten her throat again. Fearful of having to handle another distraught woman, he left her at the top of the stairs and headed out to his car.

CHAPTER 16

The wind wasn't as strong as Mr. Mascara Lashes predicted, but still blasted between downtown buildings in surging wind-tunnel gusts, pushing pedestrians and buses off track. Seth stood at the curb, weathering the wind as he fought with a sticky newspaper dispenser for the *Washington Post*. He'd left home with no particular destination in mind. Without work, filling the day would be a challenge. Reading the paper over a cup of coffee at Starbucks would be a good way to kill an hour. As he won the battle and retrieved his paper, it occurred to him that lounging alone in a public venue such as Starbucks was not something he'd have willingly done a week ago. Oddly, the notion no longer felt threatening. Maybe Paxil actually worked.

Standing at the Starbucks counter, he consciously made eye contact with the acne-faced teen taking his order. Inwardly, he laughed. Simple things like that had been so hard before. Now it seemed ridiculous to have felt anxious about it. Recalling Dong's advice, he opted for decaf, savoring it and the paper for over two hours, people-watching in uncharacteristic relaxation.

Eventually the novelty wore off, and he pondered what to do next. Bern warned against coming to work, but Seth decided that probably didn't rule out dropping by for details on Bill Steiner's funeral arrangements. As he left the coffee shop, a middle-aged couple entered and held the door for him. He thanked them with a smile. The woman smiled, too, and then did a double take, looking as though she recognized him.

He headed for the Federal Center, going east on Suitland Parkway and north on Silver Hill Road. He was about to pull into the Main Gate at Swann Road when he noticed a small caravan of news vans queued up, awaiting admittance from the guard. Media entering the Federal Center compound was a common occurrence. There was plenty to occupy them there: Naval Intelligence, the Federal Records Center, the Census Bureau, and other government operations in addition to the Ice Center. But something told him they were probably there for one reason: The Shy Samaritan. That meant cameras in his face, and questions he couldn't answer.

Eye contact with anonymous teenage mocha-jockeys was one thing. Giving interviews for the six o'clock news was another.

So he avoided the Center, flipping his blinker to the right and shooting across to the opposite turn lane for Swann Road, taking advantage of a small opening in traffic. A trailing car on his right honked its dissatisfaction with the sudden move as he passed in front, though they weren't even close to colliding. When he glanced in the rearview mirror to see how irate the driver was, he glimpsed a silver Buick Park Avenue a few car-lengths back try the same maneuver with less cushion. It caused a chain reaction of skidding and honking.

Tourists, Seth thought as he sped east on Swann.

A moment later, paranoia kicked in. Imagining that the silver Buick might be tailing him with sinister designs, he reversed direction in a horseshoe driveway and retraced his course to the intersection, where he went north again on Silver Hill and then west on Pennsylvania, back toward the District, continually checking his mirror for signs he was being followed. Two miles later, with no sign of the Buick or anything suspicious, he relaxed a bit, sure he'd overreacted but determined to keep a wary eye.

The thought of tourists sparked an idea on how to spend the day. He would drive down to the National Mall, find a public phone to call Bern instead of stopping in, and then see the monuments. Despite living in the city for over a year, he'd never visited them. He was both curious and patriotic, true, but that was where the people were. He'd never seriously considered it until now. Paxil and the need to waste daylight made it viable.

He parked in a lot north of the Washington Monument and strolled around to its east side. Spying a payphone by the restrooms a hundred yards away, he headed toward it, ignoring the concrete walkway and cutting across the dormant, splotchy grass. The feared crowd was nonexistent in the late morning on a cold and blustery December weekday.

Seth inserted two quarters in the Verizon pedestal payphone and dialed the Center as he stared absentmindedly at the unmanned souvenir and refreshment stand nearby. Sandy Page answered promptly, professional as always.

"Morning, Sandy," he said. "Is Bern available?"

"Seth, is that you? For chrissakes, how are you?"

"Other than in the last week I've been burned, robbed, labeled homosexual and crazy, accused of murder, targeted for death, and had a coworker die in my arms? Fine, I guess."

"Can you believe what happened to Bill?"

"Unfortunately, I was there."

"This damn city is a war zone. Now they're shooting innocent scientists."

"How's everyone doing?"

"It's crazy here. Lots of tears. The press is driving us nuts. They've overrun our position. They're on recon for you or anything about you. It's a circus. You're the biggest local news to hit this town since Gary Condit did the intern, or Marion Berry did the video — maybe even since the plane hit the Pentagon. Well, no. Not that," she added, quickly correcting herself. She'd lost a friend in the nine-eleven terrorist attack, and it was still a sore subject.

"You're not talking, are you?" Seth had to ask.

"Me? Are you kidding? Name, rank, and serial number is all they'll ever get from me."

"Is Bern around?"

"Yeah, but he has his finger in the dike right now. He's holding off the hordes with Sheila. Those two should be in politics. A couple of smooth operators. Can I help you with something? Anything at all?"

"Just wondering about funeral arrangements."

"Bill's sister-in-law called in for Rachel with some details."

Seth listened as she relayed the time and location. But something across the lawn caught his attention, and he lost focus on her words. A silver Buick raced past, heading north on 15th Street. It turned left on Constitution in the direction of the same lot Seth was parked in. In seconds, it was again exceeding the speed limit before Seth lost sight of it among the traffic and trees lining the boulevard.

Just your imagination?

The suspicion that he'd been tailed returned. Silver Park Avenues were plentiful, but considering recent events and the strange behavior of the ones — or one — he'd seen today, nothing seemed implausible.

"Seth, are you there?" Sandy asked, reminding him that he'd fallen silent.

"Thanks for the info, Sandy," he said blankly. "I've got to go." Abruptly, he hung up.

He stood for a moment, indecisive. Then, gathering his wits, he fumbled for his wallet and retrieved Newman's business card. He lifted the receiver and pinched it between his cheek and shoulder while he dug frantically for more coinage.

Nothing. He was out of change. Frustrated and scared, he threw the telephone at the pedestal, letting it swing and dangle, and stuffed the wallet and card back into his pocket.

Curious to see if the car had, indeed, entered the parking lot, Seth strolled back to the Monument and gazed down the grassy slope northward. But at that distance he couldn't even identify his own car.

He waited several minutes, watching for people exiting cars. His pounding heart competed with sounds of the city. Taxis honked in the distance. Pigeons fluttered and cooed. An occasional crow cawed, and the wind blew. A hint of diesel fumes wafted in the air. Still no movement from the lot.

False alarm?

It was too cold to stand around. A compelling need to satisfy his curiosity and assure his safety drove him. What if the Ice God caller, who'd surely had something to do with both the burglary and Bill's murder, had watched him leave the apartment that morning and followed him across town, with his confederates, waiting for an opportunity to shred his belly with the hot lead ejaculate of his AR-15?

As bizarre as the notion seemed, he couldn't discount it. His fingers trembled with cold and fear, but anger was building too. Anger always went unfulfilled in the past, with fear of conflict winning out over the desire to act. This was often a blessing, preventing rash acts. Other times, when it was appropriate to stand up for himself, he couldn't. That inability always left Seth feeling depressed and cowardly.

Today, anger was winning out. He relished the thought of planting another Muay Thai elbow in the man's face. Unfortunately, fisticuffs were no match for firearms.

To his right, far to the east, lay the U.S. Capitol building. The Washington Monument towered above him, with the low-slung sun casting a long shadow. He'd lost interest in visiting either. Getting into his car and away from mysterious Buicks was now his only concern. He walked nonchalantly across the open expanse toward the parking lot. There were no trees, signs, or light poles for protection, but there seemed to be no other choice. If the Silver Car People really were there, they would naturally assume he'd eventually return to his car. Perhaps they planned to await this and mow him down as he fumbled to unlock his door. He'd have to find out sooner or later.

The closer Seth got, though, the more confident he became that his imagination had only been playing tricks on him. But just inside the parking lot, seventy-five yards from his car, he saw a silver Buick parked on the near side of his Geo, with its nose facing away from the small car. He froze and then slowly backed off, trying to use taller vans and trucks as shields.

He thought of returning to the payphone, recalling with exasperation the free 911 call he could have made. But suddenly both front doors on the Buick opened and two men stepped out wearing pea coats. The driver had a cell phone to his ear. Both were looking away from him. Seth froze and was about to turn back when the doors opened on another car, parked across the aisle and on the far side of his Metro. Three more men and a woman got out. Two of the men were wearing trench coats. The woman had on a parka with the hood down, and a bandana tied over her head pirate-style. The driver

127

wore a ski jacket. He, too, had a cell phone to his ear. The two groups converged in the center of the lot. Seth continued moving backward.

Suddenly the driver of the second car, who'd just folded and stowed his cell phone, spotted Seth. After staring curiously for a second, he pointed at him and shouted something Seth couldn't hear. The others all turned and looked too. When the driver of the Buick turned, Seth recognized him immediately. Even from a distance, he knew it was the man who'd bulled his way out of the apartment three days earlier.

This man pointed at him too, and all six began running toward him. The last thing Seth saw before he turned and broke into a sprint was the trench coat of one of the men opening, and a weapon that looked suspiciously like an AR-15 swinging out.

The Capitol Building, two miles east, was open for business and full of Capitol Police more vigilant than ever following the shooting there a few years earlier, and the terrorist attacks more recently. Seth went that direction at top speed.

He cleared the end of the parking lot and took advantage of the open space before him by running an irregular path, hoping that would make him a difficult target. He executed a sudden Barry Sanders move, cutting hard and fast around the last car in the lot.

But Sanders had talent — and cleats. Seth's feet slipped from beneath him on the cold grass, and he went down hard on his side. White-hot pain exploded in his ribcage, and his head bounced off his forearm, sending shooting pains back from his predamaged nose.

The fall served a purpose, however. He heard no report, but the instant he fell, a volley of bullets shattered the windows in the car above him, showering him with glass. Had he been up and running, the bullets would have surely ripped through him.

Regardless of the pain, he didn't wait for the inevitable. Scrambling to his feet, he shot out from behind the car on a slightly different tangent and made for the Capitol.

Seth had never run for his life before. Among the flood of thoughts rushing through his head was the realization that fear and adrenalin combine for impressive result. He might lack Barry's lateral mobility, but despite the pain, linearly he was able to move faster than ever before. Carl Lewis couldn't catch him today — especially not in a trench coat and carrying a rifle.

He dashed across an empty 15th Street, dodged slow-moving cars on 14th and 13th, and was on the grass past 12th Street and into the protective trees before he had a rational thought.

Having successfully traversed hundreds of yards of turf, Seth risked a backward glance. He'd increased his lead to a safer two-hundred-yard gap over the five men still chasing at a slow, sustainable jog. The trench coats were closed. The woman was nowhere in sight. Perhaps she'd stayed with the cars in case he doubled back.

The pace was testing his heart, so Seth, too, slowed a bit. Museums lined the Mall on both sides. He considered running to one. Wouldn't they have security guards? He didn't know, but the image of a single-bullet-toting Barney-Fife-type, guarding the art inside and vainly fighting off an army of six, kept him from finding out. Nearly a mile ahead lay the Capitol Building. That had real cops, he knew. Besides, he was successfully pulling away on the run. Don't stop a good thing.

Seven strenuous minutes later, he veered left to skirt the Capitol Reflecting Pool on the north side, then zagged back east, just off Pennsylvania Avenue, toward the Peace Monument. Ahead lay 1st Street, which passed in front of the massive white-domed Capitol Building where, presumably, the antagonists would be forced to suspend their attack — unless they were hell-bent on a suicide mission. He wished he knew who they were, and why they wanted him so dead. But for now, he was content to merely thwart their plan. Safety lay across those busy lanes, down the walkways, and up the concrete steps to the marble columns.

Thirty yards from the roadway, with the statue of Ulysses S. Grant to his right and John Garfield's farther in the distance, a maroon-colored Chevy Caprice screeched to a halt directly in front of Seth. The passenger side window powered down. Inside the car, the parka-woman sat with one hand on the wheel. The other held a handgun pointing out the window at Seth's face.

Seth ducked and cut left, hearing the loud report from the gun but feeling nothing.

Did she miss? he thought.

The instinctive move left was a good one, requiring parka-woman to drive in reverse on the busy street to intercept him, a foolish move even for desperate killers.

But his mind was beyond rational thought from fear, adrenalin and anaerobic exertion. Like a wild deer crossing a country highway, he shot across the near lane at full sprint, hopping sideways and narrowly avoiding a skidding car's front bumper from his left. He was one step from safety on the far curb when his luck ran out.

Still trying to right himself after his stumbling, full-speed, bumper-hurdling maneuver, he was ill prepared for the taxi approaching from his right. The yellow cab slammed on its brakes and slid sideways. The rear end swung in toward the curb. Its right rear quarter panel caught Seth in the legs, laying him out on the trunk and catapulting him onto the concrete sidewalk. Seth's head exploded in a prism of color and pain. Then all went black.

CHAPTER 17

Seconds later, Seth regained consciousness. He sat up, dazed but numb to pain. The taxi driver, a small, middle-aged black man, was out of the cab and approaching him with a Richard Pryor-like look of shock. Behind him and across the street there was no sign of the maroon Caprice. Seth looked to the lawn beyond. He thought he glimpsed a group of men retreating west across the Mall toward the parking lot where his car remained. Maybe they thought he'd been killed. Maybe they wanted nothing to do with the group of motorists who'd stopped and were beginning to gather. Maybe they feared the three Capitol Policemen — still on heightened alert since a crazed Russell E. Weston Jr. shot up the place and killed two officers back in July of 1998 — now coming down the long walkway from the Capitol toward him. Maybe they assumed the terrorist flyover of Flight 77 in September of 2001 that killed 189 at the Pentagon had the officers trigger-happy.

Seth wanted nothing to do with them either. Nor did he want to wait around for the woman in the maroon Caprice to swing by again for another shot. Without a thought toward his condition, and to the driver's complete amazement, he struggled to his feet and stumbled to the taxi.

"Drive!" he shouted at the stunned cabbie, who hesitated on the sidewalk with legs, arms, and mouth akimbo.

Seth got the back door next to the crumpled rear panel open, and screamed more urgently at the cabbie, who this time went into action, perhaps assuming he was now called upon to provide ambulance service for his unintended victim. He slid into the driver's seat and wasted a half second by looking beseechingly over the backseat at the man sprawled in the back.

Seth had no time for delay: The Capitol Policemen, thinking the whole scene a bit odd, were now in a trot toward the car. "Go!" Seth yelled at the driver, who responded by flooring the pedal and smoking the front tires as he weaved through the obstacle course of cars stopped in the roadway ahead of them.

A few blocks away, the cabbie slowed to legal speed and turned southeast onto Massachusetts Avenue.

"Where are you going?" Seth said.

"Where you think?" the driver said. "You're messed up good. I'm taking you down to D.C. General. You shouldn't have got onto them legs without seeing whether they's busted first. You get the bones to sticking out of the skin, and you're gonna make it worse for me. I ain't never run over nobody before."

Seth's mind raced. What should he do? A visit to the hospital was undoubtedly a good idea. Adrenalin and endorphins were wearing off, and pain was setting in. His legs were surprisingly intact — he doubted anything below the waist was broken — but the chest was another matter. It felt like more ribs had cracked, and now his shoulder ached too. He had no mirror, but if his face looked like his hands and the shredded clothing on his elbows, he wasn't pretty.

Worse than pain, though, was the fear of capture by the mysterious group of assailants. If they thought there was any chance Seth survived the accident, it wouldn't take a brain surgeon to figure out where to find him next: the nearest hospital.

"We don't need to get you in trouble, friend," Seth said. "I don't need a doctor. Take a left."

The driver looked wild-eyed in the rearview mirror, but did as he was told, making the sharp turn onto North Capitol Road.

"You're crazy, Mister. You ain't gonna tell nobody I run you over?"

"It wasn't your fault."

"That's mighty generous of you, but I still got to explain the dent back there." He pointed with his thumb over the shoulder. "What was you doing coming across that roadway like that, anyhow? You fixing to shoot up the Capitol?"

Seth managed to sit up with considerable effort and pain, not interested in chatting. His mind spun out of control. He craned his neck gingerly, looking out each window for signs of the silver Buick or maroon Chevy. All he knew was the need to stay mobile, stay free — at least until he reached the police station and gave Newman a chance to protect him better.

First things first, he thought.

If he weren't stopping for medical treatment, he'd need the next best thing: painkillers. "Go left on Rhode Island Avenue," he said, half-gasping.

"You're going in circles, Mister, but that's fine. We'll be heading up toward Howard University Hospital, in case you change your mind."

Seth spotted a 7-Eleven convenience store a block ahead on 7th Street. "Pull in there and park around back," he said.

The driver did as instructed, then leaned over the backseat, looking at Seth closely for the first time. What he saw was a mess. Sweaty from the chase, dirty and grass-stained from the fall, flecked with shattered auto glass from the shooting, and with road rash on skin and clothes from the bump-

132

and-tumble with the taxi and concrete sidewalk, Seth looked as though he'd survived a train wreck — barely.

Despite that, the man still recognized him.

"Lord amighty! You're him," he said, pointing. "You're The Shy Samaritan. You're that hero all the TV folk are talking about."

Seth's head slumped. That was the final blow. The whole thing was a bad dream from which he couldn't wake. "Okay," he said, looking at the man's identification card on the dash. "You're right, Robert. That's me. But do you know why they call me 'Shy'?"

Robert shook his head.

"Because I don't want anyone to know about me. Do you follow?"

Robert gave a blank stare, and then a broad smile crossed his face. He pointed at Seth again. "I sure enough do follow."

"Our secret then?"

"Yes, sir."

Seth pulled a wad of bills from his pocket, wincing with every movement. He handed the man a fifty-dollar bill. "I'd be grateful if you'd get me a bottle of aspirin, a bottle of Aleve, a bottle of water, and a roll of paper towels."

The cabbie stared at him as if he were insane. He'd probably never been asked to shop for a fare before. But then he'd never run one over, either. And it was a fifty-dollar bill. He shrugged and hopped out.

Ten minutes later, he was back in the car with the bag of goods. He handed the aspirin bottle over the seat back first. Seth immediately flipped the cap off, discarded the cotton wadding, dispensed six tablets into his hand, and dumped them into his mouth. Rather than swallowing, he chewed furiously, reaching for the bottled water to wash them down. Next he defeated the Aleve bottle's childproof cap and swallowed four pills whole. All of this was difficult as the shock of recent events began to take its toll; his hands trembled uncontrollably and he felt pale and faint. He fought hard to stay alert.

Robert's eyes were huge.

"The Naproxin in Aleve is a great painkiller, Bob," Seth assured him, "but it's slow acting. Aspirin works quicker, especially when chewed. It's absorbed faster that way."

He swallowed a few more swigs of water. Opening the paper towels, he doused a wadded handful with water from the bottle and used it to wipe the sweat and blood from his face, hands, and elbows.

With that attended to, Seth said, "Okay, deliver me to the police station."

Robert's eyes grew again. "You fixing to turn me in?"

"No. I won't say a word. But I need to get to a safe place."

133

"Yeah, you're getting mighty popular," Robert said, "Which station you want?"

Seth retrieved Newman's business card and looked at the address. "Third District. Do you know where that is?"

"Yes, sir." Then Robert surprised him with one last item from the bag: a *Washington Post* newspaper. "I seen this in there. Some folks were talking about it. Hope you don't mind I bought it for you with your money."

Robert's reason for buying it became obvious when Seth saw the Metro Section's front page. He was the lead story. In the lower right corner of the first page was the same NIC identification photo of Seth along with a headline that read, *Forces of Evil Threaten City's First Citizen.*

Seth rubbed his temples and was silent for a moment. That's it, he thought. Forget the police. Forget Dong. Forget the Center, the bad guys, and Washington, D.C., too. Forget Corbin's pink envelopes that could foretell "disturbing bodily vibrations" such as the ones that had bounced him around today. Forget everything. He wanted out. And now.

He spotted a payphone hung on the side of the convenience store. Taking the change Robert gave him, he limped to the telephone and got Newman on the line.

"Did you see today's *Post?*" he said.

Newman got defensive. "That wasn't us this time."

"I know. It was my well-meaning neighbor. People are killing me with kindness."

"Did something else happen?"

"You could say that."

"Did our friends find you?"

"Too close for comfort." Seth recounted the events at the Mall for Newman, stopping short of revealing his run-in with the taxi — or his present location.

"Six of them, huh? And one is a woman?"

"In a maroon, late-model Chevy Caprice — with a big handgun. She was young, twenty-five maybe. Looked fit, as though she's military or works out."

"And you outran them?"

"I ... out-maneuvered them."

"Where did you go?"

"The Capitol."

"You ran all the way from the Washington Monument to the Capitol Building? There are guard stations all over the place down there, by the Commerce Building, the museums. Why not stop at one of those? Hell, the

134

White House is half the distance."

"Well," Seth said, feeling foolish, "I didn't have time to pull out my tourist guide. Besides, I needed the exercise."

Newman made a funny sound with his lips. "You might as well have kept going all the way to Camp David. I think that's where they used to hide Dick Cheney."

"Wrong direction."

"Yeah, well, I think it's time for you to come down and give us a chance to hide you."

"Actually, I was just calling to say that I won't be coming in. I've got another idea."

"Where are you going?"

"I don't know, but I think I'll keep it to myself when I figure it out."

"Peterson, we can't help you if we don't know where you are. Why won't you tell me?"

"Did you ever see the movie *The Gauntlet* with Clint Eastwood?"

"Uh … I must have missed that."

"Clint is this subpar cop chosen to deliver a small-time crook so that she can testify against the Mob. He keeps calling his boss to report their whereabouts, and every time he does, someone tries to kill them shortly thereafter. He finally figures out that his boss is in on trying to prevent her from testifying."

"I see," Newman said. "So you think I'm subpar, a conspirator, ratting you out."

"That's not it."

"You need protective custody."

"Right. Did you ever see Arnold Schwarzenegger in *The Terminator?*"

"What does this have to do with — ?"

"Arnold was a cybernetic organism sent back in time to terminate the mother of the as-yet-unborn savior of the future world. After a few narrow escapes, she ends up in police custody down at the station. Arnold simply strolls in and blows them all away."

"Except her, if I remember correctly."

"Oh, that's right. What am I worried about?"

"Peterson, you watch too many movies. Which of these leads would you have me follow up? The Mob hit men, or cyborgs from the future?"

"Newman, the point is, there's a group of people — quantity unknown but growing — who are very intent on having me dead. They're intelligent, organized, persistent, bold, and heavily armed. It strikes me as too obvious to come there."

"It's your life."

"I'll call you for updates."

He hung up and waved for Robert to swing the cab by and pick him up. With some effort, he regained the backseat.

"Take me to Dulles Airport," he said.

CHAPTER 18

At the Dulles International Airport arrivals drop-off area, Seth paid for the fare plus a twenty-dollar tip, which astounded Robert.

"I run you over, and you tip me?"

"Robert, I've got to make a special deal with you."

"Yes, sir?" he said, peering intently into the back again.

"How do you think Yellow Cab is going to feel about you hitting a pedestrian?"

"I don't reckon they'll like it much."

"So you'd be interested in keeping that fact from reaching them, right?"

"Yes, sir."

"I imagine you can create some logical excuse for the dent. Maybe some gang members kicked it in while you were grabbing a bite of fast food."

"Stuff like that happens," he said agreeably.

"And even if it was your fault, bumping into something — a pole or garbage can — would be better than having run over a human being, am I right?"

"People are too mushy to be hitting with cars. They make that real clear in orientation."

"So you'd like it if I agreed to keep our little accident secret."

"That is the truth."

"Good, because there's something I want from you."

"Yes, sir?"

"I know that after I leave, you'll eventually tell someone that you had The Shy Samaritan as a fare in your cab."

Robert opened his mouth to protest. Seth held up his hand to quiet him.

"Are you married, Robert?"

He nodded.

"Children?"

"Three."

"Well you see, it's only a matter of time, Robert. Human nature. I can't expect you to keep secrets from your family. Even if the cops or your employers don't pry the truth out of you, you'll want to share the big news with someone. That someone will tell someone else, and so on. We don't want to make an agreement that you can't keep, right?"

"No, sir."

"That's why I'm going to make it easy on you. All I want is thirty-six hours. It's afternoon now. Don't tell anyone that you saw me, hit me, drove me, or dropped me off here, until at least the morning after next. Then what you say or do is up to you. Can you agree to this?"

"Sounds reasonable to me."

"Because, Robert, if I find out you haven't held your end of the bargain, I'd obviously have to tell my version of events too, which wouldn't make providing for your family any easier." He held out a scraped hand to shake. "Deal?"

Robert smiled broadly over a set of well-maintained teeth and took his hand, shaking it firmly. "Good luck to you," he said with assurance.

Seth believed him. He was safe, at least for a while. Now he need only get out of the car and stand.

"How bad do I look?" he asked.

"You cleaned up real nice," Robert said. "You got yourself a couple of scratches on the cheek, but ain't nobody here going to care about that. Of course, you're getting mighty popular. If I was you I'd be getting myself a big old hat to hide in."

Seth pulled the lever on the door, swung his legs out, and slowly worked his way onto the curb. The aspirin was taking effect now, maybe even the Aleve, but morphine was what he needed. His right leg barely held weight, and shoulder pain now rivaled his bruised or broken ribs. Still, he could stand, and after a moment of acclimation, he shuffled toward the entrance. Robert drove off with a wave.

Inside the automatic doors on the main terminal upper level, Seth sidled over to a marble column and leaned against it nonchalantly, the newspaper tucked in his armpit, taking the weight off the bad leg and trying to develop a plan, something he lacked badly.

Must think logically.

He liked Robert's idea of the hat; and other than orange juice, coffee, and an overdose of painkillers, he hadn't eaten all day. His stomach was protesting. Spotting the Faber News & Gifts shop nearby, he set off at a slow shuffle, masquerading his movement as a bored passenger passing time between connections, rather than as the crippled car accident victim he was.

From a large selection of fitted baseball caps on an upper shelf, he chose a size seven with the maroon and yellow Washington Redskins colors and logo. It fit snuggly on his head and roughly matched the brown and gold colors of Goldy Gopher on the back of his sweatshirt, if not the smeared dirt and grass stains on the front and side. He paid for the hat and two mocha-flavored PowerBars, then crossed the wide and bustling hallway to a twenty-four-hour snack bar where he reluctantly bought a sixteen-ounce bottle of orange drink that boasted ten percent real juice content.

He found a seat in a comfortable alcove with large potted plants and sections of a current *Wall Street Journal* strewn across a central tabletop. The little rest area seated ten, but he was alone, and hoped it stayed that way. Pulling the bill of the new cap down low over his face, Seth eased his battered body into the seat. The PowerBars and sports drink disappeared in seconds, and he settled back into the seat, his breathing labored and erratic. The morning's events replayed in his head, but they seemed removed, as if he'd watched it all in a movie. It was all so improbable, so inexplicable. Yet the pain was real.

Who were these people?

A sensual female voice made announcements over the PA system. Crowds swirled by. He closed his eyes and drew a few deep breaths.

Must relax. Must think. Forget the pain. Let the Paxil do its job.

His spontaneous reaction to the shocking attack and scrutiny of complete strangers was typical: run. It led him again to the airport. He'd done this before. When the pressure is too intense, run away.

Was that what this was? Was he about to hop a plane to who-knows-where and start a new life all over again? Leave his job, his research, and this deadly unsolved mystery behind? Could he outrun it if he tried? God knows he wanted to. But he was tired of running, tired of the fear. The medication made a difference. Maybe now he could change, start doing the right thing: face his fears.

That's what he should have done before. Dong was right. He never should have let himself get on that plane and escape from Minnesota. He didn't belong here. Now look what he'd gotten himself into. The admonition from some childhood lecture rang in his ears: *Running from fear only makes matters worse.* He could write a book on that subject. But it had always been out of his control. A physical response. Fight or flight. Can the antelope rationalize in the face of a lion's attack?

Anger suddenly rose in him, like the acid reflux in his roiling stomach. He *was* an antelope. Admitting it almost brought tears to his eyes. The reasons he'd come to the airport weren't all noble and reasonable. Coworker Bill Steiner had given his life unnecessarily because of Seth's weakness, and had died in his arms. But Seth couldn't bring himself to attend the funeral. Flying out of D.C. solved that dilemma. The whole city wanted to see his face and hear his words. Disappearing into the shadows of another major city two thousand miles away might solve that too. The press would tire and drop it, and the public would forget.

But Seth never would. Add those failures to the long list. A list that was an anchor dragging him down in an ocean of opportunity. A list that now included disappointed family, shattered lives, and unfortunate death.

No. He wouldn't run. Not this time. Not ever again. They could come scrape him off whatever surface he fell onto, but he would never do it again. Newman was right. It was time to come in from the cold.

His fingers slowly stopped their trembling, and a calm came over him. Weariness settled on him like heavy fog, and he drifted off to sleep.

CHAPTER 19

A crying baby woke Seth. He sat up with a start, momentarily disoriented. Shooting pains from his bruised ribs reoriented him quickly. A Hindu woman had joined him in the alcove, cradling her baby and talking rapidly in a foreign language to a toddler who had a handful of her colorful sari. Darkness had descended outside the windows. A light snow fell and swirled on the tarmac. The airport was even busier than before.

How long had he slept?

A large overhead clock put the time at 6:30 p.m. He wasn't sure what time he drifted off, but he'd clearly slept for hours.

His rumbling stomach prodded him past the snack bar to the Lounge Café for something more substantial to eat. His right leg had stiffened severely, and his shuffle was now a hobble. There he bought a diagonally cut and pre-wrapped ham-and-Swiss-on-rye sandwich and more juice. He took an open booth along the outer wall with a large window overlooking the runways. Colored lights twinkled in the windswept blackness.

He washed down another handful of pain pills and wolfed down the sandwich. When he returned to the counter for a caramel roll, he erred by looking up at the girl working the register. She smiled and did the double take he was now used to. Her hand came up to point at him and her mouth dropped open to speak. Seth beat her to it, smiling broadly and holding a finger over his lips to shush her. She looked about to protest, but he wagged his finger at her. Leaning in, he whispered, "It's our secret," and then winked.

He left her gaping and returned to his alcove in the hallway, now empty, happy that he'd handled the encounter better than in the past. Finally, after toting it for hours, he read the newspaper Robert bought him.

Forces of Evil Threaten City's First Citizen.

They were turning him into a superhero. He skimmed the article with a mixture of disgust and suppressed pride. It contained nothing he didn't already know, but plenty he disagreed with. Charlene provided background on him: quiet, polite, neighborly, secretive, hunkish. He grinned at that.

And she disclosed the burglary. The reporter used that to flesh out the theory from unnamed sources at Metro PD and the National Ice Center that Seth Peterson, The Shy Samaritan — the man who fearlessly enters deadly

141

infernos to save the lives of helpless women and fights rampaging herds of terrorized citizens to cradle the head of dying friends and protect defenseless widows — was the target of a mysterious murder plot. They made it sound as though he did this stuff every day, and as if no one else on the planet ever would.

The article stated that repeated attempts to contact Seth for comment had failed. They posed open-ended questions: Was he really so shy? Or was he in danger, kidnapped or worse by whatever diabolical evil pursued him? Would he continue his work as city savior? Or would his own celebrity doom him? Had it already?

He crumpled the paper and threw it on the seat next to him.

Then it hit him: Dave Thornton was right, had been all along. The situation would never end until he walked into a newsroom and made himself so available that the public either tired of him or saw how ridiculous the whole charade was. Part of him secretly *wanted* to do it. Could he do it? Unknown. But he'd damn sure try.

But *should* he do it?

Pathetic fears weren't all he was running from. He was escaping submachine-gun-toting murderers, people who knew where he worked and lived. They'd broken into his apartment, pulled off a bold and well-planned public execution, tailed him across the city, and made a brash daylight attempt to ambush him. The attack this morning proved two things. One, they knew they'd killed the wrong man and Seth survived. And two, they still wanted him dead.

What could he gain by coming forward now, other than to assuage his bruised pride? With a gang of at least six, they could easily stake out his apartment and the Center again. Pulling keys from his pocket, he looked at them, pondering possibilities. The assailants had to expect, too, that he'd eventually return to retrieve his car. Good chance they'd be there waiting. Newman had warned him to stay away from home; and Bern, from work. So what if he worked up the courage to attend Bill Steiner's funeral? Wouldn't the bad guys and girl expect him there as well?

Murder in the graveyard. How apropos.

In truth, he was hiding for his life. Phobia might have led him to this point, but a commonsense will to live must guide him now. Introducing himself to the press hardly seemed wise. What, then? Take a motel room and wait them out? Hope to avoid discovery? For how long? Could he afford it? What if they decided to check all the motels? Wasn't that the next logical step for people so determined?

What did they want?

142

Maybe he should call Newman again. Seeking protection had been his first plan in Robert's taxi before he panicked and fled to the airport. But what could the police do for him? Their advice was originally to run and hide. They had no suspects, no motive. Perhaps now they would offer a safe house until they solved the mystery; but could he trust them? Secrets had a nasty tendency to leak out of the MPD like blood and brains from Bill Steiner's head.

No, he was on his own. And nowhere in Washington, D.C., was safe. With his face plastered on every newspaper and television in the city, he stood out like a neon sign saying "Here I am, kill me." The Eastern Environmental Corporation's "employees" need only tune to the daily news to find their target.

Soon, Robert would tell his harrowing tale of the brave man he'd accidentally run down; a man who then miraculously rose on damaged legs, demanding a ride to the airport, rejecting medical attention and apologies, an amazing man known more popularly as The Shy Samaritan. The legend would grow. What of the young woman in the cafeteria? He might not have the expected time-cushion before his latest location made news. He couldn't stay. But where does a man with no friends go?

Pulling the bill of his cap low, Seth limped to a bank of monitors hung from the ceiling. Two listed flight arrivals. Two others listed departures. He studied the latter. What were his options?

A listing caught his attention: Northwest Airlines Flight 621, nonstop to Minneapolis, with departure at 7:25 p.m. He looked at the big clock again. Twenty-seven minutes from now.

A desperate plan began to form.

He might have no friends, but he did have family: a mother and father in Stillwater, Minnesota, a mere thirty miles from the flight's destination. These were the parents he'd hurt so badly, leaving them in humiliation and pain when he abandoned Campbell Morrison and fled the state, the parents to whom he'd said nothing in over a year. What had Dong said? *"Think about whether continuing to hide is helpful to either of you. Think about what it might take to bring yourself to contact them and face whatever venting they feel justified in doing."*

Suddenly he knew the truth. Avoiding his parents was all about *his* wishes, not theirs. He wasn't doing them a favor by keeping a failed son out of their life; he was probably prolonging the shame. If facing fears was to be his new way, this was a good way to start. It's what Dong had known and wanted, but thought Seth should conclude for himself.

The question of whether his parents were willing to help in his time of need, after all he'd put them through, took only a second to answer: of course they would. He knew them well. They were loving and forgiving parents, though his father might be slow to show it.

Suddenly a trip home made complete sense. That's where he belonged. He could elude the peril here and mend the relationship with his parents, all without feeling as though he were still running from fear.

There wasn't much time. Seth pulled a credit card from his wallet and limped to the Northwest Airlines ticket counter as fast as his battered body allowed.

CHAPTER 20

The McDonnell Douglas DC9-30 fought a stiff westerly headwind, arriving in Minneapolis at 9:47, thirty-three minutes behind schedule. Seth worried if hotel arrangements were possible, considering the late hour. As it turned out, this was no problem; he booked a room at the Stillwater Inn with a simple call from the airport. He paid a cab fifty dollars to haul him the thirty miles out the Highway 494-694 Loop to Stillwater.

The flight was largely uneventful, and he felt confident that his "escape" from D.C. had gone unnoticed. After buying his ticket and clearing security, he'd waited to board the plane, taking a seat at the gate next to the one from which he'd actually left. If he was recognized, he hoped his pursuers would conclude he'd taken that flight to Denver instead. But he noticed no looks of recognition from those around him at the airport. On the plane, he had stared out the window or feigned sleep with his cap down, except when he used the restroom. That drew a bit of attention, as the struggle to rise and ease by the passengers seated next to him could only be done with moans and grimaces. In the restroom with his pants down, he was shocked to see the contusion that covered virtually his entire right thigh.

When the flight attendant took drink orders, Seth opted for his usual orange juice, this time adding vodka for medicinal purposes, downing another handful of aspirin and Aleve. He smiled inwardly. At the rate he was going, he might have to break with tradition and visit a doctor sometime soon — whether he needed it or not.

The temperature in Minneapolis was a chilly 14 degrees Fahrenheit, but the wind was calm and the stars were out, making for a crisp and pleasant evening. Seth watched the familiar sights on the drive to Stillwater. There was more open space — "tundra," Campbell used to call it — than around D.C. He could finally breathe again.

The Stillwater Inn was a two-story Best Western motel located "up on the highway" across from Wal-Mart, where most new businesses were going rather than in the old downtown area, which had evolved into a tourist Mecca for antique and novelty gift shoppers. Most of the downtown merchants played up the quaint, nineteenth-century lumber-business heritage of the city, selling their wares from restored brick buildings, some dating back to the early days when Stillwater earned its reputation as Minnesota's first settlement in 1847. The city's summer celebration was Lumberjack Days, featuring sawing contests, log rolling, and other thematic events.

As the cab reached the hotel parking lot off Highway 36, Seth was surprised by changes in the city. In just the year he'd been gone, the business district had exploded up both sides of Highway 5, where the sod farms he worked summers as a teenager used to be, and residential construction had crept all the way up Highway 15.

It was sad. The woods and fields he ran in as a kid were disappearing. The beautiful little town he'd grown up in was now another suburb of the Twin Cities. *How had it happened?* he wondered. The St. Croix River had a lot to do with it, he was sure. Wild, clean, scenic. Who wouldn't want to live near it? And of course, America was busy restoring its old homes, and Stillwater had some doozies, old Victorian mansions built by the rich lumber barons from their best wood stocks. These attracted the moneyed folk. He remembered thinking it was the beginning of the end for Stillwater when the celebrities moved in and called it home. First came the movie stars. Then sports heroes. Then the famous authors. Still, he preferred it to D.C., and surely never thought he'd ever leave — until the wedding.

Despite the changes, Seth entered the hotel lobby happy to be home. He checked in, found his room, and poured himself a hot bath. He soaked his weary and battered bones for an hour before slipping into bed, still mulling over scenarios of how best to confront his parents the next day.

CHAPTER 21

Seth woke to the sound of traffic on Highway 36. From his second-story window, he watched the "cheeseheads" making the Tuesday morning commute from the Wisconsin side of the river to their jobs in the Twin Cities. There were more than he remembered.

Chickadees and Northern Cardinals took turns pecking through seed mix in a birdfeeder hung on a post amidst a variety of spruce trees. A mess of fallen seedpods and bird scat dirtied the area below, contrasting with a six-inch snow base covering the landscape. Next door, a digital temperature reading of 18 degrees flashed on the old Northwestern Bank sign. Before he'd left town the bank changed names to Norwest, and then again to Wells Fargo.

Clouds had moved in overnight, covering the countryside in a heat blanket and helping raise the temperature several degrees by morning. It was still too cold for Seth's clothes. He had only a light jacket, now with holes in the sleeves. No gloves. No hat.

He showered and took stock of his naked body in the large mirror. The contused thigh was now a grizzly yellow and purple, but other than stiffness and deep painful bruising, he doubted that he'd suffered any serious damage. He windmilled his arm, checking the shoulder too: sore, but still attached and in-socket. The various scrapes on his hands, face, and elbows were minor, nothing even needing a Band-Aid. He plied his nose gently between thumb and forefinger. The movement hurt, but it felt solid enough. The black eyes had faded to a dull, barely perceptible yellow. The big problem was his chest, where no damage was visible. The car accident had erased any doubt over whether ribs were broken in there. But none of them had punctured a lung; he'd be fine. The pain, though, was nearly constant and occasionally intolerable.

Dressing again in his dirty and tattered clothes, he stepped into the brisk air and walked next door to the Wells Fargo bank. Hard-packed snow crunched like Styrofoam underfoot. He used the new drive-up ATM as a walk-up instead, withdrawing three hundred dollars — the maximum allowed — from his D.C. account. Then he hustled as quickly as his legs allowed down to Oakgreen Avenue, across Highway 36, and up to the St. Croix Mall, where he planned to buy a set of clothes and some winter-weather gear.

When he arrived, he was surprised to find that the Mall no longer existed as he remembered. The building had been purchased by Andersen Corporation, a large window manufacturer located in neighboring Bayport. Only a handful of shops and the Herberger's Department Store at the far end of the complex remained. Herberger's would have what he needed, but it didn't open for twenty minutes.

Dangerously cold, he decided against waiting, retraced his steps and shuffled past the motel to the Target store a block west. There he bought new socks, underwear, jeans, sweatshirt, wool gloves, stocking cap, and a warmer jacket. He used the restroom by the café and front door to change, throwing his old clothes in the wastebasket at the exit.

Clean, clothed, and now warm, Seth's thoughts turned to food. He hadn't eaten a proper meal in over twenty-four hours. What he craved was a good old-fashioned bacon-and-eggs breakfast at the River Oasis Café on Highway 95, under the bluffs south of downtown. Unfortunately, the way things were going he couldn't be sure it was still there. Even if it was, there was a good chance he'd be recognized.

This was a new thought. Washington, D.C., had no exclusive on Seth Peterson. Stillwater was where he'd grown up; hundreds of people here knew him. Considering how he'd left town, he didn't want his return known. Nor did he want his parents hearing the news from a third party.

He chose the Perkins Restaurant near the motel instead, where locals his age rarely hung out. He could walk there and save the taxi fare; after his purchases, his funds were limited.

Sated by a meal of French toast, link sausage, and orange juice, Seth returned to his room at the Inn and prepared to call his parents. He felt tremendous relief to be home, on familiar ground, but a knot had been building in his belly all morning. The call would be tough. Just about the time he began to sweat over it, in the corner booth in Perkins with his cap down low and his face draped over his steaming decaf, he'd thought of his Paxil. How he wished he had it now. Today he was supposed to have stepped up the dosage to ten milligrams. Unfortunately, the pills were on his kitchen counter in D.C., doing him no good.

Just when he had worked up the nerve to make the call without medication, he recalled leaving the psychiatrist's office days earlier with a starter kit of Paxil, and a prescription for more. Hadn't he stowed Dong's note in his wallet? He pulled out the worn leather wallet and sighed with satisfaction: Folded and tucked in the slot reserved for paper currency was the Paxil prescription. He ventured off again to have it filled at the Target pharmacy.

An hour later, Seth sat on his bed in the motel room, staring at the telephone. He was now safe, warm, clothed, fed, and medicated.

But he surely didn't like that phone.

He understood that Paxil was a slow-acting drug. Its effects were felt after days or weeks, not minutes. The pill he took that morning had no more effect on his courage than did the six aspirins he'd also swallowed, and he knew it. So the call to his mother and father was something he had to do of his own volition. It required a fortitude he'd lacked for thirty-six years. But it needed doing. He hadn't spent six hundred dollars and flown across the country for French toast. He owed his parents this. He owed it to himself. It was a Dr. Laura-like right-thing-to-do.

The phone went up. The phone went down.

Finally, like a skydiver braving his first jump, Seth grabbed the telephone with a tight fist and jabbed his parents' familiar phone number on the keypad. His heart pounded. Sweat rolled from his armpits. He hoped his mother answered.

The phone at the other end of the line was picked up, and he heard his father clear his throat and with a gravelly voice say hello. Seth thought he should be panicking — and he *was* nervous — but he was still in control. He paused, unsure of himself, but then just jumped.

"Dad?"

There was silence at the other end. Then, "Just a minute," and the sound of the phone being set on the table. A moment later a woman's voice came on.

"Hello?"

"Mom?"

Another pause.

"Seth? Is that you?"

"Yes, Mom."

"Oh my God." She was instantly crying. "Is that really you? I thought you'd never call again. How are you, dear?"

"I'm fine, Mom." It was difficult to talk. He was free-falling. What words could he say? "I thought it was about time I should call."

"I'm glad you did."

"How have you been? Are you doing all right?"

"Oh yes. Your father and I are fine. His arthritis is bad in this cold weather, but you know him. He says we can't afford to move south."

"Yeah. Um ... Dad doesn't want to talk to me, and I don't blame him. Is he pretty angry?"

"Never mind him. He'll be fine. Let's not talk about that now. I'm just glad to hear your voice."

"No, Mom. We should talk about it. That's why I called. It's time."

His mother paused. "For what, dear?"

"I think we should discuss it in person."

"Oh, Seth. Are you coming home?" There was a pleading in her voice, anticipation.

"I think I should."

"Yes, please do. Where have you been?"

"Washington, D.C."

"When will you come? Oh, do come for Christmas."

"Not until I can talk to Dad. I need to know that it's okay with both of you."

"I'm sure it will be."

"Put him back on the phone, Mom — if he's willing."

There was a long pause, and muffled whispering, then his dad's curt voice. "Yes?"

"Dad, I want your permission to come home and talk to you two about what I did."

A long pause. "Do you need money?"

"No. It's not that. I ... I want to say I'm sorry."

His dad hesitated. "You need to come home to do that?" he said in monotone.

"In person. Yes. I think that would be best."

"We're doing fine."

"I'm not. I want to clear the air."

"You want forgiveness."

Seth opened his mouth, instantly defensive, eager to quibble. But he caught himself. "I suppose there's some of that. But mostly I just want to apologize and ... I guess give you guys a chance to yell at me, if you want."

"Sounds easy. Nice and clean."

"Dad, I think Mom would like to see me. But I won't make the trip there ... I won't bother you guys unless it's okay with you. I'll understand."

"I'm not stopping you."

Seth read through that comment. His father wanted him to come home, but didn't want to admit it. There was no point in trying to force out of him what he didn't want to say.

"I'm already in town."

"Oh?"

"I spent the night at the Stillwater Inn up on the highway. Why don't I swing by for a visit in, say, a half hour?"

"I'll tell your mother."

"Dad?"

"Yes?"

"You guys didn't move, did you?"

CHAPTER 22

The taxi was fifteen minutes late, allowing Seth more time to fret. In silence they drove north on Washington to Curve Crest, then east to Greeley. They went past Lily Lake, where he'd learned to swim thirty years earlier, and past the softball fields, where he'd imagined sharing in the fun and camaraderie but never mustered the courage to join a league. At Lakeview Hospital, where he was born, they went east again on Churchill. This wasn't the direct route to his parents' house on Orleans Street — unless there was a change at Osgood Avenue he wasn't aware of. Maybe the driver was running up the tab. Seth didn't care. This route led into town, down familiar residential streets. Going straight at Fourth Street, he passed Meister's Bar & Grill, happy to see that landmark still there. At First Street they backtracked south a few blocks, zigging past the old Nelson School — now townhouses — and zagging east on Orleans along the old athletic field where Seth played as a child. The cab parked across from it in front of the modest two-story frame house his parents had called home for over twenty years.

He hurriedly paid the driver and made his way to the front door before his mother had a chance to rush from the house and make a scene in front of the whole neighborhood. The door opened before he got his finger on the doorbell, and his five-foot-one-inch mother bear-hugged him around the waist, nearly dropping him to the concrete stoop with white-hot pain. Had she been taller and her arms reached around him further up his torso, over the ribs, she would have dropped him. As it was, with her teary face buried in his belly, she didn't see the stretched-face grimace or understand the effort needed to contain the scream welling in his throat.

She stepped back to look him over, and then came at him again. This time he held her off.

"You're eating well," she said.

"I don't think of it as weight gain, Mom. I'm just occupying more space."

"Good. More of you to love."

"Mom, let's get in out of the cold."

"You bet." She took his hand and led him into the foyer, peering up at his scraped and fading yellow face with concern.

"You look bruised, dear. Are you all right?"

Seth waved it off. "Yeah. I tripped. It's nothing. Where's Dad?" he asked,

152

changing the subject, anxious to get the hard part over quickly.

"He's in the family room, reading."

Seth slipped off his shoes and proceeded down the restored fifty-year-old hardwood floor in the hallway. His father sat in a worn recliner with a hardcover book open in his lap. He looked up at Seth, peering over a pair of reading glasses riding low on the bridge of his nose. Seth stopped on the edge of the carpet. His mother waited behind him. No one moved or said anything.

Finally his father closed the book methodically, placed his glasses neatly on the table beside him, and rose. He'd aged noticeably in the year. He was a big man, a quiet and hardworking farm-boy-turned-mason with firm convictions and an inner strength supported by mass and muscle. Seth had feared him, respected him, envied him, loved him.

He reminded Seth now of his grandfather, Jonathan: old and wise, yet still powerful. Grandpa Jon used to sit with Seth on the porch in the hot summer and relate his aspirations as a young man to be a great Antarctic explorer such as Roald Amundson, Robert Scott, Mawson, Ross, Bellingshausen, Wilkes, Byrd, Weddell, Cook — all men whose conquests had earned them immortality in that some part of the land or sea were named after them — or his most admired hero: Sir Ernest Shackleton, the man after whom he'd named his own son.

Seth knew the oft-told ordeal by heart: In 1914, Shackleton, veteran of two previous Antarctic expeditions, with a crew of twenty-six plus an eighteen-year-old stowaway, sailed for Antarctica, determined to be first to sledge across the full breadth of the continent.

They never got there. Beset in ice floes off the coast of Antarctica, ship and crew endured a two-year trial of cold, hunger, monotony, loneliness, and despair as they were dragged helplessly around the vicious Weddell Sea by pack ice.

The ice crushed their ship before the first year was out, putting the crew onto the ice. Thus began an excruciating exercise in basic survival against all odds. The pack ice drifted interminably north, forcing them onto ever-diminishing floes, and eventually to the ship's lifeboats.

Near death, the crew finally reached hellish and uninhabited Elephant Island. This was before functional radio, and no one on earth knew the crew's whereabouts. They were presumed dead. Their only hope for salvation was for Shackleton and five others to sail the best of their three boats — an open, twenty-two-foot lifeboat — 870 miles across the worst seas on Earth to the whaling station on South Georgia Island, and return to rescue the others — if the others hadn't yet frozen or starved to death.

By some miracle, they succeeded.

The scene the grandfather painted as he recounted the story of his son's namesake left an indelible impression on his grandson's young mind. It was this incredible tale of hardship and heroism that originally fueled Seth's interest in Antarctica. He'd studied every aspect of the frozen and enigmatic continent ever since, and his life's dream was to get there eventually. It was a paradox: a place that could test his courage in infinite ways, yet in its desolation could shield him from what he feared most — people.

Ironically, Ernest Peterson never showed the least interest in such "nonsense." He'd schooled Seth in the belief that a man needn't go in search of noble deeds; that they invariably revealed themselves in due course to those who stayed put, tending farm and family, standing ready for when duty called.

Both men were right, Seth knew. He hoped that someday he'd have such conviction to pass to children of his own.

Maybe this was his defining moment. He envisioned himself as a bedraggled Shackleton, his long and lonely journey through life symbolic of struggle against enormous odds. Here he stood before his father, the Iceman, whose icy stare raked Seth's soul like the Westerlies swept Drake Passage.

He advanced with outstretched hand. Slowly, his father extended his as well, and they shook long and firmly, both men making eye contact, speaking an unspoken language of trust and understanding. Seth knew that no words could say more to his father than to stand before him as he was and shake hands.

They pulled their eyes apart and both took a seat. His mother, Irene, landed on the sofa next to Seth and pulled his hand into her lap, patting it. After an awkward silence his father finally spoke.

"So you've come back then."

"Yes."

"Feel you need to set things right, do you?"

"I'd like to try."

"And how do you suppose you'll do that?"

His mother jumped to his defense. "Ernest, there's no need to start up now."

Seth wanted no defense. He held his hand up at his side to quiet her. "It's okay, Mom." He locked eyeballs again with his father, something previously difficult. "I don't know that I can, Dad, but I thought I'd start by giving you a chance to tell me what you really thought of my leaving town."

His dad squinted at the unexpected approach, but didn't fall for it easily. "Oh, I see, I vent a little, and all is forgiven, eh?"

"I don't know. Maybe it's a start," Seth said. "It has to be better than my throwing out a bunch of excuses."

Ernest Peterson considered that. Veins throbbed visibly in his neck. "Well, I'll tell you what I felt about that. It seems to me you got yourself in further with Campbell than you expected, and then wanted out. But you weren't man enough to tell her. You weren't man enough to do anything but run at the last minute when you realized it was all wrong for you. You strung Campbell and virtually everyone in town along, making us believe you loved her. But you didn't — not enough to marry her. No, you had to think of yourself. What about the great Seth Peterson? What about *his* future? What about his plans and all the other beautiful women in the world he could have?"

"Dad, that's —"

"Let me tell you how I feel," his father said, leaning forward with nostrils flared. "I'm not a smart man. I'm not educated like you. I was never athletic or good-looking, all the stuff you took for granted. But you pissed it away." His father was pointing now, speaking loudly, angry. Irene's hand was tense, but she knew it was no time to intervene. When the going got tough, Irene Peterson shut down. "And do you know why I think you did it? Because you're a selfish son of a bitch. You come back here acting as though there were some good reason for it, but I think it was because you only think of yourself. Well, let me tell you how I feel about that. I think it stinks. Marriage is serious business. You must be man enough to call it off if you have doubts. But no, not my son. He doesn't care enough about anyone else to admit his own misgivings, to do his fiancée the favor of explaining that it wouldn't work, *before* leaving her at the altar in front of the whole town."

Ernest took a breath. Irene's head was down. Seth still faced his father, but tears welled in his eyes. He wanted to defend himself, but this was what he'd come for.

"You probably think it's the pain you caused us that hurts the worst, but that's nothing," his father said. "Maybe Korea scarred me and ruined my prospects as a good father, but if nothing else, it thickened my skin against the crap you pull. What affected us most was Campbell's pain. You left it to us to clean up the mess. You left us behind to answer the questions, but we had no answers. We were the ones who had to deal with Campbell and her family and the bills. How could you leave a good woman like that, Seth? You used her. Shame on you. *Damn* you."

Irene doubled over beside him, saying nothing. This was beyond her. Ernest's eyes were on fire. Their intensity pierced through, but Seth refused to let his gaze fall. The words hurt. His heart flopped like a fish in the bottom of a boat. His shirt was wet with sweat, but he felt an odd calm in his head, almost serenity.

"Dad, I want to tell you why this happened, but I don't want it to be an excuse."

"I don't know what the hell that even means."

"It means there's a reason, but not an excuse. I don't want your sympathy. I'm not here for … well … maybe I am. I want you to understand, but I don't know whether you can."

Shaking his head skeptically, Ernest said, "Let me guess, you're an undercover agent for the FBI and had to leave town on an important case. National security and all, right?"

"No, Dad." He rubbed his face, working up the courage to expose the truth. "Remember when I was eight? You signed me up for soccer, but I sprained my ankle and couldn't join the team? My ankle wasn't really sprained. And when I was twelve, I wouldn't go to summer camp? It wasn't because I would've had to quit my paper route. And how about when my old Monte Carlo quit on me in New Prague and I missed Aunt Laurie's graduation down in Mankato? There was nothing wrong with the car. Dad, I could name fifty other examples."

Ernest looked puzzled. "What was it, then?"

"I was scared … so I lied."

Ernest looked at him as though he were crazy. "Scared of what?"

"People, crowds, commotion."

"You're here to tell us you're a coward?"

"Well, that's what I always thought, but —"

"Listen to me. When I went to Korea in 1950 as an infantryman, I was a lot younger than you are now, like everyone in my platoon. We were just a bunch of twenty-year-old kids, never been away from home, and were facing down seasoned Chinese troops, trying to save the world from the commies. I saw grown men so scared they pissed their pants and puked their guts out. But they'd work it out of their system and did their duty. When it came time to climb out of a hole and move on, into the cold, into the bullets, they went. But you're going to tell me you were too scared to tell a woman you don't love her? That you'd rather dump her and run?"

Ernest Peterson wasn't the kind to run, Seth knew. In the Korean War, he was one of the "Frozen Chosen," the First Marine division that was surrounded and outnumbered in the mountainous region near the Korean Chosin Reservoir in December 1950. Twelve thousand brave Marines fought against over sixty thousand enemy troops to extricate themselves from a horrendous circumstance. Their escape was successful, but only after thousands were killed or wounded by the enemy, or maimed by frostbite in the terrible cold.

The Korean War never officially ended. Seth wondered whether his suffering was doomed to the same fate. He'd grown up hearing the Korea stories repeatedly. Each time they fascinated him, yet reinforced his own feelings of inadequacy. In his own way, his father was as brave as Shackleton was.

Seth couldn't even face Little League.

His mother chimed in now. "Seth, that's just silly, you being afraid. You were always such a brave little boy. You always took such risks. We worried about you. You were the one who climbed the tallest tree or jumped off the highest cliff. What about when your Grandpa Jon had the heart attack at Thanksgiving? You were only fifteen, but you were the one in the house who stayed calm. You were giving out instructions like an adult, like a doctor."

"He was calm because he didn't care," his dad said.

"Ernest, please," his mother said.

"Dad, I *did* care," Seth said, working to keep his breath even. "And as I'm learning, this isn't really about courage. It's a phobia. I don't expect you to understand, but it's something I couldn't control. In Korea, there must have been guys who lost it, jumped up and ran, or went into the fetal position in their foxhole, right? That's what this is. There's nothing you can do. It's like claustrophobia. It's fear of heights. It's fear of bridges, or spiders. It makes no sense, yet to those who have it, it's so real and terrifying, they can't control their own bodies. That's what I have, Dad: a phobia, a phobia of people."

His dad frowned hard.

"That's why I never joined the Boy Scouts or church or clubs, or why I never played football or baseball. Instead I skied, and swam, and ran, and rode bicycle — all solo stuff. Didn't you think it was odd that I never managed to make it to any weddings or funerals or birthday parties? I mean I always had some excuse, something else going on."

"You were just shy," his mother said. She didn't seem to like the idea of her son as a coward.

He blanched at her mention of the word "shy."

Ernest rose and paced. "I thought you were just too busy to share any of your precious self with others." He stopped and stood in front of Seth. "And what is this terrible thing that happens to you when you're confronted with *people*?" He shook his hands in front of him and said the last word like he'd meant "monsters" instead, mocking him.

"Passing out unconscious live on the Saturday morning news is what happens. That wasn't the flu. I lied to cover up what really happened."

"You just fainted?"

Fainting connoted dainty women swooning in the hot sun. It was never a term he liked. "I prefer 'conked out.'"

"So you've been this way all your life? You did a good job of hiding it."

"Yeah, until the *KSTP* job. That was my dream. Talk about courage. I thought if doing the weather was what I really wanted and if I just toughed it out and went in there and got past the first-time jitters, I'd be fine. Instead, my worst nightmare came true. You have to understand that it was only a few months later that I was suddenly walking out in front of everyone at that church to get married. I tried to get out of it, to tone down the ceremony, but the big church wedding meant everything to Campbell. I couldn't let her down — and I didn't want to lose her. When the moment came ... I couldn't do it. I couldn't go out there and pass out in front her, and you guys, and everyone."

"So you ran."

"Halfway across the country."

Pacing wasn't working to calm Ernest. He returned to his chair.

Seth leaned forward and spoke with his hands. "This was never about Campbell. I loved her. What I did to her just crushed me. I've been hiding ever since. I justified it by convincing myself that nobody ever wanted to see me again. I've been living in forced exile."

Ernest took deep breaths, said nothing. It was a lot to absorb.

"Look," Seth said, "my boss — at the job I have now — forced me to visit a psychiatrist after I kept avoiding a presentation I was supposed to give —"

"You saw a shrink?"

"Yeah. You don't have to be a raving lunatic anymore. The shrink diagnosed me as phobic. He explained all this stuff to me, that I didn't have full control, that I shouldn't feel guilty. But I can't help it. I've felt so guilty that I can't even face myself. It was always easier to run. But he prescribed some new medicine. I've been on it for a week now, and I think it helps a little. It helped me to come here today and do this. It was the psychiatrist's idea that maybe you two would want to get some things off your chest."

His father squeezed his forehead and ran his hand up into his thinning gray hair. This wasn't what he wanted to hear.

"Dad, I can't tell you how hard this is to admit. I feel like I'm coming out of the closet."

"That thought crossed my mind."

Seth laughed. "Join the club."

There was a long silence.

"What do you want from us?" his father said.

158

"I know what I did was unforgivable. I just want some understanding, I guess. I want a chance to make things right."

More silence. Each of them struggled with where the conversation and their relationship should go. Irene spoke first. "We love you, Seth."

"And I love you guys, Mom." He kissed her on the cheek.

Ernest sighed and leaned his head back into the chair, staring at the ceiling. "I don't know how to react to this," he said, his voice choking. "I was furious with you. I actually got used to you being gone. Nobody really talks to us about it, but I was always ready to say that yeah, we had a problem child, but he's out of our life now. Good riddance, you know? Now you show up, and it turns out you've had some terrible handicap all your life and couldn't control yourself. I'd like to say that everything is okay, but I can't switch gears that fast. There was damage done."

In his wildest dreams, Seth never envisioned his parents rejecting him, no matter what. That was what allowed him to appear at their home. It was humiliation — not rejection — that he'd always feared. Had he been wrong all along? Where would he go from here? What else was left?

"Maybe it was a mistake to come home," he said.

Ernest thought and then looked at him, puffy-eyed. "No. We're family. I have no reason to doubt anything you're telling us here, Son. That means your intentions are good. We must take you for what you are. You did the right thing. It's a first step."

Cold as it sounded, Seth knew that his father's summation had taken great effort, and meant much more coming from a man who rarely displayed emotion. Suddenly Seth saw the brilliance in Dong's suggestion to come home.

His mother stood. "I'll make lunch," she said.

CHAPTER 23

After leftover hotdish and homemade *lefsa*, Seth told of his move to Washington, D.C., and the job at NIC. True to character, Ernest said little, and Irene pretended everything was okay.

"What do you do at this Natural Ice Conference?" she asked, pulling a batch of Christmas cookies from the freezer.

Seth wanted to avoid discussion of his life in the East, especially his problems there. He didn't bother to correct her, but instead blinded her with science: "I'm in charge of a study on the stability of southern hemispheric ice. Did you know you can pull up old ice from half a mile down that's a hundred thousand years old? I've been researching deep ice cores with a new method — it's called the Optically Stimulated Luminescence and Cosmogenic Isotope dating method — as well as conventional Radiocarbon and Uranium Series methods."

That shut her down. She diverted. "They should do a study up here. We've had such a warm fall, but with lots of snow. It's very strange."

"Heavy snowfall is like an insulating blanket," Seth said. "Are they issuing thin-ice warnings?"

"You betcha. People are going through the ice right and left. KARE 11 has their snowmobile-through-the-ice body count going already, and it's only December. Tonight won't help much. A warm front is coming with lots of snow."

"What else has been going on in Stillwater?" he asked. "It seems to have grown a lot."

"It has just been terrible," she said. "The *Gazette* says Minnesota is the fastest growing state in the Midwest, and Washington County is one of the richest and fastest growing counties in the country. I have no argument with that. The countryside is disappearing, and the traffic is terrible."

"What's new with you, Mom? What have you been up to?"

"I took a part-time job at a shop downtown."

"Selling antiques?"

"What else? I'm much happier doing this."

Before he left town, she'd retired after twenty-plus years in the purchasing department at Andersen's, the window manufacturer that bought the old mall up on the highway. She liked Andersen's, but not the work she did there. He was happy to hear that she'd found something enjoyable. He smiled, and she winked.

"How about you, Dad?" Seth said.

Ernest grunted.

"His blood pressure has been a concern lately, Seth," she said, her voice quiet.

Ernest pointed a silent finger of warning at her, which she ignored. "Doctor Balder put him on some medication. His knees have been trouble too. We have my income and Social Security, though — and Medicare helps. With savings, we're doing fine."

A sharp pang of guilt over strapping his parents with the aborted wedding costs instantly stabbed Seth. It was amazing how self-centered his mental problems and the high East Coast cost of living allowed him to be. He silently committed to repaying the wedding expenses plus interest as soon as he could. He'd have to be creative with the contribution, though: His father would view it as charity, and never accept it.

Then an idea struck him. "Whatever happened to my truck?"

Irene answered tentatively. "It's in the backyard under a tarp. We had it towed here after you ... were gone a few days. We've never been able to do anything with it without keys or a title. We paid to move your stuff out of the apartment at the end of the month when you didn't return. It's stored up at Kangaroo Mini Storage on Highway 36."

"What did all that cost?"

She looked surprised, but said, "Oh, a couple of hundred for the move, plus seventy dollars a month for storage."

Seth did mental math. Two hundred for moving, seventy a month for — what was it, fifteen months? Plus a couple of grand for the wedding. Or was it a *few* grand?

"You guys sell the truck and keep the proceeds," he said. "I'll come up with the title and keys, and sign it over to the new owner when you find one. That should cover the damages."

His mom's head jerked up. "Sell your truck? A five-year-old Ford Northland Edition must be worth eight thousand."

"Probably more than ten, Mom. And that's perfect; I owe you for the wedding, too, and I'm sure there's more."

His dad chimed in. "We don't want your payoff."

"Dad, it isn't a payoff. At least not the way you're looking at it. I owe this money. The truck is the only way I can repay it now. I have no cash. It's no hardship for me. I have a car back East. If you don't sell it and take the money, the truck will just sit back there, ruining your backyard and doing

161

neither of us any good. Besides, it'll cost you something to advertise it and take time to show it. You'll be doing me a favor."

Ernest's eyes narrowed as he pondered this. He nodded.

"You'll stay for Christmas, of course?" his mom said.

"I don't know. I've got a job now, Mom. I'll have to go back."

"How long will you stay?"

"That depends in part on how long I'm welcome."

Irene Peterson used the lull in conversation to refill their glasses with milk and heap additional scoops of the meat and noodle hotdish on the two men's plates. Ernest decided to talk again.

"What about Campbell?" he said.

Seth froze in mid-chew. He looked at his mother, who performed a world-class ignore-the-whole-thing look at her plate. She was the smartest woman in the world, and at that moment, he hated her for it. His mind raced for a logical response, having conveniently ignored the entire issue. "Whatever happened to her?" was all he could manage in five seconds, as if she were an old family heirloom that finally succumbed to the draw of the antique market downtown and had been sold and placed on display in some Summit Avenue mansion in St. Paul.

Ernest's head didn't budge, but his eyes lifted and looked up at Seth, saying volumes.

"She's still around."

Oh no.

When he heard no response, Ernest Peterson pressed: "What was your plan for her with this great return-and-patch-everything-up deal you've got going?"

Incredibly, Seth had never considered it. His mind's ability to hide things he couldn't cope with was impressive. The odd serenity that blessed him earlier in dealing with his father evaporated.

"In Stillwater?"

"Oh, yeah."

Irene was up in a jiffy, clearing the table, wrapping the uneaten *lefsa* in wax paper for the fridge, and loading the dishwasher.

"I thought she'd have moved on by now," Seth said, staring blankly out the window at the white expanse on the ball field across Orleans Street.

"I don't think so."

Oh boy.

"What was your shrink's plan for her?"

Paxil or no, Seth wasn't ready to face down and own up to Campbell. "Dad, listen ... nobody other than you knows I'm in town. For now I think that's best."

"Still running, huh?"

"That's different. I didn't know where she was. Maybe she was here, maybe not. Either way, after all this time I was sure she'd moved on, got a boyfriend, a husband, maybe even a kid. You're my parents. It's not the same to waltz back into town and jump out in front of her."

His father looked at him and then threw a half-eaten roll of buttered *lefsa* onto his plate before stomping out of the room in disgust.

Seth dropped his head onto the plastic duck-hunting-scene place mat beneath him. "Mom, what am I supposed to do?" he asked as soon as she returned.

She rubbed his shoulder. "It's such a coincidence that you came home today," she finally said, changing the subject as she often did when all hope was lost.

"Why's that?" he said, with his forehead resting on the table's center leaf.

"A man called for you this morning," Irene said.

Seth's head shot up as if he'd been defibrillated. "*Who* called, Mom?"

"Some stranger. Probably a salesman. He asked for you, but I told him you'd moved away."

CHAPTER 24

Seth took extra time in his parents' hall bathroom to wash up after lunch, using it to write a brief note to his mother on a scrap of paper pulled from the wastebasket:

> *Mom, sorry. Must leave. I'm in trouble. Not with the law. Not like that. Don't say I came to see you. I'm not in town. That's very important! Matter of life and death! I'll explain when I can. Hope Dad forgives me. Love, Seth.*

There were ten more pages of explanation he wanted to leave, but no time. He placed the note on the back of the toilet and slipped out the side door, running southwest through yards and the Washington County Courthouse parking lot, then on to the Highway 36 frontage road.

A rising wind and ominous clouds were blowing in from the northwest, but he hardly noticed. In minutes, he'd run-walked his way back to the Best Western, each bouncing step shooting pain through his leg, chest, and shoulder.

He'd made the mistake of telling his parents where he was staying. They might come looking for him, might be followed, or might have his whereabouts forced out of them. Either way, he wanted to be gone when it happened. He checked out immediately and continued west across Washington Avenue on foot, unsure where to go next.

A block away from the Stillwater Inn was a Super 8 Motel. He stood in the frozen frontage road looking at its mostly empty parking lot.

Why not?

He was as safe and incognito here as anywhere — and the transportation to get here was free. He headed through the door and checked himself in.

Safely in his new room, Seth wracked his brain for the meaning of this development. Was the phone call a coincidence, as his mother believed, a telemarketer perhaps, calling him off an outdated mailing list even though he hadn't lived there for years? Possible. Or maybe Newman was trying to track him down.

Or had his mysterious adversaries already found him?

He couldn't risk his parents' lives to find out. The safest thing for them

164

was to believe — in disgust — that he'd run off again. With luck, their anger would dampen curiosity over where he'd gone, and allow them to comply with his written advice should anyone call for him there again.

He considered calling to explain his actions over the phone. But the truth would only worry them, and the more they knew, the riskier it was for them. The possibility seemed remote, but whoever these crazies were, if they were capable of public slaughterings with silenced automatic weapons, they could conceivably tap phones too. It was best to keep his parents in the dark.

Yet he doubted they could tap phones at government agencies like the MPD or NIC. Lifting the phone, he got an outside line and dialed the Ice Center. As usual, Sandy Page answered.

"Sandy, hi. This is Seth. Is Bern around?"

"Hey, you *are* alive, Seth. We were starting to wonder. Where are you?"

"Why? What happened?"

"Just another big news day for you. Witnesses report that a taxi ran over The Shy Samaritan near the Capitol yesterday. Supposedly you jumped up like Superman, drove off with the cabbie, and disappeared."

The secret was out. Had Robert broken their pact? he wondered. Or had a bystander recognized him? The "disappeared" part sounded okay, but not what followed next.

"Yeah," Sandy continued, "but the weird thing is, that same cabbie was found dead last night."

"Robert?"

"You knew him? So this is true?"

"Sandy, what happened to him?" Seth tried to keep his voice steady.

"The TV says it looked like a car accident — well, it *was* a car accident — but then they decided it might have something to do with all the bullet holes in him."

Seth was stunned.

Who were these people?

"Are you a spy or something?" she asked.

Seth faked a chuckle. "No. It's just a misunderstanding."

"Yeah, like stepping on a Claymore mine."

His mind raced.

What was happening? What should he do?

"You'd better call that Detective Newman from MPD. He's been calling nonstop for you. So have the reporters. They found your car down on the Mall. They can't make up their minds whether you're a victim or the perpetrator. You want Newman's number?"

"No. I've got it."

"Oh, and you got another one of those perfumed pink envelopes. A woman dropped it off at Gate 5 this morning. I've been holding it for you. Do you want me to open it?"

Seth was oblivious, his mind swirling with the news of Robert's death. "Yes," he said vacantly.

"Hang on," Sandy said over the sound of paper tearing.

Predictably, it held another card from Emily Corbin. The cover she described was one of Frank Hurley's famous photos of Shackleton's ship, *Endurance*, trapped in the death grip of Weddell Sea pack ice. Inside was another enigmatic quote:

Know in yourself that you are doing the right, and let the move be on the part of others ... the mental satisfaction of knowing that ye are trying makes a peace that may not be had otherwise. —1183-3.

In support,
Emily Corbin

"What's up with that?" Sandy asked.

Seth was angry and confused. Why wouldn't this weird woman let him alone? Her messages were like horoscopes he could always apply to his current predicament. Today he'd waded blindly into the buzz saw of family dysfunction, wholly unsure of himself. According to this strange woman, he was doing right. But what "move" would others be making?

"It's nothing," he said. "Just that woman from the car wanting to thank me over and over."

"Aha. Your first groupie. Hang on, I'll patch you through to Bern."

When she clicked off, Seth hung up. In no mood for conversation, he slumped on the side of the bed and didn't move. He was cursed. Everyone around him was coming up dead. Poor Robert, another innocent victim. Seth puzzled through the friendly man's mysterious death. Perhaps the woman in the maroon Caprice saw the cab number before speeding off. Even if she hadn't, maybe it didn't take much detective work to identify Robert's cab as the one involved. Maybe Robert couldn't hold his end of the bargain after all. Whatever the reason, he had to conclude that Robert shared with his murderer — by either choice or duress — that he'd dropped Seth at the airport. It wouldn't be much of a stretch from there to guess where a man in his position might go: home. And with every reporter in town on the story, the bad guys could probably learn where that might be just by watching the TV news. He knew it — could feel it. That was why his mother received the call that morning. The Eastern Environmental Corporation had tracked him here.

And the fruitcake stalker with her enigmatic messages, Emily Corbin, was still sniffing around his work and home.

It was time to call Newman and hear what the police knew. He pulled the detective's business card from his wallet and dialed the direct number to his desk.

Be there, he thought.

The detective answered after one ring and said only, "Newman," as if he were acting a part in a TV-cop show.

"This is Seth Peterson. What's going on?"

"Peterson, where the hell are you?"

That question strengthened Seth's suspicion that Newman hadn't called his parents. If he'd known Seth was in Minnesota, he wouldn't have continued to call the Center, as Sandy reported he had — not unless he was only fishing out possible locations.

"Have you been looking for me?"

"You're harder to get hold of than Jimmy Hoffa."

"I just heard about the cab driver. What can you tell me?"

"I'll remind you that I ask the questions. I need you to come down here so that I can do that."

Seth was surer than ever that he didn't want anyone to know where he was yet. "I don't have my car."

"Yeah, I know. We do. Take a cab."

Seth made a sarcastic sound with his lips. "No thanks."

"Where are you? I'll come get you."

Seth ignored him. "What happened to the cab driver?"

"He was discovered in an advanced stage of death. I assume that you intend to assert that you're not the shooter?"

"I think you know better. Let me guess, multiple 5.56-millimeter rounds, likely from an AR-15, right?"

"Were you there?"

"Nope."

"Why do you think they killed this Robert McClellan?"

Now Seth knew Robert's last name. It was better when he didn't. "My guess is they only wanted to know where he'd dropped me off. Then they killed him because they don't like to leave clues."

"Or witnesses."

"Exactly."

"And where *did* he drop you?"

"Detective, I'm uncomfortable telling you that right now. No disrespect, but I think I'm safe where I am — and I want to keep it that way."

"You don't think we're doing our job?"

"Ask Robert."

"Uh-huh."

"Have you learned anything since we talked?"

"Not much. We're going over the cab with a fine-tooth comb, but I'm not optimistic about finding anything. Rather stumped right now. We're surely getting a lot of play on this one, though. Plenty of leads and wacky callers. Just nothing concrete."

"I'm getting worried here."

"I don't blame you, Mr. Peterson. I'd be giving serious thought to this plan of yours to remain undercover. Do me a favor and at least call in every day."

"What about the papers and TV?"

"You want me to call and tell them you're okay?"

"Not particularly."

"Well, they're selling a lot of copies right now. No point in spoiling their fun."

CHAPTER 25

Seth spent another hour sprawled on the bed at the Super 8, staring at the sprayed ceiling, trying to sort out the mystery. It was like a mental version of fifty-two-card pickup. He wanted to ask Newman whether he'd been the one who called his parents, but that would've tipped off his location. Right now, he felt safer lying low and lurking. That was how he'd survived all his life. It felt familiar.

The lack of progress on the case was depressing. A group of sophisticated and organized killers was hell-bent on finding him. Their intentions were all too clear. Their identities and reasons were not.

His best plan was to stay hidden. Presumably, he was now secure. No one knew his whereabouts. By phone he could check in daily for updates on whether Newman had solved the insane mystery and put the bad people out of commission. That required him to hole up in the room and avoid traipsing all over his hometown where he might be recognized. TV would help him pass time. Otherwise, he needed only food. The motel offered no room service, only free coffee, juice, and doughnuts in the morning. Not enough to sustain his large frame. Restaurants were too risky and expensive. He threw on his new coat and headed out the door. The best and cheapest option was to buy a week's worth of groceries at the big Cub Foods supermarket a block away. He could eat meals in his room.

It was now four o'clock, Tuesday afternoon, with a building northwest wind and a dusting of snow on the roads. He assumed it was a relatively slow time at the grocery store, compared with a Saturday morning — perfect for fifteen minutes of stealth shopping. However, the large crowd of after-school shoppers he encountered dispelled that notion. Short on options, he proceeded anyway. By the time he walked through the large automatic doors with his cap slung low, he'd already planned a rough menu for the week. He could only buy what he could eat in his room without cooking, and only what he could carry back to the motel in a bag or two. For fluids, he chose two cans of frozen OJ, which he could mix with water from the bathroom sink and keep chilled with ice from the machine in the hall. The food staple was whole wheat bread, light and nutritious. For toppings, he decided on chunky peanut butter and tuna in pull-top cans. He added bananas, pickled herring, and two large bags of nacho cheese Doritos to fill in the food pyramid. No way a guy could starve in a week on that.

With cart loaded, he aimed for the checkout lane, but spotted the candy aisle. The thought that a bag of Tootsie Pops or other hard candy might help pass the time crossed his mind and turned him in that direction.

He regretted it immediately.

When he pushed his cart into the aisle he encountered a slender brunette in a matching gray sweat suit wearing a WCCO-TV ball cap pulled down over her eyes, with a ponytail neatly extruded through the hole in the back. Even though it was cloudy outside and she was inside, she wore sunglasses. Seth recognized her immediately.

Campbell Morrison.

He froze and tried to spin away, but it was too late. She looked up at him, looked away, and then did the all-too-familiar double take.

They stood staring at each other, motionless and slack-jawed.

"Well, well, well," she eventually said, cracking a wry smile. "Look who's still alive."

She settled onto one hip, cocked her head, and leaned on her cart. Seth couldn't believe she wasn't screaming bloody murder. He had no idea what to do. Every instinct told him to run, but he didn't.

Why didn't his heart fail?

He was really beginning to appreciate Paxil.

After a moment of indecision, he realized there was no escape, and oddly, he wasn't panicking. He rolled his cart slowly up to hers and stopped.

"I didn't expect you here," he said lamely.

"No, I'll bet you didn't. How long have you been in town?" She peered over the sunglasses riding low on her nose.

"Last night."

"Ah." She nodded in exaggerated fashion with lower lip stuck out. Then she just stared at him.

Paxil or no, the moment was killing Seth. The two stood awkwardly facing each other. He had to say something.

"I'm sorry, you know."

She laughed at him. "How quaint. Unfortunately, I only wish I could slap you."

He hung his head. "I wish you would."

Her arm swung out spontaneously and struck him full across the face, glancing off his broken nose. The force, shock, and pain sent him reeling into the crackers across the aisle, knocking a dozen boxes of Ritz and Triscuits off the shelf. When he regained his balance and the white spots disappeared from his vision, Campbell stood before him with her hand over her mouth and a look of surprise and horror on her face.

"I didn't hit you *that* hard," she said.

A teenaged employee in a red Cub Foods coat appeared, checking out the commotion.

More from embarrassment and habit than from panic, Seth said to Campbell, "I've got to go. I'm sorry for everything." Then he pushed his cart off fast toward the checkout.

Mentally he tried and failed to count the items in his cart, but headed for the express lane regardless. He thanked a merciful God that the lane was open. Within minutes, he was out the door and returning to his room.

Back in his room minutes later, he kept shaking his head in disbelief at his bad luck and poor performance. But he couldn't think how he'd have handled the situation better, other than having invited Campbell to hit him. What could he possibly say to her? Dong may have been right about his parents — they were family — but Campbell was another matter.

By some mysterious quirk of psychology, he'd managed to put her out of mind completely. The notion that by returning to Stillwater he might by luck or otherwise end up facing her simply never occurred to him. He always thought of her doing what he'd have done in the embarrassing position of one left at the altar: leaving town.

But as his father had said, she was still here, and he'd just run into her. *What now?*

He pondered options. There weren't many. Exposure meant risk to himself and others — even Campbell. So floating around town, trying to face the music, mend fences, or any other red-blooded American cliché was stupid. He could either fly back to D.C. and submit to the media — and murder — or stand pat in his motel room.

An hour passed. His heart settled. The answer came: sit tight.

Another hour later, a knock came on his door.

He shot up off the bed, standing erect and in pain, panicked. Who could it be?

Another knock.

There was no peephole. Unless he opened the door or called for identification, there was no way to know who it was.

An instant later, he realized no one could possibly know his whereabouts. It had to be motel staff, probably wanting to clean the room or change linen. If he didn't open the door, they'd open it themselves. Then what?

He took two steps toward the door and pulled it open.

Campbell Morrison stood looking at him inquisitively.

Seth's knees buckled. A wave of nausea swept over him.

How could this be?

"Why don't you invite me in?" she said.

Seth backed away from the open door, horrified. His only rational thought was to look for the gun she'd use to kill him.

She entered and calmly closed the door behind her. She had no gun.

"How'd you find me?" he eventually managed.

"Wasn't too hard," she said. "I checked for you at your parents' first. They acted odd, denied you were in town. Of course, I knew otherwise. I deduced you were either at their house or at a local motel. Didn't figure you'd splurge for the Lowell Inn."

Seth didn't understand how that could lead her to his door. And his look said it all.

"Stillwater isn't that big, Seth. There are only six or seven hotels you could be at. I figured you for the Stillwater Inn, but found you on the second try. I knew you'd never take a room in the Twin Cities."

"What about all the bed and breakfasts?"

"You at a B&B? Ha!"

Despite his best efforts, the EEC had tracked him to his parents' house in Stillwater, and now Campbell Morrison had dogged him to his door. For someone whose very existence depended on invisibility, it was maddening being so predictable.

"How'd you find my room?"

"You're too stupid to check in as someone else. How do you think I found you? I asked for you."

172

CHAPTER 26

Weak from lack of food, sleep, and normalcy, Seth caved easily. Maybe she'd come to kill, but that was okay. He deserved it. Better to have it done by Campbell than by the EEC.

They stood eyeing each other a moment. Snow melted from the bottom of Campbell's fur-rimmed boots into the crimson carpet. She looked the same as always: good. Green eyes, olive complexion, brunette hair with auburn highlights, pouting lips with no collagen assist, slender curves, long legs — perfect for TV news reporting. Wearing the same gray sweat suit and ball cap, she'd made no attempt to freshen up since the incident at the grocery store. That was the Campbell he remembered; what you see is what you get. Cosmetics and skirts were for the TV camera, a job necessity. Off duty, it was bare skin and old clothes. Take it or leave it. She wasn't one who cared much either way, was never much impressed by her own beauty.

Her beauty always impressed Seth, though. She'd seemed unobtainable when they first met at the WCCO-TV station on 11th Street in downtown Minneapolis. He was too cowardly to make a move. But she'd approached him, matter-of-factly stating her interest. It nearly killed him. The shock incapacitated him. But she was a woman who knew what she wanted, and for some incomprehensible reason, she wanted him. He'd worked hard to hide his cowardice and reciprocate affection. With time and Campbell's patience, their relationship became comfortable for him.

Until the wedding.

Seeing her now only made the shame of what he'd done more horrible.

"You've put on weight," she said.

He looked down at his pudgy belly, the by-product of a year's worth of sixteen-hour days at the PC interrupted by trips to the couch for TV watching. "I'm not fat, really," he said, "I've become more susceptible to the force of gravity."

She finally held out her hands and sneered. "Aren't you going to ask me to sit down?"

"What are you doing here?" he said, completely befuddled. An eerie feeling that he was now experiencing the 'move on the part of others' portion of Emily's latest prophecy insinuated itself into his scrambled thoughts.

"I see a year out East in the big city hasn't made you much of a

173

conversationalist or cleaned up your poopy attitude."

The Paxil kept Seth's heart in his chest and his head from bouncing off the floor, but it wasn't doing much for his comfort level. He opened his mouth to respond, but his mind was shooting blanks.

"Actually, I was wondering what *you're* doing here," she said, helping herself into the only chair in the room, alongside the dresser opposite the end of the bed. She stuck her finger through her key ring and twirled it like a six-shooter.

How apropos, Seth thought.

He didn't know where to begin, or whether he even should. "I came to visit my folks."

"Trying to get back on their Christmas list?"

He rubbed his face with both hands and sat on the bed, leaning back against the pine headboard and throwing his good leg onto the covers. He tried to pull the lame one up, too, but winced in pain and left it dangling instead.

"What's wrong with your leg?"

"Just a mild case of rigor mortis."

Campbell almost smiled. Seth's moment of confusion passed. She obviously hadn't come to kill. She held no weapon, wasn't dressed to conceal one, and wasn't a homicidal maniac anyway. The meeting in Cub was as much a shock to her as him. But it was short in both duration and answers. She was curious; that was why she'd come. Seth hadn't planned this, but Dong's admonition rang in his ears. He'd been right all along. Campbell, too, wanted closure, a chance at her pound of flesh. He owed her that. This was the best opportunity he'd ever get to repay it — probably the only opportunity.

"I came to apologize," he said.

Campbell laughed mockingly. "I'll bet Ernest appreciated that."

Seth nodded sad agreement and unconsciously tested his tender face with a nervous hand.

"You big baby," she said.

"It's broken."

"I didn't hit you hard enough to break your nose."

"It was already broken," he explained. "That's why I did the half-gainer into the crackers."

"Oops. I didn't realize. I didn't mean to —"

"No, it's okay." He waved her off. "You couldn't have known. And I deserved it." He quickly held up a hand. "But once was plenty. I get the message."

She squinted at him. "What the hell's going on, Seth? Why are you here? Why'd your parents lie to me?"

He sighed deeply. He wanted to tell everything, but that could place her in danger. He walked a fine line. "They lied because I told them to. I didn't want a lot of attention. I only came to apologize."

"How nice for them."

"I want to tell you, too, how sorry I am for what I did."

"Is that why you tried to hide from me, and told them to deny you were in town? That's your way of apologizing to me?"

He pulled at his hair.

"This wasn't what I wanted to happen." He bracketed an imaginary box with his hands, trying to control the situation. "Okay, the truth is I didn't come to town to see you. Only them. Campbell, I didn't even know whether you were still here. Maybe you were remarried —"

"Married, not *re*married."

"*Touché*. But I was pretty damn sure the last thing you'd want was a pathetic apology from me. Mothers are different. They never stop being mothers. I wanted to tell my parents face to face that I was sorry I hurt them, and give them a chance to vent."

"How noble of you. You're right about mothers — unlike lovers. You taught me how fickle a supposed life-partner's love can be."

"It was never a question of love."

"Oh, God." She stood. "I shouldn't have come here. You were right. I don't want to hear your pathetic groveling." She took a step toward the door.

"Wait." Seth was on his feet in a flash. This wasn't the plan. There was no plan. But somehow he knew that if he allowed her to leave now, he'd have accomplished nothing but to pick the scabs off their mutual wounds, leaving both to fester for all eternity. With a hand on each of her arms, he gently but firmly pressed her back toward the chair. She resisted, then relented. "Give me five minutes," he pleaded.

She sat slowly. He paced.

Finally he stopped and faced her. "I don't want your sympathy. I don't want your forgiveness. I don't even want you to stop being mad at me. I don't want or deserve anything from you. I just want you to understand that what happened at the wedding had nothing to do with you."

Campbell opened her mouth to protest, but Seth held up a finger to silence her.

"I've had a problem all my life, and I've learned a lot about it over this past year. Remember my weather debut?"

Campbell shrugged a "So what?"

175

"I have a phobia of being in front of people like that."

Campbell took a deep breath, tilting her head down to meet her hands. After a moment, she raised her head and looked at him. "I thought you were just shy and aloof. Now you claim it's clinical? Didn't it ever occur to you that you could just tell me? Isn't that something you'd want to share with someone you're about to spend the rest of your life with?"

"I didn't understand it then, but I realized at the last minute before the wedding that I wasn't going to make it through. I didn't want to embarrass you."

"You want to see embarrassment?" she blurted, flushed and wild-eyed now. "You should have been there!"

"No. I understand that. It wasn't a rational decision. I had no choice."

"No *choice*?" she said. Tears welled in her eyes.

This wasn't going well. Seth hung his head.

Campbell kept at him. "Haven't you ever seen *America's Funniest Home Videos*? People faint at weddings all the time. It's not a big deal. What are you, special?"

"Campbell, I know it's not *supposed* to be a big deal, but to someone with a phobia, it is. That's the problem. I couldn't have stayed if I wanted to — and I *did* want to. I was out of control. I wish I could make you understand. It wasn't that I didn't love you."

"How's that supposed to make me feel better?"

"It's not, maybe. I just don't want you to feel like it was a rejection of you, that it was in any way caused by something you did or didn't do, or that I didn't love you, because … I did."

She looked away.

"Very much," he added.

"Seems to me that love should conquer all."

That hurt. She'd nailed it. That was the very truth he'd run from for so long. *Coward.* He winced at her words. That was okay, though. The notion that having her hate him and getting the opportunity to express it vehemently was good for her. But he couldn't allow her to remain hung up on the issue of love.

"Look, all my life I've felt about myself the same way you do right now, that I was a sniveling worm, a coward."

"Well, don't stop now."

He tried not to smile, but couldn't help it. "After I ran that day, I was too chicken to face anyone. I actually believed that was the best thing for you and my parents. I figured: Well, they'll never want to see me again. I'd better help them out. At least I can do that."

"Where'd you get the silly notion you were wrong?"

"A shrink."

"You saw a psychiatrist?"

"He says I have a severe case of Social Avoidance Disorder, or something like that."

"Christ. You're not one of those alien abductees, too, are you?"

"He prescribed some medication. Without it, I'd have never been able to come back and do this."

"Hurray for pharmaceuticals. What'd they put you on, lithium?"

"Paxil."

"Paxil? I've heard of that. '*CCO* runs a commercial for it. That's the SmithKline Beecham account."

"Really? I wish I'd heard about it sooner."

Campbell shook her head. "That's just great. Now I can't even hate you anymore without feeling guilty. I'd be prejudiced against the mentally disadvantaged."

"Go ahead and hate me. I'm more comfortable with that."

She was pensive. Seth resumed his seat on the bed.

"How'd you break your nose and hurt your leg?" she said, looking at a chickadee pecking in the birdfeeder outside the window.

He didn't want to lie. He was vague instead. "It was a misunderstanding. I fell down and got kicked with a boot. It was getting better until ... well, you didn't know."

"When do you go back?"

As he pondered how to answer that question, something occurred to him. "How did you know I was out East?"

"I'm not just a reporter anymore."

"You quit?"

"Promoted. I'm an *investigative* reporter now. I made the I-Team."

"Good for you. Congratulations." Then his sudden smile disappeared. "You haven't been investigating me, have you?"

"Investigating? No, just did a bit of checking. Hell, we didn't know whether you'd committed suicide, run off with the prom queen, pulled an Andrew Cunanan, or what."

"What'd you find out?"

"I knew you took a job at that Ice Center in D.C."

"How did you find that out?"

"As I said, you're too stupid to change your name."

"How about lately?"

She offered a cute and completely insincere smile. "I lost interest a long

177

time ago."

Ouch. "Did you ever say anything to my parents?"

"Not my place."

"How about today when you called them?"

"Didn't call. I stopped by for a personal visit."

"What'd they say to you?"

"They seemed especially surprised to hear from me."

"Why, had it been a while?"

"Oh yes. I had quite a few talks with Irene after ... you ran. She was very supportive. Ernest even called me once, about a week afterward. He was so sweet. He said a lot of nice things. Asked me not to tell Irene he'd called. I got the impression it was the hardest thing he'd ever done. Your father is a good man."

And Seth wasn't.

"But we fell out of touch after a month or so. I've run into them once or twice since then, but nothing more."

"Well, what did *you* say?"

"Irene answered the door and hemmed and hawed when I asked for you. She said you weren't in town. At first I thought maybe she didn't recognize me and was just trying to protect you from ... whomever. It was weird, so I told her I'd heard a rumor you were in town. Ernest came to the door too. They both stood there and said, 'No way.' They're bad liars, but I figured they had their reasons. I said okay and went to plan B, tracking you down here."

Seth silently breathed a sigh of relief. His parents had heeded his warning. But suddenly he felt the urgent need to relocate, considering Campbell's ease in finding him. After all, it was foolish to slip into a small town like Stillwater with sophisticated assassins on your trail, only to register under your own name in one of the few local motels.

"Did you talk to anyone else?"

"You're not exactly big news around here anymore."

If she only knew how good that sounded.

"Why did you go see my parents? Why bother to try to see me?"

"Seth, you should know, if I've got something I want to see or do or say, I'm the kind who does it. I wanted some answers from you. I wanted to see your face when you try to explain what you did."

"What's your name now?" Seth asked.

"What name?"

"Your married name."

"What are you talking about?"

178

"Who's the lucky guy?"

"No, you idiot, I didn't say I *was* married. I said I'd be married, not remarried, *if* I married."

"Oh."

Awkward silence. Curiosity screamed for him to ask whether she was dating again, but he was in no mood for another slap in the face, figurative or otherwise.

"And you?" she said.

"Me? Oh, you know me," he said, trying for levity, "I'm out every night hunting feral blondes."

No smile.

"Actually, Campbell, I'm living in self-imposed celibacy. I would never do what I did to you to someone else."

"Lucky me."

"Are you still living on the North Hill?"

"For now." She stood and looked at her watch. "Your five minutes are up."

A terrible emptiness was all Seth felt. He had no great words, no way to communicate his pain, his sorrow, his remorse. There was no way to turn back the clock. No second chance. Some things can't be undone or mended. The love of his life hated him. He'd botched the apology. Now she was leaving, never to be seen again.

She stood at the door, ready to go. She'd been tough to this point, but now a heavy sadness weighed on her face. Her eyes got swampy.

Seth stood awkwardly, but kept his distance. "Are you still sorry you came?"

She made brief eye contact, and then looked away, opening the door. "No, I'm glad I came today. But I wish you hadn't."

Then she was gone.

CHAPTER 27

Seth's sadness was so profound he considered returning to D.C. to await his fate with the EEC. But then a thought struck him. He'd run out of his parents' house in fear that he'd been followed, that perhaps his presence there threatened him and his parents. And he got away clean.

How about some follow-up?

Who was to say that the threat ended when he left? If they'd guessed correctly to expect him there, wasn't it possible they would check again? Or worse? Robert McClellan could testify to that. And if he were about to switch motels for the third time and finally do it right, checking in under an alias, wouldn't it be best to make another call home before he got to his new safe house? Campbell's ease in locating him was worrisome. He was being too obvious. And his parents didn't stand a chance.

He grabbed the phone. His mom answered after three rings. "Mom, this is Seth."

"Oh, I'm glad you called again. We were so worried. We tried to reach you —"

"There's no time, Mom. Have you had any other calls for me?"

"Campbell Morrison stopped by earlier. She asked about you. We didn't know what —"

"Forget that, Mom. Have you heard from anyone else?"

"Yes, we've had two other calls for you, but we hung up."

"Did they identify themselves?"

"No, but something else strange has happened. Your father and I went out for gyro sandwiches at Phil's Club Tara and then shopping at Maplewood Mall this afternoon. When we got back, we found all our lights broken out. I think someone was here in the house. I wanted to call the police, but your father said no. He says it was probably some kind of freak power spike. I'm frightened, Seth. What's happening?"

"Was there any sign of forced entry?"

"We're still bad about locking the doors, Seth. With the way Stillwater's changing, I suppose —"

"Mom, listen to me carefully. Grab Dad right now and do exactly as I say. I don't care what it takes; you get him to listen and obey. Some very bad people are after me. Your lives are now in danger too. Get in the car and

180

drive downtown. Park somewhere on Main Street. Don't be looking around. Act nonchalant. Go in the front door at the Mad Capper Saloon. Don't stop to talk to Jeff and Tammy. Go straight on through and out the door into the back alley. Walk up through the bank parking lot and north on Second Street. Check into the Lowell Inn under the name Olson."

"But, Seth, it's snowing pretty hard out —"

"Do it! Do it now. Leave your car where it is. Don't talk to anyone. Don't make any calls. I'll contact you when I can. Do you understand?"

"We can't afford the Lowell —"

"*Mother!*"

"Okay, we'll go now."

Seth hung up without another word and hesitated only long enough to remember Campbell Morrison's phone number. He dialed it frantically. She answered immediately.

"Hello?"

"Campbell, this is Seth —"

"Funny you should call. I just got off the phone with a Detective Newman."

Mother of God.

"Campbell, shut up and listen to me. Our lives are in danger. How fast can you get here?"

She hesitated a moment, seemed to read the tone of his voice. "Same place?"

"No." He thought about his location a moment. "The frozen section at Brine's Meat Market in ten."

"I'll be there."

"Campbell?"

"Yes?"

"You know Brine's is up here on the hill now, too, right?"

She laughed.

"Hey, Seth? I suspect now isn't the time, but when I get there, plan on telling me about The Shy Samaritan."

CHAPTER 28

Grabbing his new jacket, Seth trotted the few blocks north through accumulating snow to Brine's, beating Campbell there and standing around sweating conspicuously while trying to look inconspicuous. Minutes later, Campbell arrived, still wearing the sweat suit and ball cap.

"What's the emergency?" she said, exasperated.

"Did you notice anyone following you?"

"No. Why would I?"

He watched the entrance and peered out the window for any sign of phantom adversaries. He saw nothing suspicious.

"Let's go," he said, pushing her out the door toward her car.

"Where? What's this about?"

"Go to Pioneer Park. I'll explain on the way."

Campbell dutifully drove toward the North Hill, repeatedly casting a worried glance at Seth as he slouched in the passenger seat, popping up for occasional peeks at nonexistent silver Buick Park Avenues and maroon Chevy Caprices. She opted for an indirect route, zigzagging northeast through town and taking precariously steep Chilacoot Hill. The city, tired of cars sliding into the limestone bluffs lining this roadway, usually barricaded it with snow piles. It was early in the season, though, and the road was still open. They coasted into downtown and went north on Second Street.

"This phobia thing is pretty serious, isn't it?" she said.

"How did Newman find you?"

"He called me."

"Like God called Moses?"

"I don't know how he found me. He said he was trying to locate you and he understood that we were at one time engaged to be married and did I happen to know where you were."

"And you said?"

"I said, 'And what if I did?'"

"What did you tell him, Campbell?"

"Nothing. He said we could help The Shy Samaritan defeat the forces of evil. I called him a raving lunatic and warned him to stop harassing me or I'd call the police. He said he was the police. So I hung up on him and was about to call you, but you beat me to it."

Seth sighed miserably.

"Who's The Shy Samaritan?" Campbell asked.

"Just a misunderstanding."

"You and your 'misunderstandings.' What the hell is this all about?" She pulled in and parked in the lot at Pioneer Park, overlooking downtown, the partially frozen St. Croix River, and the bluffs on the Wisconsin side.

"I wish I knew," Seth said. "Look, I didn't want to involve you, but now it's too late. Some people are trying to kill me."

"You need to up your dosage."

"Campbell, please. They've already killed two people, trying to get at me. That's why I left D.C."

"I thought you wanted to apologize."

"They followed me here, though. I just talked to my parents. This group broke into their house. If they'd been home at the time, I don't know what would have happened."

Campbell squinted into his manic eyes. "Are you serious?"

"I just talked to them before I called you. I had them check into the Lowell Inn." He pointed to the bottom of the hill at the landmark hotel, six blocks away.

"You've lost me."

"We need a safe house."

"You can come to mine, but you can't stay —"

"No way. You can't go home. If Newman found you, they'll find you. They'll kill you too."

"Who are 'they'?"

"I don't know." He gave Campbell the one-minute version of the past two weeks' events.

She kept shaking her head.

"I need a phone too. I've got to call Newman."

Campbell thought a minute. "We can go to my sister's house. They took the kids to Cancun for Christmas. I'm watching the house for them."

"Perfect. Pick up my parents first."

"Seth, I can't invite the whole neighborhood over there."

"Ernest isn't going to wait there long. He already thinks I'm nuts. He'll march right back home and get himself killed."

Campbell threw up her hands and drove off down the hill. She parked in front of the Inn and Seth warily entered alone, warning her to stay behind with the engine running, and to leave if trouble began.

At the front desk, he asked for the Olsons' room. Two minutes later, he was at their door. Ernest Peterson opened it and faced him scornfully.

"This better be good," he said.

"I'll explain in a few minutes, Dad. Get Mom and let's go."

Ten minutes later they gathered inside the home of Lynda Fritchie, Campbell's sister, who lived in an olive green and brown rambler in the Croixwood development at the west end of town. Seth spied through a gap in the closed drapes at the deepening snow for ten minutes, ignoring protests, before deciding they were safe. By the end of another ten minutes he had related the pertinent aspects — as he saw them — of his D.C. story: the burgled research, the mysteriously broken apartment and hotel lights, Bill Steiner's murder, the answering machine threat, and Robert McClellan's death. He left out all reference to the Emily Corbin fiasco, The Shy Samaritan, the National Mall shooting, the taxi collision, and all of his injuries.

Ernest, who seemed to alternate between disgust with Seth's obvious psychosis and euphoria over his tenuous reunion with Campbell, was still skeptical. "You'd better call this cop you know. I want to hear his side of this."

They all nodded in agreement.

Campbell led them down the hall into her sister's home office, from which she ran a modestly successful Mary Kay Cosmetics business. Seth dialed Newman's number into the speakerphone as his small audience, already intrigued by the MPD business card he produced from his wallet, eagerly looked on. Newman answered promptly.

"Newman, this is Seth Peterson."

"I've been looking for you."

"I know."

"So you went home?"

"Yes. How did you know?"

"Got a tip from an airport employee."

"That figures. What about Campbell?"

"That little town of Stillwell —"

"Stillwater."

"— Whatever, is small enough that a call to your chief of police can uncover little factoids such as whom you used to bang."

Seth cringed. "Newman?"

"Yes?"

"This would probably be a good time to tell you that I'm on speakerphone here with my parents and Campbell Morrison."

A brief pause.

"Ah ha, my apologies. And where is 'here'?"

184

"I think we're all finally safe for now. We're at the home of one of Campbell's relatives in Stillwater, her sister. She's out of the country. No one else has a clue I'm in town — except the killers."

"They found you?"

"Close. All the light bulbs in my parents' house came up mysteriously broken."

"Sounds like a clue."

"Speaking of which, do you have one yet?"

"We're still stumped. All I know is that it's time to call in the FBI. The bad people have crossed state lines and committed enough offenses to get the Feds' attention. What's the address there? I'll have a Minneapolis agent pay a visit."

Seth looked inquisitively at Campbell, who spoke up.

"Detective Newman?" she said.

"Yes?"

"This is Campbell Morrison. I'm sorry about the way I reacted earlier. I didn't realize the situation."

"Understandable."

Campbell gave him the house address and phone number. Seth was about to sign off, but Newman wasn't through.

"Hey, Seth, how are your ribs?"

"I'm fine," he lied.

Campbell and his parents looked at him strangely.

"I can't believe you got smacked by that taxi without breaking something."

"What's he talking about, Seth?" Irene asked.

"Nothing, Mom."

"Mrs. Peterson," Newman said, "hasn't Seth explained any of this to you?"

"Nothing about taxis or ribs."

Campbell piped up too. "Yeah, Detective, and what's this Shy Samaritan thing?"

"Goodness gracious. Mrs. Peterson, your son is a hero. He's been front-page news here for two weeks."

Seth reached for the handset, intent on ending the call, but Ernest caught his hand. "I want to hear this," he said. "Go on, Detective."

"Well, about two weeks ago your son risked his life to save a woman from a burning car."

Seth slumped. All eyes were on him.

"He apparently didn't think much of it and refused to speak to the media.

They dubbed him The Shy Samaritan. Then a couple of days later he got his nose and a few ribs broken when he tangled with a burglar in his apartment." Seth glanced up at the wide eyes and slack jaws around him.

"Then, when a hundred other people ran for their lives at the hotel where Bill Steiner was murdered, your son was the only one to run up and try to save the guy's life and comfort his wife. Still he wouldn't talk to the media. They're like rabid dogs out here. They love the story. We thought at first that some crazed fan had burgled his apartment and tried to kill him at the convention, but now we're not so sure. It looks linked more to his save-the-world research. After the crooks chased him with their machine guns across the National Mall and he got hit by the taxi — and then just popped up like nothing happened and disappeared — the papers had a conniption. He went from hero to superhero. Now that the taxi driver has been shot to death and Seth has disappeared, the whole city is worried that The Shy Samaritan is dead, too."

Seth got his other hand on the phone. "And if we don't find out whom these people are soon, Newman, I could still end up that way."

"We're working on it."

"Good. Give us a call when you find something." He hung up abruptly.

Campbell, Irene, and Ernest all looked at him in awe.

Campbell spoke first. "My, my. I didn't realize it was okay for superheroes to lie."

"About what?"

"You said your broken nose was a 'misunderstanding,' that you 'fell down and got kicked with a boot.'"

"He told me he slipped," Irene added.

"Those aren't lies. They're ... half-truths."

"You're being generous with your fractions," Campbell said.

"I don't like to draw attention to myself."

Irene shook her head. "Telling your mother that you've been run over by a car and sprayed with bullets is not drawing attention to oneself."

"Okay, I didn't want you to worry."

"That's a mother's job."

Ernest spoke up. "No, there's more," he said, directing the comments at Irene and Campbell, as if Seth wasn't even present. "He didn't want to appear as a victim. He didn't want our sympathy."

Seth looked at him, puzzled.

Ernest continued speaking to the equally confused women, but his eyes slowly swung over and locked on Seth's. "That means that his apology was sincere." Then turning to Campbell he said, "I don't know what he told you about his leaving town, but I think you should listen to him now. Come, Mother." He took Irene's arm and they headed out of the room.

"I already told her, Dad."

"Tell her again," he said, closing the door behind them.

Seth looked at Campbell sheepishly. "I think he likes you."

"As I said, he's a good man."

She pulled the swivel chair out from under the desk and sat, taking up pen and paper and pointing at Seth to sit as well. "I want you to go over this whole thing, second by second, and don't leave out a single detail, no matter how small."

"We don't have to do what he says," Seth protested.

"No, not the wedding fiasco," she said, wincing. "Tell me the story of The Shy Samaritan and everything that's happened since."

"Why?"

"I'm an investigative reporter."

"What makes you think you'll do any better than the police did?"

"I have more at stake."

Seth wasn't sure whether she meant his life, hers, or both. He was too shy to ask which.

CHAPTER 29

Seth spent an hour describing the whole story in minute detail and answering Campbell's pointed questions as she jotted notes on the yellow legal pad in her lap.

"That's about it," he said finally.

"Hmm. That's a mystery."

He nodded. "See? Where would you even start?"

She ignored the question and spun the chair around, facing the desk. She pushed the power button on the desktop PC and booted up Windows 2000, only to hit an immediate obstacle: "password required."

"Damn it," she said.

"What are you trying to do?"

"A little web surfing for information."

Seth tried to recall the names of her sister's pets and two kids. "Try 'Jenny,' 'Aaron,' 'Tyson,' or 'Zeus.'"

"I'm surprised you remembered."

"I crammed before the wedding. I figured someday there might be a test."

The first three names failed, but Zeus was a match. They were in.

"You have potential as an investigator," she said.

"I'm a meteorologist. We unlock clues to the universe."

After a minute of modem connection noise and log-on delays, Campbell aimed the browser at the *Washington Post's* website.

"What are you looking for there?" Seth said.

"I'm going to start by reading up on the local stories about The Shy Samaritan Newman was ranting about."

She found two fluff articles and a column piece in the current edition, none of which offered much of anything but speculation and over-sensationalizing. She tracked back through past articles on the same topic, getting a feel for the whole two-week media circus. Seth pulled his chair up beside her to follow the action. She looked askance at him as she read, incredulous. He just shrugged.

"Now what?" he said.

She pored over her notes, and then typed in Yahoo's search engine URL. In the search box, she entered "Eastern Environmental Corporation" in quotes for a limited query.

"Don't you think the cops already did that?" he said.

She cocked her head in thought. "Probably not."

The result was zero web page matches.

She removed the quotation marks for a broader query that returned thirty-seven related web pages, all containing one or two of the three keywords, but none with all three. A cursory scan of their descriptions revealed nothing remotely connected to whatever it was they were after.

"Try 'EEC,'" Seth said.

This yielded a list of 186 sites, including the EEC Computer Bookshop in London, England; the EEC Graphics Design Agency in West Chester, Pennsylvania; the Exercise Equipment Continuum in San Ramon, California; the Electoral Educational Centre in Australia; and one that sounded somewhat related: the Environmental Elements Corporation, makers of electrostatic precipitators. Scanning through a few pages, they found that most of the links referenced educational pages regarding EEC or EECS, both common abbreviations for college courses relating to electrical engineering and computer sciences.

"Considering that these people probably aren't so stupid as to give you their group's real name," Campbell said, "it could be any one of these."

"Or more likely none of them."

Campbell scratched her head, clicked the "Next 20 matches" button one more time, and studied her notes again. "We'll have to try something else."

Just as the browser dumped the current page and began loading the next, something in the description of one of the listed web sites caught Seth's eye. "Go back!" he shouted, jumping out of his chair. The motion knocked the chair over backwards, but he ignored it.

The sudden movement startled Campbell, who leaned away from him, rolling the casters on her chair over Seth's stocking foot. He yelped in pain and instinctively hopped out of the way, catching his bruised thigh on the corner of the desk. The pain felled him to the floor like a sack of potatoes.

He lay there quivering for a second, enduring the burst of pain. Campbell knelt at his side.

"What is it?" she said.

"My thigh," he said, moaning. "That's where the cab hit me."

"Let me see."

With the concern, familiarity, and innocence of two adults once intimately close enough to have nearly married, they worked together to undo Seth's pants and pull them down far enough for Campbell to see the enormous bruise on his thigh.

"Good God, Seth. Didn't you see a doctor for this?"

189

"No need," he wheezed.

Just then the door to the office opened, and in stepped Irene. She jerked to a halt and froze at the site of Campbell kneeling over Seth on the floor, lying on his back with his pants at his knees. "Oh my," she said, and then retreated out the door. They heard her call to Ernest as the door swung shut: "They're getting along fine, dear."

Seth forgot the pain and his face turned crimson. Campbell laughed as if it was the funniest thing ever. He pulled his pants up and covered his face. "I'll never be able to look at my mother again."

"Lighten up," she said. "Now, what freaked you out so badly?"

Seth sat as the pain subsided. "Oh yeah, hit the back button once," he said, pointing at the monitor and scrambling back to the desk.

Campbell retraced their way to the previous grouping of EEC search hits. "What?" she asked.

"Scan down," Seth said excitedly. "There!" He pointed at the description of a link at the bottom of the page. "That's what the guy said to me two times."

"Who?"

"The caller." He pointed to the words on the screen, "Ice, nature, God."

Campbell squinted at the link. "Hmm. 'Edgar Cayce — Index of Readings.' That's weird."

Seth looked at her. "Cayce? Who's that?"

"Haven't you ever heard of Edgar Cayce?"

"No — wait. Yes. He was the Sleeping Prophet. I saw a documentary on *The Learning Channel* about him. The guy used to go into a trance or something and spew out all kinds of prophecies. That was back in the thirties or forties."

"Right. He was some kind of modern-day Michel de Notredame."

"Who?"

"Better known as Nostradamus, the sixteenth-century prophet."

"Oh, him. Just another know-it-all from Notre Dame, eh?"

Campbell grinned and clicked on the link.

"Great," Seth said sarcastically. "So now I know the origin of the phrase. But what does it mean, and what does it have to do with murder?"

The web page loaded, and Campbell read through the opening paragraph. "Whoa," she said, "Get a load of this. Here's more of the quote. '*Ice, nature, God changed the poles and the animals were destroyed.*'"

They looked at each other.

"That sounds relevant," Seth said.

"Must be a coincidence," Campbell said.

"Newman doesn't believe in them. I'm not sure I do anymore, either."
"You may be right. Looky here." She pointed to a spot on the screen.
"Middle initial 'E.' Edgar *E.* Cayce."

Seth thought through what they had. "The Eastern Environmental Corporation's initials are E.E.C., but the organization doesn't appear to exist. Edgar E. Cayce's initials are also E.E.C., the bad guys are quoting him, and the quote has something to do with the pole. See whether you can find more on Cayce."

Campbell entered "Edgar Cayce" in the search box and was rewarded with twenty-one related sites.

"Click on this A-R-E link," Seth said, "The Association for Research & Enlightenment. It says it's an organization of Cayce followers."

The web site described the ARE as the international headquarters for the works of Edgar Cayce, considered the most documented psychic of all time. It was founded in 1931 to "preserve, research, and make available insights from Cayce's information."

Seth wrinkled his nose. "This is a bunch of hocus-pocus. Let's see here, he was into dream interpretation, holistic medicine, faith healing, meditation, reincarnation, spiritual growth, the lost civilization of Atlantis, and Earth changes. He sounds like a fruitcake to me. Too bad he died before his time. He'd have loved UFOs."

"Glad to hear you're so open-minded."

"Is my guy, Joe Soucheray, still doing the Garage Logic Show on Talk Radio 1500?"

"More popular than ever."

"Joe would give these guys one of his 'End of the World' sound effects. These folks are Euphorians, operating on pure flower power. I doubt they're the bad guys."

"Still," Campbell said, "I think we should try to find more on that quote of his. I seem to recall that he was most famous for a prophecy on some world calamity, a millennial disaster of some sort." She clicked on a link called "Earth changes."

"You do that," Seth said. I'm going to scrounge some chow. Want anything?"

"I suppose it's too late in the day for chicken seeds and pig muscles."

Seth smiled. It was an old inside joke between them, how they used to refer to eggs and bacon. "I'll see what Old MacDonald has to say."

He limped to the kitchen and returned fifteen minutes later with cola and tuna fish sandwiches. "Any luck?"

"You betcha. This guy gave something in the range of fourteen thousand of these trancelike prophecy 'readings.'"

"Wow, I don't know how prophetic he was, but he was certainly prolific."

"I printed a few pages. Let me read you some. 'From about 1932 to 1944 Cayce described in a number of different readings the precursors and effects of a shift in the poles during the year 2001. He often referred to this event as "The Change in the Earth Which Must Come Again." He declared that a shift in the poles had destroyed Atlantis in 10,500 B.C., and predicted another shift in the poles would occur in 2001.'"

"Atlantis, huh? Sorry, but I saw another documentary on that. I'm fairly sure they proved it wasn't a continent in the Atlantic, but a Minoan city that was destroyed by a Krakatoa-like volcanic eruption. It was in the Mediterranean on the Aegean island of Santorini — also known as Thera. And it was a lot later than 10,500 B.C. Like nine thousand years later. Either Plato, from whom the story originates, was confused, or more likely the translators got his dates and directions mixed up. He said that Atlantis was beyond the Pillars of Hercules, generally assumed to be the Strait of Gibraltar. But there's another lesser-known landmark by the same name far east of there. Also, Plato said Atlantis was larger than Asia and Africa, but the Greek word he used was one letter off from a similar one meaning 'between.' The greatest typo in history."

"Great," Campbell said, "I'll remember that for Trivial Pursuit. Now do you mind if I continue?"

Seth waved her on.

"Cayce talks about various indications of Earth Changes earlier in this century, but then in 1998 the pace of change picks up, leading to an impending pole shift in 2000 or 2001, and discovery of the Hall of Records."

"Hall of Records?"

"It's supposedly a hidden chamber beneath a paw of the Sphinx containing all the secrets of ancient civilization, presumably placed there by the Atlantians."

"Oh, please," Seth said through a mouthful of sandwich.

"Just listen. This is what was supposed to happen in 2000 or 2001." Campbell scanned the pages, reading out passages from various Cayce quotes:

"'... there is a shifting of the poles ... that day when the Earth will be rolled as the scroll ... for the heavens and the Earth will pass away ... a new cycle begins. These changes in the Earth will come to pass and there begin those periods for the readjustments.

"'As to times, as to seasons, as to places ... not given to man to know the time or the period of the end, nor to man — save by their constituting themselves a channel through which He may speak.

"'As to the material changes ... The sun will be darkened and the Earth shall be broken up in diverse places. There will be upheavals in the Arctic and Antarctic that will make for the eruption of volcanoes in the torrid areas. There will be shifting then of the poles — so that where there has been those of a frigid or the semitropical will become the more tropical, and moss and fern will grow .... Los Angeles, San Francisco, most all of these will be among those that will be destroyed before New York even. The greater portion of Japan must go into the sea. Land will appear off the east coast of America. The upper portion of Europe will be changed as in the twinkling of an eye.

"'What is the coastline now of many a land will be the bed of the ocean. The southern portions of Carolina, Georgia — these will disappear ... the sunken Atlantis ... with the change ... the temple ... must rise ... again. When the changes begin, these portions ... will rise among the first.

"'... All over the country we will find many physical changes of a minor or greater degree ... Watch New York! Connecticut, and the like ...

"'... In 1998 we may find a great deal of the activities as have been wrought by the gradual changes that are coming about. These are at the periods when the cycle of the solar activity, or the years as related to the sun's passage through the various spheres of activity become paramount ... to the change between the Piscean and the Aquarian age. When there is a shifting of the poles.'"

Seth's eyebrow did the Science Officer Spock maneuver. "Hmm. Sounds like he's talking about shifting ice sheets, doesn't it?"

"That's what I thought."

"Let me see those." He reached for the printed pages for his own perusal.

Campbell again focused her attention on her notes. Almost immediately, something piqued her interest. "Hello," she said tapping a finger at the pad.

"What have you got?"

"Another coincidence maybe."

"And that would be what?"

"Emily Corbin."

He gave her a puzzled look, but then it struck him. "No. You think so?"

"I don't know what it would mean, but wouldn't it be odd if her middle initial was 'E' as well?"

"Downright scary. Could you track her down on the Internet?"

Campbell was a step ahead of him; turning quickly back to the PC, she entered the woman's name in the search box. "How do you think I found out where you lived?"

Seth grunted.

"What do you know about her?" Campbell asked.

"Just her name, her age at approximately fifty, a good guess that she lives in the D.C. area, and that she's heavy when unconscious. I doubt there are many Emilys out there."

"Are you kidding? Emily is an enormously popular name right now."

"And how would you know that fact?"

"I read it in a baby name book."

"Oh." He suddenly realized that meant he might have wound up with a child named Emily himself, if he hadn't blown the chance.

The search results showed fourteen thousand web pages for Emily Corbin.

"Oops," he said. "You're right. Better use quotation marks."

She tried again, this time narrowing the list to thirty-three links. One lived in Springfield, Virginia.

"Is that near D.C.?" Campbell asked.

"Very. That must be her. Check it out."

Campbell proceeded to Emily's personal website while Seth perused more Cayce readings.

"Hmm," she said, "'404 Error, Page Not Found.' Looks like a dead end." She looked up at Seth, who sat staring at the printed page in hand, as pale as the gathering snow outside. "What's the matter?"

"She's involved," he said.

"How do you know?"

"These numbers after each Cayce reading," he held the papers out and pointed at what he was referring to, "like the 'Ice, nature, God changed the poles and the animals were destroyed' quote. See the numbers after that? The '5249-1'?"

"Yeah. With all those thousands of readings, they cataloged them like that. So what?"

"Since I saved her life, Emily Corbin has been sending me thank-you cards. Each has a mushy quote on it that ends with a series of numbers in that exact format. I thought they were Bible quotes. They're Cayce quotes."

"Now *that's* a coincidence."

"I just thought of another," Seth said, clamping a hand to his forehead. "Bill Steiner was killed at the Earth Environment Conference, also known as 'EEC — World in the Balance.' Hard for these people to have picked a more appropriate place to do their dirty work."

Campbell was wide-eyed.

Seth reached for the phone. "It's time to call Newman and tell him what we've got."

CHAPTER 30

Newman was away from his desk, but his cohort, Marvin Roach, paged him and asked Seth and Campbell to wait by the phone, saying Newman would return their call in minutes. He didn't lie.

"Marvin says you've got something for me," Newman said without introduction as Seth snatched up the phone on the first ring.

"Yeah, a surprise. Emily Corbin is in on it."

"Who?"

"The woman I saved from the Blazer."

"What makes you think that?"

Seth explained what they'd discovered.

"This is a strange case. I'll see what she has to say."

"Newman, can you get into my apartment?"

"We have our ways."

"She sent a few thank-you cards. They're in a small wicker basket with my mail on the kitchen counter. I think I put them back in the envelopes. We should check those quotes and make sure they're from Cayce."

"That alone won't prove anything."

"Maybe not, but the return address and fingerprints might come in handy."

"Oh, we'll find her easy enough. We've got the DMV, the police report on her accident, interviews with the media, even the phonebook if necessary."

"Let me know what you find. We aren't going anywhere. We're snowed in here."

"Which reminds me. The FBI won't be coming out. They called back and said the same thing. Asked whether you were in imminent danger. I said no. Sounds like you're getting an avalanche."

"It's going to be a white Christmas, for sure. We've got eight inches on the ground now, and it's still coming down hard. To make it worse, there's intermittent sleet. That's when there's a pocket of warm air layered in the atmosphere about four thousand feet up and as the snow falls through it, it melts and refreezes into ice pellets —"

"Peterson?"

"Yah?"

195

"I don't need to understand what causes the weather."

"Ah. Call me." He hung up.

Campbell joined Seth as he limped on his freshly bruised leg into the living room, where Ernest and Irene watched veteran meteorologist Dave Dahl doing the Channel 5 weather.

"What's he say?" Seth asked.

Ernest aimed the remote at the TV like a Star Trek Phaser and jumped to Channel 4. "He says eight to ten inches."

"He's a wimp. We've already got eight to ten. It's more like twelve to fourteen," Seth added.

"They've been all over the weather people the last few years for overstating the snowfall forecasts. He's being conservative."

"You don't base weather forecasts on the polls."

"He's still the best in town," his mother said. "Without radar, how could you know better than he does, anyway?"

"I can smell it."

Seth explained what he and Campbell had deduced about the EEC while Ernest stoically channel-surfed and Irene continually shook her head in disbelief. Outside, they heard the sound of snowmobiles racing up and down the street. Riding sleds inside city limits on the street was illegal, but in this weather they were the only means of motorized travel other than plows and the hardiest of four-wheel-drive trucks. There was little chance of getting caught. Seth occasionally peered out the window, studying the swirling ice and snow mixture, enjoying the sleds and twinkling Christmas lights.

Twenty minutes later, the phone rang again. Seth walk-hopped back to the office to answer it. Campbell followed close behind.

"We've hit a snag," Newman said.

"Lose your phonebook?"

"Might as well have. You guessed right about her middle initial. Her full name was purportedly Emily Eleanor Corbin."

"Purportedly?"

"There's no Emily Eleanor Corbin listed in the D.C. phonebook or Virginia — or the entire U.S. for that matter. We did discover that Emily was the most popular female name for American babies in 1999."

Campbell sneered at Seth.

"Really? I thought it was only for old ladies."

"Names come and go. 'Eleanor' is still on the go. Anyway, I followed up on the info from the accident report. Her Virginia driver's license lists her name as Emily Eleanor Keene. Apparently, she used the alias Corbin, and nobody noticed that it didn't match the card. We haven't located her under either name."

"What about her address?"

"You won't believe this. Since you like to quote movie scenes, did you ever see the *Blues Brothers* movie where Aykroyd and Belushi give the cops their address, but it turns out to be Wrigley Stadium? Corbin's address isn't a residence. It's a warehouse for a wholesale ice distributor called Penguin Ice Supply."

"Ice?"

"I had to laugh."

"You have a strange sense of humor."

"She worked there as a bookkeeper for the past three months."

"Past tense?"

"Recently quit. No forwarding address."

"What about the Blazer?"

"Stolen out of Virginia Beach, Virginia."

Seth sucked air. "Home of the A-R-E."

"What's that?"

"A Cayce organization."

"Fascinating. The local reporters who interviewed Emily for The Shy Samaritan worship pieces each gave us the same phone number for her, a D.C. 202 area code. They both swear they called her there more than once."

"But?"

"We called the number and it's disconnected. According to Verizon, it was previously assigned to Penguin Ice, a DID line that rang at Emily's desk."

"DID line?"

"Direct In Dial. The reporters, and anyone else, could phone her directly at work, bypassing Penguin's operator, never knowing they weren't calling her home."

"Hmm."

"It looks as if Emily is a moving target just like your EEC."

"As if she *is* the EEC."

"Hang on." For a moment, all they heard was muffled conversation at the other end. "Just got the mail from your apartment. Yeah, the return address is the same as Penguin Ice. We picked up your new mail too. Looks like you've got another card from Emily here. Do you want me to open it?"

"Might as well."

Newman opened the letter and described the usual icy photo scene — this time, a distant, cloud-enshrouded mountain image, which Seth explained with conviction was probably of Vinson Massif, which was, at 16,066 feet,

Antarctica's highest peak. Another neatly composed message was inside, which Newman read aloud:

Fulfilling that purpose as He may have in thee is a greater service, a greater joy than may be had by him who may have builded a city or have conquered a nation. —1129-2.

Your Loyal Servant,
Emily Corbin

Seth scratched his head. "I don't understand why she sends me these nice, well-meaning cards after I saved her life, but her buddies quote the same guy and are trying to kill me."

"No accounting for weirdoes," Newman said.

"Read me all those quotes and numbers on the cards. I'll check them on the Internet to confirm they're from Cayce."

The speakerphone came in handy. While Newman read, Campbell quickly typed what he read into a blank Word document. By the time Seth motioned for her to check the quotes by tapping on the pad and pointing at the PC, she was already on it.

"Have you got anything else?" he asked the detective.

"Not yet, but we've got plenty to work with now. Top on the list is locating Emily Keene. Let's stay in close contact."

"Yeah, but do me a favor and check the ownership on that Blazer. Cayce was from Virginia Beach."

"You got a hunch?"

"I don't know how or why, but everything seems oddly tied together, and it keeps coming up Edgar Cayce."

Newman signed off just as Campbell hit pay dirt with the card quotes on Yahoo, confirming their origin with Edgar Cayce. Seth's mind reeled.

"You've got a really crazy soup here," Campbell said.

"What do you think?"

Campbell sighed deeply. "Environmental Nazis?"

"This is a bit outside the Sierra Club's charter, isn't it?"

"Even Greenpeace's. No, I was thinking something really extreme."

"You think someone *wants* the ice sheet to break off and shift?"

"What other use could there be for your research? You said yourself that publicizing it to claim credit would only identify them as Steiner's murderers. Suppressing it is the only thing that makes sense. They stole the disk and killed a spokesman."

"You think these people are hoping to prevent us from finding a solution to the weak ice? Why would they do that?"

"Who knows? But they believe in *something* strong enough to kill for it."

"But they already stole the report. Why try to kill me after the fact?"

"To silence you? Maybe they're worried you can identify them from your encounter in the apartment."

Seth shook his head. "I could believe one guy might be nutty enough to do something like that, but this is an organized effort by at least six educated and well-armed individuals — seven, if you count Corbin. You can't get that many people to commit suicide for an insane cause."

"Oh? I did a report on this topic once. Remember Jim Jones and his 914 dead in Jonestown, Guyana? How about Marshall Applewhite and his thirty-eight devoted Heaven's Gate followers who all committed suicide in 1997 so that they could meet up with that spaceship hiding on the far side of the Hale-Bopp comet and ride off to Valhalla?"

"Isolated anomalies."

"And the Japanese Aum Shinri Kyo group that released sarin nerve gas on the Tokyo subway, killing a dozen and injuring thousands? Or the mass suicide of the Solar Temple cult in Switzerland — another forty-eight dead? This stuff happens."

"Okay. I get it. Bin Laden and the World Trade Center towers."

"Exactly. Fanatics. Otherwise average and educated people who came under the spell of a Svengali. How do you explain it? I don't know, but it happens."

"So we've got a cult of Edgar Cayce followers with stolen polar ice research who believe a prophecy that the poles will shift, destroying mankind, and they use machine guns to prevent all attempts to stop it."

"Completely plausible," Campbell said with a smile.

Seth wished she smiled more than she did; he'd never seen such perfect teeth. "There's one problem."

"Only one?"

"Cayce's prophecy called for the pole shift in 2000 or 2001. It didn't happen."

"Maybe that's why they're so anxious."

Seth shook his head in disgust. "It's hard to comprehend the lunacy behind this."

"Is it? Isn't much of the country in disagreement about our pro-oil energy and environmental policies lately?"

"You're not defending these kooks, are you?"

"Of course not. But the news reports I hear indicate we've been derelict in our responsibility to convert to energy alternatives. We haven't cut our dependence on fossil fuels or reduced emissions with clean, renewable sources. That's a failure some people can't tolerate."

"Hydropower is fine, Campbell, but solar and wind power are expensive. Besides, they're too inefficient to be practical yet. Sometimes it's cloudy and the wind doesn't blow. That's reality — not a government conspiracy."

"Maybe," she said, "but some think we've been heading for disaster a long time, and view the U.S. rejection of the Kyoto Protocol as the last straw. They believe that mankind is doomed, and deservedly so."

"Some may think that way — maybe even Corbin's gang — but the Kyoto Protocol was never structured to stabilize greenhouse gases. It was only a symbolic first step — a jump-start — to get public and private investors interested in alternative energy."

"But reading the newspapers, you'd get the impression that Kyoto was our last hope to reverse global warming."

"I agree," Seth said patiently, recalling Hut's statement about the media. "That *is* the impression you get from newspapers. But that doesn't make it true. Despite all the good intentions and efforts across the globe — including the Kyoto Protocol, and some others — Earth's CO_2 emissions continue to increase.

"Anyway, the Protocol only called for nations to cut greenhouse gas emissions an average of five percent below 1990 levels by 2012. That isn't much of an impact. It didn't guarantee to save the planet. And it only imposed economic hardship on the U.S., since developing nations had no limits."

"I thought that's because the U.S. is the single largest producer of greenhouse gases," Campbell said.

"Right, and why not? We're responsible for 25 percent of world economic output, yet we spend 300 percent more on climate research than any other country. More than Japan and Europe combined. And guess what? China, which produces the second highest amount, spends virtually nothing on research. And it was exempt from the Kyoto requirements. Same for India, and a lot of other developing nations. The limits won't work if they don't apply to all nations. Kyoto was a bad deal for the U.S. It would have hurt our economy without guaranteeing much environmental benefit at all."

"Wouldn't these types likely argue that it's exactly that shortsighted, bottom-line thinking that got us into this mess?"

"And what mess is that?" Seth asked.

"The warmest global temperatures in history."

Seth smiled. "Campbell, when meteorologists report that we've broken some measured temperature record, they always declare it's the coldest or hottest in history. But the history they're talking about is only one or two hundred years old. Or, okay, maybe thousands of years for climatologists studying ice cores or tree rings. But that's a pinprick in time, geologically speaking.

"Some 'experts' would have us believe that weather patterns never change. Don't believe it. Change is the norm, but Man is successful because he learned to adapt. No matter how many laws we pass, we've got both warmer temperatures and more ice ages ahead. We'd better learn how to cope with them."

"Seth, no matter what may have happened in the distant past, it doesn't justify what we're responsible for now."

"That being global warming?"

"Of course. Aren't we destroying the polar ice caps? Isn't that what these people are incensed about?"

Seth sighed in frustration. "Campbell, you sound as though you took an overdose of six o'clock news. I've studied weather patterns and Antarctica — a focal point of global warming — all my life. The truth is, ice caps come and go, always have. This stuff happens. It's not a question of who's at fault. It's going to happen anyway. Pretending that we can stop it is delusional."

"So," Campbell said, "how can you be right and all these other scientific reports be wrong?"

"It isn't that they're wrong — or at least, most of them. It's that the other side of the equation — natural influences — doesn't seem to get equal billing in the press. *That's* what causes the misconceptions, and this anti-mankind furor. It's almost as though environmentalism has become a new religion. And to those who follow it, anyone who questions any attempt to preserve some aspect of 'Nature' — no matter how inconsequential or ludicrous — is a blasphemer."

Campbell laughed and nodded. "That's insightful. The news anchor's chair *has* become the pulpit, in a way."

"Yes, but I don't believe in a media conspiracy, either. Your profession seems to be blown around by the winds of political correctness. And today it's politically correct to say that Man is being naughty to Nature. There's also the profit motive."

"How so?"

"You can sell a lot more soap with news reports that evil corporations and corrupt politicians are bringing on the Apocalypse, than that our leaders actually have our best interests in mind and that everything is hunky-dory.

"In reality, Campbell, only three elemental factors influence the climate:

201

solar radiation, atmospheric dust, and atmospheric gases. We're supposedly the culprits with the latter, but, hell, there've been reports that animal farting contributes more greenhouse gases than Man does!"

"Geez," Campbell said, giggling. "The EPA would shit."

Seth wanted to laugh, but his head ached. Too much thinking. Too much stress and pain. The situation made little sense, yet the events were terrifyingly real. A fear was building in his belly like a pearl in an oyster shell. The more he tried to suppress it, the bigger it grew. It was the fear that he was becoming the go-to guy in a mystery to which the public would demand answers. Inevitably, all eyes would fall on him.

The phone rang, startling him from his whirlpool of thought. "We made progress," Newman said, his voice ratcheting through the speakerphone.

"Did you catch her?" Seth asked, sitting up with a start and wincing at the pain in his ribs for the thousandth time.

"Emily? No, but we've got a likely suspect for the head of this gang."

"Oh?"

"Do you have e-mail at your end? I want to send you a photo."

"Uh … I don't know about Lynda, but you can send it to my AOL account. I can check it on the Web from here."

"Aha. AOL Anywhere. Good idea. I use it myself. What's your e-mail address?"

He smiled sheepishly. "It's, uh, BigIce@aol.com."

"You need to get out more, Peterson. I was expecting something more like ClarkKent@aol.com." Seth and Campbell heard keyboard clicks at the other end. "Okay, I'm sending the JPEG attachment now. Let me know when you get it," Newman said.

"Ten-four." Seth felt like he'd earned a badge.

"I traced the ownership of the Blazer to a ranking member of that Cayce group you mentioned in Virginia Beach." Newman spoke the last with obvious pride.

"The Association for Research and Enlightenment."

"That's it. I love that name. They're an affiliate of the Edgar Cayce Foundation. I had a hunch, and gave them a call."

"The owner?"

"No. The organization. They're a tame bunch, basically a peace-loving, religious crowd with a New Age twist. But I wondered whether our gang might be some splinter group, maybe former members. I asked the ARE to run a search through their current membership database — over twenty-one thousand, I was amazed — and through past lists for Emily Eleanor Keene, Corbin, or any member with the initials EEC. Got a couple of bingos. No

Emily Corbins, but Keene is a current member in good standing."

"That's great!"

"Oh, there's more. Under the initials E.E.C., we got one Edward Emmitt Carlson, ex-member. Failed to renew in 1998 after fifteen years. Ran a check on him. Interesting guy. Grew up in Richmond. Smart kid. Got into the Naval Academy in Annapolis. Studied geophysics. Did a stint on a Navy research vessel. You'll never guess where."

"Do I have to try?"

"Antarctica."

"Oh?" Suddenly, Seth felt the need to sit.

"Based variously at McMurdo Station and Siple Dome, doing ice core research below the Ice Limit, whatever that is."

"It's ... never mind."

"Right. Then he left the Navy for the Coast Guard. Wound up on a tub called the *Polar Sea*. Are you familiar with that?"

"Absolutely. A Coast Guard cutter that plays a major role in the U.S. Antarctic Program. The *Polar Sea* assists our research presence there."

"Ah. He was also a trained munitions expert."

"AR-15s?"

"That and a lot more, including explosives. Guns are small potatoes to this guy."

"Criminal record?"

"No felony convictions, but he was arrested and detained in 1997 for a protest at the Seabrook nuclear power plant in New Hampshire."

"Environmental wacko."

"That's not all. Located his roommate from his last-known address in Hendersonville, North Carolina, a Ronald James Schmig. Mr. Schmig is no longer a fan of Mr. Carlson. He was a friend for many years, but says Carlson began a downward slide after the death of his mother, Ester Jean Carlson, in an automobile accident eight years ago, about the time he got out of the service. Got weird about it. Always tried to live up to the mother's utopian ideals, but since she died in an evil, man-made machine, he'd been cheated of the opportunity to fulfill his destiny during her lifetime. Sounds like an Oedipus complex. Decided to take his anger out on Man and his machines. Schmig alleges that Carlson stole all his money and cleared out of the apartment in 1998 after leaving his job at the General Electric plant there."

"GE?"

"Yes. The world's leading manufacturer of light bulbs."

"Getting fired might explain his curious animosity toward lights."

"Didn't get fired. Quit a promising career. Good reviews. Bright guy.

Dropped out of sight after that. No known address or job since then. Hasn't filed a tax return in years. But get this: Schmig had a nickname for Edward, something his mommy apparently used to call him when she was indoctrinating him with Cayce blatherings."

"If it's Frosty the Snowman, I'm jumping out the window."

"Better than that: 'Little Edgar.'"

"Cripes."

"Hang on," Newman said, then briefly smothered the phone again. "We just picked up Keene trying to skip town. I'll have to call you back." Then, with no good-bye, he hung up.

CHAPTER 31

Seth waited twenty interminable minutes for Newman's callback, passing the time by chatting with his parents, who were still glued to the television set, watching the progress of the storm. When the call finally came, he sped back to the office and lunged at the receiver button, getting Newman on speakerphone again halfway through the third ring. "Well?" he said impatiently.

"I don't know," the detective said, hesitantly. "It's not what we thought. It's convoluted. Turns out her legal name is Keene, and has been since she got married twenty-two years ago to a Robert Keene. She was born out of wedlock and adopted by a stepfather named MacArthur. Grew up as Emily Eleanor MacArthur. It checks out. Asserts that she tracked down her biological father recently — an Irwin Corbin — and has been using his last name since her divorce fifteen months ago. Just hadn't got around to making it official. Nothing shady. No alias. She was working for Penguin Ice and sleeping there or in her car, as need be. She'd had some financial difficulty since the divorce, having been out of the workforce for a decade or two as a homemaker in Springfield, Virginia. We picked her up at Union Station, trying to grab an Amtrak train to Virginia Beach. She said she was going there to look for work."

"Newman, what about her involvement?"

"That's the interesting part. Remember Carlson? Well, it seems that our Emily was a lifelong friend of his doting mother, Ester Carlson. The two were big Cayce believers *and* also ARE buddies. Supposedly the son, Edward, called on Emily to carry out an important ARE mission: visit the National Ice Center and gather specific information on Antarctic ice. He supplied the Blazer. She thought it was his or the organization's. Swears she didn't know it was stolen. She was on her way to NIC the morning you saved her. That's why she was in the neighborhood."

"Small world, huh?" Seth said, the knot in his gut growing by the second.

"I'm guessing the call you took later — and that was Carlson himself, by the way — was because Emily never got there to complete her mission. He had to do it himself over the phone.

"The sad thing is, Emily thought she'd only be gathering info in support of Cayce's pole-shift prediction. But Carlson set her up, and she has no idea why. She didn't know that he's no longer an ARE member. The ARE has no position on polar ice-sheet collapse, never intended to interview the NIC or research the matter at all. This was all Carlson. He probably stole the Blazer."

"And you believe her?"

"Oh, she's flaky for sure, but credible enough. Just a sweet lady who thought she was serving a good cause. I'll tell you what, Peterson. She thinks very highly of three people: Jesus Christ, Edgar Cayce, and The Shy Samaritan. She's also a big believer in prophecy and fate and such. Since you, an NIC employee, saved her life while she was on mission to NIC for Cayce — or so she thought — why, that was like a good omen or something. You're a sacred cow to her — or maybe even the Messiah."

Campbell nudged Seth as his numbed mind struggled with information overload. She'd retrieved the e-mail and was clicking on the button to open the attached file from Newman.

"Hang on," Seth said, "Your photo is coming up now."

The graphic file opened slowly on the monitor. It was an older photo, black and white, but the quality was good, a studio shot, something resembling an employment photo for trade-journal releases.

Seth gasped. He was looking at the face of the burglar who'd mowed Seth down in his desperate escape from the apartment. And the man from the silver Park Avenue whose friends had tried to aerate Seth on the lawn of the National Mall.

"Is that our man?" Newman asked.

"Yes."

"You're sure?"

"Positive."

"I wish we knew where to find him."

"I'd start in Stillwater, Minnesota."

Newman was one syllable into his response when the phone went dead.

CHAPTER 32

"Newman? Hello?"

Seth checked the receiver and then held it out from his ear, looking at Campbell quizzically.

"It went dead," he said to her questioning look.

Campbell took the receiver from his hand and pressed it to her ear to confirm the silence, then looked at Seth. "The weather?"

Seth thought about it. "Could be. Snow usually won't do it, but with this sleet we may have buildup on overhead lines. Something may have gone down."

Lynda's office was in the back of the house on the main level, with no view other than neighbors' backyards. A drawn shade covered the only window. Seth approached it and pushed the shade aside with a finger, peering out at the accumulating snow as if he'd be able to determine the problem that way. The lighted room against the night sky turned the window into a virtual mirror; very little was visible outside and he immediately realized how fruitless the attempt was. He turned back to Campbell and the PC, but as he did, a movement in the window caught his attention. He spun back and looked out again at the vertical wedge of snow-sprinkled darkness. He could have sworn he'd seen a head pass by.

He hesitated a second as the possibilities ran through his overloaded brain. Then he went into instinctive action. Without explanation, he jumped across the room at Campbell, scooping her off the chair with an arm across her neck and chest and under one armpit, rudely jerking her against the far wall.

"What the hell?" she coughed.

He ignored the question, throwing open the closet door and pushing her inside, pinning her to the floor amidst what turned out to be her brother-in-law's scuba gear. Slapping a hand to her face and adjusting it to cover and silence her protests, he pressed his mouth to her ear and whispered hotly, "Do not move, no matter what you hear." Then he raised himself from her, pushing off her mouth a bit harder than was necessary, hoping the action conveyed urgency.

He closed the closet door and dashed out of the office into the living room, where his parents were still calmly watching television. He made a wild but silent gesture with his arm, warning them to move, which they completely misunderstood. They sat watching with surprised expressions. Then bad things happened.

Wood splintered loudly as the front door exploded from its mooring. Glass shattered. Shouted threats followed. His mother screamed, then was silent. The soft spit of silenced automatic weapons and the thud of punctured sheetrock and stud wall seemed thunderous to Seth as he collapsed on the carpeted floor.

People were in the room. Strangers with guns. Threatening. Pushing. Shoving. Yelling.

A week earlier, Seth would have died on the spot. No bullets required. No words would have registered. As it was, panic gripped him by the neck, choking and shaking him. Someone kicked him in the head. It hurt. Then the side, right over his ribcage. That more than hurt. Was it real? Yes. But he was frozen. A familiar voice yelled urgently. His mind struggled to identify it. His father.

Is this a dream?

Then a scream. *Mom.*

Do something. *Move.*

Then another blow to the midsection from something big and hard. A boot? Was he still cowering on the floor in the fetal position while terrorists assaulted his elderly parents before his covered eyes? He hated himself, but he didn't care; not enough to look. The pain was beyond control. Nauseated, he nearly vomited on Lynda's carpet. How would he cover up that humiliating event?

Then suddenly, clarity: *Campbell.* The woman hiding in a closet in the other room — he hoped. She wasn't the kind to stay there. Too curious. Too brave. Pure investigative reporter. But she had no idea who these people were. She didn't understand. He pictured her stepping into the room with microphone in hand, asking idiotic questions of slack-jawed murderers. Guns blazing. Blood and sinew spraying.

No.

Things were coming into focus. He made a decision. Just as the commotion in the room subsided, Seth suddenly rolled over and swung a leg out, connecting with a man's ankle, dropping him to the floor like he'd pulled a rug out from under him. The man hit the floor hard, landing awkwardly on the machine gun strapped to his shoulder. The gun didn't fire, but knocked the wind out of the man, who made an exhaling sound like a cow giving birth.

Another man moved in from Seth's other side, but he underestimated

Seth's adrenalin-charged foot speed, which he deployed as a sharp upthrust into the approaching groin. The man crumpled with a grunt, and Seth followed up with more Jeet Kune Do, a cupped right palm to the ear and left elbow to the face. The man stopped moving.

The last thing he saw was the butt of an AR-15 coming at his head like a deep-impact asteroid.

Then all was black.

CHAPTER 33

Seth woke to pain. New pain. Someone was hitting him. It wasn't hard enough to knock him out again; they were trying to wake him — and not nicely. Something cold and hard pressed to his right cheekbone. A gun barrel. Searing pain like a thousand snapping towels flashed across his face. *That would be where the asteroid landed*, he thought.

He tried opening his eyes. Only the left one cooperated. Tentatively he probed the right side of his face with shaky fingers. A golf ball-sized lump had formed over his zygomatic bone. His swelling cheek had completely closed the eye on that side. His consolation was that the rifle's gunstock had missed reinjuring his nose, and his teeth were apparently intact.

Returning to consciousness was gradual, and reality was something he was watching on a big-screen TV. The actors were good, the action intense; but he wasn't quite into it. He'd come in late. The TV wouldn't focus. What he *could* see was his mom hunched over on the sofa with her face between her knees, quaking in mortal fear as strangers stood on either side pointing machine guns with silencers in her direction. One of them was the first man he'd tripped, now obviously recovered. His dad sat next to her with an arm over her back, holding her tight. His shirt was torn. Blood dripped from his lip.

Jesus, Seth thought, *they beat up an old man.*

Despite his condition, Ernest was not hunched over. He sat erect, rigid, glaring at one of the men beside him. His face was a wall cloud, a dark and imposing expression of whirling rage and hatred, a human storm-warning of a man with a temper like an F-5 tornado. Suddenly Seth was grateful he wasn't born a North Korean or Chinese communist, facing the likes of Ernest Peterson, a good man with the courage to confront evil head-on, a man unfazed by fear. Seth envied him.

Loved him.

His father's expression was worrisome. It emitted the feel of imminent danger, like a lit fuse or a pawing bull. But he was hopelessly outmatched. He could only bring more harm to himself by acting. Seth worried that perhaps his father knew this, but had also taken in the scene, weighed his options, understood the gravity, and decided that he would be dying here today. But not sitting idle on the couch like a helpless victim. Rather, with his hands at the throat of his assailant.

"Don't move, Dad." The voice surprised Seth. It was his.

Cold steel was again applied to his face. He recoiled and turned his head. Maroon Caprice Woman stood at his right side. The cold steel was the barrel of her AR-15. With his eye shut, he hadn't seen her there.

"Talk again and I'll start pumping iron," she said menacingly, leaning in to bring her face inches away from his.

It was his first close look at her. She had a small but muscular figure topped by a thin face with a Manson-girl sweetness that might have been attractive if she bothered to work at it. Seth summed her up in a flash: no makeup, army boots — and decided that obviously wasn't her style. A strong desire to explain that her breath smelled like a colostomy bag came over him. But though she had the look of an aerobic queen, he knew her words alluded to machine-gun rounds, not weight training. He held his tongue.

He raised the finger on his left hand and wagged it at his father, discreetly reinforcing his admonition. A glimmer in Ernest's eyes signaled recognition, if not agreement.

Following the discovery of Caprice Woman next to him, he spun his head slowly around the room and found the fourth of the known six standing against the wall behind him. All four carried AR-15s. They stood silently. The fifth was the man Seth had just Thai-boxed into submission. He was now semiconscious, sitting on the floor with his back against the wall, dazed and bleeding about the mouth and nose. The TV was a smoking hulk, shot out. The acrid smell of burnt plastic and gunpowder wafted past his nose. He spotted a clock on the wall, expecting to hear its tick. Digital. Even that was silent. All he could hear was a ringing in his ears and the cold wind blowing snow into drifts beyond the six-inch walls. A lone snowmobile accelerated up the street, and its two-stroke Doppler-effect whine faded into the night.

He swung his gaze back to his personal guardian, Caprice Woman, and shrugged a silent "What gives?"

Apparently, to her, that was the same as talking. The gun barrel moved at his face again. The door to the office suddenly opened, stopping her short.

The door's movement caused a squirt of adrenalin and a flood of guilt to wash over Seth. In his fog, he'd briefly forgotten Campbell again, supposedly safely stashed in the office closet. All eyes in the room went to the person exiting the office.

It wasn't Campbell. It was Edward E. Carlson, automatic weapon in hand, psychosis on face.

Seth's heart sank.

Campbell.

211

Suddenly he was ashamed, a little boy who'd just learned a big-boy lesson. Some things are important, some things not. The fear he'd run from all his life was a minor trifle. Campbell was not. He loved her. Always had. Her feelings were no longer reciprocal, but no matter. Was it too late for her? Of course. Something had happened to her. She couldn't have escaped. Carlson had searched the house while his henchpersons held the rest captive. He was educated, clever ... and thorough. Seth had been knocked out for an unknown period. What terrible sounds had he missed? Was there more to Irene's incapacitation and Ernest's thundercloud visage than Seth knew?

Now he would join his iron-willed father at the front line of life and death, willing to go down hard. He braced himself, ready to pounce, looking for the moment, the opportunity.

Carlson brought the weapon up and moved directly at Seth, aiming it at his face.

"Where is she?" he said.

That took a moment to sink in, but those were the best words Seth had ever heard. They could mean only one thing. Miraculously, somehow, Carlson had missed her. Was he so stupid as to have ignored the closet?

"Who?" Seth responded reflexively.

Caprice Woman raised her weapon. Cold steel on contusion was imminent. Seth squinted and braced, but didn't flinch. Nothing landed. Eye open. Carlson's hand was up, holding off Woman's attack. Then he forced his gun muzzle into Seth's mouth and reiterated his request.

"Where is she?" he said more urgently, wearing the facial expression of a Jerry Springer Show guest.

The fog lifted and Seth now clearly saw that, inexplicably, the EEC had misplaced Campbell Morrison, the last of the known witnesses. That was probably the only reason he and his parents still lived. No point in killing any until all were accounted for.

Where was Campbell?

Edward's weapon thrust into Seth's mouth another inch, and the trigger finger squeezed. He was not a patient man.

"The store."

A voice. Again Seth was surprised. This time it was not his.

Carlson turned. The barrel withdrew.

Who had spoken? Brave Sir Ernest.

"What store?" Edward said, now pointing his weapon, wet with Seth's saliva, at Ernest, as if a third machine gun on him and his wife was more threatening than two plus one in his son's mouth.

Ernest appeared calm. Unbelievably so. Medium voice. Eyes focused on nothing. Eyelids half-closed like a crocodile in a swamp. Detached from fear. Amazing. Seth's hero.

"Oasis Mart," he said. "It's a convenience store a few blocks from here." Woman spoke up. "At the corner off the highway, where we came in." She threw her head and shoulder east.

Edward nodded, remembering now. "What for?" he said skeptically.

Ernest shrugged. Defiant.

Edward's gun shifted from Ernest's face to the top of Irene's head.

Ernest didn't hesitate. "She walked there just before you arrived. Too much snow to drive. Getting some supplies. Milk, toilet paper, bread, chips. Stuff like that. We thought it might be a few days."

Edward cogitated on that. He walked into the kitchen and opened the fridge. Thankfully, Lynda's family was organized enough to time their milk purchases to coincide with their vacation. Only one quart-sized carton remained to spoil.

"She should be back by now," Carlson said, shoving the half-empty carton back in and returning to the living room, apparently satisfied by the depleted inventory.

"The snow is deep," Ernest jousted. "Others are bound to be doing the same thing: stocking up for the storm. She probably stayed longer to warm up."

Carlson studied the cagey old veteran. "We'll wait for her," he said, looking at his wristwatch. "If she doesn't arrive in five minutes, the old lady gets a lobotomy the hard way."

Seth spent three desperate minutes hoping Campbell returned in time before remembering that his father's story was fiction, and that as soon as Campbell appeared from wherever she was, they would all die anyway. He invested the fourth minute in introspection on his condition and the effectiveness of Paxil. Shortly before the end of the fifth minute, he broke out laughing.

All eyes turned to him. Especially Ernest's. Even Irene looked up.

Carlson resumed his gun's focus on Seth, stepping back across the living-room carpet toward him. "What's so funny?"

Seth had no idea. But laughter was the only distraction he could come up with, and oddly, with the insanity of the situation, his laughter was real.

"Okay, Iceman," Carlson said. "You're first. I've been waiting for this."

He grabbed Seth's shirt roughly by the shoulder and hoisted him up, dragging him out of the living room and into the office. Carlson shoved him into the swivel chair by the desk. Stepping back and sitting on the other chair, with his back to the open door to the living room, Carlson contemplated Seth, seeming to savor the moment.

Seth scanned the room with his solo-eyed peripheral vision. The closet door was open, the dark cavity beyond empty. His heart skipped a beat. But there was no body. He didn't know how it was possible, but Campbell had escaped in the confusion. She must be on her way for help, he concluded. He'd have to stall if he could.

An odd calm possessed him in his last minutes of life, a calm he'd have traded ten years of life for earlier. Now it was too late. With only minutes or seconds left, he spent them on questions.

"How did you find me?" he said.

"You're predictable."

"I could see you following me to Minnesota, but how did you find her sister Lynda's house?"

Carlson smiled. Seth detected an ego. "Police band radios come in handy at times such as these."

Seth recalled Newman saying he'd called the Stillwater Police and FBI, which must have resulted in on-air chatter that gave away their location. Newman was again more harm than he was help.

"Clever."

"Shut up."

Seth obeyed, expecting the gun to come up now, to learn what it feels like to die. But Carlson hesitated. With some emergency psychoanalysis, Seth concluded that Carlson's ego wanted to answer questions, a chance to brag about whatever ingeniously heinous crime he was about to succeed at. Seth decided he really didn't care much whether he died with his mouth open or closed.

"Can you at least do me the favor of explaining why you're killing me?" he said.

Carlson smirked. "We don't like each other, you and me."

Seth shrugged. "I don't think I know you well enough to say that."

Carlson bent over, feigning a reach for his shoes, but his arm then shot up, landing an uppercut on Seth's lower left jaw. Seth's swivel chair spun and dumped him beside the desk like a skydiver with a failed chute. That side of his face had been one of his last uninjured body parts.

"Ahhh, *now* I see what you mean," he sputtered, reclaiming the chair.

"I owed you that for the elbow in the face," Carlson said.

"We're even now."

Carlson chuckled, gesturing Seth's way with the gun. "You're funny. I almost regret having to kill you."

"Almost?"

The gun came up.

Seth's mouth was faster. "Why the lights?"

"Huh?"

"What's with the bulbs? You keep breaking them."

"You're about to die, and *that's* what you're curious about?"

"I've been having trouble sleeping. The question keeps running through my mind. How about a little professional courtesy? Explain that for me before I go."

Carlson stared at him blankly, then decided to answer. "Foolish, I suppose. It's of little consequence considering what's to come, but those seemingly harmless bulbs are the final receptacles of our planet's lifeblood. Whether it's violating Earth to mine coal or drill for oil, or damming Nature's rivers for hydroelectric plants like clots in a vein, the result is the same: power. Man has evolved to the point where he kills his own Mother Earth for electricity. We've come full circle to cannibalism. We trade future generations for the instant gratification of Nintendo and blow-dried hair."

It was adding up. "I take it you've got a better plan?"

"No. It's too late."

"What do you mean?" Seth said sarcastically. "It's never too late to go back to horse manure-filled streets and mud huts. With six billion people burning firewood for heat and cooking, why, the trees would last at least a decade."

Carlson gave him a condescending smile. "You've been indoctrinated with lies."

"So you're probably against nuclear power too, I'd guess."

Carlson's eyes widened as if Seth had blasphemed by merely mentioning it. "So typical. Man always believes a bigger and better scientific response is the solution. Mother Earth is about to prove you all wrong."

"You sound as though you might be a believer in Gaia," Seth said. The Gaia Hypothesis, developed in the late 60s and early 70s by two scientists, one British, one American, held that Earth was itself a living organism, named after the Greek goddess, Gaia, who drew the living world forth from Chaos.

"And you sound like every other arrogant human uncomfortable with being nothing more than a flea on the belly of the great beast." His captor jerked his gun upward for emphasis. "But rocks and water only form the face of the great Mother."

"Right. And volcanoes are zits."

The gun started moving again. Carlson flicked a switch on the side of the weapon.

215

"What's that?" Seth said, "The safety?"

"Selector switch. One setting is semi-auto. Every time I pull the trigger, I fire one round. The other setting is full automatic. As long as I hold down the trigger, bullets keep pouring out. That's what you get."

Seth thought fast, recalling Newman's history on Carlson, and remembered the arrest for protesting at the Seabrook nuclear facility. "Why not just bomb power plants? You might have more impact than by knocking off one light bulb at a time."

"We've got bigger things in mind."

"Wiping your ass with leaves to save paper?"

Carlson squinted. But instead of shooting him, he said only, "Even bigger."

"Might it have something to do with my research?"

"You're clever."

"I'm a meteorologist."

"And a damn good one. We were lucky to find you. No, not lucky. *Fated*."

"You think that by suppressing my research you can somehow save mankind from itself?"

"Suppress it? Oh no, you've got it wrong. We're going to *use* it."

"Fascinating. Could you indulge me with a brief explanation of how you intend to save mankind that way?"

"We're not trying to save mankind. We're trying to save the planet."

Incredibly, Seth managed again to laugh in the face of all this. "Oh, boy," he sputtered, "that's a good one!"

"I don't know," Carlson said, "that you're in much of a position to pass judgment."

"Oh, you believe what you want. It's just that the irony suddenly struck me as funny: environmental Nazis on snowmobiles."

Even Carlson cracked a smile at the thought.

"Okay," Seth continued, "so you stop me from sharing my discovery with the world, the ice eventually shifts and destroys civilization, and this saves the planet. Is that about it?"

"Close."

"You know, humans exhale CO_2 as well. Maybe you should do us all a favor and just commit suicide."

Carlson glared, but the gun was still.

"And how does Cayce figure into all this?" Seth said.

Carlson's iron stare wavered perceptibly. "I underestimated you, Peterson. You know about Cayce?"

216

"Sure. 'Ice, nature, God changed the poles and the animals were destroyed.' I'm familiar."

Carlson's eyes narrowed. Seth sensed doubt behind them, as if the man were no longer as self-assured, as if perhaps the questioning was now allowed to continue to satisfy Carlson's curiosity about how much Seth knew of him, rather than vice-versa.

"Well, I don't know how much you know about Edgar Cayce's pole shift, but there are those among us who believe it will cleanse the planet of mankind, an evolutionary requirement, self-preservation, allowing the ecosystem time to regenerate and regain a natural health."

"What good will that do if we're all dead?"

"Cayce didn't foresee that all would die. Those who believe and follow his advice on where to seek refuge will survive."

"Do 'those among us' realize that Cayce's prediction called for that to occur in 2000 or 2001? It's too late. It didn't happen. Cayce was wrong. Just another fraud."

Carlson regained the smug look. "If you'd studied just a bit more, you'd know that Cayce wasn't sure of the exact date, and stated so. You'd be aware of another quote of his: *'As to times, as to seasons, as to places, 'tis not given to man to know the time or the period of the end — save by their constituting themselves a channel through which He may speak.'* You see, Peterson, he left it an open-ended question."

"Yeah, prophecies work better that way," Seth said. "But don't you think you might be misinterpreting Cayce's pole shift prediction? I read it as an actual cataclysmic displacement of the continent itself. A tectonic action. The rock literally shifting. The most devastating earthquake of all time, generating kilometer-high tsunamis and 500-mile-per-hour winds. The kind of far-fetched thing that wipes us all out within a few hours. But you've adopted the notion that only the West Antarctic Ice Sheet shifting from the pole is the event he predicted. That's a pretty liberal interpretation."

Carlson's face worked slowly into a sly grin. "I've got it on good word."

Seth looked at the man, not bothering to hide his curiosity. And then he remembered:

... save by their constituting themselves a channel through which He may speak ...

Which gave Seth the unnerving suspicion that Carlson might actually believe he was the chosen "channel" through whom God would speak on the matter. Was the boy raised as 'Little Edgar' really that insane?

"*You* believe it'll happen," Carlson said.

"Eventually."

217

"There's no 'eventually' in our plan."

"No?"

Carlson shook his head and smiled, pulling Seth's stolen floppy disk from his inside jacket pocket. "You've done us the favor of pinpointing the exact location of the most likely doomsday ice fault."

Seth scrunched his face in confusion.

"We're going to help Nature along a bit," Carlson said.

"How?"

"C-4."

"Come again?"

"Plastic explosives."

Seth recalled Carlson's military background as a munitions expert. "You wanted the research to identity the faults and plant explosives there?"

Carlson grinned. "Couldn't have done it without you, friend."

Seth's heart sank. If a volcanic eruption could accomplish what Carlson was planning, the right amount and placement of C-4 might, too. A needle-in-a-haystack long shot, but almost possible. "You'll make Ted Kaczynski look like Mr. Rogers," he said, trying not let his voice break.

Carlson smiled as though it were a compliment. He looked at his watch, and then yelled out into the living room for someone named Craig. A few seconds later, the tall man who'd been standing against the wall behind Seth when he woke on the floor appeared in the doorway.

"How's Osborne?" Carlson asked.

"Still on the floor. He'll live, but he's groggy. I think your scientist friend gave him a concussion."

"And Holtz?"

"Sore, but fine."

"I want you and Sam to take a couple of sleds down to that store and see if you can't round up this woman of his."

"Don't know what she looks like."

On the wall was a framed eight-by-ten photo of a smiling Lynda and Campbell, riding horses in a happier time. Their sibling resemblance was unmistakable. Carlson pointed at it. "Take that. Which one is she, Peterson?"

"On the left," he lied, knowing they'd never find Lynda there.

"Then she's probably the one on the right," Carlson said to Craig. "But either of them will do."

Craig left, and a minute later they heard the sound of two sleds heading off into the night.

Seth was anxious for the conversation — and stall — to continue. "What makes you think explosives will trigger the ice sheet to move?"

218

"Actually, I'm curious to hear your opinion on that."

"It sounds about as likely as setting explosives along the Rio Grande to break Mexico off Texas."

"You better than anyone should know that's a feeble comparison. Antarctica is a hotbed of global forces ... *any* of which could set that ice to sliding. I read your report. Volcanic heat has melted the underside of the ice sheet, creating a liquid cushion. Global warming is doing the same for the shelves resting on the ocean floor. And a good portion of the sheet actually rests on bedrock below sea level. Start flooding the area beneath, and that sucker could just float away. All we need now is an event to trigger the slide. The Chandler Wobble is exerting incalculable forces, enough to move tectonic plates. Twenty thousand years of warming has melted the ice and changed the weight of the poles, throwing the whole planet off balance. What if Mount Erebus erupts? How about an earthquake?"

"Or an explosion."

"Bingo."

"Well, I'm no expert, but I'd say that would require a lot of explosives."

"We have a lot of explosives."

"We'd have heard if someone stole that much."

Carlson shook his head and smirked. "C-4 can be made in a bathtub."

Committed to die trying, Seth said, "I think your plan is stupid, but if you want, I could make a call to the Ice Center for a more educated opinion."

To his utter surprise, Carlson agreed. It seemed obvious that he had no clue that the police had identified him, and that Campbell and the cavalry were surely only moments away. Seth wasted no time lifting the phone to make the call.

"Oh, wait," he said, trying to mask his disappointment, "I just remembered that the phone went mysteriously dead about the same time you and your friends arrived."

Carlson almost grimaced. "What's that?" he said, pointing at Lynda's printer.

Seth leaned over and read the label on the unwieldy electronic device covered with buttons and slots. "It's a Brother MFC 7160C, color printer, fax, copier, and scanner." He lifted the handset, and it rewarded him with a dial tone. Lynda had invested in a separate fax-modem line. "That's odd," he said sarcastically, "the weather didn't seem to affect this line."

"Put it on speakerphone," Carlson ordered.

Seth returned the handset to its cradle and punched the speakerphone button instead, praying that Bern was working late as usual.

"Just a minute," Carlson said. Then he yelled over his shoulder again for

Holtz. The man Seth had done the leg sweep on stepped into the doorway and glared at him. "Bring me the old lady," Carlson told his lackey.

Holtz returned shortly, dragging Irene roughly by a handful of blouse. Carlson motioned with his head for Holtz to leave her there and return to the living room. He then forced Irene to her knees in front of him, facing Seth, and placed the barrel of his weapon at the back of her head. She whimpered but held still, eyes straight ahead.

"Make your phone call pleasant," Carlson said. "And let's not give out any unnecessary information about our little gathering here, or the Petersons won't have a Merry Christmas."

"That goes without saying," Seth replied, holding up his hand to reassure his mother. He let his eyes fall on Edward Carlson's as he dialed the Center's number on the fax machine's speakerphone. His cold fear melted away, replaced by molten hatred.

Seth worked his way through the automated phone system to reach Bern's line, and eventually got through after a harrowing maze of menu options.

"How are you, Seth?" Bern said.

"I'm fine."

"Heard a rumor you headed back to Nebraska."

"Minnesota."

"Whatever. How's the weather there?"

Seth ignored him. "Need your opinion on an aspect of my research."

"Yeah?"

"Do you think there's any way Man could induce the movement of the West Antarctic Ice Sheet?"

"Hmm. You mean something faster than global warming?"

"Right."

"How the hell should I know? Ask Hut."

"I didn't explain the project to Dave."

"He knows all about the ice sheets. There's been a lot of discussion here on your project the last few days. He knows infinitely more than I do."

"He's not there."

"Call him at home. He'd be honored."

"Think he's home?"

"Hut? Are you kidding? Where else would he be?"

"Got his number?"

Bern supplied the number from a file, and after dialing Dr. Dave Thornton, Seth posed his question.

Dave was quiet for several seconds. "I suppose it could be feasible," he said at last.

"How would you do it?"

"Of course, you realize that the 1959 Antarctic Treaty affecting everything south of 60 degrees latitude — or roughly 10 percent of Earth's surface — suspends all territorial claims, purports eternal peaceful purposes, imposes a fifty-year mining moratorium, an unequivocal whaling ban south of 40 degrees latitude — and to the point — prohibits the deployment, use, or storage of nukes. But, ignoring all that, the obvious would be a large number of well-placed and well-timed nuclear explosions."

Seth looked inquisitively at Carlson to see whether he had any nukes. Carlson shook his head.

"How about regular explosives?" Seth asked Thornton.

"Theoretically it's possible, depending on how unstable the sheet is. But you'd need an awfully large quantity. Then again, if we were at the fault trying to mend it, we wouldn't be using dynamite. I thought you were trying to stop the ice."

"Once the research goes public, Dave, I think we'll need to cover all contingencies. The world is full of crazies." He stared Carlson square in the eye.

"Good point," Dave said, admiration coloring his reply. "Environmental terrorism. We can't patrol the whole fault line, not with a fault the size of the Texas/Mexico border. If thousands of Border Patrol can't stop a few Al Qaeda terrorists from crossing the Rio Grande, we'll sure as hell fail at keeping Antarctica safe with a SWAT team or two. That's a fascinating bit of trivia on Antarctica, Seth: an entire continent, and do you know there isn't a single cop in the whole joint?"

Under the circumstances, that wasn't a reassuring factoid.

"Anyway," Dave continued, "there are probably better ways to pull it off, Seth, such as constant vibration, hot water injection, or something else equally farfetched. But I wouldn't give any of them a snowball's chance in you-know-where of moving that ice before its time. Do you want me to work up something for your report anyway?"

Carlson dragged his hand across his throat, signaling an end to the call.

"No thanks, Dave. Just curious. I'll be seeing you in a couple of days. Appreciate your help."

As he hung up the phone, Carlson pushed Irene away and pointed her out of the room with his thumb.

Seth managed a thin smile. "Sounds like you've committed your capital offenses for nothing."

"I wouldn't be so sure," Carlson said, looking over his shoulder at the open door and lowering his voice.

As he turned his attention back to Seth, he missed the silent appearance of the Maroon Caprice Woman who, presumably curious over the delay in killing Seth, had wandered down the short, carpeted hallway to check on her mentor's progress. She now stood leaning against the doorjamb, listening to every word. Something about Carlson's odd behavior told Seth to avoid flinching at the sight of her. Instead, he maintained solid eye contact with him and didn't give away her presence.

"Speaking of capital offenses," Seth said, "why didn't you kill me when I surprised you at my apartment?"

"I wasn't sure I had the right disk. Didn't get a chance to look at the file before you came home. Thought there might be some chance we'd have to come back for a second visit. Besides, these things are great for information gathering," he said, holding up the machine gun, "and I'm not loath to use one, but I generally allow others to do what killing needs done. I hire the sheep for that. I prefer plausible deniability for myself — and shorter prison sentences."

"It wasn't you who shot Steiner and McClellan?"

"Me? No, the woman. She likes it."

MPD would love the Caprice Woman, Seth thought — a white woman who kills. A real anomaly.

"Just out of curiosity," he said, "since you already have the information you want from me, why is it necessary to kill me? I mean, we don't agree on the causes of global warming, but aren't we basically on the same side? I was doing my part for the planet. Why not let me die in the pole shift with everyone else?"

"Just a minor detail of the plan. It's obvious if you think about it. We have to destroy you and your research so that no one can figure out where we'll strike on the ice, or we'd be easily caught and stopped."

"And Bill Steiner?"

"The one murdered at the conference? That was an unfortunate accident. Still not sure why he filled in for you. Not that it matters much any more —"

Seth couldn't help thinking that it mattered quite a bit to Bill and Rachel Steiner. It certainly mattered to him.

"— but that was done for the same reason: we want the research all to ourselves. We're not stupid enough to believe that this floppy is the only copy of your research. We can't afford to leave anyone alive — especially you — who might catch on to what we're doing, help prevent it, pooh-pooh it, et cetera."

"And the rest of these innocent people?" he said referring to Campbell, his parents, and Robert McClellan.

"Witnesses for the prosecution. Collateral damage. If it helps you any, they'll be lucky to miss the devastation coming."

Seth was building the nerve to play his hole cards, but he took a chance, still dancing with the devil, probing for more information. "I'm in no hurry ... but if you aren't the shooter, why is it that you're in here supposedly shooting me, but instead asking opinions?"

"You're a perceptive geek. You see, I've always been a little skeptical of our plan to move the ice. That's why we've hedged the bet with stock puts just in case."

Something about Carlson's concern with being overheard by those in the living room made this revelation seem more like a unilateral "I've" than a "we've" action. That, and the strange expression on Caprice Woman's face.

"Stock puts?" Seth said.

"That's right. These idiots believe every word of this science fiction," Carlson said with a thumb over his shoulder. "But unlike the rest of these clowns, I've been there on The Ice. Until you've made the flight down there in a CL-130 Hercules or sailed the Drake Passage or Ross Sea, spent a few weeks in complete darkness at McMurdo Station during the Antarctic winter, or trekked onto the Beardsmore Glacier, it's easy to think of it as an abstract block of ice that can be moved at will. I was never so confident."

"So you hedged your bet by selling short on Wall Street?"

"Exactly. If I can't move the ice, I can still profit from the effort."

"Well, aren't you a bundle of contradictions: a snowmobiling environmental wacko and a communist with capitalistic designs on the stock market. Which stocks did you put? And what makes you think blowing off a few firecrackers at the end of the Earth is going to affect them?"

"Any tech stock will do, but especially those industries involved in global warming: utilities, auto manufacturers, transportation stocks, and the like. I designed a diverse portfolio. As for how to make it all work, that's the easy part. Your liberal media has already worked up the populace into a lather on environmental issues, but nothing has really struck a nerve so far. Sure, there's a bit of concern, but all the reporting is too technical, the consequences too iffy, too far in the future. Ah, but introduce a bit of human intervention, say a bomb here or there, some terroristic intent, make the outcome imminent and catastrophic, and people will sit up and take notice." Carlson smiled. "In short, you need to add drama."

"And why would the media go along with your plan?"

"You're naïve. I've already drafted a series of anonymous press releases claiming responsibility for the calving of A-38 and the subsequent ice islands of note. I'll be able to offer video evidence of the explosions, right on the continent. The media will be on this story like it was a JonBenet Ramsey of global proportions."

"But you'll never be able to prove your claims."

"And your expert friend, Dr. Thornton, just proved that *disproving* them will be equally impossible. I don't need the faith of the masses or consensus from the scientific community ... just a hard-to-disprove hypothesis drummed relentlessly by the media."

"I think your C-4 has a better chance of moving the ice than of moving the stock market."

"Too bad you'll never get to see which."

Carlson raised the gun again, now with a sense of purpose. He looked prepared to do the dirty work this time.

It was time for Seth to play one of his hole cards: "How can you kill me after I saved her life?" he said.

The gun's tip dropped slightly. "Saved whose life?"

"Your partner's."

"What are you talking about?" he said tentatively, unaware of Seth's knowledge about his link to Keene.

Here came the risky part. "Ester Carlson," he lied.

Edward's expression froze as if he'd just glimpsed Medusa. "What about her?"

"Doesn't risking my life in that burning car to save one of your gang members mean anything to you? Or are they all expendable?"

"You're insane."

"Come on, you can't deny Ester is part of your little eco-army. Don't tell me you didn't know that she's been sending me letters."

Seth couldn't decipher the look on Edward's face. It may have been rage, fear, or both, but whatever it was, it had him flushed, sweating, and quivering.

"The name of the woman you saved wasn't Ester Carlson," he said, shaking his head.

Seth played a hunch, deciding now was the time to drop the bombshell and a few more lies.

"Yes, Ester Jean Carlson, to be specific. She told me so herself. And others know about her too. She's the missing clue that helped MPD link you to the crimes."

Carlson opened his mouth but didn't speak, seeming utterly confused.

"That's right, Mister, you've been identified. Check this out." Seth reached up and gave the mouse a tap, making the advancing starfield screensaver disappear off the PC monitor to reveal Edward Emmitt Carlson's image. With both hands, Seth turned the monitor on its pedestal and sat back so that his nemesis could view it.

Carlson gawked at it in horror.

"I think I liked you better as a misguided tree-hugging extremist," Seth said. "At least you had conviction. You're nothing but a lousy extortionist. The guy that poisoned those Tylenol capsules years ago had a better stock-manipulation plan than you do. But you're going down now. We were talking to the police when you cut the phone line. They know who you are and where you are. Should be here any moment."

Carlson exploded from his chair and forced the gun into Seth's face. So much for Seth's hope the news of Edward's identification would cause an immediate exodus of Carlson and Company. It only seemed to enrage the man more.

"What are you trying to pull?" he spit into Seth's face.

"Don't you recognize your own picture?"

"Not that! With saying that Ester Carlson was in the burning car."

The impromptu lie was buying him time. "Yeah? I just got another card from her at my parents' house. So what?"

"Ester Carlson is my mother."

Seth feigned surprise. "I never made the connection. Half of the population in Minnesota is named Carlson. So Mommy was in on it? A family affair, eh? Why not? She raised you to follow the sage words of Edgar Cayce and fight for ecological purity. But things got a little warped. It all makes sense now."

Carlson stuck his distorted face inches from Seth's and hissed words like a snake. "She died *eight years* ago. What's your game?"

The words — spoken with a vehemence no man could stage — tightened Seth's stomach. His hands, which had been mercifully steady, began to quake. Carlson was hooked.

"How did she die?" Seth managed with shaky voice that served his ploy well.

Carlson seemed to buy Seth's trick, sincere in his mystification and dread over the developing implications. "She burned to death in a car accident."

Seth acted as though the words lashed him and he was afraid to ask the next question. The act came naturally. He'd known about the accident, but not that she'd roasted. The parallels were uncanny.

"What kind of car?" he said.

"An SUV. A Chevy. Why?"

Seth moaned and rubbed his temples, taking a gamble. What other vehicle would Carlson steal? "A red 1987 Chevy S-10 Blazer?"

"I know what kind of car you saved her from," he spat. "I stole it!" Carlson stood straight and backed up, slowly raising the AR-15 at Seth's head. Time for the *coup de grace*.

Oddly, Seth's thought was that though his gambit had failed, at least the AR-15 would stop his throbbing headache.

At that moment, Seth decided to play his last hole card. He allowed his good eye to shift toward the open door where Caprice Woman still stood, listening to the whole exchange with an odd expression. Carlson saw his move and hesitated, then turned his head around toward the door. Seeing the woman there for the first time, he flinched noticeably.

"How long have you been there?" he said, with an attempt at gruffness.

"Stock puts, huh?" she said. "Clowns? Idiots? *Sheep*?"

"I was just trying to get information out of him."

"Well, now it's time to get some bullets *into* him." She stepped into the room and raised the tip of her weapon from the hip, aiming at Seth. "You shoot him, or I will. Then we're all going to have a nice little chat about 'plausible deniability.'"

With the mantle of leadership having suddenly shifted like an ice sheet from the pole, Carlson looked positively ill. As he hesitated again, the Woman took aim and pulled the trigger.

A millisecond before the spit of silenced rounds whistled by his head, Seth heard an odd, rubbery twang and muted thud. Then the hot whisper of copper-encased lead breathed into his ear as it skimmed past and cracked into the wall beyond, causing Seth to spin in the chair and collapse to the floor by the desk.

He opened his good eye, surprised that he could see and deep in pain, but unsure whether it was from fresh wounds. Reality was parsed; time passed in frames. He saw none of what he expected: his own blood. What he *did* see made no sense.

A thin, quivering rubber hose hung suspended horizontally in midair across the room. One end trailed off into the darkness of the open closet. The other end terminated at an aluminum shaft attached chest-high to Caprice Woman. She stood awkwardly, with her heated weapon slack at her side and her head down, looking at the strange implement protruding from dead-center sternum.

Robotlike, Seth turned his head to see Edward Carlson standing angularly, as if he'd been ready for action but froze mid-move. His gaze, too, focused on the hose and shaft.

After several dozen frames of life passed in what probably took only a second, the Woman lifted her head and opened her mouth to speak. But only

226

gurgles and a flow of frothy blood emerged. A slow-motion moment later, she crumpled to the floor like a marionette with severed strings, landing on her side, and moved no more.

Both Seth and Carlson now saw that the aluminum shaft had continued clear through her torso. A bloody spear tip protruded six inches beyond her spine. Seth recognized it as a scuba diver's spear gun.

Carlson made the connection too, and leaped into action. But Seth was faster. He launched himself off the floor and dove at Carlson, slamming his left elbow up under the man's chin in a Thai Boxing move similar to the one that had dropped Carlson once before. Carlson's assault rifle clattered across the hardwood floor, out of reach. The two men sprawled on the floor beside the corpse, and their wild eyes met.

"I'm one up," Seth said.

Carlson twisted away, lunging for his gun.

Seth did his best 80s break-dancing move, spinning on his back and extending his toe to its limit, just managing to kick the gun another few feet across the room. Then he rolled over to pry the other weapon from the dead hand of the Woman.

Gaining control of it proved more difficult than expected. Despite her recent death, her fingers grasped it surprisingly well, and she was half lying on it.

But Carlson didn't know this. All he could see was that Seth was closer to her gun than he was to his own. So he did the logical thing, scrambling to his feet and stumbling for the exit.

When Seth finally raised the weapon, all he saw was Carlson's tail section and hind foot passing out the door. He held fire. Assuming that a rearmed Carlson, reinforced by Osborne and Holtz, would blitzkrieg through the doorway again at any moment, he skittered backward on his butt against the far wall and raised the rifle, ready to fire.

No one came. Then he heard a commotion in the living room. He remembered his parents, helpless and in harm's way, and grunted in anger, furious that he'd forgotten them and hoping his delay in chasing Carlson hadn't cost them their lives.

He jumped to his feet, oblivious to the accumulation of pain and injuries, and rushed from the room, ready for the final showdown like Butch Cassidy or the Sundance Kid.

Again, more surprises. No sign of Carlson. No weapons trained on him. Instead, he found Irene in the fetal position on the couch, breathing, apparently unharmed. Osborne was still propped against the far wall with a rifle within reach, stuporous but stirring. But most strange, Ernest was standing hunched over, pummeling something behind the couch repeatedly with a lamp from the end table.

"Dad!" he shouted, and ran toward him.

Ernest stopped in mid-blow and looked at him vacantly.

"What happened?" Seth said, as he looked over the back of the couch to find Holtz lying in a bloody heap.

Ernest pointed to the corpse. "Carlson came flying out of the back room and, to this character's surprise, grabbed his rifle, shoved him over the back of the couch, and made for the door. I thought that this guy on his back with no weapon and an old man with a lamp made for a fair fight. He shouldn't have hit your mother."

Good, Seth thought. *Revenge of the light bulbs.* "Where'd Carlson go, Dad?" he gasped.

"Out the front."

Just then, they heard a snowmobile fire up and rev wildly. Seth ran to the front door, taking time along the way to kick Osborne brutally in the head and drop him back into unconsciousness. He flung the damaged door open to see Carlson jumping a sled over the curbside snowbank into the street. He raised the AR-15 and sprayed an unpracticed volley at the rapidly accelerating target. He thought he saw a spark or two, indicating hits, but couldn't be sure. The sled raced down the street eastward in a cloud of blue, two-stroke exhaust and an extra haze that may have been smoke, or simply the blur of blowing snow.

Seth stepped back into the house and stood dumb for a second. His mind had been working on instinct, but the immediate and mortal danger had passed. Mental lethargy settled in.

"What happened in the back?" Ernest said as he advanced toward the supine and defenseless Osborne, his lamp held aloft.

Seth held up his hand. "He's good there, Dad."

Ernest looked blankly at Osborne, seeming to struggle with the opposing concepts of mercy and justice. He held off his attack, but stood guard over the limp body just in case.

Ernest's question about events in the back of the house reactivated Seth's weary brain.

Campbell!

He'd forgotten about her — again.

Using the attached strap, he slung the rifle over his shoulder, dashed down the hall into the office, and traced the rubber hose to its end in the closet. There, huddled in the corner, shaking uncontrollably, sat Campbell Morrison, clutching the discharged spearfishing gun. He knelt and hugged her close.

"How the hell did he miss you in here?" he said.

"Hid in the attic," she said, pointing up with one trembling finger.

There in the dark closet ceiling was a small crawl-space panel, a scuttle hole, which she'd cleverly scaled the interior walls to get at, managing to squeeze through in the heat of the moment.

Seth whistled. "You were there the whole time? What were you waiting for?"

"Do you know how hard it was to lower myself down without a sound and get this thing armed and aimed?"

"Come on," Seth said, pulling her to her feet. "We should go."

She hesitated. "Is she dead?"

"Extremely. You're a good shot. What's the deal with you women?"

"Hormones."

Seth nodded, then took the spear gun from her hand. "These are illegal, you know."

"What are we going to do about the body?" she asked, her eyes wide with the shock of what she had done.

"We've got to hide our own first," he said. "Those two others may be back here any second." Another thought — which he didn't share — suddenly struck him. Campbell's reappearance in the closet meant no help was imminent, unless Newman chose to phone the Stillwater PD and report their suspicious call disconnection and dead line. Even so, with the weather as it was, help could be a long time in coming.

"I don't want to see her," Campbell said as he led her out with his arm firmly around her shoulder, trying to shield her view of the bloody, pierced corpse. Even so, she ignored her own request and craned her head for a quick look as they went by.

He deposited a still-shaken Campbell on the living-room sofa, warning her to stay low in case bullets started flying. Ernest was vigilant with Osborne's gun at the living-room window. Irene joined them from the bathroom, pale as milk-fed veal.

"Is everyone okay?" Seth asked.

No one answered.

"Am I shot?" he said.

Both Irene and Campbell perked up and picked over his body, finding plenty of wounds, but none from bullets. The sense of purpose rallied their thoughts. "We should get the hell out of here," Ernest said from his post, matching Seth's earlier concern.

But Seth had reconsidered. "No," he said.

His father looked at him strangely.

"There's only one sled left out there," Seth explained. The Carlson Six had arrived on four machines; Craig, Sam, and Edward had each subsequently taken one. "We can't all fit on one snowmobile, and we can't go out in this weather on foot."

"Let's at least take the girls to a neighbor's house," Ernest said.

"No. I don't want anyone else involved. Enough innocent people have died already. We'll be fine here. The two he sent off earlier probably won't come in if they see the other sleds gone. If they do, we'll be ready for them." He patted the gun hanging at his side, unconvinced of his own reassuring words.

Ernest pulled the magazine clip off his rifle, eyeballed the contents of the forty-round magazine and, satisfied with the amount of ammo he found, clicked it back into place. He cocked the weapon with emphatic flair and smiled, apparently relishing the thought of additional payback.

"Watch things, Dad. I'll call the police."

"I thought the line was dead."

"There's a working modem line in there."

He returned to Lynda's office and recovered Carlson's rifle, draping it over his opposite shoulder, trying to avoid looking at the dead woman lying in the middle of the floor. He didn't know the local police number and called Newman instead, preferring someone familiar over 911.

He filled Newman in with an abbreviated version of the latest events, and was surprised to learn that the detective hadn't already called local law enforcement. He'd suspected foul weather, a bad connection, or another Shy Samaritan trick as the disconnect culprit. Newman promised to contact the Stillwater PD and Washington County Sheriff for help, but Seth hung up feeling no confidence that help would arrive soon, given the road conditions.

Now what? he thought as he joined Campbell and his parents in the living room. His mind refused to work. He couldn't grasp the big picture. "Did we get all the guns?" he asked his dad.

Ernest did mental math. Each of the six had come with a gun. The three who left each had one. Of the three who remained, two were dead. Their weapons were hanging from Seth's shoulders. Ernest had the last. "I think so," he said.

Irene finally spoke a few trembling words. "Let's just stay together here and wait for help."

It sounded reasonable to all — except Seth. The snow beckoned him. Out the door was an entire planet of freedom. He could run, hide, live, forget. He fought the impulse and joined his father at the living-room window instead, standing guard. Thoughts flitted in and out of his brain like bugs on a streetlight. His spinal cord did the MoonWalk. He doubled over, feeling nauseated.

"I'm scared, Seth," Campbell said.

You're scared? he thought. If only she knew what *he* was going through.

"What will that guy do, Seth?" Irene asked, speaking of Carlson.

He pondered that a moment, and as he did, an odd calm descended on him. His heart slowed and his mind cleared. Here he stood in a room full of people looking to him for guidance, for salvation. But why? What had he ever done right? He'd failed his test as weatherman, as groom, as a spokesman for the NIC. His failures had crushed lives. People had died. And somewhere out in the snow, the man who would continue to kill and charge it to Seth's guilt account was making his escape.

The Cayce quote Carlson mentioned earlier repeated in his head: *'Tis not given to man to know the time or the period of the end — save by their constituting themselves a channel through which He may speak.*

He took to pacing again.

... a channel through which He may speak ...

"Mom," he said slowly, "he's done with doing anything if I have my way."

CHAPTER 34

All three of them tried to stop Seth, but he would have none of it. He threw on what clothes he had, left one of the rifles for Campbell, and headed for the front door.

Campbell pleaded with him. "Seth, let him go. The police will catch him. This isn't your job."

He'd been considering that very thing. But Emily Corbin's cards, with their quotes, had surpassed even Cayce's purported 90-percent prophetic accuracy. Her latest offering — read to him over the phone by Newman — had played on his mind: *Fulfilling that purpose as He may have in thee is a greater service, a greater joy than may be had by him who may have builded a city or have conquered a nation.* Suddenly, Seth believed he knew how it applied to current events.

"Actually, Campbell," he said, "it *is* my job."

"You'll get yourself killed," Irene said, tugging at his arm.

"The Shy Samaritan can't be killed, Mom," he said with a weak smile.

"You won't catch him now, anyway," Ernest said.

"I wouldn't count on that, Dad. His tracks should be easy enough to follow. I may have hit something when I shot at him. He could be wounded, or the sled might be damaged. Either way, he can't go far ... he didn't bother to grab a helmet or gloves."

"What about us?" Campbell asked.

"The cops may eventually get him, but he's a wounded animal now. He'll do anything to get away. He's leaving tracks right now, but it's snowing so hard, they won't last long. The police may not find him until after he kills again. He said he has a large stash of plastic explosives. Campbell, none of us are safe until he's stopped."

He turned and faced them all. Steiner and McClellan had died in his stead. Ernest — the old man — had killed Holtz. Even Campbell, as scared as she must have been, had bagged one of the bad guys. Until now, Seth had done nothing but run. But never again.

"This is my job," he said emphatically.

No one spoke up. He wished they would. It might not have taken much to change his mind. Not wanting to think about that, he spun and trudged toward the front door and the blowing snow beyond.

Ernest yelled after him and tossed something his way when he looked back. It was a helmet; a pair of gloves was wedged inside. Seth glanced up, intending to thank him, but stopped when he saw the admiration shining in his father's eyes.

Later, Dad, he thought. *If I make it, we'll have a long talk.*

As though his father had heard his thoughts through the rising wind, he smiled and nodded.

After yanking the air-cooled Arctic Cat ZR-440 to life, Seth took time to pull on the gloves, then climbed aboard with the dead Caprice Woman's rifle strapped over his shoulder.

For all his tough talk, he knew the odds of actually catching Carlson — even if he could track him — were meager. That made his bold actions easier. But there were flashes of reality: this was a blizzard — a Minnesota blizzard — and one does not go snowmobiling as Carlson had without hand or head protection. If the subzero wind-chill didn't stop him, sledding bare-eyed into a driving snowfall would surely slow him down.

He spun the Cat around, goosed the throttle, and launched the lightweight sport sled off the snowbank into the street. Slowing at the point where Carlson had been when the bullets flew, he checked the surrounding snow for signs of blood or fluids from the sled. He was familiar with the Ski-Doo model Carlson rode, a bumblebee-colored Mach Z with the Rotax 800 liquid-cooled triple. One powerful machine. A half-inch of fresh snow already covered the tracks, burying any stains that might have been there. Seth pinned the throttle and in seconds was out of sight of Lynda's house, heading down Croixwood Boulevard to the east, doing eighty.

CHAPTER 35

It was easy at first to follow the Mach Z's trail, but as he neared the Highway 5 intersection, truck and sled traffic was more evident. Soon the road was a maze of crisscrossing tire and ski tracks. When he reached the Oasis Market at the corner, he'd lost the scent.

A plow had made a center pass on Highway 5, complicating matters. Seth knelt on the seat, alone at the intersection, ignoring the cycling streetlight, trying to pick the right sled track out of the mix with nothing but intuition on which to base a decision. They all looked the same.

He was about to retrace his way a bit to try again when he noticed something out of the ordinary: a lone snowmobile track continuing east across Highway 5 where there was no road, only homes and yards. It was a way only someone living nearby, or lost and desperate, would go. He guessed the latter.

Before following the clue, he glanced to his right at the Oasis Market Convenience Store. Pulled up in front, where cars usually parked, were two empty Arctic Cat EXT 580s. He lifted the foggy face-shield on his helmet for a better look. Ten yards past the sleds he spotted Craig and Sam at the payphone on the front side of the building, probably trying to reach Carlson's cell phone. Chasing Carlson was a time-critical mission, but allowing his cohorts to return to Lynda's and threaten his loved ones was unacceptable.

He leaned hard on the sled, spun a donut in the ten-inch powder, and motored into the Oasis parking lot. Ten yards from the two sleds he stopped, stood on his running boards, slung down his AR-15 and proceeded to shred the machines with successive bursts until satisfied they were disabled.

A drive-by shooting, Minnesota-style.

Craig and Sam instinctively dropped to the concrete walkway. Seth ignored them. Without transportation in the snow, they were nonplayers. He sped out of the lot and was across the highway before they could react with their own weapons.

The lone snowmobile track led due east through private yards in the Autumn Wood development, and up the snow-covered asphalt pathway onto Lily Lake Elementary School property. Snowmobiles were prohibited there — more support for his guess on whom he was trailing. He followed the tracks across the playground, wondering what the DNR or ATF would say

234

about exceeding the statewide fifty-mile-per-hour speed limit on school property with what was probably a stolen sled, while toting an assault rifle with silencer, forty-round magazine, and conversion to full automatic.

And he with no permits.

But most government employees were snug in bed on this cold and snowy night in December. If bad guys needed catching, he'd have to do it on his own.

He passed through another line of private yards, crossing dead-end Pine Tree Trail and stopping in the backyard at a line of houses on the opposite side. Here the trail descended into a steep and impossibly tangled embankment of trees and brush. Still, the trail led on, diving down this suicidal hill. Seth teetered at the precipice, looking down through the trees and at the white expanse of snow-covered Lily Lake beyond. Now he was sure he was on the right track. No one but a lost and desperate soul would force a sled through these short, treacherous woods. Yet from what he saw illuminated in his headlight, his predecessor had made it through, mowing down a number of good-sized saplings in the process.

With the trail blazed before him, Seth pressed on, diving into the dark woods. His only hope was to stay within the tracks of the preceding sled. After a harrowing forty-yard descent, he broke through into another row of backyards, crossed tranquil Lake Drive and another line of private property, and was suddenly on the low and level shore of suburban Lily Lake.

He braked there, pausing to appreciate his successful ride thus far. Thirty years earlier, he'd learned to swim at the public beach on the opposite shore, proudly managing to swim out to the "big dock" and personally prove the legend that if one dangled motionless in the twenty-foot water a minute, schools of hungry sunfish would nibble toes and nipples like so many toothless piranha. Ten years later he researched the same body of water for a high school project. He still remembered the data: a thirty-five-acre pan-fish lake with maximum depth of fifty-one feet in a single hole toward the eastern shore, and an average surface elevation of 845 feet above sea level. The dominant bottom substrate was a mixture of sand, gravel, and muck, with an overabundance of aquatic plants. It was an overfished lake the state stocked with Northern Pike, though catches larger than three pounds were rare.

It was all in a speech he was to deliver in class. He'd practiced it countless times until he knew the material in his sleep, yet never made the presentation. Mysterious "illnesses" kept him from school on each occasion. Eventually he'd just submitted the speech and supporting data in written form, receiving a C-minus for content.

He'd spent a lifetime overprepared but unable to act. Tonight the opposite was true. He had no idea what he was doing, only why. There was no time for practice or fretting over consequences or fears, not even the one that, as a rule, kept him off Minnesota's frozen lakes and rivers. As a meteorologist, he understood better than anyone the unpredictable nature of ice, especially early-season ice formed in a mild autumn with heavy, insulating snowfall. Irene's earlier comments about unusually thin ice this year flitted in his mind.

But a subzero gust of wind swirled past him with a whining sound that reminded him of Rachel Steiner's dreadful howl as Seth had cradled her husband and watched his brains drip out the back of his head onto the Hilton floor.

He punched the throttle and headed across the ice.

A snowmobile's solo headlamp typically provides inadequate lighting for travel across a frozen lake on those overcast nights when star and moonlight are blocked, and where ice ridges, wind-blown drifts, and crusted-over sled tracks provide deadly launching pads for speeding machines.

That and unexpected open water.

But in Stillwater the lights from the Highway 36 fast-food strip and the maximum security Oak Park Heights prison beyond reflected off the low-hanging clouds, illuminating the lake enough to allow exorbitant speeds — and for Seth to see Carlson's Ski-Doo parked aside an ice-fishing shack at mid-lake.

He'd guessed right on two counts. Carlson was the one he'd followed, and the man hadn't gone far before having to stop and warm up.

Seth eased the throttle back, moving the sled ahead slowly and quietly, stopping seventy-five yards short of the shack at a point where the wind still masked the sound of his motor. He hoped. He removed the helmet and proceeded on foot, fresh powder muffling the sound of his boots crunching on the snow.

The shack was a homemade plywood affair that someone — likely a lake resident — had constructed on a wooden sledge and probably man-hauled onto the ice ... which explained how it got there, since the ice wasn't ready for trucks yet. Five feet from the shanty, he noticed signs of violent entry. Bullet holes and splintered wood at the door handle indicated that Carlson had shot his way through the padlock — a good sign to Seth, since it meant that the shack had been unoccupied and that no one else was in danger. Or at least, he hoped so. Carlson seemed the kind who didn't mind taking a hostage when it suited his purpose ... or killing someone in his way.

He stood for a moment in the accumulating snow, rifle in hand, indecisive. What had he really hoped to accomplish? He recalled another scene from the Clint Eastwood movie *The Gauntlet*, where Clint Eastwood and Sondra Locke had narrowly escaped a house surrounded by Mob-controlled cops who opened fire on the house, releasing such a barrage of bullets that the house literally collapsed upon itself. He guessed that it wouldn't take much for him to shoot up the shack and kill or wound Carlson from right where he stood.

But he wasn't the Mob, the cops, or a cold-blooded killer. He shouted above the wind: "Give it up, Carlson. You're surrounded."

Instinct prompted him to move sideways a few feet, vacating the space he occupied when he spoke the words. No sooner had he done so than two bursts from Carlson's AR-15 exploded through the plywood exterior of the shack, aimed at where he had just been standing.

"Is that you, Peterson?" Carlson's voice rang out.

Seth circled the shack. "Yeah, and I've got one of your rifles." He kept moving and ducked behind Carlson's snowmobile.

A 360-degree spray of bullets exited the shack, blindly hunting their moving and unseen prey.

From the protection of the sled, Seth tried to reason with the man: "Hold your fire a second. I'm behind your sled now. If you shoot over here, you'll hit it and ruin your only hope of ever getting out of here."

This time, no bullets answered.

"How do I know you've got a gun?" Carlson said.

Seth aimed high and fired a short warning burst into the shack. "Satisfied?"

"Who the hell are you, Peterson?"

Seth, grateful that the wind had died down, decided to continue on the same fantasy tack he'd begun earlier. "I'm not sure anymore, but I've got an interesting idea for you to ponder. Remember that Cayce quote you dropped on me back at the house? The one about how Man can't know the time of the end '*save by their constituting themselves a channel through which He may speak*'? You believe that, right?"

"Spare me your ghost stories. Either shoot me or don't."

"I know you think you're the Channel, Carlson, nurtured by Ester, named by Cayce, chosen by God. But you're wrong."

"You're no believer. Am I supposed to be surprised?"

"Oh, I believe in the Channel. It's just not *you*."

"Is that so?"

"My mom told me something when I was a kid. I looked it up once and confirmed it. You'll never guess what the origin of Seth is. It means The Appointed One. The Chosen. Isn't that weird?"

Silence from the shack.

"You're not the Channel, Little Edgar," Seth finally said. "I am."

More silence.

"So here's the message I'm supposed to deliver," Seth continued, ad-libbing now. "The Pole Shift won't occur in your lifetime."

He waited for that to sink in, and for a clue on what to do next. Suddenly, a fierce barrage of gunfire erupted from the shack, pinging off the sled and piercing the snow all around it. Seth hunkered down and weathered it until he heard the click of an empty magazine disengaged and curses from within.

"Okay, Peterson. I'm coming out. Don't shoot."

Seth peered over the bullet-riddled seat at the door of the shack and leveled his rifle. The door opened slowly and Carlson tentatively emerged, arms spread at his sides, one of them holding the purportedly empty rifle.

"Drop it," Seth ordered.

Peterson nodded and complied. Seth stood and motioned with the rifle for Peterson to step away from the fallen weapon.

Now what? he thought.

"You got me," Carlson said. "Either shoot me or bring me in, but don't let me freeze to death."

Carlson's face showed the rigors of his escape. His hair was wet from the snow, his face ruddy from cold and windburn, his earlobes white with frostbite, and a couple of nasty red lines marked where branches had lashed him during his wooded-slope descent.

"How ironic," Seth said, "the great ice-monger doesn't like the cold."

He did a cursory once-over of Carlson's sled. Even if it started, it hardly looked trailworthy. He motioned with the gun for Carlson to start walking across the lake, back in the direction of Seth's sled.

Halfway there, Carlson, still holding his bare hands in the open air at his sides, asked whether he could pull them into his jacket for warmth. Following behind with the rifle and a ten-pace safety cushion, Seth conceded.

Five steps later, a flash of light and deafening sound exploded from the back of Carlson's jacket. Seth, startled, flinched and dropped the rifle in the snow, then covered his eyes. When he lowered his arm, he saw Carlson spinning round on him and pulling out the .45 caliber pistol he'd used to take a potshot through the back of his jacket. Seth dove to the side, rolling and scrambling through the snow as two more loud reports and bright flashes ripped the night sky. He felt nothing, but kept moving until several seconds after the last shot. Finally he stopped and chanced a peek. Carlson had fled, running for Seth's sled at top speed.

Seth crawled back to the spot where he'd dropped the rifle, dug it out of the snow, knelt, aimed, and fired off a burst. But Carlson had reached the sled, fired the engine to life, and like a stunt rider in an old cowboys-and-Indians movie, sped off on a southern tangent toward Lily Lake Beach as he hung off the far side of the sled, away from Seth, shielded from fire.

He had escaped again.

Seth flung down the rifle in disgust.

Never leave keys in the ignition.

But seconds later, with Carlson only a few hundred yards away, Seth heard an odd and low cracking sound, and felt a barely perceptible shudder through his feet. The fading sound of the revving snowmobile's engine halted abruptly, and he thought he heard a cry for help carried on the wind. He squinted into the falling snow, trying to see what happened. He could just make out the snowmobile stopped on the ice, its headlight gleaming forward. But then, slowly, the headlight beam began to rise toward the clouds with a surreal motion that could mean only one thing: thin ice.

As he watched, frozen in place just as he'd been when he watched the Blazer careen through the fateful intersection what seemed a lifetime ago, the sled went vertical like the Titanic in its final moments, then slipped rapidly from sight.

Seth peered into the nothingness, transfixed — until he heard a second cry, this one a desperate croak.

Carlson was in the water.

He scooped the rifle from the snow and dashed across the frozen lake, racing to save the life of the man whom seconds earlier he'd tried to shoot dead. The deep snow made for slow going; a full minute passed before he reached the scene. He pulled up short of the open water, a circle no more than fifteen feet in circumference. Slithering forward on his belly, keeping his weight distributed as evenly as possible, he inched forward toward the edge of the broken ice. Carlson was in full panic, pale and flailing at the crumbling edge. He'd already gone under several times, weighed down by wet clothing.

Seth knew Carlson's only chance was to gain purchase on the solid ice and belly up onto it with aid from atop. He inched closer. The ice groaned. He swallowed hard and crept forward again, near the same spot he'd learned to swim thirty years earlier. Now he might learn how to drown there.

"Relax and grab the edge of the ice," he yelled at Carlson.

He had wild animal eyes, but Seth's words seemed to calm him. His frantic and counterproductive motions lessened. He set one hand on the current ice edge and reached out with the other for help. Seth slithered as far out as he dared and then, grasping the barrel of the AR-15, swung it out ahead of him, allowing the canvas shoulder strap to reach the furthest point possible, just within Carlson's reach.

The man grabbed the makeshift life rope and pulled. Seth slithered backward, tugging as hard as his grip allowed.

"Keep your head down," he yelled at Carlson, "And your arms out. Don't move so much. If we get you started on the ice, we can slide you out of there."

Carlson understood and showed incredible presence of mind, given his position. They worked in concert, all animosity forgotten.

At first it appeared it might be possible. Carlson was still strong, full of fight. With the two of them pulling and him kicking his legs, they managed to work his chest onto the ice, almost to the fulcrum point. But then the ice gave way beneath him, and he plunged back in. Seth quickly scooted back, away from the weakened ice, and they set up for another attempt. They repeated the process again and again. Crazy thoughts of alternative measures raced through his mind. He considered the possibility of simply repeating their current routine — using Carlson as a human icebreaker — to reach the far shore. At that rate, of course, it would take days.

Carlson had only seconds.

Seth saw the man's eyes roll back in his head, and he slid under the icy water, bobbing back up a split second later. Seth shouted at him, urging him on for another try. This time Seth gave maximum effort, and Carlson, seeming to sense this was his last hope, gave a final, adrenalin-juiced surge onto the ice. This time they succeeded. Seth scrambled back, pulling furiously on the rifle. Carlson was up on the ice all the way to his waist.

Encouraged, Seth's mind fast-forwarded to the next steps he would take, including stripping Carlson of his wet clothing, which would be as deadly to him atop the windswept ice as in the cold water. Carlson was just pulling his legs free when the ice caved again. He collapsed for another full dunking, and came up sputtering and exhausted.

Seth was demoralized to tears.

He thought for a moment that Carlson had lost his grip on the strap and was doomed, but his hands came up again, one gripping the ice and the other still clinging with a death-grip to the woven cord.

"Again!" Seth exhorted him.

"No ... wait," Carlson managed to say between coughs. He calmly clung to the ice for a few seconds. Seth thought he was trying to rest for another attempt. "What you said ... back there," he sputtered, "About my ... mother ... Cayce. Was it ... the truth?"

Seth thought about it. Their eyes locked in a bottomless stare. *Truth?* The only truth he knew was his desperate desire to save Carlson's life at all costs. The right answer to the man's profound question might motivate enough to save him, or demoralize him to the point of capitulation.

But which was the right answer? Admit the truth that Seth's comments were a ploy and Ester and Edward's lifelong beliefs were a sad farce? Or the fiction that they were all major players in a prophetic ice opera of Biblical proportions?

"Yes, it's true," he lied, "I wouldn't lie to you. Not about that. Not now."

A shadow passed over Carlson's face. Then a grave and mysterious smile. "She's calling me home," he said.

With that, he released his grip on the strap and pushed off from the ice with his other hand. As Seth lurched forward, screaming at him, Carlson slipped slowly beneath the surface with his eyes held open, still locked on Seth. Even in the dim reflected light, Seth was able to watch the bizarre and horrifying descent of his eyes into the murky darkness, until they disappeared. Fifteen seconds later, a large air bubble broke the surface.

Edward Carlson was gone.

CHAPTER 36

Seth gazed into the black water for a time, not because he expected Carlson to resurface, but because his nerves temporarily quit responding to his brain. He had tried with every fiber to rescue the man, with little thought to his own safety, or of the paradoxical events that led them to this time and place.

But he had guessed wrong.

The Shy Samaritan had failed.

He'd almost begun believing in his own superpowers. Sadness overwhelmed him, and his face sank into the snow.

Eventually the cold reintroduced him to the concept of his own mortality. He backed off the open water, rolled to the side, and crawled across the ice for fifty yards before gaining the confidence to stand again. He returned to the ice shack, tried Carlson's snowmobile to no avail, and rummaged through the damaged structure for dry clothes. The effort with Carlson had soaked his jacket. He found a thick wool shirt hanging on the wall with only one bullet hole. Discarding his jacket, he donned the wool and headed on foot for the north end of the lake at a sustainable trot. He grounded on the dead-end at Hemlock and turned left on Pine Street, aiming for Lynda's, a little more than a mile away.

As he climbed the Pine Street hill, he heard distant sirens. A good sign. Minutes later he reached the Amoco station where he had disabled the two snowmobiles. It appeared that the police had enlisted the help of the DOT, as Highway 5 and Croixwood Boulevard were both well plowed. A Washington County Sheriff's four-wheel-drive SUV and a Stillwater PD squad car were in the parking lot, lights flashing. He spotted two men in the back of the squad. He wasn't close enough to be sure, but assumed they were Craig and Sam.

He didn't stop to find out, but continued toward Lynda's instead, arriving there a few minutes later, wet, cold, and exhausted. A half-dozen emergency and police vehicles surrounded the area, with enough lights flashing to put any Christmas display to shame. A sizable crowd of bundled-up neighbors was braving the blizzard to gawk at the mysterious goings-on.

Seth trotted through the throng and up the driveway, making the mistake of forgetting the assault rifle slung over his shoulder. A lone cop standing guard on the front stoop spotted this disheveled intruder approaching and sounded the alarm. Before Seth knew what hit him, he was again facedown in the snow with a knee on the back of his head and another buried in his spine as four animated officers plied his arms, legs, and neck in ways they shouldn't go, especially when bruised and battered.

The Rodney King video had taught him not to struggle in such instances.

They clamped on handcuffs and used them to lift him rudely to his feet, stretching his damaged ribs to excruciating limits. He was dragged roughly up the front steps and into Lynda's house by a cop on either side. They planted him on display in the foyer, doubled over in exhaustion and pain with wet matted hair, wearing a stranger's fish-odor shack shirt. One eye was swollen shut and the other blinded by snow.

He heard a familiar voice.

"Good God, you fools, that's my son!" Then Ernest Peterson was at his side, parting police officers like the Red Sea. "Take those damned cuffs off him. You caught the good guy."

Irene arrived to fawn and paw at him. Questions rained down on him as the cuffs came off. The warmth of the room felt glorious. Someone wrapped a towel around his head, then a blanket over his shoulders. Without even realizing how he got there, he found himself sitting on the couch, a crowd around him. He was laughing — or crying, not sure which. Maybe both. He talked as best he could, explained the chase, the firefight, the ice, the end. Then the crowd thinned, and reality returned.

Campbell had stayed out of the fray, choosing to hold off by the kitchen counter, absorbing the scene like an innocent, wide-eyed child. The cops stepped away and were milling about, talking, making phone calls. Seth was recovering with his mother at his knee and his father standing over them. Finally, she approached.

Ernest looked hard at her, and some silent understanding passed between them. He gave Irene a gentle foot-nudge and motioned with his head for her to follow him out of the room, leaving Seth and Campbell alone.

"Why does this stuff happen to me, Campbell?" Seth asked her.

"You're not going to like it," she said, her eyes both shrewd and worried. "I'm no prophet, but I'd say maybe Cayce was right."

"You mean there's a higher purpose to my being a loser?"

She smiled with those teeth. "Oh, you're no loser."

"Well, I'm looking forward to going back to being one. The Shy Samaritan died out there too."

"I'm afraid it won't be that easy."

Seth squinted his one good eye at her. "Why not?"

"It isn't mission accomplished yet."

"What the hell could there possibly be left for me to do?"

"Seth, you know me. I don't beat around the bush."

His head went in circles. "That's the truth."

"We have a wedding to finish."

The words shocked him so much he jerked back, causing his entire body to sing with pain. Then he looked at her and slowly broke into an irrepressible smile.

But Campbell wasn't smiling back. She was deadpan, frowning even.

Seth had a horrible thought. "Oh, I see," he said. "A cruel joke. Payback time. *Touché.*"

She shook her head. "No, you idiot. I'm completely serious. I love you, Seth, and I'll still marry you. But only under one condition."

He cocked his head. "Keep the toilet seat down?"

She shook her head. "Worse."

"You want the TV remote?"

Another shake.

Seth felt a twinge. "You still want your big wedding?"

She thought a moment, then wobbled her head. "That's negotiable."

"What then?"

"I'm still an investigative reporter."

He put his hands up like Joe Pesci. "What? You think I'd make you quit your career to wait on me hand and foot?"

"You can be so dense," Campbell said. "No, the condition is that I get the exclusive on The Shy Samaritan. I helped crack this case. And the story is Pulitzer Prize material. You're going to be famous whether you like it or not. You may never have to do another live weather broadcast in your life, but you're damn sure going before the TV cameras. *For me.* I want to be the only reporter you speak to."

"Oh, I see. You're using me."

Campbell leaned down and whispered hotly in his ear. "You ain't seen nothing yet, Shy Boy."

***